D

ELIZABETH family in rural educated on the Isle of Wight and was then tempted to London to work for a magazine editor, before pursuing a career in public relations. She lived for ten years in south west London before opting for the peace and tranquillity of the countryside in order to concentrate on her writing career. *Daddy Darling* is her third novel, following *The Corporate Wife* and *Making Up*.

Acclaim for Elizabeth Harrington

Making Up

'A light and luscious romantic thriller'   *Living*

The Corporate Wife

'A fast-paced, warm-hearted romantic thriller: the sex and skulduggery will keep you racing from start to finish'   SALLY BEAUMAN

Also by Elizabeth Harrington

THE CORPORATE WIFE
MAKING UP

ELIZABETH HARRINGTON

Daddy Darling

Dearest Jeni & Frank

with lots of love

Liz xxxx

3/6/96.

HarperCollins*Publishers*

HarperCollins*Publishers*
77–85 Fulham Palace Road,
Hammersmith, London W6 8JB

A paperback original 1996
1 3 5 7 9 8 6 4 2

ISBN 0 00 647328 8

Set in Linotron Palatino
at The Spartan Press Ltd,
Lymington, Hants

Printed and bound in Great Britain by
Caledonian International
Book Manufacturing Ltd Glasgow

One of the nicest aspects of completing a novel, for me, is the opportunity to thank all those who have helped and supported the book over the long months of production.

When I first had a vague idea for the book which would eventually become *Daddy Darling*, I tracked down the man responsible for a publication called *Trace* magazine which lists details of stolen art and antiques in order to help retrieve missing heirlooms, masterpieces or simply items of great sentimental value. That man, Philip Saunders, proved to be wildly imaginative, inspiring and enthusiastic; full of scams, trade secrets and encouragement! *Daddy Darling* would not have been possible without his help.

Allan Jones of Allan Jones and Company, Solicitors, Hereford proved the extent of his friendship and patience by meticulously checking over legal facts and scenarios. Howard Townson of Clyde and Company, London furnished me with information about the Law of Market Overt, delving into dry legal texts going back many centuries.

A certain barrister who asks to remain name-less provided inspiration and authenticity – a charmingly soft lady with a wit as sharp as a pitchfork!

To Rachel Hore and Allison Walsh for all their ideas, encouragement and hard work; and to Yvonne Holland for her painstaking efforts checking out the facts.

Lastly to my family: to Peter for his ideas, his never-ending support and long-suffering ability to read my novels-in-production five times over and still say he likes them, and of course to my two children Jamie and Poppy to whom I dedicate this book:

For Jamie and Poppy
with all my love

Prologue

Dickie Crowborough stood slightly back from the crowd, watching the frail figure of his goddaughter. His heart went out to her. She was such a brave young thing. The bitter wind howled around the mourners, stinging through their overcoats, but she stood resolutely beside the gaping hole where the coffin had just been lowered. In her hand she held a tiny pink rose which she placed on her lips, and then threw gently down into the grave. She looked alone and lost, frightened and insignificant beside the huge looming hole – a terrifyingly cold and unremittingly final resting place.

How unfair that she should have to face such sadness at such a young age. But he knew she was a spirited girl. She was clever and quick-witted, and she would get over it.

As everyone else started to move away, unbelievably she seemed to have been forgotten. She remained, rooted to the earth. Dickie walked to her side. Gently he put his hand on her arm, and pulled her away.

'Come on, my dear . . .'

Chapter One

❦

1992

Gus pushed her tortoiseshell-rimmed spectacles hard up against the bridge of her nose and squinted into the worn mirror. Her cheeks were flushed pink from excitement – and the unseasonal warmth of the mid-May evening. Her clear grey eyes shone with anticipation at the importance of the evening ahead.

The small ladies' room was dark and airless, and the gown felt heavy on her shoulders, but Gus didn't mind its weight, or the heat. Nothing could take away from her happiness tonight. She'd worked towards this moment for a good portion of her twenty-two years. Telltale bruises beneath her eyes gave away the fact that she'd hardly slept a wink all night, and she put another layer of cover-up stick over the top, in an unsuccessful attempt to hide the damage. That would have to do. She deposited the stick back into her pocket and shrugged the shoulders of the gown back into place, feeling like a voluminous bat and wishing she had plumped for a slightly smaller size.

Still staring at her reflection, Gus turned her head sharply from side to side, and then gave it a dog-like shake, testing the scratchy wig's gripping power. It hung on, limpet-like, giving the barest glimpse of her chestnut-brown hair where it poked out behind her temples to be caught in a sober knot at the nape of her neck. She hoped that the discreet knotted-gold earrings were not going to look *de trop* – she thought of them as a good luck token,

3

for they had been a Christmas stocking gift from her father a few months before.

Willing the butterflies in her stomach to settle down quietly, she squared her shoulders beneath the flowing robe, gave a large 'good luck' wink to the reflection in the mirror, and set off to keep the appointment she had spent the last four years working towards.

It was a pity that her father was unable to make it to the traditional family drinks party held while the ceremony was in progress. He'd told Gus he'd tried very hard to reorganize his schedule, but he had business commitments he simply couldn't cancel. Instead, he had agreed to meet her for supper afterwards. Gus felt a warm glow as she looked forward to celebrating later on with her only parent, and the person she loved most in the world. What a night it promised to be!

As she almost skipped up Middle Temple Lane, Gus saw several other similarly robed individuals heading purposefully towards the ceremony. She glanced up at the grand façade of the Middle Temple to the flagstaff where the Union flag caught the sweep of the pleasant May breeze. Windows were thrown open to savour the unseasonably warm late afternoon air. Gus could hear the gentle clacking of computer keyboards and the sounds of voices drifting out across the square towards her. Those were the chambers, or sets, of the noble members of which profession she was officially about to enter. Soon she would be taking up her apprenticeship alongside some of the cream of the British judiciary. Gus would be styled Augusta Lawrence, Barrister. She wanted to savour every moment of the evening. Though her gown flapped unfamiliarly around her ankles and her stomach felt full of nerves, she couldn't stop smiling to herself.

'Gus, Gus,' someone called. 'Wait for me.' One of her fellow students raced after her, and then another, until they were quite a little band, all similarly decked out,

4

and just as nervous, overcome at the thought of the honour ahead of them.

A steward directed them down past the Great Hall where everything was soon to happen, and towards the inner recesses usually reserved for the Masters of the Bench. Gus's crowd squeezed in, but Gus paused in the doorway of the packed anteroom for a few seconds to collect herself, and to freeze the moment in her memory. Fifty to sixty others stood chattering over their sherry glasses. Here assembled were the bright hopes of the legal system's future. As she downed her dustily dry sherry she glanced around, noting the bizarre cross-section of candidates. Voices mingled noisily with a colour and variety synonymous with those of a country cattle market. Oxbridge brays overshadowed hesitant but precise interjections from students of foreign and Commonwealth origin. The fast-increasing population of those from the lesser but perhaps trendier universities – or, God help them – polytechnics, regarded the elitist majority with a fair degree of disparagement and mockery, equalled only by the nose-curling distaste that clouded the old school's view of them. Reformers were not welcome here. The temple of advocacy was governed and administered by the intellectually glittering and arcane masters of British justice whose supremacy would only be assured through perpetual exclusivity and the patronage of like-minded men – oh, and just a few women!

'Gus, you look radiant.' Gus found her cheek being kissed noisily and enthusiastically by the enormously tall, gangly figure of Anthony Hopton-Jones, one of her friends from Bar School.

'Thanks, Anthony.' Gus gave him an answering peck on the cheek, noting that he too had an unaccustomed glow about him. Anthony swept the long gown around his knees theatrically.

5

'Makes a change from the old miniskirt, eh, Gus? No more teasing for us in mess after tonight? No longer students any more, we'll be the real thing soon. Only six months before we can stand up in court. Ah look, they're calling us through. Onwards and upwards, dear girl. The night belongs to us!'

They were ushered through to the Great Hall and the ceremony began. They lined up, four rows deep, shuffling sideways and then forwards, as each new barrister was created.

At last it was Gus's turn. Her eyes were fixed on the Reader who stood beside the other Master of the Bench. 'Master Treasurer,' he said, 'I present Miss Augusta Lawrence . . .'

Augusta stepped forward. 'Miss Lawrence, in the name of the Masters of the Bench, I call you to the degree of the Utter Bar.'

She shook the Master Treasurer's warm hand and moved on to sign her name in an enormous leather-bound tome. Now, at last, Augusta had finally achieved her ambition. As she left the Great Hall she felt inches taller. Her spine tingled with pride and achievement. Ever since she'd been a teenager and had first been told what a barrister's job involved, she had never wanted to be anything other. The role had caught her imagination and all through her school examinations and then university, she had pushed her mind to its limits so that she might one day be able to fight for truth and justice. And now she was very nearly there . . .

Returning to the bright sunlight, she noticed there was a lot of hugging and kissing going on. Several of her contemporaries were disappearing into serious clinches with boyfriends and girlfriends. It wasn't often that she had time to think about the lack of romance in her life, but she would be kidding herself if she didn't admit to the tiniest spark of envy at those who had someone to share their moment of glory with. There hadn't really been anyone in her life – there'd hardly been any time for anyone – since Jonathan back home in Guernsey when she was seventeen. Although it was just five years ago, it seemed like many lifetimes back. She couldn't help remembering him with affection, in spite of his betrayal, thanks to her bloody stepsister for leading him on. Jonathan had been just a game to Mirabelle. He hadn't stood a chance.

Now she had a career to think about and the last thing she needed was some man getting in her way.

Anthony caught up with her and kissed her vigorously on each cheek once more. 'Congratulations, sweetheart,' he said affectionately. 'Well done. Feeling proud?'

'I guess if I'm honest I'd admit to maybe just the smallest feeling of satisfaction. You?'

'You bet your little ponytail I am. What are you up to?'

Gus looked at her watch. 'Off to meet my father in a couple of hours.'

Anthony brushed the top of her head playfully. 'Still, there's time for some champers. You can join my mess for dinner. George Lavenham's coming, and maybe we might pick up other interesting people . . .'

'Interesting women you mean!' Gus was very fond of Anthony. His witty good humour made him fun to be with, but she despaired of his love life. He was for ever on the pick-up, trying to impress the less worldly lady pupils. Gus had never been remotely involved with him on a romantic level. But they were firm friends.

'What rubbish, Augusta. I am escorting you and have eyes for no other. Come on, this is just the right temperature,' he coaxed, holding up a bottle of champagne beaded with condensation. '. . . Been in the fridge all day.'

Gus laughed at his high-spirited enthusiasm. 'Thanks, Anthony. I'd love to. I've got to try not to eat too much though; I'm supposed to be dining with my father later.'

'Me too. And Ma. But we have to keep up tradition and dine in Hall first, Gus.' He waved the skirts of his robe around the backs of his knees. 'Aren't you looking forward to eating in a long gown for once?'

'Anthony, I'm beginning to wonder just what your vocation really is, all this talk about dresses. Has anyone ever told you what a poseur you are, crowing about how we no longer have to wear the student number? Yes, of course I'm looking forward to it, only I'm just a little more discreet,' she teased.

'Oh come, Lawrence, it's our turn to annoy the students now. We've joined the club.'

Gus was well used to hearing herself referred to by her surname – not that she much liked it. The Inns of Court were not unlike a boys' boarding school – and were still a little uncomfortable about having let the girls in.

'Well, we've almost joined the club, Anthony. We may have swapped our short student gowns for these rather fetching long ones, but we've still got our year's pupillage to serve!'

'Killjoy!' he hissed teasingly. 'Tonight I intend to be a barrister, learned counsel, skilled advocate –'

'You mean pupil barrister – probably inebriated barrister too, I shouldn't wonder. Just remember, Ant, that if you do decide to throw up later, then try and make it out of Hall first, okay!'

Anthony looked into Gus's clear grey eyes, remembering with a degree of sheepishness that she had witnessed one of his little 'celebrations' in the past. And one that he would really rather forget – not that he remembered much, but Gus had stolen every available opportunity to let him know, in irritatingly spartan instalments, just how badly he had behaved. He really enjoyed Gus's company, for she had a dry and cryptic sense of humour, and a shrewd intuitiveness which, coupled with her undoubtedly clever mind, would send

8

her far. And besides all that, he fantasized about pulling the glasses off that pale, perfect face of hers and whiling a few hours away horizontally. Actually, Anthony thought, as he considered this fact, there were quite a few lady barristers that he had similar ideas about . . .

He shook his head to clear it of such lecherous thoughts and concentrated on not letting the freezing bottle of champagne slip through his numbed fingers as they made their way into dinner. Gus followed Anthony through the long lines of narrow trestle tables as he searched for his mess, stopping every now and then for more noisy congratulations. The atmosphere was like that of the last day of the school year, great excitement and the hint of mischievous behaviour which one knew would be overlooked on the basis of justifiable high spirits. Anthony dragged Gus behind him as he looked for George and whoever else might be joining them in their mess. Another tradition of the Bar was that diners separated themselves into groups of four for dinner, known as messes, supposedly to enable the younger pupils and junior counsel (or barristers) to meet and talk with the upper echelons of the profession. Juniors, through this system, would have the opportunity to listen to great cases of the day and how their more experienced peers or, if they were really lucky, QCs, had dealt with the day's business, and thereby absorb some of learned counsels' wisdom. Of course it also gave them an opportunity to hear all the gossip too. But the sad truth of the matter was that very few seniors ever dined in Hall because they had perfectly nice families to go home to instead. Numerous other rules had to be kept within the messes and in the early days Augusta had felt that the whole system was so alien and intimidating as to make her wonder what the hell she had got herself into. Still, she had persevered with her dinners. One had to. In order to qualify as a barrister, she had to eat twenty-four of them! What other profession had the eating of dinners as a prerequisite of qualifying?

Anthony was gesticulating with his champagne-free hand. 'George, here we are. Come on,Gus,' he called over his shoulder.

Augusta clambered between the chairs to get to her place. Anthony placed the bottle in the centre of the table and George Lavenham roared his approval.

'Well done, old chap. Glad we met up earlier. Oh, and well done to the pair of you.'

'Thanks, George, and congratulations to you too,' Gus breathed as she got to her place.

Her wig was making her head uncomfortably hot and itchy and she longed to remove it. Thankfully they were only required to wear wigs on this ceremonial night. Just another hour or so to get through and then she could rush home and get into some normal clothes before meeting her father. George and Anthony were becoming more and more outrageous in the heady spirit of the evening, leaving Gus the restful option of listening. There was a spare seat to Gus's left, and she hoped that it would be taken by someone fairly easy on the ear. Some of the fellows had such loud voices that they had given her a headache even before the coffee arrived. She scratched at her hair buried beneath the thick woollen wig and watched eagerly as Anthony unwired the cork.

Right on cue, Charlie Brewer grazed the chair legs across the floor as he pulled his seat up beside her. Her light heart sank. Charlie Brewer, QC was renowned for his difficult manner towards students. While Gus had never met him personally before, she knew of his reputation and had heard about some of the casualties. Rumour had it that he wasn't quite as nasty to the women as he was to the men, in that he had a reputation as a ladies' man. But he was a snob, and Gus couldn't stand anyone who gave themselves such airs as Brewer did.

But even Brewer's company couldn't spoil the atmosphere tonight. Pretending to listen to his arrogant drawl, Gus sifted mentally through her wardrobe for later, settling on the little black Jasper Conran dress with the cutaway shoulders. It made her look older, more sophisticated. Gus had been thrilled at her father's suggestion that they celebrate together, just the two of them. For once he had had the sensitivity to realize how important this particular night was to Gus, and her stepmother, Elena, had little interest in Gus's career. Gus felt a warm glow of affection towards her father as she accepted Anthony's champagne.

Just another couple of weeks and she would be starting her pupillage with Henry Apsley-Collins – a specialist in civil matters such as divorce, children, property disputes and the like. For the next twelve months she would remain glued to Henry's side, learning all – or some – of the skills necessary to enable her to stand on her own two feet in court. In the second half of her pupillage in just six months' time she would be able to accept briefs from her own clients.

The year in Bar School had gone amazingly quickly. Gus could hardly believe that she was almost ready to be let out on her own. There were times when the prospect scared her half to death, and other times when all she could feel was a delicious anticipation at the opportunity to test herself, to find out whether she was as strong as she hoped she would be, whether she'd cope with the work, the stress, the anxiety of being responsible for preparing and presenting an argument which could mean the difference between a person's liberty or detention. She had a lot to live up to. She had won an award for advocacy and so people expected great things of her. She had been fortunate in getting a pupillage in one of the most blue-chip chambers in the Temple, while many of her contemporaries were struggling to find places *anywhere*. Many more pupils than pupillages existed and the competition was immense.

11

Grace started. Augusta bit her lip, willing the arrival of the moment when she could finally have a drink. The full glass brimmed enticingly on the table, but she was not permitted to touch a drop until the four members of her mess had silently toasted each other, and bowed their heads to each in turn. Only then could she slake her thirst. By now her head and neck were beginning to steam with the heat. She eyed the jug of water which the steward had placed on the table in front of her. If only she could pour it over her blasted wig. Suddenly Anthony kicked her under the table. She started to speak but Anthony got there first. 'Brewer was talking to you, Augusta.'

'Oh. Sorry,' she muttered. 'I'm afraid the heat . . .'

'Wig giving you a problem? Don't worry, you'll get used to it. Won't be long before your head starts to feel odd without it, you'll see.'

Augusta smiled gratefully, but refused to believe it.

'I was asking if you were the same Lawrence that picked up the Advocacy Prize this year.'

'Yes, I did have that honour . . .'

'Good. Well done. I shall look out for you – to see how you progress.' Augusta smiled.

'Excuse me, Miss Lawrence.' A steward appeared at Gus's side. 'This note has just arrived for you.'

Gus thanked the man and took the envelope. Recognizing her father's writing she excused herself and ripped it open.

Darling,

So sorry, but I am unable to meet you as arranged. Something has come up which I can't avoid. Please forgive me. I know that you will be busy celebrating with your friends and I send you all my love and congratulations.

Daddy.

Attempting to hide her upset, Gus slipped the paper

12

into her pocket, but she hadn't fooled Anthony.

'Everything all right, Gus?' Anthony sounded concerned. 'You look very pale.'

She tried to force a smile. 'Everything's fine, Anthony. Just the heat.' Inside she felt sick with disappointment. Her appetite died. She chased the food around her plate despondently. How could he let her down tonight of all nights? When he knew how much it meant to her? What could be more important than helping her to celebrate something which he was at pains to stress at every opportunity made him so proud?

Gus had an awful suspicion that his detainment elsewhere could well be something to do with Elena. She could be very possessive at times, and particularly so where Gus was involved. But surely her father wouldn't allow Elena to interfere on a night like tonight?

She struggled to listen to, and to join in with, the conversation. She kept smiling until she felt her head ache with the strain of it. Charlie Brewer talked on and on about his many successes. George and Anthony listened like children. Somehow she managed to make the right noises, nodding here and there encouragingly, until at last it was time to go. Charlie would go home to his family; George and Anthony on to meet their parents for more celebrating. Gus would go back to her house to nothing.

'Enjoy your dinner, Gus,' Anthony called after her just as she slammed the cab door. She waved and then turned her face away, fighting back the hot sting of tears.

How could her father not realize that all her friends would be celebrating with their own families; that after the traditional dinner everyone went their own ways – into the bosom of their loved ones? He really didn't seem to know *anything* about her life these days. Gus hated to admit it, but they seemed to be growing further

13

and further apart. She wasn't even sure if she really knew *him* any more after tonight's fiasco.

Piers Lawrence loosened his bow tie, and watched as his wife slid the zip of her dress down over her slender body. The fabric glided with a hiss of silk over her legs and on to the floor. Gracefully she stepped out of it and stooped to retrieve it. She caught him watching her with cool blue eyes, holding his head to the side – the famous Lawrence look, well known in the art world when he was viewing something he liked. He gave a low laugh. Throwing the dress on to the bed, she walked towards him, giving him the full benefit of her carefully corseted figure. Elena's breasts ballooned out from her chest like ripe grapefruits with a gravity-defying splendour. Piers knew very well that silicone had more to do with the effect than nature, but nevertheless he much appreciated the power they had over him. Elena was very accomplished at the sexual arts. She had been schooled to behave like a whore in the bedroom, and a lady in the drawing room. She was one of those women who seemed to delight in doing everything simply to satisfy their man. She could be as malleable as a kitten and as voracious as a tiger. She knew that even at the age of forty-three she still had a great body. She put a lot of time, effort and money into keeping it that way. The corset was purely decorative – a deliciously tantalizing silk and lace confection that nipped her waist into a neat twenty-two inches, cut high up over her hips, extending the line of her long legs.

'Not still angry with me, darling?' she murmured as she placed her slim fingers on the lapels of his jacket and slid it carefully from his shoulders. Her perfume filled his nostrils and he felt the heat in his loins spread as Elena started to unbutton his shirt. Piers grabbed hold of her, pulling her close to his chest, holding her so tightly that she squeaked. Her soft lips yielded under his hard mouth. He pushed against her, forcing her neck backwards. Eventually when he released her she sagged like a string puppet and then, recovering, she pulled him over to the bed, where she lay down on her back, waiting for Piers to join her.

'Guy Chippenham wants to buy the Canaletto . . .' Her voice was seductively low. Piers could see the triumph in her eyes.

'I know that, my love, but he can't afford it.' Piers' hand slid up Elena's thigh and expertly set to work on unpopping poppers.

'He says he'll give you what you wanted.'

'The full £1.5 million?'

'Well, that is what you wanted, isn't it?'

'Aren't you a clever girl?' Piers sighed with pleasure as his fingers found what they were searching for.

'Just think,' Elena murmured as she squirmed against his hand, 'if you hadn't joined me tonight, you still might not have a buyer for it.' She felt Piers' body stiffen.

'You could have gone on your own, Elena, as I suggested.'

'Oh no, darling. Guy would have been deeply offended. When I suggested dinner I told him quite firmly that you would be with me. He would have been insulted if he'd thought that you had accepted another invitation. And you can hardly go upsetting the director of the Welbeck Museum, can you? You had no choice, Piers, but to accompany me.'

'I let Gus down very badly. I had promised to take her to dinner.'

'You indulge her too often. Besides, I bet she had lots of friends to celebrate with.' Elena found Piers's attitude towards his wayward daughter frightfully irritating. 'If it wasn't for your business, Piers, she wouldn't be living in such style. If she makes a fuss, perhaps you should remind her of that.'

'The house is no big deal, Elena. It was, after all, your idea to use it as a tax write-off. I wish I could do more for her. The trouble is she's so damned stubborn that she won't let me. To be absolutely honest I feel very bad about tonight, about letting her down. You put me in a bloody awful position, Elena. Don't spring any more last-minute dinners on me like that. It's just not on . . .'

Piers could only console himself with the fact that the deal had, thanks to Elena, gone splendidly well. All he had to do now was make it up to Gus. He would deliver her gift in the morning, having fully intended to give it to her over dinner tonight. He was so desperately proud of her – his only child – making her mark through her cool intelligence. What a strange world that could create such a talent from such an unconventional cocktail of genes. She was so unlike her mother – and worlds removed from him! Only a God with a large sense of humour could have mapped out such a course for the daughter of Piers Lawrence.

'Come and show me what a clever wife you think I am . . .' Elena cooed seductively, bringing him back to the present.

Everything would be fine, just so long as the past and the present never collided!

Chapter Two

Piers eased his black Mercedes convertible into a space outside Augusta's house. It was in one of those rather bijou Chelsea mews, where the occupants painted their front doors in dark gloss colours, and the brass door furniture received a weekly polish. Even Gus had found time in her schedule to cover the sills with windowboxes crammed with blue and yellow irises and white tulips. The cobbles beneath Piers's feet had worn smooth over two hundred or so years, and had the appearance of being clean enough to picnic on. He glanced up at the top, second-floor window which he knew to be Gus's bedroom and noted the closed drapes on the other side of the glass. Piers glanced at his watch. It was almost eleven o'clock and he'd been up for three hours already. No doubt Gus had had a hard night's celebrating.

Trying to extricate himself from Elena's side had not been an easy task. He hated it when Elena sulked. It could drag on for simply days on end. He'd stop off at Harrods on the way back to the hotel and sort her out. Life had been so straightforward in his single days after Cat's death. Sometimes he wondered whether remarriage had been such a wise move. But without any doubt Elena had her advantages, both to his business and to his home life. She had some very heavyweight Italian friends who had replenished his client list when the recession hit the rest of Europe and America, and as she was for ever reminding him, she was an inventive and entertaining bedmate. She also put a stop to the seemingly endless queue of women who had tried to get him to the altar. While Elena was expensive to keep, she was a useful expense. Rather like a good accountant, he mused. If only she could resolve her problems with Gus then life could be very sweet.

It was true to say that Elena could be difficult, he knew that. She was a typically spoiled rich woman. Her late husband had been a very good client of Piers's, and upon his death Elena had called upon Piers to advise her as to what to do with Giorgio's art collection. Piers was aware that Elena had set her sights on him, but at least he knew she wasn't a golddigger. Elena's inherited fortune was sizeable. Between them they had done some pretty good deals together, to their mutual advantage, and under Elena's gentle but persistent persuasion, he had eventually decided that the time had come to settle down once more. He had put the moment off for long enough. At the time of his marriage to Elena, Augusta's mother, Cat, had been dead fourteen years. The single-minded teenage Gus needed a female figure in her life, a role model other than himself. He loved her desperately, but he knew he couldn't possibly provide all the emotional needs required by an intelligent young girl. She needed a mother, for heaven's sake! But the entire venture – at least from that point of view – had been a bloody nightmare. Matters weren't helped along by the fact that Mirabelle, Elena's daughter, and Gus seemed to be permanently at war. Piers had hoped that Gus would be thrilled at a ready-made sister, just two years older than herself, but they were such opposites! Sometimes Piers felt he deserved a UN peace-keeping medal for smoothing things over between all of the women in his life. Elena always took Mirabelle's side, and then got mad at *him* if he didn't! Privately Piers felt that Elena was blinkered when it came to her daughter's behaviour. She could be a devious little madam, but there it was ... Didn't he have enough on his plate without having to sort out these little domestic squabbles?

On this occasion, though, he knew he had been a bit of a heel, letting Gus down. It had been her night. He should have been stronger with Elena, and insisted for once.

Clutching the present safely in his pocket, he wondered what he would say to her. This was not a new situation and he had a shrewd suspicion she'd be angry with him. It could quite possibly be one of their more awkward meetings, but he must brace himself, face her and apologize. He pressed Gus's doorbell firmly, keeping his finger on it for several moments. He was prepared to keep it there for several more, knowing what a difficult task it was to wake his daughter, but within seconds he heard the soft thudding of light footsteps coming down the stairs.

As the door opened, Piers stepped in, and then stopped in his tracks.

'Oh. Who are you?' he said bluntly, not bothering to cover his surprise at finding the barely dressed coffee-skinned lady in his daughter's house.

'Flora,' the girl said, extending her hand towards him. 'I'm sharing Gus's house. Who are you?'

'Augusta's father. I didn't know she had a lodger.'

'Oh well, there you go,' the girl said turning back towards the staircase. 'Gus is asleep. Do you want me to wake her up?'

'If you wouldn't mind.'

'Come on then,' she said, leading the way on up. Piers tried not to notice the way her slim hips swayed beneath her thin cotton nightshirt. Her bare ankles flashed delicately in front of his nose. He forced his eyes down towards the carpet.

'Sit down,' Flora invited, pointing to the sitting room. 'I'll tell Gus you're here.'

Piers paused in the doorway. The girl had invited him

to sit, but it would have taken a fair amount of ingenuity to clear a space large enough. Nearly every available surface, including the floor, was covered in piles of books, files and notepads. Piers hovered in the centre and then decided he'd better not move anything as he had the definite feeling that there was some strategy in the mess – a kind of order which he could very easily upset if he so much as shifted a pen. Instead, he found himself drawn towards a painting on the far wall. Augusta's walls were lined with paintings but this one had a peculiar attractiveness. It wasn't a large canvas, but it still had the ability to catch one's attention, the sort of star quality that made Piers' spine tingle with the knowledge of the very rightness of it. He stood in front of it, marvelling in the quality of the light which poured through the opened window into the small, almost brutally bare room where the subject kneeled. The young woman's face was clouded with a deep sorrow which one could only guess at, but she held her sadness with dignity. Her small white hands were clasped neatly in her lap, her shoulders set squarely, her neck held high. There was a pride in her bearing, showing through the veil of sorrow. It was a sad, stark painting, but at the same time it was deeply moving and beautiful. Gus had wanted it from the very moment she had set eyes on it when she had been what, no more than eight?

Piers remembered the day so vividly. He had arrived at her school in the morning at the designated time, ready to take her out for the day as the rules permitted. She could escape once every half term so long as she was returned by six o'clock. It was the first such outing they had had together even though Augusta had been at the school since she was barely six. She had not settled at all well and the headmistress had most strongly advised Piers to stay away for the first couple of outings, telling him firmly that it would only serve to unsettle

Augusta, and that it would be better to stick to the school holidays for exeats. Reluctantly, and without knowing any better, Piers had bowed to the experienced woman's judgement.

Augusta had appeared solemn and miserable. Her huge grey eyes had studied him suspiciously and, he was sure he wasn't mistaken in this, accusingly. Piers had felt awkward and stiff with this strangely silent little girl. All thoughts he had had of whisking her up into his arms and filling the day with cuddles and laughter had melted away. Augusta had put her hand out. 'Good morning, Daddy,' she had said stiffly.

They had been to the zoo, the waxworks and to Fortnum's for tea. Piers couldn't recall Augusta smiling once. And then, in desperation, he had whisked her into the Royal Academy at the last minute where there was an exhibition of works by the final-year students.

Augusta had viewed the pieces silently but studiedly. Piers had tried to explain a little about various influences in the work, as he saw them, but he felt that this small child was much too young to know what on earth he was talking about. And then she had found this painting. She stood in front of it with her hand clapped to her mouth. Piers stood behind her, expecting her to move on, but she didn't. It was as if she were devouring every minute detail of the work: the bare white walls; the window with its chipped paintwork, looking out on to a blue, cloudless sky; the glorious light which surrounded the small kneeling figure in the foreground, almost as if she wore a halo. Piers was shocked to realize that he, too, was deeply moved by the picture.

'You like the painting?' he had asked Augusta needlessly.

'It makes me feel funny,' she said eventually. 'The lady looks so sad that I'd like to reach out and touch her. And her room – it's such a sad room, Daddy, with no things in it. Look, there's no carpet on the floor, the walls

21

are bare, she doesn't even have a mirror. And her clothes . . . why do you think she's dressed in black?'

'Perhaps it's because someone she cares about has died,' Piers had said softly, stroking the silky hair on top of Augusta's small head.

Augusta said nothing more, but continued to stare deeply into the painting, as if she were searching the woman's very soul. Piers took a few steps away, expecting his daughter to follow, but she remained, transfixed.

When he had returned to the Academy the following day, he found the damned thing had been sold already. It had been the devil of a job to track down its purchaser and persuade the woman to sell it to him – for treble its value, of course. But the look of pleasure and disbelief on Augusta's face the following Christmas when she unwrapped her gift had made all the effort worthwhile.

'Gus says it reminds her of her mother.' Flora's voice cut sharply into his thoughts.

Piers's shoulders stiffened and he turned, his expression darkening. His thick black brows knitted together in a frown of irritation. 'Oh?'

'Yes,' Flora continued, as she walked towards him. 'It must have been awful – her dying so young like that.'

Piers's blue eyes glittered at her coldly. He didn't discuss Cat's death with anyone. 'Is Gus coming?'

'Sure, she's just crawling out of her sack. I expect you know how difficult it is to drag her out of bed.'

'Lived here long?' Piers turned his back on the painting, fearing that the artless girl might return to the subject.

'A couple of months. Feels longer, though. It's a lovely house. I haven't been used to having this much space before. All those bedrooms. I couldn't believe it when I first saw the place. Four bedrooms and only one person. Two bathrooms – just amazing. So Gus said I could move in, and we can study together. It helps a lot.'

'Study together?'

'Sure.' Flora licked the tip of her forefinger, having placed a last corner of toast in her mouth. She finished chewing and then continued, 'We were at Bar School together. We're based at different Inns, though. Gus is in the Middle Temple and I'm at Lincoln's Inn.'

'So you're a barrister, too!'

'Yes. Well, at least I will be when I've done my year's pupillage. Only unlike Gus I haven't found it quite so easy to get a place.'

She stopped abruptly and looked at her watch. Her eyes widened in horror. 'Oh my God, I'm supposed to be meeting someone in five minutes. Sorry, umm. I've gotta run. Nice meeting you.'

Piers watched the young woman retreat. Augusta had always had a penchant for waifs and strays.

'Daddy!' Piers grinned affectionately at the bleary-eyed vision in the doorway. Gus's long brown hair fell in a tousled mess around her shoulders. Her cheeks carried the rosy bloom of sleep and she hugged the enormous towelling gown tightly around her. 'Heavens, what's the time? How long have you been here?'

'Not long, maybe five minutes. I met Flora.'

'Yes,' she said, folding her hair behind her ears. 'She was having to live with her mother way up in North London somewhere.'

'But I thought you preferred living alone. You've always professed to like your independence so much, I'm surprised that you wanted company . . .'

'I love having Flora here,' Gus said crisply. 'She was finding it difficult to study at home and we get on brilliantly . . . anyway, I'm sure you aren't terribly interested in Flora's problems.'

Piers sensed her hostility growing. 'No, no. It's none of my business. I'm just interested in what you do, seeing as you're my only child and your best interests are always uppermost in my mind.'

'It's a pity you couldn't make last night.' Augusta pushed her arms in front of her chest and folded them protectively, her grey eyes glittering at him accusingly. 'I imagine *someone* managed to dissuade you from keeping your appointment with me.'

Piers shuffled from one foot to the other uncomfortably. 'It had absolutely nothing to do with Elena.' He felt distinctly awkward with the fact that his daughter usually knew exactly when he was lying. That was partly why boarding school had been so damned convenient. 'It was business, darling. Look,' he made a step towards her and reached out to take her arm, 'I know how important it was to you, but I would have been there if I could – you know I would – and, besides, I bet you had lots of friends to celebrate with.'

Gus looked at him, watching him squirm. Should she tell him how she had celebrated the remainder of her evening after dinner in Hall? How she had come home to an empty house and opened a bottle of champagne which she had drunk while reading her text books?

'Sure, of course I did.' She twisted away from him and perched her bottom on the arm of the sofa. 'So, did you sell it?' she asked coldly.

'Sell what?'

'Whatever it was you were selling . . . last night.'

'As a matter of fact yes, I think I did. A Canaletto – the Welbeck Museum. Elena managed to negotiate the price.'

'So Elena was with you, then?'

Piers flushed. 'Yes, yes, she was.'

'Well, I'm glad you had a successful evening.'

'Oh come on, Gus. Stop giving me such a hard time.' Piers was starting to get irritated. He always did when he was being put into a corner. He reached into his pocket. 'I've got something for you.'

Augusta watched impassively as her father dug into the inside pocket of his jacket. Her arms, crossed in

24

front of her chest, tightened and her mouth twitched as she fought to conceal her emotions. This was, after all, his usual pattern. He felt guilty over last night, and now he would give her a trinket to assuage his conscience. He held out the oblong box and Augusta regarded it without moving for several moments. Eventually she took it. 'Thank you,' she said. 'It's very kind ...' She placed it into the pocket of her gown.

'Open it,' her father commanded. Really Augusta could be very stubborn and tiresome at times.

Sighing, she pulled open the narrow case. She gasped when she saw its contents. 'But it's fabulous! It must have cost you a fortune.'

Piers shrugged. 'That's not important. What is important is the fact that you deserve it, darling. Now, shall I put it on you?'

Augusta held her hair away from her neck, as her father deftly draped the three-stranded pearl choker around her slender neck. Once it was fastened she stood up and examined her reflection in the mirror over the mantelpiece. The huge oval cabochon sapphire sat at the base of her throat, surrounded by the pure white fire of glittering diamonds. 'It's superb,' she said. 'I don't deserve it ...'

She watched her father's reflection as she stared into the mirror. He placed his hands on her shoulders. 'Remember, Augusta, that I love you dearly. You are my only child and I am extremely proud of you.' Their eyes met for several moments. Cool grey held ice-blue.

Augusta's fingers traced the fine gemstone as she spoke. 'Do you think Mummy would have been proud of me?' she said in a voice which he had to strain to hear.

Piers swallowed hard and Augusta noticed the small twitch of the muscle in his left cheek which always signified anger. 'Yes, I'm sure your mother would have been,' he said almost coldly.

'Oh well,' Gus said, deciding to lighten the moment, 'how about coffee?'

Piers checked his watch. 'I'd love some, darling, but I really have to dash. I promised Elena I'd meet up with her...'

''Course you did.' Gus bit her tongue, resisting the temptation to carp at her father yet again. 'Don't worry, I know how demanding she can be.'

'It's been good to see you, darling.'

'And you, Daddy.'

Piers bent his head down to kiss his daughter lightly on each cheek. 'I expect to see you in Guernsey at the end of August, Gus. I'm giving a party for Elena.' Gus frowned but managed to stay silent. Piers turned towards the stairs. 'Oh, and by the way, Gus,' he said over his shoulder, 'good luck in chambers!'

'Thanks.'

The front door thudded closed behind him. The house was so still and quiet. Slowly she removed the necklace and carefully replaced it on the satin cushion in its neat little box. Then she snapped the lid shut. She couldn't fail to love the gift, but the best gift of all would have been to have her father to herself for once. Gus couldn't remember when she had last had that treat. Since Elena had taken over his life – what, five years ago? – they had at most only been alone for a couple of hours. Gus couldn't help but think that Elena was jealous of her. She wanted all of his attention on her, all of the time, and on her daughter. But it wasn't Gus's style to point it out to her father. He should have the intelligence to work it out for himself, and deal with it. If Gus mentioned it to him, he'd only think that it was she, Gus, who was jealous and insecure.

Well, in a way maybe she was. Hadn't she had her father to herself for just about fourteen years? Okay, she'd been away at school, but they had spent a lot of time together during the holidays – trips around

26

Europe, cruises with friends of her father, wonderful stays in beautiful houses and villas around the world. All very privileged and protected and all the while she had been made to feel the most important thing in Piers Lawrence's life. There had been many other women before Elena, but none that he had chosen to commit himself to. Gus had tried, but found it difficult to like most of them. It took Gus up until the age of twelve to work out just why they were always mean to her when her father wasn't around. She was something that got in the way, something that took up a large chunk of his emotions, thus removing that part of him from them. Thankfully her father had always been loyal to her, and had protected her interests above those of his lady friends, up until the arrival of the Angeletti team. Ironically, though, Gus had been delighted for him in the early stages of the relationship. Elena had seemed so kind and loving. And Gus had even been persuaded that her ready-made sister would be a wonderful addition to her life. For her father's sake, and for her own loneliness, she had tried very hard to care for Elena and Mirabelle. But they had turned out to be just the same as all the others. Worse!

Perhaps one day she might learn to stop snapping his head off and then he might find her company more enjoyable. Sometimes she could be her own worst enemy.

Gus felt very alone. The oppressive silence of the house crowded in around her, bringing back last night's feelings of isolation and loneliness. Flora had been out until the small hours, still celebrating her call night which had been a week before Gus's.

She knew it was childish to mind so much, but she had a horrible sense of being abandoned, in the same way as she had had when she had been sent off to school, at the age of six. Then the separation from her father had been unbearable. She could still remember

27

the pain of the rejection she had felt. She had pleaded and begged her father not to send her away, not to leave her like that, but he had woodenly explained that his business affairs made it impossible for him to be able to be with her at home all the time, but that they would make up for being apart in the holidays. She reasoned to herself that she must be being sent away because she was getting very much in the way. She had tried very hard to be good after that. It had been easy to settle down and get on with work and the business of learning. That way she didn't have to think about how much she missed both her parents. But still she counted off the days to the next time she would see him.

She knew that he loved her. She just wanted to pretend sometimes – not very often – that he was still her special person, that somehow they could re-enter the happy world they inhabited in her memory. A time when he had been her world, and she his. She had been a sensitive child, and she had had to toughen up her hide in order to deal with the separation from her beloved father. Most people now thought of her as fiercely independent – and strong! But they didn't know how vulnerable she could feel deep inside.

She stood by the window, watching as her father edged his car out of the tight space on the street below. She leaned her head against the cold glass.

'One day you'll find time for me, Daddy,' she sighed sadly. 'Maybe you'll realize what's happening to us.' Then, straightening her shoulders, she turned away from the scene. 'Until then I'll manage on my own, just like I always did. I'm going to work so hard that you'll be really proud of me, Daddy, just see . . .' she said softly to herself.

As Piers pulled out of Gus's road, his carphone rang. 'Lawrence.' He pushed the remote button.

'Ah good, glad to catch up with you, me old mate.'

Piers's face darkened. There was no mistaking that voice. 'What the hell do you want? And how did you get this number?'

'I can get anything I want if I try hard enough – or had you forgotten?'

'What do you want?' Piers growled, slamming his foot hard on the brake as the lights ahead of him changed to red.

'Just a chat. A proposition.'

'No, Thompson. Just stay out of my life – and don't contact me again!' Piers disconnected the phone, sliding down the window and gulping in deep breaths of the polluted London air. But even that tasted sweet after hearing Thompson's poisonous voice.

Chapter Three

'God this case is fascinating!' Flora wriggled in her seat and continued to scan the bundle of papers on the table in front of her. 'There's just so much evidence to support our side. I can't see how the prosecution have a case at all.'

Gus leaned back in her chair at the opposite end of the table and eyed her flatmate enviously. Gus had spent the morning in court with Henry, her pupil master, making an application for a non-molestation order against a separated husband who had got into the habit of entering his estranged wife's bedroom late at night, flashing his parts and saying, 'Look what you're missing, you old bitch.' Unbelievably the judge had been initially reluctant to grant the application, but after some smooth talking by Henry he had eventually been persuaded that the level of distress suffered by the hapless woman was sufficient grounds.

All very interesting stuff ... while Flora was defending in a murder! Ironic, thought Gus, that Flora's work should be looked on as being at the bottom of the profession – the lowliest of the low, overworked, poorly paid and the keeping of dubious company! Flora was specializing in criminal stuff, while Gus was privileged to be dealing with residence orders and battles over who should get the washing machine and who should get the dishwasher.

Whilst it all had a degree of importance, she didn't feel she was doing an enormous amount to advance the quality of life of fellow humanity. To Flora's pupil master's clients, a decent job by counsel could mean the difference between life or death – or at least life or a shorter sentence. As Gus was reading the affidavit to support the application based on a semi-detached house, domestic bank statements and a few unimpressive share certificates, Flora was poring over forensic reports and police statements. As Gus was weighing up the technicalities of property value against projected income, Flora was assessing the alleged murderer's physical ability to do in someone twice his size with his bare hands.

It had been nearly eight weeks since Gus had started her pupillage. And in that time the only respite from matrimonial and ancillary matters had been an invitation to stand in for someone else's pupil who was 'off sick' when needed to take notes during her pupil master's case. Henry hadn't forewarned her that day. James Kentish had poked his head around Henry's door and ahemmed in Gus's direction. Henry had waved Gus off with a blithe, forgot to mention it, but cut along there, dear girl, sort of attitude. Obviously Gus had fallen over James Kentish before, but she didn't really know much about him. Although members of the same chambers worked in the same place, they were very much independent of each other, each being self-employed rather than in partnership. Chambers were more a pooling of resources and a spread of expertise designed to benefit collectively and individually each barrister, than an association working together. Like Flora, he practised at the Criminal Bar – the supposedly mucky side of the profession, although just by looking at him one could see how much he appreciated the finer things in life – and those were more usually attained through a career in civil or chancery matters.

They were defending in a rape case and James confided to Gus on the way to the Old Bailey that he had an ulterior motive in taking a lady pupil with him. 'It does the jury good to see that the alleged rapist has a woman on his side. Makes it seem that the chap can't be that much of a monster if an intelligent-looking woman is helping him. In an ideal world Julia Montgomery would have defended, except she's had to take early maternity leave. Some kind of ghastly complications, I gather. You see, to have a pregnant barrister defending you is a real one in the eye for the prosecution. The psychology is bizarre. There is the poor jury faced with the ultimate contradictions: the rapist – the misogynist who defiles women and is rightly hated and feared by women – and the representation of all that is yielding and vulnerable, the essence of femaleness, standing up for the rapist. Ergo the man can't be a rapist. And even if he is, he must have been severely provoked. You get the gist of it?'

'So what do you want me to do?' Augusta was still reading the gory details of the case, and fast realizing that she had certainly got the gist of it. James Kentish's pupil probably wasn't ill at all – he was simply the wrong gender for this particular trial.

'Well, as I'm sure I can't persuade you to stuff a pillow under your gown, just deliver the odd note to him. Smile encouragingly. Make it obvious that "we're with him". You know the sort of thing.'

'Is he guilty?'

'Augusta,' James said stiffly, 'you know very well that it is not our job to judge. That is for the jury to decide. We merely have to put our client's case as professionally and competently as possible in order to ensure him a fair trial.'

Augusta swallowed hard and tried not to take the rebuke to heart. She should have known better than to ask the question.

'Between the two of us,' James's voice dropped to a whisper, 'I think the little sod's as guilty as hell!'

What had most impressed Gus about the entire three-day event was James's handling of the case. He had held the jury spellbound with his oratorical gifts. The prosecution had been made mincemeat of by Kentish. As every bit of solid evidence was presented, he tore it to shreds. Time and again he reduced to tears the poor woman who had allegedly been raped. Gus was sickened by the attack upon her, needing to summon up all her professional training, her supposed hardness and objectivity, to appreciate the tactical instruments employed, to divorce herself from emotion. Their job was to put the case for their client, and to put it better than the other side. It was a game played for very high stakes. This man would be put away for a very long time if he was convicted. Whether he was innocent or guilty was not for she or James to decide, but for the jury. Always she must remember that.

James was almost uncomfortably smooth, leaving Augusta unsure as to whether she admired or disliked him. Either way, he certainly knew how to play to a jury. It had been a welcome diversion from the misery of divorce. There was something almost bloodcurdlingly exhilarating about the criminal courts which Augusta knew she would never feel when arguing the toss over whether a wife deserved to be paid as much as a nanny.

Ridiculous now to think how it had seemed that Flora had got the bum deal, being out on a limb in some down-and-out chambers, handling drossy legal aid stuff while Gus would be nodding wigs with the cream of the profession at the hub, the very centre of operations. The fact of the matter was that Flora was having a wild time cutting her teeth on meaty criminal cases, watching her master coddle a jury, and meeting the less uptight, and arguably cleverer, members of the Bar to boot. The highlight of Augusta's day was not being mistaken for Henry's secretary. Still, it was only for a year. After that she would be able to make grand plans for her future. In the meantime, she intended to pump Flora voraciously

33

in order that she might offload some of her new knowledge in Gus's direction.

Gus collected her papers up neatly, retying the red ribbon in the centre of the bundle. She had thought a great deal in the past four weeks about her experience in court with James Kentish, about his extraordinarily riveting performance resulting in a not guilty verdict, and the slightly teasing way he had said to her as they parted that day, 'By the way, give my regards to Daddy!' She must remember to ask her father how he knew James.

Quietly, leaving Flora bent over her work, she went to the kitchen and set about her task, humming lightly to herself. It was almost 2.30 a.m., but even so, Gus was after information and she knew how to break Flora's defences.

With a final flourish of salt and vinegar, Gus carried the chip-laden plate through to Flora. Flora's nose had already started to curl suspiciously. Gus pushed the giant pile of crinkle-cut oven chips towards Flora, who groaned with the agony of one who is about to be broken. 'How could you?' she moaned.

'Because I know how much you like them,' Gus said, helping herself to the rather large specimen on the top of the pile.

'So what do you want to know?' Flora said, as she pushed aside her papers and set about feasting on Gus's wicked bribe.

'Everything,' Gus said, rubbing the fat from her fingertips. 'Just everything. Since seeing James Kentish's performance I've got very interested in criminal practice.'

'Hussy,' Flora giggled.

'Professional interest,' Gus confirmed. 'He's not my type. Far too old.'

'Oh for God's sake, Gus, every woman on the planet would find James Kentish sexy. There's just something so smooth about him.'

'My admiration is purely professional – unlike yours.'

'Of course, Augusta,' Flora said, mocking her primly. 'Besides, you gave up men when you were seventeen, didn't you, thanks to that delightful stepsister of yours?' Gus's grey eyes clouded for a moment and Flora immediately regretted her taunts which were meant in fun. 'Hey, I'm sorry. I guess I shouldn't pull your leg in that direction. Come on, help me with this disgustingly good feast and I'll tell you all about it.'

As Gus settled back to listen to Flora's animated recounting of her forays down at the Old Bailey she had to admit that she had found James Kentish extremely attractive, but finding someone attractive was no reason to think of remapping her career. No, there was something deeper in her that had been stirred by her experience with him – a sense of being closer to the edge, of real, animal excitement charged by the fact that everyone was playing for high stakes – stakes which were lost or won with tactics and intellect. The adrenalin had buzzed through her veins as the Court waited silently for the foreman of the jury to give the verdict. How could she ever feel the same way about these petty civil squabbles? She would keep her ears open and maybe, at the end of her pupillage with Henry, she might get some experience in criminal stuff. Gus knew that it was not going to be easy bearing in mind all her training would be pushing her towards civil matters. But Gus liked a challenge and she knew, somehow, she'd find a way in.

Chapter Four

Gus snapped the seat belt across her lap and a few moments later they were airborne, on the short flight to the small Channel Island of Guernsey which her father had made his home seventeen years earlier. She wished Flora had been able to join her on this trip, but Flora had her own plans for the Bank Holiday which involved trekking through the Peak District with some friends.

Piers had demanded her presence. As usual Gus had tried to make excuses, but he wouldn't hear of it. He and Elena were holding an anniversary party to mark their first five years of marriage and Gus's presence was expected. No buts! Besides, she was all too aware of exactly how much Piers had done to support her throughout her long years of training. The house had been a gift to her upon her twenty-first birthday. He had tried to buy her a Porsche for her eighteenth, but she had managed to persuade him that a nifty little Peugeot would be far more practical for student life. Unlike her stepsister, who revelled in being a material girl, Gus found the ostentatious trappings of her father's wealth to be something of a hindrance in her life, always creating a barrier between herself and the rest of the world. However hard she tried to pretend to be just any normal girl, something would happen to let those around her know that her father was a multimillionaire and she would be treated differently until she managed to convince people that she was just a normal everyday sort of girl.

Before the arrival of the Angeletti women Gus had

always looked forward to returning home to Guernsey. The house had held so many happy memories of time spent with her father.

They had moved there from Sussex after her mother's death – not that Gus could remember much about the house in Sussex. She had been only three at the time. Sometimes, though, the strangest things would evoke memories of her mother and the house. Wafts of a particular scent, or the pear-drop smell of nail varnish would bring back the feeling of being safely cocooned in a maternal bosom. Sometimes drifts of music or maybe a certain type of incense. She had no clear memory of her mother's face in her mind's eye, although she had a few faded photographs of her. Her hair was a shade darker than Gus's, and Gus always felt that her mother had a vitality which she had, sadly, failed to inherit. Gus had vague recollections of windswept walks with her parents across the rolling Downs, when her short legs found it hard to keep up with them. She couldn't remember how they were, though. She fantasized that she remembered what a loving family they all had been, yet she had no clear pictures to recall. Since that time, Gus had carried the feeling that life could never be perfect again. She had never dared ask her father if he had felt the same way. Whenever she mentioned her mother he grew sad or angry, so that over the years she had avoided asking about her. Now, with countless silences between them, to ask straight out would be to take on a very big issue. She assumed that the reason he had sold everything up so quickly was to leave the void behind him.

Having safely landed, Gus collected her two suitcases and was quickly ushered through the VIP route. A few minutes later, she stepped out into bright sunlight. She looked around for the familiar figure of her father as she placed her sunglasses on her face.

'Hello, Gus,' came a silky, almost feline voice behind her. 'Long time no see.'

Gus's heart sank into the concrete below her feet. 'Well, well. I hardly expected to see you, Mirabelle.'

Thick blonde hair spilled around her stepsister's shoulders. Her face looked tanned, as usual. The freckles across the bridge of her nose were accentuated. Her aquamarine eyes glittered at Gus and the bracelets around her wrists jangled noisily together as she brushed the blonde locks from her face in an affected sweep back towards the crown of her head. Her long legs were set off to best advantage with a garment which could almost be described as a skirt. Gus had to call on all her self-control to stop herself from spinning on her toes and catching the next flight back to London.

Mirabelle walked beside Gus as they made their way to the car park. Although Mirabelle was aware of Gus's struggle with the luggage, she did not offer to help. Always so busy proving herself, Mirabelle thought, let her get on with it. She knew how disappointed Gus was not to have her father meet her. It had taken a lot of persuasion to get Piers to agree to Mirabelle's suggestion that she come and pick up Gus. God, they could be insufferably close, the pair of them. It almost made Mirabelle want to be sick. She couldn't remember his ever turning up to meet *her* at the airport! Always his precious Gus! Piers had eventually acquiesced on the basis that he thought what a nice idea it would be for the two girls to try to get on together. That was a joke! But at least she'd managed to keep the pair of them apart for a little longer.

'I haven't had a chance to congratulate you yet ... and,' she continued in her affectedly deep voice, 'I couldn't wait to show you what Piers has given me.'

Gus shook her head in amazement. When would Mirabelle grow up? She behaved like a ten-year-old.

Gus could see straight through her motives. She always had been so competitive.

'Piers was going to come and get you himself, but I'm afraid I insisted. I explained how I hadn't seen you in an age, Gus. And he understood that we'd want to spend some time together.'

'How thoughtful of him,' Gus said through gritted teeth as they reached the shiny red Mercedes convertible that Mirabelle was so keen to show off. How on earth could her father have possibly thought that Gus would want to spend time with Mirabelle? She struggled to heave her suitcases into the rear passenger seats, ignoring Mirabelle's wince of concern over her champagne leather upholstery.

The house was a twenty-minute drive from the airport, separated from the main road by twelve-foot-high security gates, a uniformed guard and a mile-long sweep of a drive. As soon as the tyres hit the golden tarmac it was a cue for Mirabelle to push her foot further to the floor, shooting Gus backwards in her seat. Gus's white-knuckled hands gripped the door handle to stop her from sliding across into Mirabelle's lap as they flew round the sharp right-hand bend that brought the house into view. Then, mercifully, the brakes were hit and the car skidded to an ungainly stop outside the Lawrence mansion. The sun blazed onto the glaring cream façade of the neo-Georgian property. Two twenty-foot-high Corinthian columns towered above them from the summit of the three wide stone steps that led to the vast front door. As Gus struggled to reclaim her suitcases the door opened and Patrick, the butler, greeted her in familiar soft Irish tones. 'It's good to see you, Miss Augusta. It's been some time since you've been home. You look in need of a rest, if you don't mind my saying so.'

'No, I don't mind, Paddy. Frankly, I'm exhausted. I was rather looking forward to one of your Pimm's specials. The truth is I've been dreaming of it. The weather here must be ten degrees hotter than in England. I can't wait to get out of these clothes.'

'Your room is ready for you. I'll bring the cases up right away. Then what about drinks by the pool in half an hour?'

'Perfect,' Gus beamed gratefully, enjoying the cool interior of the marble hallway. The gleaming surface of the George II breakfast table in the centre of the hall reflected the pinks and peaches of the old-fashioned roses spilling out of a blue and gold Sèvres vase. The scent wafted under her nose, immediately pulling her back to hot childhood summers running through the rose walk. She would visit it later on, perhaps after her swim.

'Where is my father?' She turned back to Paddy, ignoring Mirabelle.

'Out until much later, miss. Some business to attend to . . .'

'As ever,' Gus sighed, trying not to let her disappointment show. Even though Mirabelle stood behind her, she could feel the malicious satisfaction emanating from her. Collecting the smaller of her two bags she climbed the long curve of the stairs to her room.

The French windows that led out onto the balcony were thrown open and the white voile drapes fluttered diaphanously in the gap. Her bed, a Dutch pine four-poster chosen by her father for her twelfth birthday, added an almost rustic simplicity to the plain white room. Mirabelle had called it her nun's cell. Gus supposed it was rather plain, but she had considered it her escape from the flamboyant luxury of the rest of the house. Anyone would be a fool to consider the room too simple though, as a closer inspection of the rough, sepia-tinged architectural sketches of Florence's domed church of Santa Maria del Fiore revealed their creator as a young Leonardo da Vinci. Gus had begged her father for them when a private collector had put them secretly up for sale the year before Piers met Elena.

Gus tore off her clothes and left them in an untidy pile on the bleached pine floor. At last her body felt free. The breeze cooled her travel-weary skin as she started to hang up the few obligatory dresses she had brought with her. When she closed the mirrored wardrobe door, she caught sight of her own nakedness. Her flesh looked so white, almost alabaster. She was long and lean, and lacking in the curves department. Her breasts could never be described as voluptuous. More like pert, or athletic perhaps, she thought, as she sneered down at them. Her long brown hair had turned even more wavy in the heat, and it curled annoyingly into the nape of her neck. She gathered it up and twisted it into a ponytail, showing off her slender neck. Like a goose, she thought, critically.

Oh well, her charms were subtler than those of the sexy Mirabelle. Gus might not have the blonde hair, or the big tits, or the curving hips. But she did have the brains! As she let her hair fall back to her shoulders, Gus smiled at her reflection, comforting herself with the thought that Mirabelle's looks would reach their sell-by date a lot faster than Gus's grey cells.

After a brief cold shower she slipped into her swimsuit and stepped out onto her balcony that overlooked the pool. Looking around to make sure no one was watching, she clambered over the parapet and dived expertly into the clear blue water below.

Elena Angeletti Lawrence peered down from her elevated position at the balcony overlooking the pool. The girl was such a tomboy! When would she learn to start acting like a lady? Really, Elena despaired. That's what came of being brought up without a mother. Piers had spoiled the child miserably. She barely knew how to behave. Thank goodness Mirabelle was home. Elena never stopped hoping that some of Mirabelle's grooming and polish might rub off on Augusta.

A sharp knock at the door signalled Mirabelle's appearance. 'You've seen her?' Her daughter plonked herself down on the blue silk chaise longue.

'She's swimming. I haven't spoken to her as yet.'

'You're not missing much. She didn't say a word all the way back from the airport. I feel sorry for Piers. Imagine being lumbered with a bore like that. No sense of humour, no sense of fun. She's like a miserable blob just sitting there looking disapproving. I wish she'd made another one of her famous excuses and stayed away.'

'Well, she couldn't. And Piers must be terribly grateful that he's got one daughter he can be proud of!'

'He's not my father. I do wish you wouldn't try and pretend that he can just slot in and take Daddy's place,' Mirabelle sighed. It was a conversation they often held. Elena had tried so hard to replace her child's precious father with Piers, but nobody could take his place. Mirabelle had known that she was special to him. With Piers she just couldn't understand why he didn't seem to want her as much as he did Augusta, who was such a plain, dull thing. He must be blind or stupid – and quite possibly both.

Piers was not enjoying meeting his last client of the day, the Conte di Fiorenzi and his ladyfriend Giovanna Lucciani. He was finding it a struggle to remain civil, but he knew he must. For one thing he was a good client – mostly; and for another Elena had invited the pair of them to the bloody party! But the man was a Philistine. He didn't deserve to own such a stunningly high-quality Matisse. Piers had successfully outbid two other dealers to get it knocked down for just one million and the bastard had quibbled over Piers' commission. The Count had preserved his anonymity and saved himself almost half a million against Piers' estimate of what it should have gone for. Now the man was asking if Piers had landed him with a pup of a painting that was destined to lose money. It had been no good explaining to the fool that with the panic in the air after Giffords sale in New York last week where several paintings had failed to meet their reserve, the Matisse had fetched a seriously good price taking into account there was such a drop in confidence in the market generally.

Piers disliked being railed at in Italian. While he could speak the language fluently, the content always sounded a lot louder and a damned sight ruder than if it came through in English. It had been a long and difficult day necessitating his attending a viewing of a private collection in Paris in the morning, followed by taking instructions on a possible private sale. Then he had flown back to the gallery in Guernsey to show the Matisse to his ungrateful client and his companion – a man-eating vamp who had spent the entire time flashing her long legs in Piers' direction while pretending to be attentive to the old Count. Piers guessed that the main reason the Count had been so damned difficult was because he was growing jealous over his girlfriend's behaviour. Getting involved in other people's domestic nonsense was not something he relished. But Piers kept reminding himself that the Count was a lucrative contact, and the couple would be attending the party that night, thereby making it difficult for Piers to let the pair of them know just exactly what he thought of their attitude. Piers would arrange for the Matisse to be shipped to Rome within the next few days. He was relieved when their business concluded.

He turned to the computer to access the New York gallery. The screen flashed up the latest auction catalogue details together with the anticipated price tags. Piers knew better than to judge a painting by its price. One bad sale could make the entire market jumpy; one good one could send prices rocketing. Playing the art market was almost like gambling. One had to have the necessary nose – and head – for it. Piers had burned his fingers in the past by buying in the odd painting expecting to be able to double the price when he passed it on, only to find the market then plummeted. One could either accept a lower price, or lock the painting away for a few years until the market recovered. At the end of the day it rather depended upon one's cash flow and, thankfully, Piers's cash flow was pretty sound these days. He was well able to weather the recession. Prices were still pretty low, but Piers knew that he could move something special even in troubled times. While Britain had been a lousy market with nothing happening on New Bond Street for months on end, Rome had been almost buzzing, and thanks to Elena's contacts through her late husband, Piers had gained many valuable customers.

Unlike many of his competitors, Piers had survived the past two years fairly well. After all, many of his customers hardly bothered to ask the price. Funny how much he disliked acting for those sorts of customers these days. Like the ungrateful Conte di Fiorenzi, his 'special' customers had no sense of a painting's intrinsic value, no appreciation of the artistry involved when it was that quality alone that could leave Piers feeling as if he had quite suddenly had all the wind knocked out of him. Some of the works that passed through his hands were astonishingly beautiful and he couldn't quite get over the sense of awe that haunted him, knowing that he might be one of only two or three people to feast their eyes on such masterpieces for years to come. Such paintings would be committed to some safe somewhere, too valuable to be shown, too valuable to have their whereabouts or even their owner published. He imagined his position in the world art market must be fairly unique bearing in mind the types of customers he serviced, for he must know the whereabouts of almost every major work of art that had been sold or stolen in the last twenty years.

As Piers made a last check on the catalogue, the private telephone on his desk trilled into life.

'Yes?' Piers said.

'Piers old man,' the smooth voice travelled across. 'Been trying to track you down. Secretary's chased you in London, Paris, Rome ... you ought to have a radar signal ... make you easier to find, old chap. Last place we try is Guernsey. Still, should have known. Guess you're getting ready for the do?'

'Dickie! Yes, in fact I was supposed to be home two hours ago. You've just caught me. Are you still going to make it?'

'Wouldn't miss it for the world. I told the Chief Whip that I had an extremely important function to attend – of international importance, in fact – and that all things being considered I could damned well miss a vote brought in by some bloody crackpot lefty wanting to ban showjumping because it's cruel to horses or some such twaddle. Ludicrous ... ludicrous. 'Sides, I want to see my goddaughter. I haven't set eyes on her for yonks. Gather she's quite a clever gel these days.'

'So it seems. She gets to practise on real people now, I understand.'

'Jolly good. Just the ticket. At least I'll know where to go to when I need some advice. I suppose divorce is on her list ...?' He guffawed into Piers' ear.

'How is Belinda?' Piers enquired politely.

'Belinda who?' Dickie said baldly.

'Your wife.'

'Oh, that one ...' Again Dickie brayed with laughter. 'Only joking, old man. Wouldn't be without her for the world. 'Course she'll be joining us tomorrow. She'll be coming under her own steam, not with me. She hates what she describes as a flying bubble car. Anyway, thing is, I just thought I'd let you know about security. The chopper's going to drop me off about sevenish. Thought I'd stay over for lunch on

45

Sunday. Got a proposition to put to you. I could tell you then.'

'Righto, Dickie. I'll have the Scotch waiting.'

'You're a fine man, Piers. Cheerio.'

Piers replaced the receiver. Sir Richard Crowborough, Minister for Arts, was one of his oldest friends. Piers looked forward to discovering his latest business proposition. Over the years, he had also been a loyal and lucrative client.

Gus was so deeply absorbed in her book that it took her a while to notice just how much the daylight had diminished. Curling up with Joanna Trollope was a far more alluring proposition than attending the party. However, there was no way out of it. She pulled on the white dress she had chosen for the evening. It had the simplicity of a nightgown, with its bias-cut line fluting out around her calves as she moved. The thin silk fabric clung to her hips like a second skin.

One thing Gus knew she had inherited from her mother was her love of good clothes – when she was in the mood for them, that was. It was easy to get used to her drab uniform of black suit and white shirt; easy not to have to think every morning about what she must wear, but it made a pleasant change to feel utterly feminine for once.

The music from the band grew louder as Gus came downstairs. A few guests were milling around inside the house. She slid past the flamboyantly dressed art critic Nigel Gordon, who was holding court in front of the Van Gogh in the drawing room. She spotted her father, deep in conversation with Melanie Hughes, Channel Four's doyenne of all things cultural, and decided to leave them to it. She didn't yet want to face one of those 'darling' type discussions which her father's associates were so good at. She couldn't shrug off the odd sense of being rather apart from everyone there.

She felt unsure of herself, and a little shy. This was the house in which she had grown up – or at least where she had spent most of her school holidays. This was where she had spent her most happy – and most unhappy – times. Every room, every picture, every piece of furniture held a memory for her. Every inch of the place was as familiar to her as the features on her own face. Yet she felt isolated and ill at ease. So un-at-home.

The garden looked like a magical fairy grotto with paper lanterns dangling from the trees. The breeze played with the lights, making them dance like distant dragonflies. Gus's skin chilled and she shivered, rubbing the goosebumps on her arms. A dance floor covered the top of the swimming pool and even now, at this relatively early hour, a few people were stepping out to the sounds of the jazz band. To her left a circular marquee had been erected where the sumptuous banquet would be laid out. Salmon had been flown in from Scotland, oysters from Ireland, truffles from Périgord and the finest beluga caviar direct from St Petersburg. Elena had pulled out all the stops as usual. Gus wandered through the garden, searching out familiar faces until someone pushed a glass into her hand.

'You must be Piers's daughter,' the man said. He was around her father's age – maybe a little older – fifty or so. He was looking at her intently, his eyes studying her face with an expression of such open interest that it made Gus feel uncomfortable.

'Yes, that's right, I'm Augusta.'

'Of course,' he grinned at her. The way he held himself, the way he smiled, the tilt of his head, reminded her of a rodent. 'I'm Frank Thompson. Your father and I go back a long way. Pleased to meet you.' Gus detected the flat sound of East London in his speech.

'Are you a dealer?' she asked, curious.

He laughed. 'You could say that. I have done business with your father over the years.'

'I see. Then you must know plenty of people here.' Thompson looked around and, at the same time, drained his glass. 'No, not really. I move in slightly different circles, you see ...'

I can imagine, Gus thought to herself. This man was not her father's usual type of business contact, although admittedly there had been some fairly colourful characters passing through their lives on occasions.

'It's been a long time since I last saw you,' he went on.

'We've met before?' Gus couldn't remember. Strange, because she had an excellent memory for faces.

'You were very small, maybe three.'

'When I was little?' Gus's curiosity was more deeply stirred. How had this man known her?

'You have a look of your mother, you know.'

Gus's hand trembled and she steadied it with her other, clutching her glass between them. 'You knew her?' Her sense of excitement grew. Barely anyone in her life had ever discussed her mother with her. It was as if they were always afraid to raise the subject, afraid of her feelings, afraid of opening up sad memories.

'Darling,' Piers cried with pleasure as he grabbed her arm, 'I've been looking for you everywhere. There's lots of people I'd like you to meet.' He almost yanked her away from Thompson, with barely a nod to the man.

'But ...!' Gus protested. 'Daddy, what are you doing? I was talking to that man, he said he knew Mummy. Who is he? Frank something, Thompson, yes, that was it. He says he knew me when I was little, and that he also knew Mummy.'

'Later, darling. I'm sure he'll still be here later. Now I have someone very special waiting to say hello: James Kentish. I gather you've already met ...'

Gus's reluctance to leave the mysterious Mr Thompson diminished at the prospect of meeting James outside of chambers. 'He's here?' she cried delightedly. 'How come?'

'He's a client, darling, a rather important one. And he's also mentioned you a few times. Now I left him over here several minutes ago – ah, here we are . . .'

Gus had to take large strides to keep up with her father and she was aware of the silk dress riding up her legs, exposing her calves. What she wasn't yet aware of though, was just how prominent her nipples had become through the thin fabric. Many an admiring glance was cast in her direction as they passed among the guests.

Gus was the first to catch sight of Mirabelle's glamorous head, her thick blonde hair cascading in ringlets down her bare back. She was dressed in a gown of silver and white, as delicate as gossamer. The man she was in conversation with seemed mesmerized by her. Mirabelle had this ability to make men fall instantly in love with her. For one angry moment Gus remembered Jonathan.

'I take it you're impressed, then.'

'Seriously,' she grinned at her father. No wonder Mirabelle had got her claws in first. As Flora had already pointed out, James Kentish was what an old-fashioned girl might call devastatingly handsome. He had aquiline, almost Byronic features and lustrous brown hair which was usually well-hidden underneath his wig. James's back was turned towards them as they approached the table, but Gus was quick enough to catch Mirabelle's look of dismay. Naturally in the midst of a party she would want *every* man to herself!

'James, I think you've met my other daughter,' Piers said by way of introduction.

James Kentish found himself looking at the most magnificent pair of nipples underneath what looked like a nightie. Rather different to the young Lawrence he'd seen in chambers and in court.

'Augusta,' he said smoothly, 'how very nice to see

you!' Augusta's glance had followed James's as far as her chest where she had become uncomfortably aware of the effect the chill was having on her. She crossed her arms defensively, wishing she could be as brazen as Mirabelle about such things. 'Mirabelle, your sister, has just been telling me about her work in television. It sounds very different from what you and I do, does it not? Though a good barrister has to give a good performance, play to the jury and make a trial good theatre, bring the story to life, don't you agree, Gus? I do feel we're all frustrated actors.'

'I'm sure you're right,' Gus grinned, 'but thank goodness we don't have to submit ourselves to the critics. Can you imagine if we had our performances analysed and spread over the newspapers?'

'Sometimes that's exactly what does happen. Just wait a few years until the time comes when *you've* made a name for yourself. You'll see just what I mean.'

'It's a pity they don't allow cameras inside court as they do in America,' Mirabelle interjected. 'I think it's certainly in the public interest to do so.'

'Well, the public might think so, but I don't believe the judiciary would accept your views. Just look at what's happened since they've televised parliament. Everyone's realized just how childish the whole business is and how as often as not, half a dozen members are dozing the day away. Can you imagine what Mr Clapham Omnibus – or Mr M25 as I should now say – would make of some of our judges? Some of them are almost unable to stand up, let alone sit in the highest courts in the land.'

'But surely that's the point,' Mirabelle continued doggedly, 'to expose the silly old fools for what they are and get a change in the system – a decent retirement date for judges – and a more open method of selecting judges in the first place –'

Gus interrupted: 'All televisation would achieve would be to sensationalize the trials – cinéma vérité gone crazy! At least with the system as it is at the moment if some poor man stands charged of, say, a particularly grue-some murder, and is found innocent, he can leave the court and hopefully get on with his life. If every fact and every witness account was broadcast to several millions of people, then you'd find people taking justice into their own hands. Not only that, but imagine the extra pressure placed on terrified witnesses, knowing that their every utterance is going to be heard by the entire country! I think it would jeopardize the entire system of justice. I know that there's room for massive improve-ment, but I don't believe that letting Mr Couch Potato dictate what those improvements should be is a step in the right direction. My God,' Gus continued with pas-sion, 'we'd only be a short step away from having public executions!'

James's face was full of admiration. 'I couldn't agree more, Augusta. The thought of such "Americanization" fills me with horror. Younger judges are one thing, television cameras quite another.'

'But the media does have its uses, doesn't it, James,' Mirabelle rallied, 'especially when it comes to miscar-riages of justice . . .?'

'Such as?' James eyed Mirabelle with polite interest.

'Such as that case you defended – the one where the defendant had a mental age of eight and was tried for rape and murder! The one who got two life sentences!'

'John Ocklington?'

'It was the media who broadcast the reconstruction of that particular crime and who demonstrated quite clearly that that man was not capable of carrying out the crime. The medical evidence – all that, remember?'

'Of course. The Home Secretary was lobbied to such an extent that the file was reopened and the conviction was quashed on appeal. That would have happened without the media's intervention.'

'How can you be so sure?'

'Because, dear girl, I was his counsel, and I was in the

51

middle of preparing his appeal based on exactly the information that the programme in question revealed. If anything, the revelation of such information at such an early stage jeopardized the appeal's success. But that, of course,' he nodded conspiratorially to Gus, 'is purely my professional opinion!'

Piers, who had been hovering in the background, broke into the conversation. 'I think you're all getting far too serious. Come on, Mirabelle, your mother asked me to find you at least half an hour ago. Let's leave these two to talk shop – or otherwise.' Piers winked at his daughter and led Mirabelle away.

'I didn't realize that you knew my father so well.'

'He's done me some decent deals on paintings over the years. He's an enormously likeable fellow. Which anniversary are your parents celebrating?'

'Elena's not my mother, she's my stepmother.' Gus hated people to think that Elena could be her mother.

'I'm sorry, one should never make assumptions like that.'

'Don't worry, it's a mistake people often make.' Gus changed the subject rapidly. 'What sort of art do you like?'

'The Impressionists. I confess I'm rather a sentimental at heart.'

Gus tried to hide her cynicism. The last thing she'd ever hear James Kentish described as would be sentimental.

'Funny,' she said, 'I'd have thought you'd prefer something a little more political – such as nineteenth-century realism, perhaps.'

'On the contrary, I get too much of real life myself. I need to escape. I could easily depress myself without staring at a bleak prospect of peasant life. Even such staunch radicals as I have to have an escape from reality.'

'I'm surprised you describe yourself as a radical when

ours is one of the most Establishment chambers of the lot . . . and your father was a red judge, wasn't he?'

'You're remarkably well informed.' Gus found herself gazing into his deep brown eyes. He *was* very attractive even at his age. No wonder he was the gossip of the ladies' robing rooms.

'I believe in fighting from within the ranks. I find it gets you a lot further in life. You'd do well to remember that, Augusta, in your future profession. It's all very well being a bit of a thorn in the Establishment's side when in court, but one must always be able to soothe the ruffled feathers over dinner later on. It's the Establishment that wields the power at the moment, and you'll find yourself more powerful if you respect it rather than try to knock it down.'

'Thank you, I'll think upon it.'

'How's life with Henry?'

'Oh, fine.' Gus couldn't help sighing rather wistfully. 'I wish I could spend some more time at the criminal courts. Trouble is at the moment I mostly work on divorces and civil stuff – property disputes between landlords and tenants, civil damages, all terribly dry, I'm afraid.'

'So why don't you switch masters for your second six months? My present pupil is just finishing off her year. As of next term I don't have a pupil. Why not come and be mine?'

Gus's eyes widened. 'Are you serious?'

'Yes, of course I'm serious. I've seen a few potential pupils but there's no one I'd promised. Besides, I know that you're supposed to be a very clever girl and I'd be interested to teach you what I can. I'll sort it with Henry. Poor old bugger's used to losing pupils halfway through!'

Gus's mind raced. It was like a dream coming true. One of the country's leading criminal barristers was offering her the opportunity to be his pupil. She just couldn't pass up an offer like that. Henry would understand . . .

'How long do I have to decide?' She already knew what her answer would be.

'Speak to me in chambers next week. Now enough of this serious talk. I suppose it would be all right for two barristers to be seen dancing? I must confess to a particular liking for jazz – perhaps you might humour me?' He extended his arm and led Gus towards the dance floor.

James Kentish hoped very much that Augusta might accept his offer. Tonight had revealed that she had a body every bit as potentially stimulating as her brain . . .

'Nice-looking daughter, mate.' Thompson's slimy tone made Piers's flesh crawl.

'What the bloody hell are you doing here, Thompson? I told you weeks ago that I wanted nothing more to do with you! How dare you turn up here, and how dare you go near Gus. I should have you thrown out, you little –'

'Oh yeah? Just you try it, mate, and I'll shout so loudly the whole of New Bond Street will hear me.'

'What do you want?' Piers hissed. 'I thought we had a deal. I paid you a lot of money to stay away from me, Thompson. You agreed.'

Thompson laughed. 'Honour among thieves, eh, Pete? Well, I'm sorry, but there's no such thing. I've missed you . . . missed doing business with you.'

'Nothing would induce me to do business with you ever again, you bastard. I'm clean now. I want to get on with my life, with my family. A quarter of a million pounds, you creep, and you agreed never to infect my life again!'

'Yes, but life doesn't always go the way we plan, does it? Like I said, I miss our little deals, and I wouldn't want you to think that I'd forgotten all about you, me old mate Pete – oh sorry, Piers!'

'Just get out of here –'

'I could just make your life rather uncomfortable. Nice daughter, as I said.'

'You're a ruthless bastard, Thompson.' Piers knew that he couldn't allow any potential risk towards Gus. 'I'll talk to you – but not here. Call me next week.'

'That's better. Much more friendly, Pete. I'll just enjoy your party a bit longer and then I'll be on my way.'

'Just get out now before I have you thrown out.'

'I'm a police officer, Pete. Police officers don't get thrown out of parties – we usually do the throwing.' He drained his glass and handed it to Piers. 'See you around, Pete.' Then he disappeared into the shadows beyond the lawn.

Piers wiped his brow and realized he had been sweating.

Gus lay naked in a battle zone of cotton sheets and scattered pillows. She tossed and turned, her eyelids fluttering and her lips framed, ready to cry out in terror. She clutched onto the pillow and then started to beat it with her clenched fists. A thin film of perspiration broke out over her entire body.

'No, no, please, don't . . .' she cried aloud. They were on the edge of a cliff – the three of them – her mother, father and herself. Her little legs wanted to run, but they wouldn't move. She watched helplessly as the dog bounded between her parents. The grass field sloped upwards away from her, towards an abrupt horizon where, Gus knew, the land disappeared with a sheer drop ending on the rocky beach far below. The wind blew against Augusta, forcing her back, further away from her parents. Her hair was whipping around her face, sticking in front of her eyes like tentacles. She tried to brush it away but the wind just put it right back, blinding her. She tried to shout, but her words were carried away on the roar of the wind. Tears streamed down her face. Then, when she could at last see again, her father stood alone against the horizon, his face fixed on a spot far below.

'Mummy .. ' she screamed in her head. Then came the sound of the dog barking, barking and barking as if it would never stop; her father trying to catch the dog with the lead flailing uselessly in his hand. Then her father coming towards her with his arms outstretched, vshaking his head, his face as grey as the worn boulders around them. Then suddenly she woke. She always awoke then. Her father never quite reached her, and she never quite knew what had happened. Frank Thompson's face had jogged something in her subconscious, triggering the recurring nightmare.

There were periods in her life when Gus had had the nightmare so often that she had been relegated to the sick bay at school for weeks so that she wouldn't disturb the others with her calling and her tossing and turning. Everyone had told her that she would grow out of it, and it had certainly become less frequent, only visiting her about once every six months now. The problem was that she never quite understood what had happened to her mother. Her father had always flatly refused to tell her, and there were no relatives around who were prepared to give her a reasonable answer to the mystery. Gus had been so terribly young when Cat had died. Apart from what she gleaned from the dream, the only thing Gus could remember about her mother's death was standing frozen in the cold cemetery, watching as a large box was lowered into the ground. Her nanny had given her a small pink rose to throw down into the hole and Gus had been afraid to do it, protesting that the rose might not like it down there. Then, as she watched the earth being heaped into the hole, crushing the rose, Gus had cried and asked to get it back.

As Gus lay in the middle of the night darkness, listening to the sounds of the old house breathing into the silence, she knew that the nightmare would keep on returning until she knew exactly what had happened on the day her mother died.

James Kentish was in a rare state of semiconsciousness – not quite awake and yet not quite asleep. As the sunlight struggled to filter through the curtains, so he pulled himself awake. For several moments he was unsure of where he was. Whatever nightcaps he had been given last night, they had certainly blown his head apart! He'd remember to steer clear of Armagnac next time. He felt as though a tight piece of metal ran around his temples, making his whole head throb painfully. As he attempted to open his eyes he caught a glimpse of a shoe. Not a male sort of a shoe, but a high-heeled wisp of a sandal. James's eyes flew fully open as he stared curiously at the untidy pile of clothes strewn over the chaise. Was that a silver ballgown draped over the arm? If so, who the bloody hell's was it? Very slowly, cautiously and tentatively, he turned his head towards the other pillow.

'Morning,' sighed Mirabelle, sleepily.

'Damned attractive, that wife of yours, Piers.'

Piers smiled amiably and refreshed the champagne in Dickie Crowborough's glass.

'Thanks.' He sat down on the chaise beside the older man. The marquee people were busy taking down the tent, the caterers still retrieving glasses and plates from around the garden, while sundry other guests were partaking of Elena's hangover cure in the house. Piers and Dickie had managed to find a private spot away from the general mayhem in order to have a quiet chat. Dickie adjusted his sunglasses and settled back.

'Well, this is the life, old boy. Makes a pleasant change to be away from bloody Westminster and all those blessed whingers. Nothing very exciting happens these days,' he continued morosely. 'No budgets to do anything with, no art worth talking about, even the bloody theatre consists of damned musicals. Where's the art in that? The Royal Academy's turning into an upmarket caff and some of the exhibitions I've been to see . . . D'you know, Piers, I wouldn't be at all surprised to find an embalmed stiff on show one of these days. It's getting to the stage where one can wrap up one's own turd and call it art. I just don't understand any of it any more. I just hope to God that if there's another reshuffle before we get kicked out for good I get a decent port-folio. I wouldn't want Arts again – doesn't exist . . . No, what I'd like is Education. I'd soon sort the buggers from the boys. We should never have got rid of the grammar schools . . .'

'Yes, yes, quite, Dickie . . .' Piers was keen to put an end to his friend's diatribe. He had a habit of drifting on in no particular direction – perhaps he'd spent too many afternoons in the Commons' tea-room, Piers mused.

'Anyway, what was I saying? Ah yes, your wife, dear chap. Quite a stunner. 'Course you had a habit of going for stunners. Still haven't forgiven you for stealing Cat from under my nose all those years ago. You were an absolute cad, Piers.' He started to laugh quietly. 'Re-member the scandal? God, those were the days, what? I remember her father, old Harris – beside himself he was! He had a heart attack a couple of years before the . . . er . . . accident, didn't he?'

'Yes, he did,' Piers muttered.

'I remember he thought you were highly unsuitable. I think he rather hoped for a title for his only daughter. I believe I was in with a good chance there before you turned up, you know. My, she was a wild one, wasn't she? I can see a lot of her in Gus.' He smiled to himself as he thought fondly of his goddaughter. 'You must be very proud of her, Piers. She's done so well. I always knew she'd be a clever girl. Of course, she's only like her mother in looks, not character!'

Piers frowned and his lips tightened.

Dickie continued: 'Sad, really, the way things went . . .' His voice trailed off awkwardly. 'Still, look how happy you are, dear chap. And Gus has turned out splendidly, just splendidly.'

'Yes, hasn't she?' Piers murmured vaguely. 'You said you had a business proposition.'

'H'm? Oh so I did, yes. Actually it's an opportunity for you. There's a very important body looking for an art adviser. Very generous fees, so I understand. It's all very hush-hush. One of these pension fund thingies. I thought I might push your name forward. Sort of thing you'd be interested in?'

'Of course. Providing I've got the time.'

'Always so damned busy these days, Piers, flitting between your galleries. How many now?'

'About ten.'

'I still remember you as a young slip of a lad when you opened up your first gallery in Piccadilly. I've really got to hand it to you, Piers, you've done bloody well, old boy.'

Piers smiled politely at Dickie. 'Thanks, Dickie. And I remember you when you were a bright young MP – desperate for cash when your father threatened to disown you because you had run up a couple of debts!'

Dickie roared with laughter as he, too, remembered how it was in their misspent youth.

Piers stared into the middle distance, silent and inscrutable. He hated these conversations. One never knew quite where they would lead. He placed his empty glass on the table.

'I'd better go and see how the other guests are getting along. Excuse me for a few moments . . .'

As he left Dickie relaxed and soaking up the rays, Piers wondered, not for the first time, if he could ever get away from his past. Seeing Frank Thompson talking to Gus last night had caused him a physical pain, like a

59

knife twisting deep inside his gut. However much distance he tried to put between himself and his early life he always failed to keep it at bay, it seemed. More than anything he would have liked to tell Frank Thompson just where he could stuff his nasty little schemes, instead of agreeing, like some pathetic, frightened coward, to meet him once more. But he couldn't afford to let any of his seedy past affect Gus's life. She was the embodiment of all that could have been good in his life, all his hopes and his dreams. Maybe if he could have looked into the future all those years ago he might have acted differently. Dear God, how he wished he had!

Chapter Five

❧❦❧

1965

The young lad shifted his weight from one foot to the other, stamping hard in an unsuccessful effort to get the circulation back into his toes. Breath billowed from his mouth in a frozen cloud, mingling with the predawn fog. His ears were trained for the rattle of a particular engine, as the various lorries and vans started to arrive in the bleak, almost deserted marketplace. Strange, twisted, skeletal shells of the stalls faded surreally into the fog. Within an hour, though, the place would be bustling with vendors and customers hellbent on making a fast buck or picking up a bargain. Pete's stall had been inherited from his mum's dad some eighteen months ago, after the poor old sod had finally put the lid on his last deal. Pete had spent much of his time down here with his granddad, learning about the market and picking up tips from the seasoned traders. Now Pete had grander plans. It had always frustrated him to watch the old man fiddling about with crap second-hand furniture and stupid little knick-knacks that Pete hated but which his granddad assured him were their bread and butter. Sure enough the wives flocked to buy the sordidly tacky brass plate candlesticks, and the wood veneer mantelclocks, and the occasional plastic seated kitchen chairs that were sold individually or in sets of six. 'This is what people want and need, son,' had been his creed to his grandson. 'Find what they want, turn it into a need, and you'll always have customers. Folks'll always need furniture and bric-à-brac, son. Keep it cheap and cheerful so the wives will think they can afford it.'

While the old man's marketing strategy was sound, Pete didn't have much of a taste for bread and butter. He was more of a cake and jam sort of bloke. Over the months he had been carefully cultivating just the right contacts, building up his business, expanding and diversifying, so to speak. His deals were slowly becoming bigger, and far more interesting.

His reverie was interrupted by the sound he had been waiting for. The big lorry slowed to negotiate the entrance and Pete watched as the pinpricks of headlights grew bigger and stronger as it rumbled closer to him. Pete checked his watch and sniffed hard. They were pushing it a bit. The sun would be up in half an hour at most. Pete nodded an acknowledgement as the driver jumped down from his cab and grunted in Pete's direction. His partner joined them as, wordlessly, they made their way to the back of the lorry. Waiting for the tailgate to be opened, Pete speculated on what juicy items could be on offer this particular night. Jimmy Jones and his friends rarely disappointed, but more often than not it was quantity, not quality, that they tended to concentrate upon. Whilst they were masters of their own rather specialist trade, they lacked the expertise for assessing the merchandise. That was where Pete came in . . .

Once the three of them had climbed aboard, the door was ceremoniously closed behind them, leaving only the weak yellow glow of the interior light to see by. Pete waited while Jimmy Jones, the driver, used a crowbar to lever the lids off several wooden packing cases. His accomplice, whom Pete didn't recognize, started to pile up the hoard, enabling Pete to pick his way through the items. An Aynsley coffee service, the usual collection of silver salvers, candlesticks, cruets, an assortment of Georgian and Victorian silver photograph frames, plated cutlery, fine china figurines, a couple of Victorian miniatures and then the jewellery cascaded onto the floor. But Pete wasn't too interested in the latter, knowing the gems were destined elsewhere.

'Any pictures?' He watched as a mound of blankets was lifted off what appeared to be a scrappy pile of rolled-up rags, torn and greying. Reverently, Pete unrolled the first, carefully spreading the canvas out onto one of the clean blankets. Even to his fairly inexperienced eye he could tell it was nothing spectacular. He had studied hard at Billy Smith's evening classes and as a result had a rough idea of what to look for and what to avoid. The fact that it was nothing spectacular made it worthwhile making Jimmy an offer for it. Anything too well known was asking for –

'Jesus Christ!' He stared disbelievingly at the next canvas. 'You gotta be kidding. Do you know what this is?'

Pete hardly dared to touch the canvas. He'd just entered kamikaze land. Anyone handling this was surely heading for one hell of a lot of trouble.

'What's up, mate? Keep the bloody noise down, will ya? The old bill'll be 'ere any bleedin' minute if ya keep up that racket. We done good, yeah?'

Pete ran his fingers through his neat black hair. He struggled for tactful words. These guys were looking at a seven-year stretch, no trouble, courtesy of this pretty lady. Pete was certain he had seen a picture of her in one of the books. They'd only gone and nicked a bloody Gainsborough!

'This,' he said slowly, 'will be shit hot. So hot that your tyres'll have left a burn mark right the way from Norfolk to bloody Bermondsey.' His mind raced as he tried to work out what, if anything, he could do with it. The most sensible thing would be to stick it in the post and send it right back to where it came from!

' 'Ow d'ya know we was in Norfolk?'

63

'Well, an educated guess tells me you were at Deptford Park, seat of Lord Eltrington. This is one of his lordship's ancestors – the Lady Anne Chesham. This particular painting fortunately survived a fire in the ancestral home, hence its fame. It's a rather rare example of Thomas Gainsborough's early period. Any fool who knows about art could tell you that.'

'Amazin'!' Jimmy's sidekick exclaimed. 'You ought to be on one of those quiz shows. Fancy you bein' able to tell all that –'

Jimmy interrupted: 'Ya mean the police will be on to us?'

It seemed that the significance of young Pete's words had sunk in. 'Right on bloody top of us, mate,' Pete confirmed. 'So, what are we going to do with it?'

'Well, I was 'oping that you'd fence it for us, as usual.'

'It's not worth anything! Except a pile of trouble,' Pete snapped.

'But you just said it was famous – Thomas wotsit.'

'That's why it's not worth anything. I can't flog it, can I?'

Jimmy's black leather jacket creaked as he squirmed inside it. He seemed bemused by this latest piece of information. 'Can I leave it wiv ya. See what ya can get?'

'I tell you, mate, five years for receiving! You'll be lucky to get a couple of hundred nicker. No one will want to touch it.' Pete shook his head slowly, expressing the depth of his consternation. 'Tell you what I'll do,' he said, after Jimmy had sat himself down heavily on the top of one of the packing crates. 'I'll take the silver and the miniatures, and the paintings for five hundred. I'm taking a risk. I can't see how I'll ever get shot of the bloody thing. And if I end up in the nick –'

'No, Pete, I can't let you do it,' Jimmy said, his voice full of paternal concern. He'd known this kid for a long time and he knew he was a good'un. Too bright for his own good, maybe, but he was okay.

Jimmy's accomplice, who had remained silent throughout this exchange, suddenly spoke. 'Take it, Jim. 'Arf of it's mine. I says take it.'

Jimmy shrugged towards Pete, relieved to have the responsibility of landing the kid in the shit removed from him. 'What can I do?' he shrugged helplessly. 'I got a business to run. Looks like we got a deal, Pete.'

Pete snorted. 'So, you owe me, Jimmy,' he laughed. 'Maybe you should come to Billy's classes with me. Then you'd know what to nick and what to leave behind.'

'Nah,' Jimmy sighed derisively. 'I'm too old to learn new tricks. Ooever 'eard of a con giving evening classes in fine art? The modern world ain't what it used to be, son. I 'spect you'll soon be gettin' a job down Bond Street, won'tcha? Wot's that place ... Soveby's? Bermondsey won't be good enough for the likes of you no more, you mark my words. Art expert, that's wot you'll be, Pete.'

'Yeah, you may be right, Jim. But for the moment I need the open market to get rid of this stuff. And if I'm not mistaken it's dawn already and I need to get it out of the way. Is it a deal then?'

Jimmy sniffed and then threw open the rear door, hawking into the grey light. Pete's stomach churned in revulsion. 'Yeah. Take it.'

Pete pulled a wad of cash out of his trouser pocket. 'Five hundred. There's no need to count it.'

Jimmy pocketed the cash while his partner loaded the stuff into an empty packing case. Pete waited patiently until the lid was safely in place, and then manhandled the box off the lorry, nonchalantly looking around before he left the safety of the lorry park. Experience taught you who was a regular, who was a customer and who was the old bill – even in civvies they stuck out a mile.

Antiques dealers flooded in from around the country to see what bargains they could pick up, or what they could offload, taking advantage of the very special trading conditions surrounding the ancient market overt charter with which Bermondsey was privileged. It meant that anything sold in market overt passed good title to whoever purchased it, provided the goods were sold in the open between the hours of dawn and dusk on a stall whose custom it was normally to sell such goods. So stolen items sold in market overt became legally owned by the purchaser and there was nothing the previous owner could do to recover his goods – without paying for them, at any rate. Bermondsey street market and various shops within the City of London operated under the charter and while Pete's private ambition was to own one of the three art galleries who also carried out their business in market overt, he knew the chances of ever getting close even to running any of them were extremely remote. No new galleries could be opened up within the City because of the market overt charter, and the existing galleries were very tightly held by the families concerned with them. Pete had taken some paintings into all of them at one time or another, and he had received a similar flea in his ear from each. Their special privilege understandably made them very cagey about the origin of certain goods. While the police couldn't prosecute them for stolen goods traded openly in the shop, in full view of the public through plain glazed shop windows, they could very well prosecute the galleries concerned for receiving. Naturally, because of this, the police had a habit of checking the galleries' deals and stocks on a fairly regular basis.

Pete had very quickly learned that subtlety was by far the best approach, and he had got into the custom of using some of his hard-earned cash to reinvest in fairly minor artworks bought legitimately from country auctions, or from other dealers he had got to know. Thanks to Billy Smith's evening classes, he had developed a reasonable eye for sifting out the rubbish. Billy was revered by the underworld as being one of the finest cat burglars of the forties and fifties. He was a real gentleman of a thief, who had used his agility and ingenuity to carry off some daringly ambitious art thefts. He had never handled a gun or any other offensive weapon in his life. Of course he had been caught and banged up several times, but he had viewed his time inside rather philosophically, considering prison to be a spartan boarding school where he could expand his education while taking well-earned rest and relaxation. Through the naïve kindness of prison visitors and prison librarians, he used his time to learn more and more about the art he had 'collected', and to help him decide where he would visit upon his release.

Now that Billy was in his seventies, and his days of precariously scrambling over lofty rooftops were well behind him, he had taken the entrepreneurial step of teaching newcomers to the business the secrets of his craft, which included a thorough grounding in art history and appreciation! Pete had been one of Billy's most voracious pupils, gobbling up every fact, chewing his way through every book on the subject he could lay his hands on, and forever pushing Billy to go into greater detail on what separated the masterpieces from the mundane.

As Pete's knowledge grew, and his taste in paintings became ever more sophisticated, little by little his relationship with the smart gallery owners of not only the City but of Bond Street too was growing in confidence and trust. It was clear to them that here was an extremely bright young man who was fast developing an eye for a good picture. From the dealers' side of the fence, they were just as keen to nurture young Pete as young Pete was keen to get in with them.

'Well, this looks like an interesting bunch of items . . .'

Pete was busy finishing laying out the goods on his stall, so busy that he hadn't noticed the dark figure approaching. His heart started to pound in his chest as he looked up, taking in the dark uniform, the silver buttons, the wide belt. Only the old fucking bill! He forced a smile on to his lips. 'Morning, guv,' he said brightly. 'Anything you fancy?'

'Yeah, plenty. I expect the owners might like to know about some of this stuff. What's your name?'

'Lawrence, Pete Lawrence.'

'Well, Mr Lawrence, looks like these,' he pointed to a pair of Georgian silver candlesticks which Pete had bought in from Portobello a couple of days before, 'are hot. Nicked! Where d'you get them?'

'I don't remember. Some dealer, maybe an auction,' Pete stammered, determined not to tell the bastard where he had bought them. How the hell could he know they were nicked? Even Pete wasn't sure of their origin – unlike the stuff which still lay under the stall fresh off Jimmy Jones's lorry. Catching a bloody Gainsborough would probably make this bastard's career!

'PC Thompson . . .' Pete recognized the soft voice of Mr Levy. 'You're out bright and early!' Maurice Levy owned a gallery just down the road and he was a regular customer of Pete's. 'Something the matter?'

'Yeah, I'm a little suspicious about the origins of some of these items here.'

Pete watched the exchange. Obviously these two knew each other, although Pete hadn't seen the weasel-faced policeman around before. Pete was stunned into shocked silence as Levy spoke confidently.

'I can vouch for everything on this stall. Usual arrangement, Frank. Come and see me later on, all right?'

The policeman's eyes roved slowly over the items on display. Pete realized he had been holding his breath. He let it go, hating the tension, the fear which had clutched his belly. He willed the copper to go away. Anything, only please not let him find the bloody Gainsborough.

' 'Spect you've got some pretty interesting stuff

68

stashed away down there.' The weasel eyes had caught on to something in Pete's face.

'Nothing, nothing at all.' Pete's voice sounded breathy and nervous.

'My name's Thompson, by the way. Frank Thompson. Any friend of Maurice's is a friend of mine.' He grinned crookedly and Pete was amazed when the man put out his hand towards him. Pete slowly pushed his forwards, still in shock, and they shook hands.

'Pete Lawrence,' he said.

'I'm wrong,' Thompson decided, glancing at the candlesticks once again. 'Now I see them properly, they're really quite different to the ones I thought they were.'

Pete nodded. 'Good.'

Then unbelievably, the copper winked at him, patted Maurice Levy's arm, and wandered off through the market.

'Shit!' Pete breathed in relief.

Maurice Levy also watched the copper walk away, then he turned to Pete. His gaunt face looked pale as ever, but his smile was warm, revealing the neat set of very white false teeth of which he was inordinately proud.

Pete had always had a soft spot for Mr Levy. He had heard his story through market gossip. He, his wife and two children, and his twin brother with his wife and family, had been in Poland when the Nazis had begun rounding up Jews for shipment to the death camps. Sadly, Maurice had been the only member of the family to survive to the end of the war. He had made his way to London where he had relatives, and within ten years of his arrival, he found himself inheriting the Gillespie Gallery – one of the privileged galleries within the precincts of the City.

'Good morning, Pete,' Mr Levy said cheerfully, raising his dark grey trilby. 'And how are you this morning?'

69

'What did you mean you could vouch for everything?' Pete still couldn't quite believe what had just taken place.

'Trust me. I know how to deal with the PC Thompsons of this world. Lucky for you I happened to be around, though.'

Pete scratched his head, unsure of what to say next. Maurice Levy behaved as he normally did, as if nothing had happened.

'What have you for me?'

Pete followed his cue. 'Nothing. It's been a quiet week, I'm afraid.'

'Oh dear, dear.' Mr Levy sighed his disappointment. 'I always look forward to your pictures. Wait a minute ...' His small blue eyes crinkled shrewdly as they fell on the rolled canvases. 'Have I spied something ... over there?' He pointed a bony finger at the top of the packing case and Pete kicked himself for not making sure that the lid was covering them sufficiently.

Pete spoke quickly. 'There's nothing you'd be interested in. It's rubbish. I wouldn't insult ... ' He didn't intend to get burned twice in one day.

'Nonsense, my boy. Pass them here.'

Pete knew that the smaller of the two was the insignificant painting. Taking a deep breath, he passed it over to the older man. Maurice Levy unrolled it, being careful not to touch the other items which Pete had carefully arranged on his stall. But as he lay the painting flat, he knocked a miniature, which had been perched unobtrusively on the edge of the table top, onto the floor. He stooped to pick it up.

Forgetting the painting – which Pete quickly rolled back up – he started to examine the miniature. He drew a jeweller's loupe from his pocket and turned the frame around carefully, examining the hallmarks punched into the silver.

'This is really most interesting,' he murmured as he

pressed his eye close to the small image of the serious-faced woman. 'Most interesting . . .'

After several moments, he tore his gaze away and removed the loupe from his eye. He gave Pete a long and rather knowing look which made him shift uncomfortably from one foot to the other, giving him the feeling he had experienced at school when he had been copped for something by one of the teachers. Knowing that shiftiness didn't pay, he returned the look evenly, managing a small, friendly sort of smile.

'A Holbein if I'm not mistaken,' Mr Levy said with relish.

'What?' Pete said, unable to mask the shock in his voice.

'A Holbein. One of the greatest miniaturists ever, Pete. Early sixteenth century, I believe, worth a vast sum of money, and as there are several well documented in private collections, and a few others scattered around important galleries of the world, I wouldn't have expected to find such a thing at a street market. Most interesting.'

Pete swallowed hard. Fuck Jimmy Jones! Numbers ran through his mind. If he were put away now, how old would he be when he got out? Twenty-five? Maybe twenty-two if he got time off for good behaviour. His mouth felt dry and his stomach suddenly leaden. He stared at the older man, like a petrified rabbit unable to take his eyes away.

'Interesting. Very interesting,' Maurice Levy continued to repeat. 'I would like to buy this from you. How much are you selling for?'

'I . . . um . . . ' Pete struggled to answer, trying to think bloody quickly. 'It's a bit expensive, that one.' He took a gamble. He had no idea what it was worth. He'd never studied miniatures. But a Holbein? Jesus, what did a bloody Holbein go for? Whatever, it probably had several noughts on the end of it. But this stuff was hot, and it was going to be even hotter later today after the burglary was publicized. He was looking at a proverbial gift horse, and he didn't want to lose it. 'I was thinking about three hundred.'

'Pounds or guineas?' Mr Levy said, as he reached for his wallet and began counting out the cash.

'Er, guineas,' Pete said quickly, finding it hard to swallow as his tongue was sticking to the roof of his mouth.

'Here we are then,' said Mr Levy as he deposited the wad of cash into Pete's palm. Pete quickly stuffed it into his pocket with a grunt of thanks. He was still trying to work out what exactly was going on.

Mr Levy slipped the tiny painting inside his tweed overcoat. As he lifted his hat by way of thanks, he glanced again at the rolled-up canvases. 'And by the way, you'd better bring both those canvases round to the gallery later on. I might well be interested in whatever it is you have.'

'Oh, right ... yeah ...' Pete muttered. As he watched the small, slim figure walk away, he realized he may have totally misjudged this Mr Levy.

Chapter Six

'I have a proposition to put to you,' Maurice Levy said, passing Pete a cup of tea. 'Sugar?'

'Thanks,' Pete dropped four lumps into the dark brown liquid and stirred it until the granules had dissolved. Then he chinked his spoon loudly against the teacup before setting it back in the saucer.

'Forgive me if I have misunderstood anything, but I feel that there are certain items of merchandise which you might find a little awkward to dispose of, shall we say?'

'I'm not quite sure I get your meaning,' Pete said, all too conscious of the rolled-up Gainsborough sitting inside the brown canvas holdall on the floor at the side of his chair.

'Art is a somewhat specialist market in certain areas. It is true to say that ironically the more valuable and rare a piece is, the harder it is to sell.'

'Yeah. I guess . . .' Pete tried to sound noncommittal, and took a sip of tea.

'If I can be frank, there are only a limited number of people who are interested in buying the better known works of art. These collectors are shy people – they hate publicity – and they are very difficult to locate because they never make it known publicly that they have a collection at all. In my line of business naturally over the years I have come to know quite a few of these rather reticent collectors. My instinct tells me that it might be of mutual benefit to you, to me and to these, er, contacts of mine, to perhaps collaborate in some way.'

'I'm not sure I take your meaning.' Pete again sipped his tea, keeping his face expressionless. If this bloke was trying to say what Pete thought he was trying to say, then things could get very interesting.

'Show me your paintings, my boy, and I will explain.'

Pete set his cup and saucer down on the table beside him. What had all his mates taught him? You don't get anywhere without taking a gamble, Pete. You've got to risk a bit to win a bit more. Well, this was one hell of a risk, but he had no option and the gains could be pretty useful! He passed Mr Levy the larger of the two paintings.

'Thomas Gainsborough, of course. How interesting. You knew, didn't you, that you had a difficult piece here?'

'Yeah, I s'pose I did. That's why I didn't show it to no one.'

'And of course the miniature – you didn't real-ize . . .?'

'Never hardly looked at it. Just goes to show what a lot I've got to learn.'

'My boy,' the older man said gently, 'you will go on learning about art until the day you die. Every day I learn something new. And in our side of the business it becomes more and more fascinating as each year goes by.

'So, you are faced with a problem. You cannot sell this painting anywhere because it is so well known. However, legally the painting is yours, and were you to take it through to the shop and there sell it to me, in full view of anyone who happened to be passing by, or who happened to call into the shop for a browse, then the painting would be mine. But of course there would still be massive legal implications.'

'Yeah. I should never have bought the bloody thing. I knew it would be a mistake.'

'No, no, do not be downhearted. As I said, I think if

74

we were to somehow pool our resources, you could solve your problem and I could solve mine.'

'Yours? What's your problem then?'

'Supply and demand. Or demand and supply. You see, some of my collectors are very acquisitive. But there is only so much of what they want in circulation. Therefore one requires to somehow increase the artworks in circulation. There are limited ways of doing that. But that is where I think you might assist.'

'How?'

'By making sure that when your friends decide to clean out a stately home, they steal the right items.'

'You mean you will tell me what you want, and I will tell them what to nick.'

'Precisely. More tea?'

Pete shook his head in wonder at Maurice Levy's benign face. 'So what's the deal.'

'Commission, of course. That's the way most art dealers work. And that is what you want to be, isn't it? An art dealer?'

'Yeah, I suppose I do.' Pete grinned with pleasure. 'So, how much are you going to give me for the Gainsborough, Mr Levy? Know anyone with a penchant for such things?'

'Oh, indeed I do, Mr Lawrence. I anticipate doing the deal with my client tomorrow, but I would have thought we should be asking in the region of £150,000. In this instance and as a gesture of goodwill, I suggest that we split the profits two-thirds to you and one-third to me? Is that all right by you?'

Pete gasped. 'One hundred grand to me?'

'I hope that would be acceptable. But if I might advise you, Mr Lawrence, better not go spending it all at once as people might think your stall had done rather too well.'

'I wouldn't dream of it, Mr Levy. I'll probably save it for a rainy day.'

'Then we'd better hope we have a dry summer, Mr Lawrence, to avoid temptation. If you would care to come and see me at, say, two o'clock tomorrow . . .?'

Pete balanced the snooker cue and took aim, watching with satisfaction as the black ball skilfully nudged the red the necessary twelve inches to the hole, where it plopped gratifyingly into the pocket. He blew the chalk from his fingers and handed the cue back to his opponent. 'Sorry, Alf. Let's have a rematch later on. I 'spect you'll get your own back.'

'I'll get my money back, more to the point,' Alf McNicholls chuckled as he handed over a five-pound note. 'This is getting expensive. I should never have taught you to play so well.'

'Come on, I'll buy you a drink.' Pete squeezed through to the crowded bar. 'Two Scotches,' he called out to the small, wiry Irishman behind the bar, 'on the rocks!'

As he waited, the scent beneath his nose changed subtly from a sort of comfortable whiff of stale nicotine and beer to something which made him want to know just where it was coming from. It was sweet – almost cloyingly full of the fragrance of flowers – like walking past old Dot's stall on a sunny summer's morning when she had buckets full of lilies. He spied the brunette a couple of feet away from him. She had thick eyeliner across her eyelids which swept out from the corners, and when her eyes lifted to meet his, she looked like a small cat. Her lips were coated with sugar-pink frosting, like a sherbet sweet. The thought quite suddenly made Pete's mouth water. He found himself returning her smile.

'Drink?' he said as the barman handed him the two whiskies.

'Yeah, Scotch would be fine,' she said, taking the glass from his hand. He opened his mouth to speak and then, looking around for Alf and being unable to spot him, he chinked his glass against hers.

'Chin-chin,' he said, watching her lift the tumbler.

She had long slim fingers, and ridiculously long nails immaculately coloured with that same sugar pink. There was something about her, a sort of dolly-birdishness, that set her apart from the usual girls who came to the club. She had class. 'Cheers,' she said, slowly sipping her Scotch, while at the same time staring into his face with those feline eyes. He noticed that her eyelashes were so long that they touched her brows.

'I'm Pete,' he said, raising his voice to make himself heard over the racket.

'And I'm Catherine,' she said, extending her hand to his.

He shook it formally, then feeling self-conscious, he touched the knot of his tie, making sure it still sat squarely beneath his Adam's apple.

'My friends call me Cat,' she added almost invitingly.

'I haven't seen you here before.'

'No,' she said, casting her eyes around at the East End lads whose club this was. 'I haven't been here before. I heard it was rather . . . colourful.'

Pete shrugged and glanced around, too. Then he grinned ruefully. 'Yeah, I suppose colourful is an okay word for these old crooks.'

'I'm here to get a good look at crooks.' Her voice was an odd mixture of smart English and trendy London. 'I thought it might be exciting to meet some villains. Chelsea can get awfully boring. Tell me, are you a crook, Pete?'

Pete took a swig of his whisky. 'Er, no. No, I'm not. Least not tonight, any rate.'

She continued to gaze into his eyes, as if she might learn whether he was telling the truth. Pete touched her elbow and started to lead her away from the bar. 'Let's find somewhere to sit . . .'

'Catherine!' They both turned towards the voice. 'Catherine . . . ah there you are.' Pete took in the lanky figure, the suit, the voice. This guy was a square if ever he saw one. 'I wondered where on earth you'd got to. Excuse me,' he said, turning his back on Pete as he squeezed his way to the girl's side.

'We was just – '

'Very kind of you, I'm sure,' the bloke interrupted, again turning his back on Pete. 'Catherine,' he whispered loudly, 'let's get the hell out of here. It's very dangerous coming to a place like this. I must have been completely mad to bring you. I promised your father I'd take care of you, and look at us, in a right den of thieves – and murderers, no doubt. I'm taking you home right now.'

'Oh Gerald, don't be so stuffy. Why don't you let me introduce you to this charming young man who kindly bought me a drink? Gerald meet Pete . . .'

'Good evening, Pete. It really was most kind of you. Now I'm afraid the young lady and I must go.'

'Sounds like she wants to stay.' Pete drew himself up to his full five feet eleven inches. 'Do you want to stay, Cat?'

Her eyes glittered at him, teasingly. 'I thought things were beginning to get interesting . . .'

'Drink up, I'm taking you home now. Come along, Catherine.'

Catherine knocked back the last half-inch of whisky without so much as a cough and handed the empty glass to Pete. She blinked at him, setting her large brown eyes to best advantage.

'She doesn't want to go,' Pete said. 'And I don't want her to go either.'

Gerald grabbed her arm and pulled her gently away, towards the door. Catherine was giggling, turning back towards where Pete stood.

'Sorry, Pete, I guess I'd better behave myself, like Gerald says. Shame though. Nice meeting you!' Her long legs tripped after the toff. Pete noted with admiration that her skirt was so short he could have sworn he'd seen her knickers.

As soon as they had left the bar, Pete realized that he wanted to see her again. Perhaps he could get her phone number, or at least find out where she lived. He struggled to get past a crowd of ten or so people who had just entered the bar.

'Here, steady on, mate,' one of them called out, disgruntled, as Pete fell over his bird.

'Sorry ... sorry ...' he said tripping down the stairs two at a time.

As he got out onto the street, he saw the tail lights glowing on a red sports car. The engine roared once, settled into a throaty purr, and then sped off into the night. Class, that's what the girl had. Real class. Well, he may not have the class, but he certainly had plenty of dough burning a hole in his pocket, thanks to old Maurice and his propositions. Fucking prat, Gerald. Pete kicked some railings bad-temperedly and turned back to the club. Soon he'd be in the big league. No upper-class twit was going to pull a bird from under his nose like that. Pete's grand plan was already taking shape, and now he could hardly wait to get into action. Tomorrow he'd get to work on it. But for now he still owed Alf that Scotch.

Chapter Seven

1992

As the sun glared through the voile drapes, Gus's head felt as though it had been clamped in a vice all night. Her eyes felt grainy and sore, grating against the inside of their lids. She must have had far too much to drink. She remembered dancing with James, and then being dragged off by Dickie Crowborough's 'Excuse me' for several more dances where she had been thrown around like some kind of wild dervish by her exuberant godfather. By the time he had finally released her, hot and exhausted, James had disappeared from view. Gus vaguely recalled being plied with several glasses of champagne by some young and very intense artist her father was in the process of launching. After that, she must somehow have fallen into bed and into a sleep disturbed by the old nightmare. Now, in the late morning, the feeling of abandonment and confusion hung around her like an old soggy raincoat – an awful sense of disquiet, of unsettlement which the bad dream always gave her.

As she slicked back her hair in front of the mirror, staring into her grey eyes which, though rimmed with pink, looked so like her mother's – at least so the few remaining photographs seemed to show – Gus wondered about the man she had met so briefly last night, the man her father seemed so keen to drag her away from. Hadn't he said he knew her mother? That he knew Gus when she was tiny? Maybe he could tell her something. Why had Piers dragged her away like that? After lunch she would talk to him. Even though he had always fobbed her off in the past whenever she had tried to solve the riddle of her mother's accident, wasn't it her right to know? A fine criminal counsel she'd make if she couldn't even get information from her own father.

Lunch had been laid out on the terrace, a picture of casual elegance, with various decorative women draped around the table, in between several men looking somewhat the worse for last night's festivities. Piers had taken his seat at the head of the table, while Elena was wafting about, making sure that the army of staff were looking after all the guests. Gus had hidden herself behind a pair of Raybans and slid unobtrusively into one of the remaining seats two down from James Kentish and across the table from the Italian Count and his lady. Mirabelle was holding forth, as usual, about some TV shoot, and was casting some rather obvious looks in James's direction. James, in turn, was heading them off by engaging Piers in conversation about his art collection. The young artist, all long black wispy hair, gangly and awkward, was chain-smoking Gauloises and listening intently to Melanie Hughes's advice on his forthcoming exhibition. Elena finally seated herself beside Nigel Gordon and everyone tucked into the giant platters of langoustines. Gus's mood sat too heavily on her to feel easy about making conversation either to the Italians seated across from her, or to Nigel Gordon on her right. In any case, Elena was monopolizing the great art critic, and the Italian woman was sending hot looks down the table to her father, while the old Count glowered into his wine glass. Piers had always attracted loads of women, and Gus hadn't made it her business to know whether or not he remained faithful to her stepmother. Her feelings towards Elena were so ambivalent she supposed she wouldn't really care if he was still playing the field. She contented herself with listening to the various conversations around her, while picking at the food. She avoided the wine, but drank large amounts of Evian water, hoping that her headache would soon go. The combination of the heat and the noise, and the effort to appear interested in what was going on around her, was almost too much, so she was relieved when the first of the guests got up to leave. In the bustle of goodbyes Gus saw James smiling across at her. He got to his feet and was about to come to the newly vacated chair beside Gus, but was headed off by Mirabelle appearing at his side and insisting that she show him Piers' Monets. Gus stood up from the table and, as no one appeared to notice, she quietly slipped off across the lawn down towards the rose walk, to be alone with her thoughts and to try to shake off her ill humour.

Inside the long shaded stretch of arched roses, the air was cooler and filled with heady scents. Gus lingered here and there, pushing her nose into the fragrant petals, and then came once more into the sunshine where a narrow stone path led down the slope to a small lake. Gus sat down beside the water, pulling off her sandals and dipping her toes into the deliciously cool water, then splashing it on to her face and neck where it prickled her skin as it dried. The voices were a long way away, and if she closed her eyes she could almost imagine that she was back in her childhood, newly returned for the summer holidays, with the prospect of weeks with her father ahead of her. She lay back in the soft grass, closing her eyes against the still fierce sun, and dreamily tried to remember the good things in their lives.

When footsteps whispered through the grass some twenty minutes later, Gus had dozed off. Piers stopped short when he saw her peacefully sleeping a few yards ahead of him. He always knew where to find her. This was her spot, where she came when she was happy, or sad, or simply wanting to be alone. The lake formed the centrepiece of a small glade, surrounded by rhododendrons which each year stole a little more of the surrounding garden, too beautiful to restrict, with their heavy waxed leaves and flamboyant flowers, yet endangering everything around them.

Piers silently lowered himself onto a wooden bench and watched his daughter in her peaceful slumber. How grateful he was that she had turned out so different from her mother. If there was any character trait which he could attribute to his first wife, then maybe it was her determination and her bravery – a will which she could exercise with total single-mindedness, but with Gus it was in such a positive way. She would, he thought, use her drive to achieve great things, far removed from the world that Piers and Cat had known at Gus's age. It was as though every negative gene she had inherited from the pair of them had been purified in Gus. Piers' tough old heart ached with love as he watched her lovely face – not obviously beautiful like her mother's, but softer, somehow more refined. She had inherited Cat's colouring, and though Gus's eyes were grey, they had the same feline tilt which made them unusual.

A bee landed on her bare foot, and Piers brushed it away with his hand. Gus woke with a start and a little splutter of fright. Then, when she saw who it was, she sat up and smiled with pleasure. 'I thought you'd be busy with your guests,' she said, stretching her arms above her head and then pulling herself up into a kneeling position where she could see her father properly.

'I was but they're all drifting off now. I've said my goodbyes. I needed a break and I guessed you might be down here. I know you're going back this evening and I didn't want you to leave without our having a moment to ourselves.'

Gus felt warmth spread happily through her body. She almost purred with pleasure. 'I'm pleased. Sometimes you just seem so busy, so tied up with things.'

'I expect you still haven't really forgiven me over your call night, have you?'

'It's a long time ago, now – nearly four months. I've forgotten, really . . . ' she lied unconvincingly. Stupid to be upset though; it couldn't change the fact he hadn't been there.

'I'm very proud of you, you know, Gus darling.'

'Thank you. It's important to me to know that.'

'Well, don't ever forget it. I know how you feel about Elena and Mirabelle – that it's not always easy for you. I know, too, that Mirabelle plays up. I imagine she thinks that you're more special to me – which, of course, you are – but lately she does seem to be making an effort. I was pleased she came to meet you yesterday from the airport. It would be nice for us all if we could get on as a family.'

Gus bit her tongue to stop herself from saying something ghastly about the pair of Angeletti women. She couldn't imagine ever feeling a part of any family connected to those two. Gus knew exactly what Mirabelle's motives for coming to the airport were – to show off the new car, and to keep Gus and Piers apart.

Piers gazed into the dark water, absently tugging at the little blades of grass around his feet. A song thrush warbled in the bushes behind him, and overhead Gus could see several white trails crisscrossing the cerulean sky. There was a sense of timelessness, of languor and warmth which had almost thrown off Gus's previous mood. As she realized this, she also realized that the atmosphere between them was better, closer, than it had been in many months. It was so rare for them to be alone for more than the time it took Elena to replenish

84

her lipstick or powder her nose. Maybe now was the time to approach him, to break down the barriers of secrecy that always stood between them whenever she brought up the past and her mother. She knew that there was a connection between her past and the man at the party. If her father hadn't interrupted them the stranger would have talked, Gus felt sure of it.

'Last night, that man, who was he?' she said softly. Immediately, she saw her father's face grow tense and the muscle in his jaw twitch. She knew he was struggling to remain calm. She felt uneasy, knowing the relaxed mood between them had been broken – as always happened when she tried to raise the subject of the past.

'What man?'

'The one you rushed me away from. He said he knew me when I was little, that he knew Mummy.'

Piers's hands tightened on his knees. Why, after all this time, did his past keep on coming back to taunt him? Bloody Thompson turning up like that, daring to talk to Gus!

'No one important. No one you'd want to know, darling.'

'But I'm interested,' she persisted. 'How did he know us?'

'I really can't remember.' Piers had his face turned away from Gus towards the lake. He refused to meet her eyes.

'Did he visit us in Sussex?' Gus continued, all the while watching her father's face, searching for clues, as if he were in the witness stand. 'I suppose he would have done if he'd known Mummy, too. Then he must have known you quite well.'

Her father had paled. Gus felt the killer instinct rise within her. This was just too important to let go. She knew he was struggling for composure. 'Why won't you tell me what really happened? Does that man know?'

Piers snapped, 'Enough. That's enough, Gus. You

know how I feel about that time. Why do you have to keep on dragging it up again and again?'

'Because there's something missing. I know there is. The dream ... I had it again last night. I know that seeing that man brought it back – ' She broke off, feeling tears stinging behind her eyes. 'There was just something about that man ...'

'He did business with me, all right?' Piers was hissing now, angry, cornered and cold. 'He's just someone I knew a long time ago. He's not a very pleasant character. That's why I didn't want you to be bothered by him. There's nothing more to it.'

'But what was he doing here then?'

'Just business, like most people who come to see me. You know what my life's like, Gus. I know all sorts of people, from all walks of life. He's just one of the sort I'd rather not have around my family.'

'You were worried he might talk to me about Mummy. That's why you interrupted us?'

Piers could feel anger throbbing through his veins. But he also felt very afraid. Gus was far from stupid. Had she remembered what had happened? God, he hoped not. He dared not allow himself to think that she could have remembered from all that time ago ... He had to think quickly of something to explain, to stop her searching back, in case even a three-year-old might remember.

'When you were very young Thompson used to ask me for help. He's a policeman. He was involved with the investigations into a few robberies and he thought I might get to hear about some of the items. You know about fencing, don't you, Gus? Well, Thompson thought I might be approached – innocently, you understand – and asked to fence some pieces. But it wasn't so good for my business to be involved with Thompson. It made some clients nervous. Art dealers have to be very careful. I was building the business, the galleries, my

86

reputation ... you know what the art world's like. That's all. He visited us at home a couple of times. Maybe you saw him.'

'And now?' Gus's mind was racing ahead. 'What was he doing here? Is he still chasing stolen paintings?'

Piers forced himself to laugh. 'Seeking a few tip-offs, I expect. Maybe he thinks I've got a few heists up my sleeve. After a promotion, maybe, through insider knowledge. Unfortunately for him I don't move in those circles.'

Gus stared at him levelly. She knew her father so well. 'I know you're not telling me everything.'

Suddenly Piers erupted. 'That's enough! I will not be interrogated as if I were one of your criminals, Augusta. Now stop this at once.'

Gus stood up. 'I know you too well, Daddy. I know how you behave when you're cornered. You react in exactly this way. You're hiding something and you can't fool me! But have it your way, as usual!'

She rushed away from her father, blinded by angry tears. All this talk of fencing. What nonsense. He was trying to fob her off. She just knew that somehow that man Thompson had something to do with that day in her recurring nightmare. She almost ran headlong into her stepsister.

'Ah, here you are, hiding away.' Mirabelle stood, hands on hips, unable to hide her irritation at finding this cosy little scene, but then, on closer examination, deeply curious as to why the pair of them looked so upset. A little row, if she wasn't mistaken. She knew better than to ask Gus. Maybe she'd find out from her mother later on. Mirabelle smiled to herself. What a successful weekend it had turned out to be!

'Everyone's looking for you, Piers. And James wants to play tennis, Gus. Mixed doubles. You're partnering Nigel Gordon.'

* * *

87

That night, and much to Mirabelle's further irritation, Gus and James returned to London on the same flight. She listened to his chatter, enjoying his easy wit, and the flight passed reasonably quickly. But she couldn't drag her mind away from the scene she had had with her father. When they eventually shared a cab back into London James promised to talk further about her pupillage, but not even that could distract her from her father's conversation. She hoped James didn't notice how woodenly she was behaving. But she just knew there was a part missing of her father's story. She had seen his reaction, the anger on his face. And she had seen something else. Something that was now gnawing away at her, giving her a sick feeling in her gut. Fear.

Chapter Eight

❧

1968

Pete turned right off Piccadilly into St James's Street, walking the few yards down to where the new gallery stood. His step was light, as it always was when he walked through St James's. Since his little deal with Maurice he had come a long way. But while Maurice had provided the cash, it was his own shrewd eye which had landed him his fast-developing position in the art world. Each night had seen him poring over fat books stuffed full of photographic reproductions of paintings, devouring everything he could possibly find in an effort to educate himself in this field. His memory was superb and he had learned about every artist, and every painting, but it was his eye that gave him a talent which gained him entry to the upper echelons of the art world. He had an almost unerring ability to know when something was right, and when it was wrong. It was a strange skill to be genetically passed down from market traders and dockers, an accident of nature. Now he received privileged invitations to private viewings from all over the world. Rich new clients contacted him for advice. People watched him at auctions, interested to see what he would go for. Oh yes, he had arrived all right.

The gallery's window was small, but the goods were impressive enough. Not that the actual goods were on view -- that would have been too tempting to an opportunist thief -- but well-produced photographs mounted on glossy boards showed the newly acquired view of the Grand Canal by Tintoretto, circa 1570, along with a luminous green caterpillar by Dürer. The originals were safely locked away in the strong room, along with Pete's fast-growing collection of worthy works of art. It had been his idea to open up the new gallery as a way of doing something useful with his earnings. Maurice had leaped at the idea, granting him a partnership arrangement in the venture, but giving him overall responsibility for the day-to-day running of it. The marketstall in Bermondsey had been taken over by one of Pete's cousins and he now only visited it on very rare occasions. He preferred to deal with his 'contacts' on a more anonymous basis these days. In the three years since he and Maurice had first had their little chat, he had come a long way from his market days. His suits were now bespoke by tailors in Savile Row and his shoes were handmade by Lobb just across the road from the gallery. His ties came from Dior and Gucci, and his pants and shirts were of the finest Sea Island cotton. His image had undergone quite a change. And so had his name.

'Morning, Piers.' The young blonde receptionist stooped to pick up the pile of post from the mat. Her long hair fell over her face and as she stood up, pushing it back into place, Piers admired the way the sun shone through the silky gold mass.

'Morning, Veronica.' He smiled as he adjusted the alarm system. It was good having such an attractive bird around the place. Piers had been amazed at just how many of them had answered his ad in the *Evening Standard*. He had been tempted to get Veronica into bed almost immediately, but the fact was she had turned out to be a great little receptionist, and he feared that if it all went sour after fucking her then he might lose her. So he had kept himself celibate so far as the gallery was concerned.

Of course, outside was a different matter. Now that he seemed to have achieved respectability amongst the Establishment with his new money, he was spoiled for choice between the young chicks who were prepared to lift up their micro minis for him. His dad would have turned in his grave with all this promiscuity going on. The pill was becoming as much a fashion accessory as were these peculiar new things called pantyhose. Piers approved heartily of the former, but he wasn't at all sure about the latter.

Veronica delivered a cup of coffee to his desk, together with the usual pile of stiff invitation cards. He flipped through them. It never failed to amaze him how well he and Maurice had managed to develop the business. While in the first few months they had had to scour the pages of *Burke's Peerage*, the *Tatler*, *Country Life*, the *Lady* and the National Trust's guide to houses open to the public in order to find out who lived where and what they'd got, Piers now found himself attached to the guest lists of most of the smart parties.

Being in the City had helped his rise up the social ladder. It had been handy to get to know several bankers, brokers and dealers – some of whom used the gallery almost like a pawn shop, selling in a painting one week to raise the cash for some deal, and buying it back later on when the deal went right, all before the wife noticed! Sometimes a masterpiece had to be off-loaded, very discreetly, of course, in order to meet school fees. Piers had adopted just the right manner when dealing with these City types: discreet, charming and not too subservient. It was far better to let them know subtly the extent of his expertise and thereby win their trust so that they brought their business back again and again. It was more than convenient to them that Piers should attend any house parties they happened to be having. They even joked with him that that way he could view the paintings without their ever having to leave the house. He could give a valuation on sight, as it were.

Piers picked his time very carefully when it came to passing on the details to his 'removal men'. The last thing he wanted was to have a burglary linked with his visit to a place. Luckily, the legitimate side of his business seemed to be growing in direct proportion with the other.

Veronica poked her nose round the door. 'Don't forget you're going to the Crowboroughs' tonight.'

Piers nodded and thanked her. He hadn't forgotten. This was one party he wouldn't dream of missing.

'Oh, and Piers, there's a man out in the front asking to see you. Frank Thompson, he said to tell you.'

Piers' dark brows knitted together in irritation. What the bloody hell was that little shit after? No doubt another fucking payoff! Thompson was becoming an expensive liability these days – and he had a nerve, turning up at the gallery!

'Show him back here, would you, Veronica?'

'Pete!'

Piers cringed inwardly at the way Thompson was grinning. Even though Piers was well used to dealing with villains, there was something ultraslimy about Thompson and his methods. He had a way of popping up just after a major job, demanding money for silence. Blackmail and extortion were Thompson's hobbies, and unfortunately he was too much of a risk to ignore. His swaggering sense of self-importance had recently become even more unbearable since his promotion to *detective* constable.

'What is it, Frank? Don't you think it's a bit risky, turning up here in broad daylight? I don't suppose anyone would believe you're a punter, now would they?' Piers couldn't keep the sarcasm out of his voice.

'Ah well, Pete, me old mate, that is where you're wrong. Well, not me personally, but – how shall I put it? – a certain friend of mine has an interest in your business.

Thinks you might be able to help out. Could be a good deal for you, if you know what I mean.'

'Such as?'

Thompson helped himself to the whisky from the coffee table between them and then sat down on the small sofa beside Piers' desk.

'My contact wants to buy a painting. Something special. He's got quite a bit of ready cash.'

Piers couldn't imagine that anyone Frank knew would have the kind of money needed to buy his sort of stuff. 'What sort of amount are we talking about?' Piers sounded mildly bored. Frank was wasting his time.

'Around a million!'

Piers let the breath whistle between his teeth. He just couldn't stop it. 'A million *pounds*, we're talking . . .?'

Frank grinned smugly. He liked the fact that the arrogant sod had been way off the mark. Put him back in his place. 'So should I take my business elsewhere, or do you think you might be able to help him?'

'Depends what your friend is looking for. What's his taste?'

'Something special. Something which can readily find a market later on.'

'Is he a collector?' Piers decided to dig a little, find out what sort of friend of Frank's could afford a million.

'Not exactly, but he's very rich. I think he's probably prepared to take your advice on what's good.' Frank's weasel face split into a suggestive leer. 'I told him you wouldn't let me down.'

Piers chose not to answer. Instead he stroked his chin as he thought about his stock. 'Is he a businessman or what?'

'Oh come on, Pete, client confidentiality and all that. I'm afraid I'm not at liberty to divulge.'

Piers smiled his understanding. 'Tell you what, I'll give it some thought. Where can I phone you?'

'Oh, I'll call you in a day or two. And, Pete,' Frank

drained his glass and placed it heavily on the table as he stood up, 'make sure you sort it. He's a pretty important bloke.'

'Yeah.' Piers stood up too. 'Thanks, Frank, for the contact. It's good to know I can always rely on you.'

Frank shrugged at Piers' insincerity. 'That's what friends are for, me old mate.'

Piers watched him go. Then he poured himself a Scotch and sat for a few moments, attempting to work out just what Frank Thompson was up to this time.

Piers nosed the British racing green Lagonda through the twin stone pillars on each of which was perched a chimaera. With their lions' heads, goats' bodies and serpents' tails, they were a fitting emblem for a folly on such a fabulous scale as Hollyworth House. The car swept Piers along the curving drive, and suddenly the house came into view. The clash in architectural styles was almost surreal, as if the original owner had found it impossible to decide which style of house he particularly liked and so had tried a bit of everything. The doorway was flanked by Corinthian columns which rose majestically towards the crenellated façade. The left wing of the house had windows enveloped by pointed gothic arches and the far end was marked by a tower cut into the corner of the building. To the right gracious Georgian windows ran from floor to ceiling on the ground floor, while slim, iron-fretted balconies ran along the upper floors. The only saving feature of the place was that someone had had the foresight to paint everything white – the only attempt at unity in the whole scheme. But Piers, far from thinking the place hideous, found its imperfections rather charming – like a tart attempting to pass herself off as a lady, or like a barrow boy trying to be a gentleman.

He strode through the open door, hearing the rise and fall of the well-bred voices coming from the other side of the huge entrance hall. It had been a long hot drive from

London to Kent in the Friday night traffic. He accepted a glass of champage from a passing flunky and thirstily drained his glass. He stood and looked into the crowded room for a few moments, enjoying the spaciousness and cool of the hallway.

A curved staircase twisted around the wall ahead of him which in turn was adorned with several portraits of the Crowborough ancestors. The Crowborough Collection was internationally renowned and there was one particular piece which Piers was more than curious to see hanging. He climbed the stairs, two at a time, hardly bothering to glance at the portraits. He headed along the corridor towards the salon where the stars of the collection could be found. The double doors were closed, but Piers pushed them open, noticing immediately the way the paintings had been wired into the wall. Any attempt to remove them would be met with all hell breaking loose. There were two Rembrandts, a Gauguin, three Monets, a Goya and a Raphael. But the painting that caught his attention was the small study below one of the Rembrandts. He peered into the scene, examining the canvas minutely. Unable to stop himself, he pushed his fingernail into the oil where it met with the slightest resistance before giving way to his gentle pressure. It would probably take months to dry out properly, but in the meantime there was no reason why anyone should discover that the Manet was a fake – arranged on Dickie's behalf by Piers.

All the paintings in the Crowborough Collection were fiercely guarded by trustees, keeping them secure for future generations of Crowboroughs. They could never be turned into cash – at least not legitimately. Dickie had run up some pretty large gambling debts and needed some hard cash to pay them off before his father, who had already threatened to disinherit his son once before, got to hear about them. In desperation Dickie had come to Piers for help, having heard via the young boys' network that Piers was a bit of a fixer. At first Piers had been reluctant to let on to Dickie that he was up for the job, but when he had heard the extraordinary story of the Manet's history, he had been persuaded to change his mind.

Bizarrely, Dickie's grandfather had fallen out with the Frenchman responsible for cataloguing Manet's works, the artist's *catalogue raisonné*, and the latter, through pique, knowing that Alistair Crowborough had acquired this particular painting, had decided to leave it out of the catalogue, thus throwing doubt upon the painting's provenance and potentially reducing its future value. The story had only come to light a couple of years before, when the Crowborough Collection was revalued and recatalogued. Dickie had learned the story from his mother who had been most amused to hear about the revenge eked upon her late father-in-law.

Piers had realized that because of the painting's obliquely shady past, it would be a difficult one to trace backwards, as there was no real record of its existence.

As long as Piers was careful about who he sold it on to, he knew he – and Dickie – would get away with it! Even now it was at the gallery, carefully and anonymously stored. As Piers stared at the canvas he had a shrewd idea as to just who he might sell it on to!

Closing the doors behind him he headed back along the corridor towards the grand staircase feeling very pleased with himself. As he turned a corner in the long passageway he heard a cough, almost a little choke, coming from one of the rooms off the passage. He pressed his eye to the tiny crack where the door wasn't quite closed, curious as to what was going on inside the room. He caught a glimpse of someone standing, swaying oddly in the middle of the room. It was a woman and she appeared to be in some discomfort judging from the sounds coming from her lips. Piers silently inched the door wider to get a better look, at first thinking the woman might be ill, but as the door swung open, he stopped abruptly, shocked and intrigued by the scene in front of him.

The woman's dress was pulled up high around her waist, and below she was naked save for a flimsy suspender belt and stockings. She stood with one leg lifted up, her stilettoed foot resting on a stool to the side of her. She was circling her pelvis, rocking her cunt, over the eager mouth of the man who kneeled between her legs. For several seconds Piers stood watching the scene, trying to take in what he was witnessing: Dickie Crowborough suckling the woman, drinking her, completely oblivious to the intrusion.

As Piers started to edge back out of the room suddenly her eyes flew open and he realized with a start where he had seen her before. Those eyes, so catlike and unusual. Her mouth spread into a lazy smile. Her lips were open, the breath coming in short but quiet little gasps. He could see that her mouth was moist. Even as she smiled at Piers, realizing she was being observed, she continued to rock on to the eager tongue below her, her arms resting on her hips, holding her skirt high. She looked triumphant, exhilarated, not at all fazed by Piers' presence.

Piers turned on his heel and retreated. He ran back down the stairs two at a time, and grabbed another glass of champagne from the nearest waiter. He was amazed to find that his hand trembled as he lifted the glass to his mouth. The vision of her was stamped across his mind. He could feel his erection throbbing. The sheer, hot eroticism of her, the joy with which she was abandoning herself to the moment, giving herself to pleasure without the vaguest sense of guilt. Suddenly Piers knew with a boiling certainty that he would fuck her. His loins were aflame with lust for her. It was almost as if in allowing Dickie to suck her, she was granting him an enormous privilege. A kind of arrogance exuded from

97

her, from the way she stood looking so damned pleased with herself, as if Dickie was a slave to her cunt. Jesus, he couldn't remember ever being so excited by anything in his life before. He had to have her. But not tonight. He had to get out of the place before he exploded!

Frank hardly bothered to look at the painting. 'Manet, you say. He's all right, is he?'

'Well, he's pretty dead, actually,' Piers was used to Philistines like Frank but that didn't mean he had to humour them.

Frank growled, 'Cut the cleverness, Lawrence. You're making a killing on this deal I expect.'

'No. Not much. I'm selling on behalf of a client. Here, you'll want this I expect.' Piers handed Frank a piece of paper. 'Your receipt.'

'Not on your books, then,' Frank regarded him slyly. 'Dodging the tax, are we?'

'I didn't know you were that interested in my business affairs.'

'Oh believe me, I'm interested in all your affairs, Pete. You wouldn't believe just how interested I am in what you get up to!'

Bastard! Piers thought. When could he ever get shot of the slimy little sod? After this deal he would refuse to do anything else. Thompson was becoming boring.

'So, I hope your client's satisfied with his purchase. Unusual for him not to want to see it . . .'

'Yeah, well as I said before, he might want to sell it on. Maybe you could arrange it?'

Piers's mouth twitched. So that was it. Just as he had hoped and counted on! This so-called friend of Frank's was laundering!

'Maybe.' Piers was thinking quickly. 'Perhaps a sale in New York might be more, er, lucrative for your client?'

Frank grinned at Piers's quick understanding of the situation.

'Tell you what, for being so helpful, I'm going to arrange for a small token of thanks.'

'How kind.' Piers poured a drink for Frank and handed it to him.

'Yeah, £25,000 sound all right?'

Frank knew Piers would bite his hand off for a backhander. He was just as bad as the rest of them. Once a thief always a thief. Something else for Frank to use in the future.

'That sounds absolutely fine, Frank. How quickly does your client want to arrange the next stage of his business?'

'Straight away. Why don't you hang on to the Manet and sort it?'

'No problem.' Piers raised his glass in a toast. 'I'll let you know when it's going to be auctioned. I'll get on to Giffords at once. Leave it all to me.'

Piers was as good as his word. Funny how well things could work out. Dickie Crowborough was happy – he had a nest egg stashed away in Switzerland large enough to keep him going for many years. The Manet was safely out of the country, the saleroom was buzzing with interest, and Piers would earn a fat commission from Giffords for the introduction of the painting. Maybe he'd split the commission with Frank and get even more future insurance on the creep. Now, he reasoned they were more or less quits. Piers had about as big a hold over Frank as Frank had over Piers. And Piers had the last laugh bearing in mind Thompson's nice little deal was centred around a hot painting! Piers settled back to enjoy the show as lot number nineteen came to the podium.

Piers wasn't the only person in the audience showing an interest in lot nineteen. Stephen Wallace shifted in his seat unable to keep still for the tension. He had decided to cross the Atlantic almost on a whim. He'd never been to one of these smart auctions before, and what made it doubly interesting was the fact that lot nineteen was his painting! Thompson had done a great job finding this guy Lawrence to sort things out. By the time he had the cash in his pocket it would be squeaky clean – twice over! He settled back into his chair, his excitement growing almost by the second when it became clear that there were two very serious buyers after the painting. It was certainly turning out to be a most interesting – and lucrative – evening.

Piers' life became even more interesting some two weeks after the New York sale.

'Haven't we met before?' The voice startled him. 'You look terribly familiar, I'm sure I've seen you somewhere. Were you at Julia's ball last week? Or was it Belinda's twenty-first?'

'What?' he began slowly, before he realized who was addressing him. He had just closed a deal with a rich duke at his latest private viewing party when the voice interrupted them.

As the Duke drifted back to his Duchess the feline eyes regarded Piers with some amusement. Her lipstick was slightly paler than before, creamier, emphasizing the peachy tint of her fresh young skin. She wore an elegant black and white bouclé suit – the skirt of which skimmed the tops of her knees by a discreet three inches or so.

'I've got it . . .' she said, after she had gazed at him for several moments. 'That club down the Mile End Road, or whatever it was. Oh, and ghastly Gerald. Gosh, did I behave very badly?' She moved closer to Piers and as her scent wafted under his nose, he was carried back to that night, such a long time ago. Then there was the last time.

'Cat, isn't it?'

'How clever of you to remember me.'

'It's not easy to forget someone who fucks like you.'

She looked puzzled but not shocked. 'Have we...? Did we...?' She studied his face clearly trying to remember when they had been to bed together.

'No, we haven't,' he said, putting her out of her misery. 'Dickie Crowborough, remember? I watched you and Dickie. It was quite a scene. I must say I enjoyed it enormously.'

She laughed, a husky, deep-throated chuckle. 'Of course, I remember now. You should have stayed a bit longer,' she narrowed her cat's eyes at him, 'it got far more interesting after you left.'

'I was worried I might have seen too much of a good thing. Besides, I didn't want to spoil my sense of anti-cipation, my exploration of the unknown.'

'If you mean what I think you mean, you're taking an awful lot for granted.'

Piers grabbed her arm and pushed his head close to her ear. The scent of her filled his nose, his mind, his veins. 'I have every intention of fucking your brains out before the night is over!' He felt a delicious shiver run through her body as she turned her head towards him. The same lazy, almost lascivious smile played around her mouth.

'What makes you think I'm interested?'

Piers slid his hand up her skirt, oblivious to those around him, who in any case were all too intent on the paintings to notice what he was up to. He cupped his hand against her mound, his fingers resting softly against the swelling of her lips. Her underwear felt damp.

'You're ready for it,' he grinned back at her. He could see the glazing in her eyes, her mouth open just that little bit more. He felt the tremble in her leg against his. He released her and then took her by the hand, leading her firmly through the crowds of guests until he reached his office at the back. As soon as the door was closed behind them he felt her fingers fumbling for his zip.

'What was your name again?

'Piers, Piers Lawrence.'

'Piers, hm? Posh name for an East Ender . . .'

'Yeah, me mum 'ad delusions of grandeur.' Piers slipped back into the vernacular.

Their breathing quickened. Cat placed her long forefinger inside his trousers, her eyes fixed on his. Her lips had the faintest smile playing around the edges as she gazed at him wantonly. Piers grabbed at her teasing hand and held on to it tightly, pushing it against his hard cock. Cat's eyes widened with pleasure.

'It's huge!' she cried awe-struck. 'However did you manage to grow one that big?'

'I didn't, you did!'

Piers released her hand, then he grabbed Cat by the shoulders and pulled her closer to him. Her mouth looked so soft and yielding, her lips swollen and ripe and impossible to resist. Slowly, savouring the moment, he lowered his mouth against hers, satisfyingly conscious of the way in which her body seemed to go limp in his arms, moulding into him. Piers' tongue searched deep into her mouth. God, he wanted her. Their breath joined in harsh, almost rasping, need. His kisses travelled down her neck as Cat arched her head backwards, leading him towards the place where her breasts heaved against the bodice of her blouse. She slid her knee up the outside of his thigh, where he caught and held it, pressing his fingers into the warm, firm flesh.

'I want to fuck you!' Piers whispered against her ear.

'And I want to fuck you . . .' she moaned.

Piers's hand was riding higher up her leg, his fingers kneading into the soft skin around her buttocks. He knew that if he didn't take her very soon he would explode. Without another conscious thought, he pushed her onto the floor and ripped at her knickers. Her legs were wide open, inviting him to take what he wanted, what they both wanted ... At last he entered her, savagely almost, with an intensity of passion so fierce it sent a shudder of ecstasy right through his entire body. He burst into her almost immediately, but she was right there with him. Their cries of satisfaction mingled into one, and then faded into astonished but happy gasps.

Piers was the first to move, raising himself up on to one elbow from which angle he could watch the lovely face below him. Her eyes were closed.

'Just like the cat that ate the cream,' he murmured, reaching out to stroke the rich brown hair which fell in an untidy mess around her head. He admired the clever sweep of deep brown liner which curved along the crescents of her closed eyelids, and flicked out towards her brows. Her skin was smooth and flawless, coloured by a flush of peach on her cheeks. Her lips tilted upwards seductively. Piers could already feel his passion rising once more. He wanted to take this lovely creature again and again. Only slowly, this time, in order that he might savour the experience. He wanted to enjoy her nakedness; to explore those enticingly secret parts of her which he had only enjoyed so fleetingly.

'Let's get out of here! The party's getting boring. I want to take you somewhere where I can have you again and again. This floor's too bloody hard.'

Cat giggled as he pulled her up, scrabbling in the darkness for her underwear. 'You're a pretty fast worker, Mr Piers Lawrence. What if I say no?'

'I'll fuck you here. It's up to you.'

'You'd better take me somewhere a little more comfortable. Besides, I need food before sex. I'm starving.'

'Has anyone ever told you you're like an animal?' Piers helped her straighten her dress.

'Why the hell do you think I'm called Cat?'

Chapter Nine

1993

As Gus trotted along in James's wake through the grim bowels of the Old Bailey, she realized with a start that she had been with him for almost three months. The time had simply rushed by. Working beside James was like trying to survive next to a raging tornado. It was impossible not to get whisked up by his boundless energy and enthusiasm and his seemingly endless capacity for work. Gus had often wondered what it was like for his poor wife at home. She must hardly ever see him. During the week, so far as Augusta could gather, James dragged himself back to his flat in the Barbican where she supposed he must simply fall into bed with exhaustion – rather like Augusta herself. Then, come the weekend, he would pile up his briefs and trek out of London to his main residence in Surrey to catch up with marriage and children.

Clearly James wanted to keep them very separate and she respected his professionalism. London was all about the business of being a barrister. And in that he was a joy to behold. Gus's arm was nearly dropping off with the weight of the beribboned bundles. Her body bent over sideways at a curious angle, while her master strode out, black robe flowing majestically behind him, with not even a pen to burden his passing. Gus could feel a sweat breaking out on her forehead with the force of her labour, although she should be used to it by now. At least she hadn't yet had to use one of those sack trolleys, as many of her fellows did.

The instructing solicitor, David Lewis, caught up with her. 'Ah, Miss Lawrence, how are you? Let me help.'

'Thanks, David,' Gus smiled gratefully, 'and, please, call me Gus. How's the client?'

'Remarkably cool and still protesting his innocence. I'm afraid I haven't persuaded him to change his plea, even though the evidence against him is colossal. Maybe Mr Kentish will have more success,' he added, hopefully.

'Well, if he doesn't, our client is going to go down for a very long time indeed. Wasting a lot of public money on an unnecessary trial, holding up a jury, besmirching witnesses, et cetera, et cetera – all of which can really get up a judge's nose,' Augusta warned.

The cold concrete stairs led down to the cells underneath the courtrooms. The stairwells rang with the sound of footsteps, the clanging of iron bars, and the clunking of giant keys in locks. Gus always felt chilled down here. James, on the other hand, seemed perfectly at home and was whistling merrily under his breath. If Gus wasn't mistaken, it was an attempted rendition of 'Colonel Bogey'.

The police officer let them into the cell and locked the door firmly behind them. Kevin Lawton was sitting up on the bare mattress, looking awkwardly stiff in his smart blue suit, white shirt and tie. Even his shoes looked freshly polished. His hair, which had receded some way from his forehead, was oiled and combed straight back, and tapered neatly into his collar.

'Morning, Kevin,' Gus smiled. 'You look very smart today. How are you feeling?'

'Like a right dick'ead,' Kevin sniffed. 'Still, if you finks this'll 'elp get me off then it's wurf it.'

'Hello, Kevin,' James said smoothly as he shook the client's hand. 'Nice to see you looking so well. Now I don't want you to worry about a thing today, you just leave it all to us and we'll do the business.'

'You think you'll get me off, Mr Kentish?'

'No, Kevin, I don't think I'll get you off, but we'll have a jolly good run at it. Trial lasting five to seven days – jury out for two hours – unanimous verdict and the maximum sentence. That's my prediction, dear boy! We'll take care of it, though, don't you worry.'

'But – you don't think I'll get off?' Kevin sounded staggered by this news, even though David had been telling him the same thing all the previous week.

'I don't think you've got a cat in hell's chance, as they say. But you see the thing is, Kevin, you're the client and at the end of the day I act on your instruction. I advise you what to do, you listen – or not, as in your case – and then you tell me what you want. You've decided to enter a plea of not guilty therefore the case must go to trial, the judge will get severely pissed off and you'll get banged up for a very long time. I go off to fight somebody else's case and that's the end of it – for me at any rate.'

'Why, you cold-hearted bugger –'

James laughed gruffly. 'Yes, that's exactly what I am, Kevin. And so are the jury and so is the judge. We're all going to be very cold-hearted buggers in that courtroom and the most cold-hearted bugger of all will be prosecuting counsel. Whom, I might tell you, is extremely good and will pull more holes in your story than you can count in that string vest of yours!'

'So what you sayin' then?'

'Plead guilty, dear boy. That way you can show remorse for what you have done, we can plead mitigating circumstances – that is, make excuses for why you might have acted in the way you did – emotionally disturbed, cry for help, the usual rubbish, and you'll get a reduced sentence.' James smiled reassuringly, turned to the others. 'Come on, troops,' he called jauntily. 'See you in court, Kev,' and with that he banged on the cell door and the three of them left poor Kevin to ponder his fate.

'I don't know how you dared do that.' Gus felt as if she were letting her breath out for the first time in ages. 'You were really quite mean to him, James.'

'Mr Kentish, I feel I must protest on behalf of my client,' David Lewis panted as he tried to keep up with James's stride. 'You've destroyed his confidence and left him not knowing what he should be doing!'

Suddenly James stopped dead in his tracks. He rounded on the unfortunate solicitor, his face a picture of ferocity. Even Augusta felt like shrinking backwards. 'Have you taken leave of your intellect?' He brought his face close to Lewis's. 'That client of yours has a bucketload of evidence against him. Three witnesses saw him stab the shopkeeper. Kevin's fingerprints were on the knife which had actually snapped off inside Mr Bundhu's chest. Mr Bundhu's blood was on Kevin's clothes. What kind of idiot goes and pleads innocent?

'Now I'll suggest that by the time our Kevin has got up to the dock, he'll have changed his plea to guilty. That way he'll have his sentence reduced from twenty-five to eighteen years, and he'll be out after serving nine. If he pleads not guilty he'll serve at least twenty years. Now who's looking after your client's best interests?'

'I don't know how you can be so confident that he'll be found guilty!' David said gruffly.

'You instructed me because I'm one of the best there is. That is how I am qualified to know these things. Now, if you'll excuse me for a few moments I should just like to have a brief chat with my pupil. Augusta . . .'

And as ever, James had been proved right. Kevin passed a note to David, and David passed it to James. As Kevin stood up in the dock, the judge's clerk read out the charges and asked Kevin how he pleaded.

'Guilty,' said Kevin weakly.

James then sprang into action, eloquently and articulately explaining that the unfortunate Mr Lawton had been suffering from acute depression which could well have caused paranoid delusions, and as such would milord like to see a doctor's report recommending that the defendant be sent for further medical reports prior to sentencing.

As expected, his lordship readily granted the request and suggested a date two weeks' hence for sentencing.

Once outside the courtroom James cast his robe in Augusta's direction and, nodding only briefly to Mr Lewis, sauntered towards the exit.

'Amazing,' David Lewis sighed to Gus. 'I tried for a whole week to talk Kevin into changing his plea. Perhaps I should practise some rough stuff like Mr Kentish.'

'It's up to you, but don't forget there's something about the wig and gown that puts the fear of God into the poor client. It does give counsel an advantage.'

'Yes, quite an unfair one when it just comes down to fancy dress.'

Augusta giggled. 'We need to be disguised, David, we're in the front line, remember.'

'Yes, well I suppose it's cheering to know that it'll be you lot the client beats up, not us humble solicitors.'

Augusta laughed. However unsavoury the cases, however seedy the clients, the work she was doing now was inordinately more interesting than the stuff she had been poring over alongside Henry. Luckily Henry had been very understanding about her leaving him. He had wished her well and been extremely complimentary about the work she had done while with him to the extent that she had felt incredibly guilty about going and, consequently, unsure of her decision. However, a week with James had banished all doubts. Cases ranged from burglaries to sadistic murders. Because of James's seniority he tended to get the more serious crimes – unless the client happened to be particularly well-heeled.

Back in chambers Gus settled down to work on her papers. Unfortunately, James had taken himself out for lunch and nobody seemed to know his whereabouts for the rest of the day. She was disappointed, but soon lost herself in her work. She had to trawl through lengthy witness statements, police evidence, forensic reports and medical reports to get a clear picture of the case. The hours ticked by and she worked on contentedly, happy in the knowledge that she was getting much more of a feel for the work. On days like this, she was permitted to use the spare desk which was situated in a corner of James's rather grand room. A huge marble fireplace was the focal point and, as the weather had grown colder, it was James's custom to build a log fire in the late afternoon. Gus realized that she would be working on for several more hours and, while not being sure as to whether or not James would return, she decided to kindle the pile of logs. The sound of the gentle hiss and spit of wood and flame was very soporific and relaxing.

Although it was a large room, it was also remarkably cosy. To either side of the firebreast were shelves stacked full of gold-tooled leather-bound volumes recording the Acts of Parliament, and thousands upon thousands of cases and commentaries. Over the mantelshelf hung an oil painting of James's father – Lord Justice Kentish – looking sternly down at her, solemn and uncompromising in his scarlet robes. A marble and ormolu mantelclock ticked soothingly into the peace of the room. Gus stretched her arms, feeling the tension in her neck. She could barely remember what it felt like not to be stiff. Life outside chambers was barely existent. She arrived early for work, and dragged herself home late into the evening. She and Flora seemed to pass like proverbial ships in the night. Gus laughed to herself. How green Flora had been when she learned about Gus's new pupil master. She had almost fainted with envy. And now, rather than Gus having to pump Flora for every little snippet of information, Flora was the one to pounce on Gus, begging to know how the great barrister was performing!

Gus recognized the footsteps as they approached the room. She felt a warm, pleasurable sense of anticipation at the prospect of seeing James. It would have seemed a very flat day if she had eventually gone home without having spoken to him since Kevin's brief appearance in court this morning.

'Augusta, ah, so glad you're still here,' James said warmly as he divested himself of his Burberry raincoat. 'And you've lit the fire, clever girl. You must have read my mind.'

He stood in front of the glowing hearth, warming his hands behind him. Gus couldn't help but admire his athletic frame. He was much older than other men she had previously found attractive, but he had kept well in shape for his forty-one years, and his thick brown hair carried not a trace of silver. 'I thought we might dine together tonight, Gus, unless you have any other plans?'

'In Hall?' She queried, thinking about the rather dry prospect of Hall formalities.

'Heavens no, I thought we might enjoy ourselves. Go to a restaurant ... what do you think? I looked in my diary and realized you're nearly halfway through your time with me – that's something to celebrate. Besides, I'd like to treat you. We spend so much time working that I fear we are in danger of becoming dull. Quite frankly I'm tired of putting up with the bores in Hall, or

111

the alternative frozen offering from Marks and Spencer which my dear wife stocks the freezer with in case I should starve to death. I don't know about you but I'm beginning to forget that eating is actually one of life's main pleasures.'

Gus's pulse quickened inexplicably. The prospect of dinner with James – a real dinner as opposed to a professional dinner – filled her with a strange sense of excitement. 'I'd love to, but I feel a little, well, plainly dressed,' she said, staring down at her drab black suit and plain white shirt.

'Tell you what, let's make a proper evening of it,' James said enthusiastically. 'Go home and put on one of your drop-dead gorgeous dresses and I'll take you somewhere really special.'

Gus beamed with delight. 'That would be very nice.'

'You've worked so hard it's the least I can do. Leave all those papers and go and get yourself prettied up. I'll send a cab for you at, what shall we say, eight o'clock?'

All the journey back to the house, through getting changed and on the way to the restaurant, Gus kept telling herself that she was foolish to feel such a nice sense of anticipation. This was her pupil master, for goodness' sake. Female pupils invariably had crushes on such debonair masters as James. It stood to reason, after all, being in his presence all day long – she spent more time with him than his wife did! And James's charisma, his worldliness, his knowledge, were a heady mix for a young and impressionable female. She wasn't young and impressionable, though. She was a professional through and through who knew very well that mixing one's profession and one's love life was not a very clever thing to do. Gus would not fall into that ridiculous old cliché.

But when she saw James stand to greet her as she crossed the bustling restaurant, her wit betrayed her. He looked so attractive dressed in his beautifully cut light grey suit. This was almost the first time, apart from the party in Guernsey, that she had seen him in anything other than his black wool barrister's garb. Gus sat down carefully, arranging her dove-grey silk trousers to avoid creases, and watched James signal the waiter. She barely noticed anyone else in the entire restaurant, or what food they ate, or how long they were at the table. It was as if her normally cautious, sane mind had gone AWOL. By the time the coffee arrived, she found herself with both elbows on the table, leaning her chin on her hands, gazing lasciviously into James's eyes.

'I know just the place for a nightcap,' he said, as he handed over his credit card to the waiter. 'Feel like one?'

'Hm, lovely idea,' she sighed, aware that if James had suggested a vending machine at Leicester Square it would have been okay with her.

Gus didn't hear where James directed the taxi to. She recognized the Barbican though when, a short time later, the cab deposited them outside.

'My flat,' James explained. 'It'll be more relaxing for us here.'

Gus bit her lip and started to feel a tiny bit sober. She stared at the pavement. Now was her chance to leave. If she stayed she knew exactly what would happen and if she left, it wouldn't. Her fate was in nobody else's hands but her own. James had not forced her to come back with him. It was now or never – never to know what it could be like . . .

'You'd better lead the way,' she said, noting how her voice appeared to have broken.

In the lift there was a conspiracy of silence between them. As she waited for him to unlock his front door, a deep, gut-hollowing excitement grew in Gus. She couldn't remember wanting a man as much as she now knew she wanted James Kentish. She respected him, she admired him greatly, and boy, did she fancy him! As the door closed behind them, James's mouth closed

113

on hers, and she felt herself melting down towards the floor as her legs started to jellify beneath her. With awe-inspiring strength, James swept her up in his arms and carried her through to the bedroom where he laid her gently down on the enormous double bed. Still with their mouths burning hotly on each other, Gus helped peel away James's jacket. Then her fingers fumbled with his shirt buttons. Soon that too was discarded and she could at last feel James's naked skin beneath her hungry fingers. His chest was broad and smooth. Almost without her noticing, James had managed to divest her of her trousers and blouse and Gus and he now lay, almost naked, luxuriating in the joy of discovery. James ran his hands through Gus's hair, then with a surge of passion he kissed her mouth, then her neck, on down to her breasts, closing his lips around her nipple, sending agonizingly wonderful shivers of pleasure through her body, down to her centre. Gus craned her body against his, realizing it had assumed a will of its own. All control had left her. She was powerless to stop, as the tremors rippled over her skin, and her pelvis thrust wildly. She was James's, totally and completely, for him to do with what he would. Her only consciousness was her desire to open up to him, to press herself on to him, to feel him deep inside, hard and pulsating and real. Suddenly she reached her climax and as soon as her cries had subsided, he started to move again, slowly and teasingly at first, while her body recovered from hypersensitivity. James's skill was limitless and as his thrusts grew deeper and faster, Gus felt herself, unbelievably, climbing once more with him. As he whispered her name, over and over again, his lips pressed against her hair, Gus wanted to scream aloud. James's moans mingled with her own, and as his body shuddered, spilling into her, Gus once more reached the cloud with him. He was wonderful, a superb lover. As they lay together, spent but satisfied, Gus smiled with pure happiness.

114

This was going to be extremely complicated. James was her master, they worked together, he was married! But as she snuggled into the warm curve of his body, she decided that, for the moment at least, she could handle it.

Chapter Ten

Mirabelle never particularly enjoyed the Wednesday Afternoon Meeting knowing that, more often than not, whatever ideas she came up with usually met with a fairly negative response from the illustrious controller of Maverick Productions. John Stapleford was ultracautious about what new commissions the production company undertook, aware how difficult it was to sell their programmes on to the TV networks. Game shows, that's what he wanted, more and more daft game shows! He told them all to spend their time watching European game shows on satellite TV and see if there was anything they could work on importing to the UK. And some of the stuff was bizarre in the extreme!

Mirabelle had spent the last week researching whether British couples would be prepared to discuss graphic details of their extramarital affairs while their surprised spouses would have to guess who they were having an affair with! Even Mirabelle felt they should draw the line somewhere, and she, along with her colleagues, had tried to explain to John that some of these cuckolded husbands and wives just might blow a gasket if they found out on prime-time TV that their other halves were having it off with their best friends! Thank goodness they had managed to persuade him of the stupidity of the idea. Mirabelle had yet to forgive him for making her stand on Waterloo station five nights in a row where she had to stop complete strangers and ask them whether they liked a bit on the side or not. But what was even more astonishing was the fact

116

that the great British public didn't appear to mind being asked! Everyone wanted their five seconds of fame, it seemed, and despite her predictions, several adulterers had said they would be prepared to play the game, provided they got several thousand pounds in compensation! Perhaps, Mirabelle supposed, it was one way of increasing the marital assets.

Her ears pricked up as Fran Jeffries, the production manager, reached Mirabelle's suggestion: *Justice on Trial*, a series of interviews with the cream of the British legal profession getting some heavyweight opinions on the ways in which the system is changing, including solicitors rising to the challenge of being able to act in the higher courts in the same way as barristers do, and using interviews and cases to illustrate the various interviews. Mirabelle saw the idea as a cross between a consumer magazine and a hard-hitting in-depth profile of the law and lawyers, with a few of the myths exploded. She smiled to herself. That was always a good phrase to tempt a director – a few myths exploded!

'Yes,' John Stapleford was saying, 'I rather like this one. Mirabelle, it's one of yours, isn't it? Would you like to do me a fuller report on how you see this developing? Perhaps we could put together a pilot, see what we can come up with? Do you have any contacts who might be willing to talk to us about their roles in the judiciary? It might be hard to get hold of a judge. They're notoriously camera-shy. You'll have to go for the retireds. Unfortunately some of those are a little suspect, I gather. Can't always guess what they're going to do next. Still, why don't you put together a couple of scripts and I'll have a look at it again?'

Mirabelle couldn't believe her ears. This was the first time John had taken the slightest interest in anything she had proffered. 'Of course, John. I'll get to work on it right away.'

'Come and talk to me later, and I'll give you some

more pointers, if you like. Now, anyone seen any good game shows this week?'

Gus thought she must be seeing things. She blinked twice just to make sure. She had just stepped out of the clerks' office when she saw the vision – Mirabelle – walking down the corridor towards the stairs which led up to James's office. Her jaw dropped and she stopped dead. What on earth did *she* want? It certainly wasn't Mirabelle's style to make social calls on Gus.

'Mirabelle!' Gus called after her. 'Hey, are you looking for me?'

Mirabelle turned around and her eyes swept over Gus's drab suit with an expression that at once expressed pity and disdain.

'Oh Gus, hello. Er, no, as a matter of fact I wasn't.' Her wide lips split into a deliciously self-satisfied grin. 'I have an appointment with James! See you.'

She turned back towards the staircase, leaving Gus unable to decide whether to follow her and demand to know what the hell she was doing here or to mind her own business. Gus could feel her cheeks growing hot with anger and frustration. The girl needed psychiatric help! Every time Gus had a potential love interest Mirabelle moved in on him. But not James . . . She couldn't! James wouldn't be remotely interested in Mirabelle. No way was she his type. James was far too intelligent for Mirabelle! No, stupid of her to think anything . . . but what on earth was she doing here? No doubt trying to muscle in, like she usually did. But Gus was older now, more experienced. She wasn't going to be as vulnerable as she had been over Jonathan.

James was attractive, a wonderfully exciting lover, and an extremely interesting companion. But he was married to some homely wife who reared their four children. James had hinted that Esme couldn't meet his needs these days – probably one of those marriages where one partner had simply outgrown the other. It happened. No doubt Esme was a bustling, capable sort of housewife, on all the local committees, keeping her house shipshape and spotless for the return of her weekend husband. James clearly needed more than that – to be stimulated and entertained. But whatever James decided to do about his unhappy marriage was his business. Gus was enjoying the affair at the moment. Maybe something serious would develop – but for now she was going to protect herself by not becoming dependent upon him. That way she was less likely to get hurt. She had carefully planned everything out in her mind. However, her plans did not included accommodating Mirabelle – in any shape or form.

Gus returned to her own room. Compared to James's it was small and impoverished. Where he had grand drapes at his three-quarter-length window, Gus had a grubby old Venetian blind which obscured the view out over the back of the building and on to the rear of the building beyond that. She shared her room with another of the pupils – well, it was really more of a cupboard than a room. Mostly she spent time with James, in his room, where even the spare desk was twice the size of the one she now poured her papers on to. She had a case to prepare – a drink-driving in Guildford Magistrates' Court in a few days' time. It was only the third case which she had taken on by herself, and she was justifiably nervous about it despite her success with the previous two. The rest of the afternoon had been set aside to look at it.

Steeling her will, Gus pushed her specs up on to the bridge of her nose and opened the brief. Words swam before her eyes as she tried vainly to concentrate on the evidence in front of her. All she could think of was blasted Mirabelle and whatever it was she was doing with James! She would not give in to the temptation. Even as she tried to close her mind, excuses kept insinuating themselves into her head as to what she

119

would say to James when she interrupted their meeting. She bit her lip with frustration. Mirabelle would be triumphant if Gus appeared; immediately she would have scored a point against Gus. God, it was so bloody stupid.

The problem stemmed from the fact that Mirabelle's own father had died when she was a young teenager, and while alive he had spoiled her rotten. She had never got over losing him, and then had been unable to cope with the fact that Piers didn't worship her in the way she felt a father should. The ridiculous thing was that Piers lavished everything he could upon Mirabelle – probably because he felt guilty about the fact that he loved Gus more. But then Gus was his only daughter. Mirabelle was not his flesh and blood. Gus knew he had tried to love Mirabelle, but it was Mirabelle herself who made it hard, being always so competitive.

It was all rather sad. At the beginning, when Gus had worked out just what Mirabelle's hang-ups were, she had tried to understand her, but had discovered that the girl's only currency was her beauty. She was obsessed with her looks, trading in the superficiality of skin-deep appearance, trying to compete with Gus on her own twisted terms of self-worth.

Mirabelle held out James's shirt for him and lay back on the bed while she watched him dress. The idea of getting him back into bed had only struck her halfway through their meeting – well, perhaps seeing Gus had sewn the seed of the idea. Mirabelle had wanted to laugh out loud when Gus 'just happened to be passing' James's office. Mirabelle had bet herself it wouldn't take Gus long to come and check out the competition. And then James had almost blown everything by suggesting the three of them go out for a drink. Luckily boring old Gus had work to do so she couldn't join them, giving Mirabelle just the opportunity she wanted.

120

Feeling well pleased with herself, she continued to enjoy the scene. James had a very good body for a man his age – rather like Piers, she mused. She had often wondered what her stepfather would be like in bed. She doubted that he would be quite so exciting as James. Anyway she'd probably never know unless she asked her mother directly.

'I think Gus was a little curious to know what I was doing in your office this afternoon.'

'She doesn't know about the TV deal. I'll explain tomorrow. She's busy preparing a case tonight.'

'I don't expect she'll be too happy about the prospect of my being in your chambers for a few days.'

'You and she obviously have a problem, er, between you.' James flipped his braces up on to his shoulders.

'Well, I don't suppose I'd be here like this if we were close ...' Mirabelle's lips curved upwards in a highly suggestive smile. James stepped forward towards the bed and stroked Mirabelle's ripe breast. 'It was fun, wasn't it,' Mirabelle grinned encouragingly, 'rather like after the party in Guernsey?'

Suddenly James's face clouded. 'I'd appreciate it, Mirabelle, if you didn't let Gus know of our ... of our ... well, you know what I mean!'

'As if,' Mirabelle said sweetly. 'No, what you and I have, James, is a sort of friendship. I really had no idea that you and she were – well, an item. She hadn't mentioned it to me.'

'I didn't think you were particularly close.'

'Oh, we have our ups and downs,' Mirabelle said, finally climbing off the bed and heading towards the bathroom. 'If you hadn't told me I'd never have guessed.'

'But I didn't tell you,' James protested. 'You knew. You asked how my affair with Gus was going!'

'I was teasing. It was my little euphemism for you two working together. The last thing I expected you to say was that you and she were spending so much time together.'

'I assumed Gus had told you, otherwise I wouldn't have been so open about it.' James was angry at himself for being so indiscreet. Still, Mirabelle was hardly likely to go blabbing about their activities to anyone, least of all Gus!

He stood in front of the mirror combing his hair. 'I'll leave first, shall I, and deal with the bill?'

'That's good of you, James,' Mirabelle smirked. 'I suppose I could put it down on expenses *re* the programme. What do you think, something like "Entertaining prospective interviewee, double room, Savoy Hotel, afternoon rate"?'

'I don't suppose it would be the first time a hapless interviewee had been "had" on the casting couch.'

Mirabelle propped her hands on her naked hips. 'You really have a pretty dim view of us TV types, don't you?'

'Having heard what your scripts are full of, I could say that you TV types have a pretty poor view of the legal world. Unfortunately, I seem to have agreed to allowing your unsympathetic cameras into my chambers, for better or for worse.'

Mirabelle strode over to James and stood before him, gloriously naked. Her long blonde hair cascaded down to her nipples. James could feel temptation rising. He cleared his throat and thought of Gus.

'You'll be famous, James. More famous than you are already. Your name will be known in every household. You'll have women all over the country falling for you. Clients will be demanding that you take their cases for them. Just think of the number of lady solicitors who'll be queuing up to brief you. You'll be fine. I'll make sure of that.' She kissed him lightly on the nose and then stepped into the bathroom.

James stood fiddling with his tie, deep in thought for several moments after Mirabelle disappeared. Appearing in Mirabelle's programmes was just the kind of high-profile exposure he needed right now, provided he could check over the scripts. The candidacy selection was coming up soon, and he would stand a far greater chance of becoming the next Labour candidate for Bulsworth if he had media credibility. Funny how Mirabelle had turned up just at the right time with her idea. A few months back he would have sent her off with a flea in her ear, but now ... well, she could be enormously useful to his proposed new career as an MP.

'I hope you know what you're doing, James.' Esme Kentish regarded her husband somewhat sternly from her seat at the opposite end of the refectory table. She dabbed her delicate mouth with the starched linen napkin and splashed some more claret into her glass. She watched as James mopped up the last of the beef fillet and then stood up to collect the used plates. It was Friday, and she had given Maria, the Filipino housekeeper, the night off so that Esme would have ample chance to speak to James.

He topped up his glass as he finished the remainder of his mouthful. As ever, Esme had provided a simply delicious supper and he never ceased to wonder how she managed to fit everything into her busy schedule and succeed in doing it all so beautifully. He watched, admiringly, as her slim figure crossed the vast but homely kitchen, then bent to place the china into the dishwasher. At thirty-nine she had retained the body of a twenty-five-year-old. Her black hair was as sleek and dark as ever, without a trace of grey. That was partly the trouble with Esme, of course. She was so damned immaculate and perfect that she could be extremely intimidating – even to him. He knew exactly what she was talking about, but he decided to hedge, nevertheless. Experience had told him that it was advisable, if at all possible, to avoid the straight answer so far as Esme

123

was concerned. One could never quite be sure where her needle-sharp mind was leading!

'About what, darling?' he answered vaguely.

'This bloody television series, James. You do think it's the right thing?'

'Apparently I shall be a household name, darling. I shall become the new media barrister. That, after all, must be good for business.'

'And if you get selected for Bulsworth when Max Fowler dies?'

'It'll bring the whole thing forward. I should think I'd have far more chance of winning the seat after a load of television exposure, wouldn't you?'

'As long as it's good, James. That's what worries me. You know I'd hate to have anything jeopardize our long-term plans. But if you really think this will place you in a better position to stand, then I suppose it must be good news.'

James smiled at his ambitious wife. Politics – the logical step for a bright barrister who didn't want to spend the rest of his days arguing the toss for the underclasses. In an ideal world there was absolutely no reason why he shouldn't be able to pick and choose what and whom he represented, take silk even, while fulfilling his role as a Member of Parliament. He knew he couldn't put off the decision too much longer. At forty-one he was getting a bit long in the tooth for entering politics. He needed to get a decent seat – a high-profile, fresh addition to Labour's collection – not some marginal full of problems and headaches destined to do nothing for him but lose him his seat at the next election. He had to be choosy about where and when he stood and he was keeping a very keen weather eye on Max Fowler's constituency. Old Max was known to be terminally ill. It was only a matter of time before there would have to be a by-election in Bulsworth. This television exposure could only help his cause.

Esme was the granddaughter of Henry Macpherson, the great post-war socialist Prime Minister, and daughter of Charles Macpherson, the former Chancellor of the Exchequer and Foreign Secretary. He had been only narrowly beaten for the leadership post by Michael Foot back in 1980 much to the family's disappointment.

'One thing worries me though, James.'

'Yes?' he asked carefully.

'These – how can I put it? – dalliances of yours, they're really not going to do you much good, are they?'

'I'm really not sure I'm quite with you, Esme darling . . .' James eyed his wife evenly. She appeared to be half preoccupied with spooning coffee into the cafetiere.

'Please don't be coy, James. You know exactly to what I am referring, and I think you should be aware that whatever you do in your private life from now on could very possibly be open to public scrutiny sometime in the future. Whilst I know it's very hard for you to keep your zipper closed I do think it would be circumspect of you to try. Otherwise I'd hate all we've worked for to be blown for the sake of one of your tarts.'

'But –'

Esme raised her hand as if she were addressing one of the children and was tired of explaining the obvious. 'Let's leave the matter there, shall we? I don't think either of us wants to get embroiled in discussing detail. We have a fairly busy weekend ahead of us, James, and I'd quite like to relax and enjoy it.'

James let out his breath in silent admiration of his wife. If she were a man, she'd have balls of steel.

Chapter Eleven

Gus made her way to the magistrates' court across the road from Guildford railway station trying to convince herself that her jangling nerves would disappear the minute she stepped into the courtroom. Since James's decision to let her out on her own, she had mitigated a plea of guilty by a burglar by outlining the combined effects of drink, divorce and unemployment, resulting in a twelve-month suspended; and pleaded guilty to assault and got six months in custody. The outcome of the cases had been pretty certain from the outset and thankfully on both occasions the client had seemed to be grateful for the result. James would hardly have given her anything too heavyweight to cut her teeth on – it wouldn't have been fair on the poor client. Her main problem was to convince her client that she had been practising for years and had every confidence in both herself and the outcome of the case. She couldn't allow the client to notice her quaking knees, or her shaky hands and wobbly voice. She must look as if she had been doing this day in, day out for at least ten years. The fact that that would have made her twelve years old somehow had to be overlooked!

The only good thing about her impending ordeal was the fact that it kept her mind off James's revelation that he had agreed to allow Mirabelle into chambers to make some crappy-sounding programme about the system. Gus had been so angry that it had temporarily rendered her speechless. The whole thing was just too awful to bear contemplation! She would face it after she had got this case out of the way.

The solicitor's face clouded over with disappointment when he saw such an obvious novice approaching the bench where he sat with his smartly suited client. His frown deepened as Gus thrust her hand forward by way of introduction.

'Mr Jennings,' she said smoothly and confidently, 'I am Augusta Lawrence and I trust that I may represent Mr Gilbert this morning . . .'

'But I thought David Forbeson was coming. When I spoke to the clerk last week he said that we would definitely have Mr Forbeson . . .'

Augusta could feel the hostility like an icy wind around her. This was something she knew she would have to get well used to over the next few years. No solicitor client liked to be fobbed off with a youngster, but it was an unfortunate fact of life that they couldn't guarantee getting the barrister they had originally briefed because other cases didn't always run to schedule. David Forbeson had been defending in an armed robbery, the trial had overrun its estimate by four days already, and the judge had only just started his summing-up. In a way it was fortunate for the younger barristers that these things happened, otherwise they might never be given any briefs at all!

'I'm so sorry,' she said in her most appeasing voice, 'but I am afraid that my colleague Mr Forbeson's case rather overran the clerk's expectations. As you know, these things happen and all I can do is to apologize on Mr Forbeson's behalf and assure you that I have had ample opportunity to acquaint myself with the file.'

'I should hope so,' the disgruntled solicitor snapped. 'Were you Forbeson's pupil?'

'Er no, James Kentish's actually.' She didn't enlighten the man as to the fact that she still was his pupil!

'James Kentish as in *the* James Kentish?'

'Yes, that's right,' Augusta allowed herself a small smile as she detected a faint note of admiration in the solicitor's tone.

'Well, that could indeed be most fortuitious. I assume that you know James Kentish rather well, then?'

'Naturally.' Gus's thoughts immediately flew to a mental picture of James at the opposite end of her bath. She felt her cheeks begin to turn pink. She cleared her throat and adjusted her gown. 'Yes, indeed . . .' she added rather weakly.

'Then, as I said,' Mr Jennings continued chirpily, 'we should have rather an advantage.'

'Oh, why is that?' Augusta could predict what the answer would be. James's cases always received massive press coverage, and as such if the average Mr M25 was asked to name a leading barrister they would more often than not come up with the name of James Kentish. Clearly Mr Jennings hoped some of James's kudos would have rubbed off on Gus.

'Because Mrs James Kentish is Chairman – of the Magistrates. But how silly of me, I expect you knew that already. She can be rather a toughy, can't she? But socially I expect she's quite different.'

'What did you say?' Gus was reeling. Had she just heard correctly? James's wife was Chairman of the Magistrates in front of whom she was about to perform? Surely this couldn't be possible. Jennings had got it wrong.

'Mrs Kentish. She's Chairman of the Magistrates . . .' Jennings confirmed.

Gus had to strangle back the sound of an expletive. 'There must be some mistake,' she blurted weakly. 'Probably a different Mrs James Kentish. Probably a distant cousin or something. The family has very strong ties with the legal profession, you know.'

'Esme Kentish – who is Mrs James Kentish,' Jennings affirmed. 'It's most definitely the same one. You see

128

they live locally and Mrs Kentish has been on the bench here for the last eight years or so. She was one of the youngest magistrates ever to be appointed, but with her outstanding qualities, she was deemed to be eminently suitable for the job.'

'How nice,' Gus stammered. This was positively surreal. How on earth was she going to put up a proper performance for poor old Mr Gilbert and his drink-driving charge?

'Have you met her?' Jennings asked.

'No, as a matter of fact I haven't,' Gus said, swallowing against the rising tide of nausea. 'Would you excuse me for a few moments, Mr Jennings?' she said, and then quietly slipped into the ladies' loo where she promptly threw up.

The members of the bench filed into the courtroom and Augusta tried to guess which of the two ladies was Mrs Kentish. As they shuffled to sit in their correct seats, centre stage was taken by a woman in a striking red and black dress. Gus watched, mesmerized, as a beautifully manicured hand, complete with the exact same shade of red nail varnish, deftly poured a glass of water. It had to be the other one! Surreptitiously Gus took in the rather frumpy beige dress and jacket, the spreading hips. Yet it was the other, glamorous, creature who occupied the centre chair – the one reserved for the Chairman. As prosecuting counsel began his speech Gus was unable to take her eyes off the scarlet woman seated high above her. Whatever preconceptions she had had about James's wife, no way could they have ever hit upon reality. Stupid Augusta! What had she thought? Some wifey little mouse of a woman, complete with apron and spotless kitchen, more interested in her garden than her bedroom, with the ubiquitous string of pearls and a floral frock for public occasions?

This woman looked like a vamp! As Gus's eyes remained transfixed upon the perfectly made-up face and

129

the piercingly intelligent blue eyes, Esme Kentish turned her head towards Gus, raising her eyebrows as if to say, 'Was there something you wanted?' and questioning Gus's impudence. Gus was forced to look quickly away in embarrassment.

James was a bastard not to have warned her! Not one hint had he passed her about what she was about to endure. For someone who was supposed to care about her he had a pretty poor way of showing it. And just look at his wife! She was not at all like James had suggested – dull, uninspiring, unattractive ... God, had she really fallen for the old 'my wife doesn't understand me' routine? What a bloody twit she was.

'Lastly Your Worships,' her colleague was reaching the end of his speech for the prosecution, 'the defendant has two previous convictions: for driving whilst having a blood alcohol level three times over the legally permitted limit, for which he received a two-year ban from driving; and for driving whilst having a blood alcohol level twice over the legally permitted limit, for which he received a five-year ban from driving, and was fined plus costs. He is forty-two years old and has been on police bail since February.'

'So this is his third offence?' Mrs James Kentish regarded the hapless Mr Gilbert sternly.

'Indeed, Your Worship.'

'I see.' She scribbled daintily on her notepad. 'Well, is there anything you wish to say on your client's behalf, Miss Lawrence? At least he's been sensible enough to plead guilty.'

Augusta stood up and promptly sent her sheaf of papers flying all over the floor. She dithered between whether she should answer or whether she should collect up the embarrassing mess around her feet. 'I'll get it, I'll get it,' Jennings hissed, irritated. Gus cleared her throat, desperately trying to forget that this intimidating female was married to the man whose bed she had climbed out of only a few hours ago!

'May it please Your Worships, I would submit that there are certain mitigating facts of this case which bear relevance to the court's normal sentencing practice in these circumstances. While one understands that this is Mr Gilbert's third offence, there is substantial mitigation by way of the fact that Mr Gilbert attended a party at his business partner's home where he was given a glass of what was described as a fruit cocktail. It was a very hot day and Mr Gilbert ill-advisedly downed the drink in one, before realizing that it was liberally laced with rum. Mr Gilbert had not eaten during the day and so the drink was taken on an empty stomach . . .'

Mrs Kentish tapped her pencil on her pad impatiently. 'Indeed. Go on, Counsel, get to the point.'

Gus cleared her throat and continued even more nervously. 'During the party Mr Gilbert received a telephone call from the family's babysitter informing him that his son had slipped down the stairs and had a suspected broken arm. Mr Gilbert drove a mile to his house where he collected his small son and set off for the casualty department of the local hospital. On his way there he was stopped as part of a spot check. I would submit that the principal mitigation here is that Mr Gilbert did not intentionally take an alcoholic drink that night, that he had been misled, and that under normal circumstances, once he realized the mistake, he would have had time to eat something and it would have been several hours before he had to drive again, and I would remind Your Worships that Mr Gilbert was only just over the legal limit.'

Mrs Kentish raised her eyebrows towards the ceiling. 'There is always someone you can telephone. I believe we do still have emergency services in this country . . .'

'Indeed, Your Worship,' Gus persevered. 'Er . . . in addition, I would submit that Mr Gilbert has only recently been divorced and has had agreed access to his two children sorted out to both his and his ex-wife's satisfaction. His ex-wife and his two children are entirely dependent upon Mr Gilbert's income which is derived from his business as a self-employed financial consultant. Mr Gilbert has been mainly off the drink since his last conviction some eighteen months ago and on the rare occasions that he does drink socially, he always makes arrangements whereby he does not have to drive. As he has said himself, after two such convictions he had really learned his lesson. Finally I would submit that a custodial sentence would be devastating not only to Mr Gilbert's business, but to his family. The recommendation therefore, Your Worship, is for a non-custodial sentence. I would invite the Court to deal with Mr Gilbert in the light it sees fit, and to consider the global circumstances surrounding Mr Gilbert's business and family, and pass sentence which is more lenient.'

Augusta sat down again, wondering whether she had managed to get everything in and wishing she had worded things differently. In her eyes she had sounded like a complete prat and clearly Mrs Kentish was having none of it.

She watched disbelievingly as Mrs Kentish leaned to the woman seated on her right and said in a loud stage whisper, 'How many times have we heard this nonsense before?'

Gus stared down at her notes, trying to hide her scarlet face. What a bitch this woman was! Gus had thought she'd be some old-fashioned homely little jam-maker, and here she was, a cutthroat cow!

'Stand up, Mr Gilbert,' Mrs Kentish ordered. 'Your counsel has argued for this Court's lenience with you. I hardly need to remind you, of all people, that this Court treats all drink drivers extremely seriously and as no doubt your legal representative will have told you, bearing in mind this is your third offence in three years we have to consider seriously a custodial sentence. However,' Mrs Kentish regarded Mr Gilbert sternly, 'we also have to consider the circumstances of the case and the fact that the level of alcohol in your blood was relatively low. Therefore we have decided that a period of community service will be the most appropriate sentence.'

Gus let out a sigh of relief on Mr Gilbert's behalf.

'In addition,' Mrs Kentish continued, 'you will be disqualified from driving for a period of three years and thereafter you will be required to retake your driving test.'

As Gus stood up to clear her desk, she realized her knees were still quaking. Did Mrs Kentish know? She felt that glamorous face burning into her back as she wobbled out of the courtroom behind Mr Gilbert. Just what wouldn't she say to James when she saw him!

Chapter Twelve

James stared at Augusta almost as if he wasn't seeing her. He seemed removed – off on some tactical ploy regarding the case notes in front of him. She wondered if he had been listening to a word she had said.

'Your wife, James, at Guildford!'

He smiled pleasurably. 'Ah yes, Esme. You were in her court were you? What was she like? Fair or not? I've heard she's really quite good . . .'

'James!' Augusta rebuked him. 'Don't you think it would have been a good idea to let me know that I might be performing in front of your wife? I had no idea that she was a magistrate, let alone Chairman of the Magistrates at Guildford. The shock nearly floored me!'

'So I heard,' James said pointedly. 'The instructing solicitor contacted Forbeson and mentioned that you seemed to be a little, well, how did he put it? . . . disorganized!'

'What the hell do you expect?' Gus snapped indignantly. 'I was in front of your bloody wife, James. Don't you think any normal person might have been a little disorganized? I damn near fainted with shock! And, I might ask, does the delightful Mrs Kentish know about us?'

'Good Lord, of course not!' James brushed off the idea as if it were too ridiculous to consider. 'Why on earth should she?'

'Because I just thought she might not have been quite so objective as one might have expected.' Gus bit her lip wondering just how much she wanted to say about his wife. It was not in her nature to be bitchy, but there were times when even Gus could be pushed too far.

James sighed. He pushed his chair back from the desk and clasped his hands in his lap. The clock ticked into the quiet of the room. 'Because you lost your case?'

Gus took a step backwards. She had been leaning forwards, her hands placed on the front of James's desk. There was something in his tone, something that in spite of the current circumstances surprised her. A sort of killer instinct – was it the hard edge to his voice? The way his eyes had turned cold? The way he was so obviously wishing that she would leave him alone to get on with his work? Not at all what one might expect from the man one shared a bed with at least three times a week!

'I find your attitude hard to believe.' She decided to leave him to it. She was stunned to realize that he really couldn't understand how she must have felt, what it must have been like to get a surprise like that.

'Just remember, Gus,' he said just as she reached the door, 'you should be ready to face anything. All through your career you will have nasty surprises thrown at you – from opposing counsel, from witnesses, from defendants and from the bench. If you can't handle a little thing like Esme then you'd perhaps better start thinking about your career.'

'Why you ...' Gus almost wanted to hit him. The arrogant, pig-headed, unsympathetic ... 'And for the record, I didn't lose. We got a non-custodial.'

'Morning, Gus.'

Gus was blocking somebody's way. She turned at the voice and came face to face with Mirabelle.

'Excuse me, I've got to get James wired up.' She squeezed past Gus, who remained frozen to the spot, mesmerized by the way James's face lit up.

'Ah, Mirabelle,' suddenly his whole tone had changed, 'how lovely to see you.'

135

Gus snorted down her nose and slammed the door behind her.

Gus opened a second bottle of wine and waved it in Flora's direction. Flora placed her hand over an already full glass and listened, silently, as Gus continued to tell her all about her ghastly couple of days.

'So now you can't move in the place for cameras, wires, microphones and Mirabelle's cronies. Really, Flora, it's like some sort of nightmare. I just can't believe how the girl has managed to do this to me.'

'What is it that she holds so much against you?' Flora couldn't imagine what it must be like to have such a vengeful person dogging one's life. Her family was remarkably straightforward in comparison to Gus's.

'Believe me, I've wasted many hours trying to work that one out. I think she's jealous, basically, because her father died and mine's still around. She thinks that Daddy loves me more than he loves her, and that she's neglected. She seems to think that she's somehow getting her own back, proving that she's better than me – or at least prettier, which is all that counts in her book – by stealing my men.'

'Do you think she'll succeed with James?' Flora asked cautiously. She wasn't quite sure how far she should push on the sensitive subject of whether James would succumb. From what Flora had heard about him, it would be a big surprise if he didn't. He was known as the biggest skirt-lifter in the business. She had tried to warn Gus, but would she listen . . .?

'Probably already has,' Gus said darkly.

She couldn't get out of her mind the way James had welcomed the cow so warmly into his office yesterday morning. Mirabelle didn't usually hang around if she was in with a chance. Since the episode with Jonathan anything was possible. The way she had wormed her way into Gus's trust, just after Piers and Elena had got together, then suggested the three of them – Jonathan, Gus and herself, go off on Piers's yacht to France for a couple of nights. All so very nice and cosy. Jonathan was Gus's first love and it had been barely a week since Gus had given up her virginity for him – all of which had been confided to Mirabelle! Gus had agreed to go shopping and then returned to the boat, having forgotten her purse, to find the pair at it, oblivious to her presence; blind to the fact that she was standing at the side of the bunk watching them. The memory still made her want to throw up.

Gus dragged herself back to the present. 'Having met his wife, Flora, I really feel as if I've been well and truly taken for a ride. James had led me to believe that she was some frump of a woman who couldn't understand either him or his work, and she turns out to be ... well, drop-dead attractive, highly intelligent and quite likely knows exactly what her husband is up to. James is not going to leave her, she's far too much his style. I do believe he's using Mirabelle's television programme to boost his chances of being selected as a candidate for Bulworth. God knows what he was using me for.'

'Sex, of course!' Flora clapped her hand over her mouth, immediately regretting what she had said. 'Oh Gus, I'm sorry, I shouldn't have said that.'

'No,' Gus said bleakly, 'you probably shouldn't. But it's the truth.' She downed the remainder of her wine and banged the glass on the table. 'You know, Flora, I really feel stupid over the whole affair. I should have seen through him. What a cliché, pupil and master. Hah!' she laughed bitterly. 'I'm beginning to think that life's a lot less complicated without having a man around. I should have better things to think about than the James Kentish types of this world.'

'I can't blame you for falling for him. Anyone would, Gus. It's more than any female could stand, having undiluted Kentish pheromones shoved under one's nostrils ten hours a day. I'd have done the same!'

Gus reached out and touched Flora's hand affectionately. 'You're very kind to give me such an easy time, Flora. But I do think I should have known better. Of course I'm sad – I fell for him – but I can't let it jeopardize my career, not after all this sweat and graft.' She stared into her empty glass, twisting her fingers around the stem.

Flora could tell that she was fighting back the tears. She kept quiet, and waited for Gus to recover. Gus started to nod slowly, as if she had just talked herself into a decision.

'I'll be fine. I'll cope. I've got plans and I don't need a bastard like James to mess them up!'

'Atta girl!' Flora cried encouragingly. 'You're worth a hundred of him. Let Mirabelle have him.' Flora couldn't suppress a giggle. 'They deserve each other!'

'Right, James, that's lovely, very nice, if I could just –' The make-up artist deftly flicked James's curl across his forehead and then mopped a tissue across James's brow. James wrinkled his nose at the unfamiliar feel of the face powder.

'Is all this completely necessary?' he asked gruffly.

'Yes, if you don't want to appear shiny-faced. Trust us, we do this all the time, you know.'

'I can imagine,' James muttered as he watched the rather camp artist pick up his box of tricks and retreat to the sidelines. The room had been transformed into a makeshift television studio. Bright lights glared down at James and state-of-the-art cameras and monitors surrounded him. Mirabelle winked at him reassuringly from her corner and gave him a thumbs up sign. Gay Swift, the interviewer, sat opposite James but the camera was trained on James's face. Mirabelle had explained that at the editing stage they could cut in on the

138

interviewer where necessary. Gay Swift introduced him and then briefly explained a little about James's background, then she posed him a few questions about the changing role of solicitors and barristers within the two branches of the profession, and his opinion on the various changes. James answered easily and confidently about his hopes for both the future of the Bar, and for the role of solicitor advocates in the higher courts. He also touched on the training of pupil barristers and briefly explained how the training works. After about twenty minutes, the producer was satisfied. 'Okay, guys, that's enough for tonight, thanks very much,' he called.

'What a lot of setting up and fiddling about for such a short interview.' James could hardly believe that it had taken about three hours to get everything into just the right place in order to produce such a short piece of film.

'I suppose one gets used to it,' Mirabelle said as she clambered over the spaghetti-like pile of flexes. We've got a few more pieces to do on life in chambers, and then we can get on to some case reconstructions. Maybe at that time we can ask you to comment upon them.'

'I think not. Professional etiquette and all that, I'm afraid, forbids us from discussing proceedings with the media if we're personally involved. I can only comment on concepts, as it were.'

'I'm sure we could work round it,' Mirabelle said, perching on the edge of James's desk. James couldn't avoid noticing the way her miniskirt slid up her thighs revealing a tempting bit of shadow between her legs. If he wasn't mistaken he could have sworn she wasn't wearing any knickers.

His cock throbbed into action, reminding him of the rather pleasant afternoon he had spent with her. 'Er, Mirabelle, what are you doing for dinner tonight?'

'Me? Oh nothing. I thought I'd have an early night, spot of television, boring stuff like that. Why?' She raised her eyebrows innocently.

'I was wondering if you'd like to join me for supper. We could discuss the format of the programmes, perhaps.'

'Of course I'd love that, James. I'll just get my things together and tell the others I'm off. What shall we do, meet outside in five minutes?'

'Five minutes it is,' James said, grinning broadly. As he watched Mirabelle's legs stride gracefully across the room, he realized he had a rather large appetite tonight!

Just a couple of miles away, as Gus slept alone in her house once more, the dream visited her again. She woke, in the middle-of-the-night darkness, covered in a film of perspiration. The room felt stuffy and hot. Flora must have forgotten to turn off the heating, Gus realized, sliding her legs over the edge of the bed. As she reset the boiler and gulped down a glass of water, she recognized just how utterly alone she now felt. She had to face up to just what an idiot she had been to allow herself to be seduced by James. She was no better than all the women she had despised for being taken in by chambers Casanovas like James. She had managed to get herself into just such a messy relationship. Would she ever make a success of love? Or was she destined always to get hurt, always to be the one left pretending to be tough and in control when inside she was shredded into little pieces?

Right now, she could have done with a comforting shoulder to lean on. She'd lost one parent, and now was in danger of losing the other. Since the party seven months ago, apart from a polite Christmas when they had no chance to talk privately, she had only had a couple of very brief, curt telephone conversations with her father. She knew he was was willing to make up, but she still felt angry. But how could she feel close to him when he persisted in being so secretive, and in lying to her? And even if she did know the truth about the relationship between her father and mother, about what really happened that fateful day, would she then be happier? It was all so damned complicated. At least during her affair with James she had managed to keep her mind off this other business. It had been so easy to allow herself to be swept along in the romance of the situation, to feel wanted and loved by him, so that the loneliness didn't feel so acute.

As she stood feeling sorry for herself, she heard vague stirrings coming from Flora's bedroom. Quickly, taking the glass of water with her, she returned to the darkness of her room and climbed back into the dishevelled bed. At times like this, she would have dearly loved to turn to her mother. Gus knew they would have been firm friends – she could just sense it in her being. They could have talked about everything and she could have helped Gus through this hideous emotional mess. As Gus drifted back to a kind of semiconscious dozing, she tried to imagine what her mother must have been like, to remember, as she had so many times before. But it was hard. Gus had been so young. Everything was blocked out but the vaguest recollections. In her fantasies her mother cradled her gently, sang to her. Gus could imagine the sound of her laughter, the lovely feminine smells and warmth of her breast. Such a young age to lose a mother – not to remember what she was like.

As Gus turned over, and started to drift down into the blackness of sleep, she realized there was one person who did know the answers, and that he must be aware she was old enough to ask the questions. Dickie Crowborough would tell her!

Chapter Thirteen

1969

Whatever expectations Piers might have had about his marriage to Cat, the reality of the situation was several thousand miles removed from them. Cat was anything but conventional in nearly every aspect of her life. She loved to shock people; to test the limits of their patience; to be outrageous. Cat would rather lose her right hand than ever be accused of being dull. Therefore Piers guessed that she had agreed to marry him partly because she professed to love him, and partly because she knew that in doing so she would upset her parents, ruffle the feathers of most of her friends and be the object of nearly every gossip column.

The realization hadn't bothered Piers overmuch. He, after all, knew that marriage to Cat was advantageous in many ways, not least being the fact that her father was an extremely wealthy northern millowner. Old man Harris had made his fortune through lucrative clothing contracts during the Second World War and he was a bit of a rough diamond himself. Even so, he and his quiet little mouse of a wife had made it their ambition to turn their only daughter into a lady. Unfortunately for them Cat had had her own ideas on the matter.

She had been expelled from three schools in total – the first two for relatively minor misdemeanours such as smoking and drinking, but the last was for the bald seduction of the headmistress's virginal seventeen-year-old nephew who had only come to the school for a long weekend.

Despairing of finding any more institutions to control his daughter, barring a female borstal, her father had installed a private tutor who had managed to cram enough education into Cat to scrape her through a few O levels. Cat had enjoyed the ministrations of her private tutor not least because she soon started a rather lurid affair with him. The summerhouse at the far end of the magnificent ten-acre grounds of the Harrises' mansion had been a haven for the lovers for an entire academic year and Cat had luxuriated at her lessons in front of a roaring log fire in the winter, and under the hot sun in the gloriously endless summer. Her tutor, a man of some thirty-five years, had taught her the bedroom arts almost as successfully as her maths and English. And after the examinations her tutor had left heartbroken and vowing to return to marry her, while Cat had patted him on the head and told him that he was, after all, far too old for her and he should go back to his wife and children and forget all about her.

There had followed a stint at a Swiss finishing school where, Piers gathered, the most important thing they had taught her was how to keep her knees together when getting out of a sports car. Usefully, though, she had found a stepping stone into her smart circle of friends. Cat's parents had hoped that she would marry a duke or, at the very least, an earl so when Piers did the old-fashioned thing and asked Harris for his daughter's hand, the old man had flatly refused. Then he had threatened to disinherit Cat, at which point Piers had decided he really must step in and help matters along. A couple of Impressionists, on what Piers had termed a permanent loan to the old sod, had done the trick. So grateful had Harris been that he had almost fallen on his knees to thank Piers. While he had money aplenty, style was not something that had been acquired along with

143

the mill and so a couple of serious oil paintings did marvels for the family's kudos. After that, he had decided that perhaps Piers wasn't quite so bad and he had begrudgingly given the happy couple his blessing. Of course Piers had the last – private – laugh. The Monet and the Matisse were hot enough to burn a hole in the wall. Some 'friend' of Maurice Levy's had decided they needed a holiday from their previous home in Germany and they had mysteriously found their way to Maurice and then on to Piers.

Cat eschewed a big church wedding and instead had opted for the far trendier venue of Chelsea Register Office. King's Road had been jammed with guests' Porsches, Ferraris, Lotuses and Lagondas as the happy couple stood and faced the paparazzi immediately after the service. Cat wore a pair of completely diaphanous white bell-bottomed trousers and a skimpy, bare midriff top designed by Yves Saint Laurent. Piers had been persuaded by Cat to don a white suit and they were swept to the reception in a white Rolls-Royce.

Pop stars, artists, interior designers, photographers, boutique owners and the aristocracy dominated the guest list. No members of Piers's family attended, and pitifully few of Cat's relatives had made the journey south from Leeds. At the reception marijuana flowed as freely as the champagne and even though Piers touched none of the drug himself, the fumes had been enough to make him light-headed.

He and Cat had then jetted off to Marrakesh, a place that had just about finished him off. Cat drifted in and out of consciousness for a couple of days while getting over the wedding, only to stone herself out of her mind once more as soon as she could get her hands on some Moroccan gold. Piers hated Marrakesh. It was hot, dirty, full of flies and exceedingly foreign. Everything about it was strange, including the art. He couldn't wait to return to London and the house awaiting them in

Holland Park – a wedding gift from Cat's parents. Cat disappeared for hours at a time and reappeared zombied out of her head. Piers' anger hadn't seemed to have any effect on her whatsoever and so he had taken to visiting the mosques and the temples and the souks, buying rugs and vessels here and there.

In anyone's terms, the honeymoon could not have been classed as a success, but Piers was not a man to judge his new wife too harshly for her excesses. After all, he had known she would be quite a handful from the first night he had seen her all that time ago in the East End club.

The sex, though, was superlative. Even when high as the proverbial kite, Cat had the ability to drive Piers wild. There was no trick she hadn't picked up. She was as inventive and as skilled as a professional whore. There was nothing she wouldn't – and didn't – do! Piers thought he'd been around, had experience, learned a few tricks in his time, but boy, how wrong he'd been. Compared to his wife he was a total naïf. She exhausted him and then aroused him with consummate skill. She had searched and teased his body in every conceivable place. There was no part of him that Cat hadn't explored and charted. She was as supple as a snake and as voracious as a black widow spider. And there was something equally dangerous – equally, animalistically, unpredictable – about his wild, abandoned, new wife. But in his youthful arrogance, it never occurred to Piers to ask himself whether he had, in fact, bitten off more than he could chew.

They returned to London and embarked together upon their married life. Piers continued to build up his contacts in the world of fine arts while at the same time wheeling and dealing with his former associates, including Thompson. After the successful sale of the Manet in New York, Frank's friend Stephen Wallace had bought a couple more paintings from Piers, in the same way.

Much as Piers hated dealing with Frank, the commissions involved had been hard to turn down. And it was amusing to spot Wallace in the smart auction rooms getting so excited over the sale of his latest 'acquisition'. Were it not for the fact that Wallace was a nasty little drugs dealer, his enthusiasm would almost be touching. Immediately after the successful auctioning of the Manet, Wallace had insisted on taking its new owner, oil tycoon George Kennedy-Hughes, out for a champagne celebration!

Piers would have liked to suggest to Wallace that he keep more of a low profile, play the whole thing down, keep it private – between themselves. But if Piers had told Wallace to keep his mouth shut, then Wallace might have wondered what Piers was trying to hide. Luckily the Manet scam had worked like a dream and everyone had come out happy. It seemed that Piers just couldn't fail in his business life. Through having a highly respected and well-known gallery, through being able to direct any robberies on a kind of demand-and-supply basis, he could profit from selling on the stolen property to his reclusive clientele, and he could also profit from the fact that those who had had their goods stolen came to his gallery to spend their insurance cheques.

He luxuriated in the immense gratitude from all those he dealt with. Small and large gifts were showered upon him and Cat from satisfied customers, hoping that when Piers came across a really good 'find' they would be the first to be tipped off. The Lawrences had their pick of the use of luxury villas around the world from the Bahamas to Indonesia. Several private jets were at their disposal if they chose. Their social circle consisted of the aristocracy, members of the government, newspaper proprietors, brewing magnates and several foreign royal families – along with the trendies whom Cat surrounded herself with.

146

To a large extent the Lawrences led fairly separate existences. Cat would disappear for days on end, tripping out with her hippie friends, while Piers got on with the business of art dealing. They maintained a kind of status quo, whereby there was an unspoken agreement between them that each would get on with his/her own business without interfering with the other overmuch. While Piers disapproved vehemently of Cat's druggie friends, it suited him to have her otherwise occupied and not asking too many questions about his business affairs or associates. Piers knew that Cat had guessed his dealings were not all they appeared to be but her questions had always met with Piers's tight-lipped secretiveness. Suspicion was one thing, knowledge was quite another, and he wouldn't ever like to be put into a position whereby Cat's learning exactly what he was doing could place her in a compromising position. He was the protector of several identities within the underworld, and within the sphere of master smugglers. He knew the whereabouts of some of the greatest international masterpieces, which could well remain missing for several generations and, in the wrong hands, his knowledge could be severely abused. So to keep Cat in ignorance, Piers conducted most of his meetings either in the gallery, or at a suitable hotel so that she wouldn't recognize any of his contacts. It hadn't occurred to either of them to discuss what effect starting a family might have on this rather convenient state of affairs.

Cat's shriek could be heard right through the house as far as Piers' study on the top floor. Halfway through dialling out a telephone number, he threw the receiver back on to its cradle and raced down the three flights of stairs to the morning room where he guessed she would be.

'I don't fucking well believe it,' she hissed at him as

she paced up and down the stripped floorboards. 'How could I have been so bloody stupid?'

'What is it?' he cried, his voice full of concern. He couldn't remember the last time he had seen her in such a state. She was almost foaming at the mouth.

'My bloody doctor just called me . . .'

'Yes . . . and?'

'I'm pregnant. That's what. Can you bloody believe it? Pregnant! Me! It's just the worst thing that could possibly happen. I'll have to get rid of it. I just couldn't bear the thought of it – a revolting little baby . . . uggh. I loathe children, Piers, you know I do. And my body – can you imagine – it would grow fat and ugly and distorted. I might even get stretchmarks. No, it's simply out of the question. We'll have to arrange an abortion immediately. I simply don't want children. The very thought of them makes me feel quite ill. Piers, you'll have to sort it out. It is, after all, completely your fault!'

Piers collapsed down into the pale calico cushions which were scattered along one side of the room. Pregnant . . . it took a good few minutes for the idea to sink in. Cat was pregnant with their baby – at least he assumed it was his. A spark of excitement glowed in his belly.

'But . . .' he started to speak as he watched Cat expertly roll a joint. Her fingers, though, were shaky and awkward. She prattled on, almost oblivious of his presence.

'The whole thing is just so bloody inconvenient. I was supposed to be going to St Tropez with Julian, Justin and Saffron next week. Now I suppose I'll have to book into a bloody abortion clinic. Oh God, how ghastly!' She stuffed the fat joint into her mouth and lit it, drawing hungrily on the aromatic smoke. Her eyes closed as she held the smoke deep in her lungs and then after several moments she exhaled, swallowing down the last of the smoke before taking another long drag.

'That's better . . .' she sighed as the drug soothed her conscious mind. Abstractedly she offered the reefer to Piers. He shook his head, trying to hide his distaste, and watched her as she continued to pace across the room. Her small bare feet had hardened skin across the soles which clicked on the stripped wood as she walked. Silver anklets festooned with tiny beads tinkled against each other. Her ankle-length gold and red kaftan had slits up the side to her thighs which showed glimpses of her smooth brown legs. Since their marriage Cat had lost weight and whereas before her body had been nothing short of voluptuous, she was now almost painfully slim. Her breasts, though, were as magnificent as ever and Piers noted that their outline could be clearly seen beneath the fine cotton garment. If anything, they seemed to be riper than usual. Her cheekbones stuck out from her skin more prominently, but they only added to the unusualness of her beauty, ever catlike and deeply exotic with her slanted eyes and long curved lashes.

She was a very different woman to the one he had seen at Dickie Crowborough's party that night. Their marriage had presented Cat with the freedom to dress and behave almost exactly as she pleased without any form of restraint. Piers wasn't at all sure that it was his role now to be a responsible guardian to his young and beautiful wife. Should he be weaning her away from the drugs – preventing her from jetting off all over the world with whom she pleased? Shouldn't he start taking some responsibility for her welfare for once instead of turning a blind benevolent eye on her antics just because it was convenient to have her pursuing her own lifestyle rather than prying on his? Just what sort of a husband was he turning out to be that he should blithely watch while this lovely young woman got on with the business of destroying herself simply because he was too busy to do anything about her?

149

Suddenly he knew exactly what he had to do. Raising himself off the cushions he stood up and waited until she drew near to him, then he reached out and snatched the reefer from her lips. He crushed it into an overflowing ashtray.

'What the hell do you . . .?' Cat shrieked as she tried to rescue the concertinaed joint. 'I was enjoying that.'

'You're pregnant!' Piers whispered in a voice that was at once threatening and authoritative. 'It's not good for you.'

'I know it's not good for me,' Cat screeched back at him. 'That's why I intend to get shot of it.'

'I want you to keep this baby. I forbid you to get rid of it. This is my child – at least I assume it's my child?'

'I haven't screwed anyone else in the last month so it must be yours! And I don't think I screwed anyone in the month before that – and the month before that – so it must be yours, goddamn it! But I will not have it!'

'Cat,' Piers softened his voice, but there was still an icy note to it that hinted at hidden menace, 'I demand that you do nothing to harm this child and that you will have it. We need to appear as a happy family. Just think how pleased your parents will be about it – and so shall I. Believe me, I will make it up to you once the child is born. But just do this for me. You may even love it when you've got it.'

'No! I will not. This is my body and you can't expect me to be used like some bloody brood mare just to breed at your whim. It's my body that's going to bloat up like a dead sheep. It's my body that's got to go through the agony of expelling the bloody thing in approximately eight months' time, and my body that has to feel so damned sick, tired and ill. You want a baby, find someone else to have it for you. I've made my decision!'

Her eyes flashed angrily at him. She spun on her bare feet, heading for the doorway. Piers's voice cut through the air like the crack of a whip. 'No!' he commanded.

'You are my wife and you will have this child. If you don't I shall tell your father of your behaviour and I guess he will disinherit you, and I shall divorce you and make damned sure that you can't get your hands on a penny of my money. Or you can stay and have this baby and be treated like a queen, by me and by everybody who comes near you. I shall make sure of that. That is my promise to you. In return I would ask that you cut out your drugs, you live healthily until the child is born and after that you can do what you like – within reason, of course. The choice is yours, Cat. You never know, you might even get to enjoy the attention you no doubt will get when you convince everyone what an earth mother you are going to be.'

'My father would never disinherit me over something like a baby. And you wouldn't divorce me, Piers. You love me too much for that.'

'You're right about one thing, and that's that I love you. But because I love you I won't have you getting rid of a child which we've made between us. Don't be silly, Cat,' his voice softened. 'It's only natural that we should have children sometime. I must admit that I hadn't given the question of a family too much thought, but there's no reason why we shouldn't start now.'

'It's just your bloody lower-class philosophy coming through. That's what a wife's for, isn't it, a baby-making machine. I guess you've got fantasies about me with a string of ten snotty little bastards tied to my gingham apron strings. Well, I tell you now, I'm not interested.'

'Then I shall have no choice but to carry out my threats.'

'Do that. I am not having this baby!'

Cat's belly had already started to blossom when Frank Thompson called around to see Piers several weeks later. He was surprised to realize who she must be. Somehow, although he'd heard Piers's wife was pretty

151

wild, he hadn't been prepared. Her face was as white as alabaster, but her eyes were encircled with thick black lines, like a panda. A filmy white cheesecloth dress fell straight from her shoulders to her ankles, but her breasts could be seen through the thin fabric, ripe and swollen above her round stomach. She held the door open and then turned away, walking back down the hall, leaving him wondering whether to remain on the doorstep or follow her. He stepped inside and closed the door.

'I've come to see Piers,' he shouted to her back.

'Oh yeah?' she called over her shoulder. 'Who the fuck are you?'

Even hardened young Frank was shocked. Well-bred birds weren't supposed to talk like that. Frank didn't hold much with women swearing – something to do with his old-fashioned upbringing, but she was a real looker. All hippie-like, smelling musky, of joss sticks, or dope . . .

'Is he here?'

'Dunno,' she shrugged. Then she turned back to have a good look at him, her black eyes sweeping over his suit and his brown suede shoes. 'I think he's in America. Got any fags?'

Frank fumbled in his pocket and found his packet of Players. 'Here,' he said, offering her one. Her long fingers closed around the packet in his hand while her eyes seemed to mist over as she stared into his face.

'Thanks,' she said as she took the entire packet from his hand. Frank looked at the space in his palm where the box had been, and then smiled. 'I'm up the duff, you see,' she stabbed her finger towards her stomach. 'Not supposed to smoke, or anything. It's a real fucking bore. But as Piers isn't here, he won't know, will he?'

'It's not good for the baby,' Frank found his eyes fixed on the swell of her breasts. 'What's your name?'

152

'Cat. But it's all right, I won't sharpen my claws on you. Who are you?'

'Oh, just a friend of Pete . . . Piers's.'

'Ah,' she said knowingly. 'From way back then. You've known him long?'

'A fair while.'

'Funny,' Cat's laugh broke into a husky little cough, 'he thinks I don't know what he gets up to, but I do. It's just that we have different interests.' She spread herself down, cross-legged on one of the floor cushions in a huge room off the hallway. It was beautifully light and airy – no curtains, no carpet, just white walls and highly coloured rugs, and weird paintings which, to Frank's eye, could have been executed by a five-year-old.

'Drink?' She waved him towards a bottle on the floor between them. He looked around for glasses. 'Hand me the bottle,' she commanded, and then took a big slug before passing it to him.

'I bet Piers doesn't like you doing that either.' Frank couldn't work out whether he was appalled by her, or attracted to her. But he was certainly mesmerized by her. Here was Pete struggling up the social ladder while this bird, his wife, was busy throwing herself right down to the bottom. Frank sensed that, somehow, building a relationship with this woman could be useful. She gave off a sense of a craving for something bad, something definitely debauched, self-destructive and dangerous. Pregnant she may be, but she was no madonna. Sexy, dirty and desperate . . . and Frank had an idea he knew just what it was that she was really after.

Chapter Fourteen

1993

There weren't many occasions when Gus doubted her chosen profession, but today's trial was one of those rare times when she wondered if she really had the stomach for it. She listened to the horrifying tale of sexual abuse coming from the young woman in the witness box as James gently put her through the whole story. In the dock was her father, a small, grey, rather frail-looking man, shrivelling into an overlarge cheap suit, pale blue eyes made larger through his National Health spectacles. He was the sort of man one might have stood aside for in a bus queue. Insignificant, slightly helpless and, most of all, harmless.

By any standards it was a tragic tale of terror and neglect. The mother had died when the girl was only seven years old, leaving the father in sole charge of her and her small brother. As the children grew bigger, the abuse got worse. Listening to the highly articulate and detailed recounting of events, Gus could feel every person in court, from the public gallery to the members of the jury, hanging on to the girl's every word. No horror movie could more graphically illustrate the sense of fear, of utter despair and of hopelessness. James was standing, listening, directing, at times turning his face away in order to spare the girl his own emotions. Gus was seated at counsel's table, scribbling on her notepad, trying not to let her own feelings show on her face. It was a relief when the judge decided it was time to adjourn for lunch.

As the relatives bustled the woman away from the courtroom James offered to buy Gus a sandwich and a glass of wine at El Vino.

'Thanks, James, but I think I'll just take a walk – unless you need me. I feel like some air after listening to all that.'

'Pretty unsavoury, wasn't it? Shame she didn't bring charges earlier. The fact that she's left it so long rather weakens her case.'

'But then there's the other witnesses, the brother and the sister-in-law, and the evidence that he tried to tamper with the five-year-old nephew.' Gus knew the brief backwards. The woman had suffered severe psychological problems in the past but had not wanted to go through the ordeal of prosecuting her father. Now that he was practising his old tricks on the next generation the family were united in their wish to bring him to justice.

'Well, it will be most interesting to see what Edward Boothby comes up with for the defence. No doubt we shall have the false memory syndrome and all that tosh . . . Sure I can't buy you lunch?'

Gus shook her head. They parted at the entrance to the court. Gus strode off towards the park. Hearing this morning's evidence had killed her appetite, and she didn't feel like coping with James. That might mean she would have to tell him that they were finished, and she wanted to pick the right moment. In just six weeks' time she would complete her pupillage and she had been offered a tenancy in the chambers after that. Gaining a tenancy in a good set of chambers was vitally important to a young barrister. Without a tenancy it was impossible to get the work. Clerks were employed by all the members of chambers and they acted like salesmen, or brokers, between the solicitor clients and the barristers. Oddly enough it was the clerks who wielded most of the power in chambers. Acting as buffers between barristers and solicitor clients, it was in the clerks' hands as to which barrister would be given which case, slotting any new work into the diary of whichever barrister seemed most appropriate. Gus knew she would stick with criminal work, if she possibly could. Despite the ugliness of this morning's evidence, she could feel she was actually doing something worthwhile, and the cases were extraordinarily diverse. She wouldn't have a minute to think about anything except her work and, knowing she would have to spend the foreseeable future bumping into James almost every day, hard work would be just the right antidote.

When she eventually returned to court, fifteen minutes before the appointed time, Gus spotted James deep in conversation with Edward Boothby. When he saw Gus he broke into a huge grin, waited until Boothby withdrew and then turned to her.

'Well, well, what an interesting time I've been having while you've been enjoying your walk. It seems the defendant, upon hearing his daughter's evidence, has decided to change his plea to guilty!'

'What? But why now? Why not before? Why did he put her through it? Couldn't he have done that earlier and saved everyone the ordeal? I can barely believe it!'

'My theory is the dirty old bugger wanted to hear it all. Probably got some sort of thrill out of it!'

Gus recoiled in horror. 'You don't seriously think so, do you?'

'Oh undoubtedly, Gus. I know it may seem ghastly, but these sex offenders seem to get pleasure from reliving it all. You'll see it happening time and time again. No doubt Boothby gave him a pretty stiff talking to. So all we have to do now is go back in and the judge will adjourn everything for sentencing, the jury will be thanked for their time, and we'll all come back in a few weeks after all the necessary social reports and so on. So

... all in all a good morning's work. Tell you what, let's have dinner tonight. The champagne's on me!'

'Sorry, James, but I'm afraid I can't. I've got an appointment.' Gus felt relieved that for once it was true. She was having her long-awaited meeting with Dickie Crowborough and nothing in the world would get in the way of that. She'd spent the last few weeks dodging extracurricular activities with James. Every excuse in the book had been used from work to illness to exhaustion, family ... anything. She knew he must suspect that the relationship was over by now. Two reasons stopped her from coming right out and telling him: first, she didn't think his behaviour actually warranted such an honourable termination, and secondly, she wanted to bide her time until she felt properly strong emotionally, and safe in the knowledge that her tenancy had been formalized.

'Another night, then.' He sounded cross, rejected. Gus shrugged and headed into court.

Mirabelle sat in the low chair beside John Stapleford's desk, ostensibly watching the giant TV monitor, but surreptitiously peeping at the man known as 'God' to read his expression. John was stroking the side of his nose as he watched James Kentish talk directly into camera, and Mirabelle felt a satisfyingly warm glow flow through her. Most of John Stapleford's idiosyncrasies and mannerisms were well catalogued within Maverick Productions, together with a dictionary-like interpretation of what they all meant. Nose-stroking was definitely a good sign – a very good sign indeed. Chin-stroking, on the other hand, was a definite sign of displeasure. Mirabelle permitted herself a small smile of self-satisfaction.

Justice on Trial had been far more successful in production than she ever dreamed possible. Of course James's good looks and charismatic charm were seventy per cent responsible for its potential success factor, together with the public's growing interest in opening up things traditionally cloaked in secrecy and inaccessible to the average mortal. James had, thankfully, talked very candidly about his criticisms of the 'system', as he called it, and had – despite his earlier reluctance – cited several cases as examples of what he perceived to be justice gone haywire. Mirabelle guessed what was going through John's mind right now. The series of six programmes would be both commercial and controversial.

'This guy is good – very good. Where d'you find him?' John was almost talking to himself.

'It's a long story,' Mirabelle murmured, knowing he wasn't listening.

'I think with a bit of editing we can do something with this. It's certainly got potential . . .'

Bastard! Mirabelle thought to herself. It had more than potential. No doubt he thought if he told her how good he thought it was – and therefore she was – she'd probably ask for a raise and/or promotion.

'Yes, I think it's good too. Presumably you'll be thinking of selling it to the networks, John – not just London regional?'

John regarded her thoughtfully. His black hair was thinning on top, leaving him with a widow's peak in the centre. With his narrow nose and dark, almost black eyes, he brought to people's minds the image of a vampire – especially when he carried the pallor of too many hours spent in a hot, dark studio. God or vampire, he never gave away much at one time.

'Maybe. We'll have to see what it looks like after it's been edited. This guy Kentish, he's not likely to object to anything, is he? I don't like upsetting lawyers – it makes me nervous.'

'Oh no,' Mirabelle allowed him her most dazzling smile, 'he won't be any problem at all, I'll make sure of that, John.'

John grunted and turned back to the pile of scripts on his desk. Mirabelle knew she was dismissed. No matter

– she had had a good afternoon. Now she couldn't wait to call James and tell him the good news. Too bad he hadn't returned her calls over the weekend – she was looking forward to enjoying a repeat performance of their collaboration. She smiled her inimitable smile of gratification and if anyone had happened to be passing at that particular moment they would have seen that she looked quite astonishingly beautiful.

All her plans were bearing fruit, at last. Once again she had proved to Gus how easy it was to pull her men. Poor brainy Gus, blessed with a brain, but not one ounce of glamour. Well, not that Mirabelle had ever noticed any! Men were afraid of women who were too clever. That's why James had been so quick to fall under her own spell. Mirabelle loved watching James's appearances on the series. He looked edible. Drop-dead handsome! The series was bound to turn him into a sex symbol. And he was Mirabelle's for the time being.

He'd be so grateful to her for giving him such a push in his new career that he'd probably even leave his wife for her! But Mirabelle hadn't yet decided if she'd want that. She liked to be free, to play the field. One never knew what opportunities were lurking around the corner, and she'd be the last person to miss any . . .

'I don't get to see you often enough, Gus my dear.' Dickie Crowborough stroked her hand as they nestled into a deep sofa in the Lanesborough's lounge, having retired there after a feast in the restaurant. Gus had led him to the quietest corner, well away from prying ears, so that she could have every confidence their conversation would remain private.

'Well, you're always so busy, being a high-flying cabinet minister.' Gus was terribly proud of her godfather, even if she did doubt his motives on occasion. She knew that Dickie had a far too acutely developed taste for the finer things in life to be totally altruistic. Gus privately suspected that he had mostly got where he was through always backing the right team, putting right words into right ears, and generally directing all his energies into being thought of as an all-round good chap. Now he was getting his reward. Next stop would undoubtedly be the Lords in the very near future.

'You seem to have been doing your fair share of high flying, Augusta. Who'd have thought of that little shadow of a thing I remember so well – you must have been three or so then, frightened to say boo – turning into such a brave and talented young woman?'

Gus leaned into Dickie's shoulder affectionately. 'Do you remember those days well?'

'In parts. 'Course, some of the things I prefer to forget,' he laughed to himself.

'You've known Daddy for a long time, haven't you?' They'd had the conversation before, but Dickie usually found some excuse to change the subject. Tonight he wasn't going to find it quite so easy. Gus had made sure her glass remained full, while Dickie's had been emptied several times over. Besides, she was a lot more practised at keeping someone on a difficult subject these days.

'How did you meet?' she asked brightly.

'Damned if I can remember.' Dickie frowned into his cognac, struggling through his archives. 'At his gallery, some viewing, something like that. Someone must have introduced us, I suppose ... He did some marvellous deals for me.'

'Maybe it was Mummy,' Gus sighed, leaning back into the cushions.

'No, I don't think so,' Dickie continued, obviously relaxed. 'In fact I rather think I was instrumental in introducing your parents.'

'I've been thinking about her lately. I just wish I could remember what she looked like. Was she like me, Dickie?'

Dickie's kind blue eyes roved affectionately over Gus's

160

lovely, intelligent face. She had the same wide brow as her mother, creamy skin and lusciously thick brown hair which curled around her shoulders. Her eyes were lighter than Cat's, but there was, indeed, a strong resemblance.

'Yes, you are like her, darling. She was a beauty, and you've certainly inherited her looks. Obviously there's a touch of your father in there somewhere.'

'The stubbornness,' Gus volunteered, and then placed her coffee cup down on the low table in front of them. 'Dickie, what was she like?'

'Your mother?' Dickie hated this line of questioning. Poor dear Gus had lost her mother at such an early age. But what a mother! How could one possibly tell a child just what a parent she had lost?

'Well, as I said, she was very beautiful, like you. And clever. But she wasn't channelled like you. It was the sixties, remember, and the ethos around us was to party all the time. Work was for squares. We were the privileged young. Too much money, and too much time to waste.'

'Did you like her?' Gus couldn't hide the raw need for information. Her eyes searched Dickie's face hungrily.

'H'm.' Dickie thought for a moment. 'Like her? Oh yes, I think everyone liked her.' But there was something in his voice, the way he hesitated, that alerted Gus to a hidden agenda. 'She was good fun, wild, you know . . . a bit of a party animal.'

'Sex, drugs and rock and roll, you mean?' Gus held her back ramrod straight as she stared down into her lap, willing Dickie to talk, to open up.

'We were all experimenting at that time, I suppose. Sex was new to us – girls had the pill. Cannabis was the cool thing. We had music. Funny, isn't it, how this new generation is so much more puritanical?'

Gus felt him drifting away from the subject, so she didn't bother to contradict him.

161

'Did you know Frank Thompson?' She watched as Dickie reached for his brandy. He took a long draught of it and slowly placed the empty glass on the table. He looked down at his hands.

'I don't believe so, my dear. Why d'you ask?'

'He was at the party in Guernsey. He told me he knew Mummy and that he'd met me when I was little. I asked Daddy but he just told me some silly story about the connection. He didn't want to talk about it. I thought perhaps you might have met him if he knew Mummy and Daddy.'

'Maybe. I don't remember. Your mother mixed with all sorts, darling. Cat was certainly no snob. Not that your parents led separate lives – they had lots of friends in common. Your father was completely devastated by what happened and that's why he doesn't want to talk about it. But I'm glad you and I have had this little chat.' Clearly the meeting was about to be terminated. 'Any time you feel you want to talk things over, you know I'm here for you. If you prefer, I won't tell your father about this. But don't you worry. The future is what matters now. There's no point in looking back through the past, darling.'

Gus kissed him on the cheek. 'Thank you, Dickie, you've been most understanding.'

He gave her a hug and walked her to the door. 'Any time, my darling. Now here's a taxi. Hop in and keep in touch!'

As he waved her off, Dickie let out a long sigh. He hoped he'd satisfied her curiosity. She was a lovely girl and she deserved to be protected from the truth.

But Gus was far from satisfied. Dickie's words were spinning around her mind as she analysed them over and over. The good deals her father had done for Dickie – what sort of deals were they? And if Dickie hadn't remembered Frank Thompson then why did he immediately pitch Thompson into the 'all sorts' category? He knew Thompson. Gus was sure of it. And she was also absolutely certain that Dickie, like her father, was hiding something from her.

Chapter Fifteen

Piers didn't let his concentration waver for a second. The bids were coming in thick and fast from all around the room. A bank of about ten telephones was manned by Giffords staff, as international bids competed with those in the room. Although only two bidders were active, Piers knew that when one of the two dropped out that would be the time for someone else to take over in the competition. As ever, he was supremely conscious of the eyes which burned hotly upon him, watching to see when he would make his move, keenly eyeing the paddle held loosely, nonchalantly, across his lap. Once he was seen to lift it, to join the bidding, it would incite even greater interest in the painting. The art world knew that if Piers Lawrence was after something at a particular price, then it might be worthwhile having a go for it. The multiples were going up in leaps of tenths of millions, and so far the bids had reached two million pounds. The auctioneer, Jeremy Hanson-Bewdley, exhibited the classic *laissez-faire* coolness of the true pro. As the bidding threatened to raise the gilded ceiling, he didn't even raise a well-bred eyebrow. Placed upon a small easel was the painting that all the fanfare was about. At least four museums were desperate to own it, as were another six or seven private collectors. Four heavily armed security guards flanked the masterpiece. Collars tightened nervously, and Piers glanced around the audience as the bidding reached £4 million. He felt his heartrate quicken with the thrill of the chase.

'Do I have five million?' Jeremy requested calmly. 'Five million? I have 5.5 million on the telephone, are we all done at five and a half million pounds? Do I have 5.6?'

Piers' hands remained still. Only a slight twitch of his jaw betrayed the tension in his body.

'I have 5.6 million in the room, do I have 5.7 million? I am bid £5,700,000 . . .' An almost tangible shudder of disbelief went through the audience. Someone else had entered the bidding. Again heads turned to look at Piers, but his body was devoid of movement save for the casual smoothing of his jacket sleeve. Then all eyes rested on van Jorgaan, the newest member of the race, a dealer not normally up for this kind of money. He must be buying for somebody, but who?

The painting was already fifty per cent over its estimate. But Piers knew his client was desperate to own it. Money wasn't the point. Finally, at six million the hammer came down in van Jorgaan's favour. Piers permitted himself the smallest of smiles. The painting would be charged to his account, and would earn him a fee of £500,000 for his trouble. In turn, Piers would reimburse van Jorgaan for his efforts on Piers's behalf as a straw man. If Piers had done the bidding himself, the price might well have approached a half-million more. All in all, it had been a good afternoon's work.

He would go back to the gallery, make a call to the client, and then head back to the hotel for a shower. He would have been happier if the painting had been closer to its estimate of 4.5 million, but that was the joy of the art world: one just never knew which way the market would jump. Today's sale was a clear sign that things were picking up. Four years ago a major Renoir such as this one might only have fetched £1.5 million. Now he had to arrange export licences and such like, and deliver the thing personally to Italy and its new owner.

165

Gulio Capeletti was one of Italy's richest new art collectors with a fortune acquired through diverse and definitely dubious means. Piers was trying to wean himself away from such contacts, though it was impossible to keep one's nose entirely clean, as many of his so-called legitimate customers had come by their wealth through some devious ways back in their pasts, but Piers kept a sort of self-integrity by never asking too many questions regarding where certain monies came from.

This introduction had come not from his past life, but from Elena. Her late husband had regarded Capeletti as one of his most important clients – who had invested heavily in Angeletti's corporations.

Piers, for once, was alone in London. Elena couldn't make Italy because she had to supervise the flowers for some charity luncheon back home in Guernsey the following day. Therefore he had called Gus to arrange to meet her for dinner – just the two of them. They'd been on poor terms for months now and he fervently hoped they might be able to smooth over their differences at last.

Gus had been more than pleasantly surprised to get her father's call. Although he often passed through London, he was usually accompanied by Elena, or tied up with business meetings, entertaining clients, or visiting influential people in the art world. It also gave her yet another excuse to turn down James's persistent invitations. For the past few weeks she had successfully managed to keep away from him. He had been more than busy with his selection campaign, rushing off to local party meetings and trying to convince the Bulsworth Labour Party that he was the right candidate for the job. Gus dearly hoped that he'd be successful. If he ever became an MP he'd spend less time in chambers, leaving her to get on with forgetting all about him and building her career. The problem was, whenever their paths did cross, he seemed to be keener than ever. His latest suggestion had been that they zip off to Paris the following weekend! She'd have to come up with a good reason for turning that one down or else finally face the prospect of telling him just how she felt. For tonight, though, Gus determined that she would push all thoughts of James out of her mind, and just enjoy herself.

Gus's grey jersey dress was cunningly cut on the cross-grain, so that it flattered the figure. The skirt fluted out a couple of inches above her knees, and the two thin shoulder straps sat comfortably. She smoothed the silvery pearl choker around her neck and ran her fingers through her hair. It was good to be able to wear it loose seeing as it spent ninety per cent of its time cooped up in the old-fashioned bun she was forced to wear for work. She had let it grow slightly longer, discovering that, with extra length, it was easier and quicker to wind up in the mornings, so that it now curled almost level with her breasts. As she stood sideways on to the mirror, regarding herself somewhat critically, she knew she would never be as glamorous, or as sexy, as Mirabelle. For one thing the long blonde mane guaranteed Mirabelle would be noticed wherever she was. And she had legs far longer than Gus's, and tits much larger. She also wore a lot more make-up than Gus. Gus pouted into the mirror, examining her medium-sized mouth with its dark pink natural colour. She hardly ever wore lipstick, except when she was nervous. Funny how it gave her an extra boost of confidence. Nor did she wear much facial make-up. She had got used to seeing a pale face stare back at her, and her skin, on occasion, had an almost translucent luminescence. Her big grey eyes widened as she flicked a tiny bit of brown colour onto her lashes. Then she stood back. Mousy, mousy. That's what she was. She got the brains – she could hardly have expected beauty as well!

She collected up her silver leather purse and locked the door behind her, mentally telling herself that tonight she would not fall out with her father, she would not be bitchy about Elena, and she would behave properly.

'Daddy ... darling!' she called delightedly as Piers turned in her direction. He stood up and held out his arms.

'Gus! You look beautiful. Come here!' She fell into his arms, and let herself be taken over by the wonderfully cosy feeling of fatherly protection. The wool of his suit felt comforting against her chin, and the smoothness of his jaw was eminently rubbable. However, she restrained herself from poking her fingers over it. As a child, when she had been rocked to sleep on his knee, she had a habit of worrying at his chin. She especially liked the feel of it later in the day, before he had his evening shave, when the whiskers were just beginning to poke through and her hand would make a strange rasping sound across the wiry surface. She smiled at the memory.

He looked immaculate in his perfectly cut suit, his equally perfect shirt and, she correctly guessed, his Hermès tie. She had never ever known him to look less than immaculate. His hands were manicured, his hair cut in the same style, side parting and wave of thick dark hair falling slightly, almost boyishly over his forehead. Not a trace of grey adulterated Piers's natural darkness. With a jolt in her chest, she realized that in some respects he resembled James. With just five years between them, they had very similar styles, and they were even of the same build. God, what would a psychiatrist make of that one? She flushed as Piers ordered her dry martini.

She remembered the first time he had allowed her to sample one – it had tasted absolutely disgusting, but she had persevered and eventually developed quite a taste for the cocktail with its incredibly dry and somewhat bitter taste. The green stuffed olive bobbed in the bowl of the glass like a dismembered eyeball and would, she knew from experience, taste absolutely delicious by the time she had finished off the drink.

For the moment, Gus decided to push aside the fact of their row, which had preyed on her mind for months now. It had been two weeks since she had met Dickie, and since then she had almost convinced herself that she was suffering from extreme paranoia so far as her parents were concerned. She had decided to try to follow her godfather's advice and look forward, instead of trying to dig up the past all the time. Naturally she was keen to get to the depths of the mystery, but a very big part of her was desperate not to have another ghastly scene with her father when she saw him so rarely.

'So what are you up to? I must say it was a wonderful surprise to get your call. No doubt you're negotiating some mega deal, knowing you.'

Piers grinned. 'I had an interesting time at Giffords this afternoon. Picked up a Renoir for someone which I have to deliver to Florence tomorrow. I hope he'll be pleased with it.'

Gus sighed. 'You lead such a glamorous life, Daddy. I've been taking statements in a remand cell all afternoon, ready for a trial the day after tomorrow. I don't think we've got a cat in hell's chance of winning . . .'

'What, the great James Kentish losing a case? Surely not!'

'James isn't working on this one. He's getting rather tied up with his new interest – politics. Haven't you heard? He's preparing to stand as the Labour candidate for Bulsworth.'

'He'd never struck me as the socialist type,' Piers smiled ruefully.

'No, more of a champagne socialist, really. Full of gas and wind . . .'

Piers's antennae, always sensitive to Gus, wavered curiously. 'What's wrong?'

'Wrong? Nothing's wrong. Why should anything be wrong?' she said, chasing the olive around her glass with her little finger.

'Still enjoying work?'

'Sure. It's going really well. I've actually handled a few court appearances myself, drafted half a dozen opinions which have not been rewritten, and done some statements of claim which I gather were sent directly out to the client.'

'That's marvellous, Gus,' Piers said enthusiastically, though not entirely sure just what it was his daughter had done so successfully. Legal jargon was way over his head. 'So how long is it till you finish your pupillage?'

'Four weeks till the end of term. It's gone so quickly, I can hardly believe it. Then I shall be a fully fledged barrister ready to be let loose on the poor unsuspecting criminal world.'

'Your mind is set on this criminal business?'

'Yes. I know you don't approve. I suppose it grates rather with your smart friends, doesn't it?' Gus giggled as she felt the martini go to her head. 'It's not quite the thing, is it, having a daughter associating with the underworld?'

Piers squirmed uncomfortably.

'I understand that the really clever barristers go into the Chancery Division. I would have thought that that would have suited your academic brain far better than dealing with legally aided down-and-outs.'

'Oh Daddy, don't be such a snob,' Gus chided him lightly. Perhaps she was like her mother, after all. Dickie had said that Cat liked to mix with people from all walks of life. Maybe that's what was making her father so uncomfortable – bringing back painful memories.

'Can you imagine just how dry and boring Chancery would be, getting bogged down in trusts, or taxation

170

and such like, with hardly ever an opportunity to appear in court? It may be absolutely terrifying, but it certainly gets the adrenalin going. It's what I want to do. I had a taster of divorce and messy matrimonial matters. Frankly I find a good assault far more diverting!'

'Gus, really!' Piers admonished her. Privately he was beginning to wonder if she had inherited more than just a *chip* off the old block. There was definitely something rather unsavoury about his daughter's tastes.

'No, Daddy, I'm sorry if it offends your sensibilities, but you'll have to get used to the fact that I like dealing with criminals.'

Piers shook his head hopelessly. 'Come on, my little moll, let's go and eat. And please, let's talk about something other than assault over dinner. The other diners do find it most offputting.'

Gus's joking made Piers feel deeply uncomfortable. Although he struggled to remain light, underneath he knew that her work might take her closer to his past than she could possibly imagine, into the depths of the underworld. It was time for him to take some action on her behalf. He needed to clean up his operation, so that there was no possibility of any threats to himself, or more importantly, to Gus in the future. After the Italian business, he'd make sure he avoided any more dodgy contacts.

Neither Gus nor Piers noticed the shadowy figure stepping quietly a few yards behind them as they walked away from the restaurant. But the tall, long-haired man, lean legs scruffily wrapped in baggy cords, ambled along for several yards, before nipping into a car conveniently parked a short distance down the street, and waited for the inevitable taxi to be hailed by Lawrence and his companion.

Chapter Sixteen

However often Piers visited the hills beyond Florence, he still felt the same sense of stunned awe at the absolute beauty of the countryside. Paintbox colours filled his mind – raw sienna hillsides, burnt umber villas, ochre vegetation, all muted and blended and bathed in that special light so loved by artists. Piers gazed about him, playing a sort of spot-the-composition with his mental reference library of paintings. As the car rounded the last bend, the vast terracotta and pink-washed *palazzo* came into view.

Piers had stayed in Gulio Capeletti's Tuscan home on two previous occasions: once when Elena had introduced them, and then when he had delivered another painting to Gulio – the Vermeer. The Vermeer had only been in Gulio's hands for a couple of years. Piers remembered the sale too well. Gulio had been desperate for it. Any work by Vermeer was a desirable addition to a collection both for the fact that he was attributed as one of the greatest artists who ever lived, and because his paintings were so rare – only about thirty-five canvases were authenticated as the true work of the Delft master. Nearly all, bar two or three, were in the hands of museums and this particular canvas was, up until St Patrick's Day 1990, in the hands of the Isabella Stewart Gardner Museum, Boston. Piers had a shrewd idea who had carried out the heist, one of the most audacious in recent times. Including the Vermeer, works by Rembrandt, Manet and Degas were stolen, valued at about $200 million all together. The thieves, posing as policemen checking out an invented attempted break-in, had overpowered the guards and then leisurely carried out the hit. With a value of anything up to £25 million, the Vermeer was a work a lot of people in the world would have liked to get their hands on. Piers had not wanted anything to do with it. It was far too hot. Suicidally hot! Piers had tried very hard to dissuade Gulio from his ill-judged acquisitiveness, but Gulio was immovable. He must have the painting. It was to be a mark of the power of his money. By having the painting, he could say to himself that he could, quite literally, buy anything that money was capable of buying.

For Piers it had meant retracing old steps which he had no wish to follow again. His so-called new life had taken him away from having to deal with the criminal fraternity on any kind of direct level.

Piers liked to feel that he had risen so far beyond his roots that he had completely reinvented himself. He was Piers Lawrence, successful art dealer, investor and businessman. His legitimate business netted him several million and the last thing he needed was to be dredging up his murky past. He had his family and his reputation to protect. Even so, he had helped Gulio out – but on the strict understanding that the Italian hung the painting in his Swiss apartment for the statutory period of limitation according to Swiss law of six years – after which time he would become the legitimate owner of the Vermeer, providing nobody spotted the painting as stolen beforehand. That way Piers felt he could absolve himself from any potential legal wrangling likely to come up in the future. In short, he wanted nothing more to do with what, arguably, could be classed as one of the hottest paintings in the world. Even before Gulio's request that Piers find it and start negotiations with the thieves, Piers had watched with interest any developments regarding its whereabouts.

Indeed, most of the art world had been on the edge of their seats, hoping that it would turn up sooner rather than later – and not be consigned to some despotic collector's safe for another generation or three. With Piers' contacts in the underworld, it hadn't taken him too long to track the painting down. Even without his contacts he could have whittled down the number of likely homes to a handful. Eventually, through some hard bargaining, a deal of £15 million had been struck between the two crooks. To Piers' disquiet, unfortunately, the two men had discovered more than a mutual love of hot paintings in common.

Having been shown into Gulio's beautiful drawing room, Piers couldn't see his host anywhere around, but he took the proffered glass of excellent chilled vintage champagne. He stepped through the glazed doors on to the magnificent terracotta-tiled terrace at the rear of the *palazzo*. Piers sniffed at the scented night air. The lemon and orange groves were in full blossom, below the stone steps were the rosemary, lavender and box hedges of the knot gardens, intersected with standard bay trees dotted amongst the beautifully manicured parterre. In the distance he could see the illuminated fountains and the ancient walled gardens. All was silent except for the gentle splash of the water, the occasional clash of a pot far below in the kitchen quarters as the staff prepared their master's dinner, and the almost hesitant rasping of a cricket. Listening to the still night air, Piers eventually recognized Gulio's deep voice, with its melodic rise and fall, passing instructions to the staff. Although underneath his acquired polish Gulio was a hardened villain, he retained that charm peculiar to Italians of being rather old-fashioned and gentlemanly to the point of diffidence in his manner – unless of course he was ever betrayed!

'Piers ... welcome,' he smiled and embraced his guest. 'So sorry to keep you waiting. We will eat soon,

174

but first let us walk around the garden, and you can tell me all about the sale . . .'

As they walked slowly through pathways of crumbling honey-coloured flagstones, breathing in the heavily perfumed evening air, Piers could almost believe that this was the home of an Italian aristocrat. The elegance, the sheer sumptuous but faded grandeur of the *palazzo* – all belied Gulio's trade. If there was one small thing that could be said in his favour, he certainly had a lot of style. Not for Gulio solid gold glitz and wall-to-wall Jacuzzis. He had a fine eye for art, a wine cellar to be proud of, and a jewel of a house. Piers could almost relax and enjoy himself. Almost . . . but it was never prudent to lower one's defences fully with men such as Gulio.

He appeared pleased with the purchase of the Renoir, despite the fact that it had cost more than Piers had anticipated. But from his manner Piers guessed he was holding something in reserve. The Renoir wasn't the only thing on his mind this evening. Piers was shrewd enough to read the signs – he was being prepared for something big!

He had to wait until after dinner to find out just what that something was. The two of them sat at either end of a fifteen-foot-long trestle table, feasting on the most delicious of Tuscan fare. Although the servant returned again and again to replenish Piers's glass with the renowned Capeletti Riserva Chianti Classico, Piers kept pushing his hand over the top of his glass. He sipped slowly and abstemiously, while Gulio appeared to knock back vast quantities.

'I have a buyer for the Vermeer,' he pushed his chair away from the table and stared hard at Piers. 'I want you to deliver it.'

Piers raised an eyebrow in a gesture which bade Gulio to continue.

'To a lady friend of mine. Giovanna Lucciani.'

'Ah yes, I've met her.' Piers remembered the woman. An outrageous flirt who clearly collected rich Italian playboys as other women collected baubles. She had behaved very badly indeed when she had accompanied the Conte di Fiorenzi to the anniversary party. He thought better of mentioning the connection to Gulio.

'She is an old friend of mine, an old and very dear friend. She fell in love with the painting ...' Gulio shrugged, 'and what could I do? You know how women are.'

Piers gave a small but knowing smile. He knew exactly how this woman was. She was extremely glamorous and she had chased Piers in a terribly obvious manner. Elena had been livid, and although she had denied to Piers that the woman had needled her, Piers knew full well the cause of her annoyance. Giovanna Lucciani was also extremely wealthy. Gulio would not let the Vermeer go for less than he'd paid for it – a cool £15 million.

'She remembers you, Piers, and she asked that you deliver it personally. That way you can check it out for her, can't you?'

'I can't imagine there'd be any need for that,' Piers answered smoothly. 'Where is the lady?'

'Oh, not too far away,' Gulio chuckled. 'I'll have the car take you down there tomorrow.'

'If she's just down the road, why on earth don't you deliver it yourself?' Piers had the annoying feeling that Gulio was playing out some private game and using him as a pawn.

'Believe it or not, it's part of the deal. She specifically asked for you. I think you must have made quite an impression on her.' Gulio had his reason for wanting to send Piers down with the painting; he meant to teach Giovanna a lesson for not being able to keep her legs closed to other men while she had been with Gulio. The painting was the best fake Gulio had ever seen. Even

Piers Lawrence would be unable to spot that it hadn't been executed by the great Dutch master. Piers' involvement with the transaction added that certain stamp of authenticity to the fake Vermeer.

Piers sighed. As usual it would be difficult to say no to Gulio. Well, he would just deliver the damned painting and then leave to get on with his life in peace.

Giovanna Lucciani was an extremely beautiful woman – the fact of which she was more than aware – and she had spent almost three decades honing the combined deadly effectiveness of her exquisite body, beauty and brain. She watched the arrival of Piers Lawrence from her salon and smiled as she experienced the faint fluttering of excitement in her belly. It had been some weeks since she had entertained and she was looking forward to the diversion of Mr Lawrence's company. She remembered meeting him before – and his ghastly possessive wife. Now she had him all to herself . . . A shiver of anticipation rippled across her skin.

Piers knew he was going to be in for an interesting evening from the moment Giovanna passed him the champagne. 'How very nice,' he said admiringly as he swirled the wine around his tongue. 'Bollinger RD if I'm not mistaken.'

'How clever of you to recognize it. Do you know as much about wine as you do about art?' Giovanna stood close to him, so close that the smell of her strong scent filled his nostrils. He recognized that too: Shalimar – exotic, foreign and a little dangerous. 'I enjoy drinking it.'

'Then maybe I can organize some surprises for you – to accompany our meal. Something different followed by something very exciting.' Having a conversation with Giovanna was remarkably like engaging in foreplay.

At the table, the butler splashed some wine into Piers's glass and Giovanna watched him expectantly, almost mischievously. 'Tell me what you think.'

Piers tested the nose and then the colour. Finally he tasted. Giovanna's black eyes glittered with anticipation, her deep red lips as rich and full-bodied as the wine he was about to sample. He relished the unmistakable silky texture of the wine, the aroma of blackberries and violets that was pure pinot noir.

'Well?' she asked eventually as Piers's tongue searched the complexities of the superb burgundy. It was unmistakably Romanée-Conti.

'My dear Giovanna, I am honoured. This is quite simply one of the finest burgundies in the world.'

After a wonderful dinner Piers leaned back into his chair feeling replete and at ease. 'Delicious,' he smiled as he mopped the corner of his mouth with the tiny linen napkin. He was surprised to find that in spite of his misgivings, he was actually enjoying Giovanna's company. His stomach felt pleasantly full and his head nicely relaxed. His hostess was charming, well-informed and amusing. The staff had tactfully withdrawn, leaving them alone with wine, candlelight and a soft aria in the background. Giovanna's silk dress slipped above her elegant knees as she crossed her legs on the sofa beside Piers. Their heads were no more than eighteen inches apart as they gazed at the newly hung Vermeer. Giovanna sighed her satisfaction. 'I remember the time I first laid eyes on The Concert ... at Gulio's. My breath was quite literally taken away. It's taken me months to persuade him to sell it to me. I really never thought he would. Especially now that we're not exactly the best of friends.'

'Oh? But he told me you were an exceptionally good friend of his.'

'Sweet, isn't he?' Giovanna's soft lips glistened invitingly in the candlelight. 'I'm so pleased that he's forgiven me.' Piers felt her body soften against him. 'It really is quite extraordinarily beautiful.'

Piers eyed the masterpiece appreciatively. The three figures concentrating on their music, the girl seated at the clavecin so intent on her music along with the instructor and the second woman – the singer. The mystery of Vermeer's placement of the two paintings upon the wall – Baburen's *The Procuress* with its three figures also intent on music, but in direct contrast to the genteel scene below them – the woman's breasts spilling over her dress licentiously; and then the other painting in the manner of Jacob van Ruisdael which included a dead tree trunk, again in contrast with the gentle scene of rustic paradise depicted on the lid of the clavecin.

Giovanna slipped some more wine into Piers' glass. 'Of course the theme of music in Dutch art is generally associated with love and seduction.' Her hand rested lightly on his thigh. He swallowed hard and pretended not to notice the way her fingers started gently to knead at his flesh. 'The tree trunk represents death and decay.' She moved closer to him, pushing her leg tightly against him. 'Did you know that some say the three figures in the Baburen are supposed to represent the relationship between the three figures in The Concert?'

Piers's jaw twitched. He found himself looking into the Baburen again. The buxom wench was being ogled by two men – one gazing into her eyes, the other gazing at her breasts. She was leaning back into the arms of one while playing her lute and singing to him.

'Do you suppose that she is about to bed one of them?' Giovanna murmured against Piers's ear. 'And do you suppose that the music master is also about to bed one of these prim young women?'

'Vermeer has always been rather a mystery to me,' Piers confessed and tried to sit up. Giovanna's grip on his leg tightened.

'For me it is one of the greatest paintings in the world.'

179

Piers cleared his throat. 'My dear Giovanna, let's not be coy. This would be a masterpiece for the rest of the world too. Now you must promise me that you will take great care as to whom you show it to. I find your little gadget here most intriguing,' he added, changing the subject.

Giovanna giggled and pressed a combination of numbers on a remote control pad which rested in the arm of the sofa. Immediately an entire section of fire-breast, upon which hung the Vermeer, revolved through 180 degrees and where before they had been viewing a grand Dutch master, they were now looking at a good quality but relatively unimportant example of nineteenth-century realism.

'A Daubigny, if I'm not mistaken.'

'When is the great Piers Lawrence ever mistaken?'

Piers grinned and helped Giovanna to some more wine. 'Sometimes, though thankfully not very often, these days. Mistakes get more and more expensive.'

'Mistakes are always expensive,' Giovanna sighed, 'and not just in the world of art.' Her soft doe eyes looked desperately sad, as if she were about to dissolve into tears.

Piers touched her hand. 'Giovanna,' he said gently, 'what is it?'

She seemed to snap out of whatever spell she had temporarily slipped under and forced a smile back on to her crimson lips. Her ink-black eyes glittered with moisture. 'Nothing, sweet Piers, nothing at all. I suppose that sometimes one thinks that if one could live one's life over again, one would change certain things, things one wishes one had maybe not done. Would you change things in your life? If you had the chance, if you could start all over again? What regrets do you have?'

'Too many to burden you with. But I have learned there is nothing to be gained in allowing oneself the

180

luxury of regrets. Regrets never change anything. We have to deal with what is past and accept it.'

'My past is my present and my future. For me my regrets will always be my constant companions. I am not allowed to move on, you see, to start again. But ...' she fiddled with her control gadget once more, returning the Vermeer to pride of place, ' ... my life does have its advantages. Come, you are my guest, Piers, I must not be so morose.'

She tipped her lovely face up towards his. The candle-light flickered over her alabaster skin. Her small oval face looked so fragile and vulnerable. Without even realizing what was happening, Piers leaned over and kissed her firmly on the mouth, savouring with pleasure the sweetness of her soft lips. When Giovanna's hot Latin blood had been stirred it only took a kiss to ignite all her passion!

Within seconds Piers was on the floor with Giovanna astride him, her dress riding high up over her thighs. He realized with a fast-increasing sense of destiny that she wasn't wearing any underwear. She was, in every way, perfectly ready for him. Piers pushed himself up on to his elbows, his eyes popping at the sight of Giovanna's bush being thrust towards him. It was a fine, silky-looking bush and it didn't take many more seconds for Piers to do the only natural thing and place a tentative finger into the stiff curls. Giovanna pressed herself on to his probing hand, at the same time pulling her dress up over her hips, wriggling in order to let her breasts swing free and gloriously pendulous over his head. Then she was naked above him. Too late for thoughts of Elena and his almost unblemished record of fidelity. Here was a gloriously juicy cunt, pink, ripe and inviting thrusting over the giveaway bulge in his pants. Giovanna's fingers expertly unzipped his fly where-upon he popped out in full magnificence, proud, ready and willing.

181

'Oh Piers,' Giovanna moaned as she slid her hand down the entire length of his shaft, 'you are so beautiful, so big, so . . . throbbing . . .'

She closed her eyes and placed her other hand upon her large brown nipple. Piers took this as an invitation and grasped both her breasts in his hands. They were almost like melons, only softer and warmer, and they swelled in his tremulous hands. Like a hot knife through butter he slipped easily inside her. Their breathing joined in heavy rasps as they both concentrated on their own private pleasure centres, ripples of hot ecstasy blossoming out from where they pounded into each other. Giovanna bounced above him like a doll on strings. Her cunt consumed him, sliding over him, enveloping him in its silky depths. He felt his climax surging through his balls. Giovanna froze for a moment, crying out, screaming her rapture. Piers held on to her buttocks, squeezing his fingers into the warm firm flesh. Then she crumpled on top of him, leaving them both breathless and spent.

As Piers' pulse returned to normal, and his mind returned to the real world, Giovanna lifted her head, her gorgeous eyes filling with softness and joy. Piers smiled back at her. Maybe visiting Giovanna hadn't been such a bad idea. A little diversion such as this with an excitingly physical woman – the kind of woman who obviously indulged a healthy appetite, and who understood the pleasures of the flesh. Uncomplicated sex, far enough away from home, just the ingredient for a perfect one-night stand!

Chapter Seventeen

Gus came out of the Head of Chambers' room feeling as though she were skipping on air. 'We are delighted to invite you to take up your tenancy here, Augusta. We feel that you have fitted in excellently with the team, and that with your fast-developing skills, you will be a huge asset to the set.' Hubert Farquharson, QC had grandly offered her his hand in congratulations, and then they had sealed the offer and Gus's acceptance in sherry. Now she could feel fully settled. No more worrying about what would happen if she were out on the street, with nowhere to practise. No more worrying about James and the politics of their relationship. How free she felt. And in control of her life once more.

She picked up the phone and called Flora, then Anthony and George, and quickly fixed up a party for dinner that night, suggesting that they bring along anyone else they could think of. This night would not be a repeat of her call night. She would celebrate with her own friends, on her own terms.

Just as she replaced the receiver, James knocked on her door. 'Gus, I've just spoken to Hubert and he told me that he'd given you the good news. I knew about it yesterday when we had our meeting.'

He walked towards her, with his arms outstretched. 'Darling Gus, how proud I am to officially welcome you to our set. Let's have dinner. Champagne, the works. Do say yes, we haven't been out together in *weeks*!'

Gus looked him up and down. Thick black hair, curled into his collar. Chiselled jaw and aquiline nose.

Black suit covering a beautifully preserved body. Long fingers and manicured nails. Wasn't he just a bit too good to be true? Looking at him now she wondered how on earth she could have been so daft as to fall for it all. Maybe it had been his mind! She laughed at herself and saw James's puzzled expression.

'I'm pleased to see you're amused by my invitations,' he said gruffly.

'Oh but I am, James,' she teased him, enjoying herself and her new sense of freedom. 'You see I know you so well now. After these last six months you've no idea what an education it's been working with you; being trained by you. I've learned more than I've ever dreamed possible.'

She watched, further amused, as James puffed out his chest like a strutting cockerel.

'Well, I pride myself on my ability to teach, Augusta. It's up to us, as the experienced, to pass on our knowledge; we have a moral duty, I feel, to guide and to educate. I can only say what a real pleasure it has been to have you alongside me, in more ways than one!'

'Yes, well I rather wanted to talk to you about that.' Gus took a deep breath and sat down on the chair behind her desk. 'You see I've known about your affair with Mirabelle for some time.' She watched with satisfaction as his face reddened.

'But ... why didn't you – I mean, what affair, for God's sake?'

'Actually, James, I'd feel much happier if we could just put it all down to experience. I hardly think we should demean ourselves by going into the detail of it.'

James spluttered. 'But Gus, whatever you think –'

'It really doesn't matter what I think, James. It's purely the facts, as you've always been so good at pointing out to me. Now let's be grown up about this. Thanks for the invitation, but I have an appointment with friends.'

James straightened himself up, gathering his composure around him as if he were robing up for an appearance. 'Very well. Then I wish you good luck.'

'Thank you,' she smiled at him graciously. 'Now, if you don't mind, I've got a few papers to go through.'

As he strutted through the door, Gus had a struggle trying to fight an attack of the giggles. How could she have ever . . .!

They had managed to clear the restaurant of other guests, and now the proprietor was making closing noises, but the party was far from breaking up. Ten barristers-at-law had put themselves the wrong side of twenty bottles of wine, including eight of champagne. Gus's head was already throbbing, but she was loving every drunken moment.

'A toast,' Anthony attempted to stand up, but his long legs wobbled beneath him as if he were negotiating a storm-tossed sea.

'Sit down, Anthony,' George Lavenham brayed across the table. 'We've had ten already, and my glass is empty.'

'Call for wine!' Julian Symonds ordered the reluctant proprietor. The rest of the staff had long since left. Another bottle appeared and was ceremoniously splashed into various glasses.

Anthony started again. 'To all of us. Gus, Flora, George, Julian, Sarah, Kate, Andrew, Michael, William and, most importantly, me. The illustrious members of the class of '92. To us all,' he repeated drunkenly, 'to our tenancies and to our glittering futures. May we stand proud . . .'

'You're always standing proud, you dirty bugger,' George wailed.

'. . . and fight each other to the death. May we kill each other in court . . .'

'The only way you'll kill in court is through boring them to death,' George added good-naturedly.

'Oh shut up, Lavenham. Just because you're slinking off to the CPS. And we all know what a cushy number *that* is. So ladies and gentlemen, learned friends, I ask those of you who are still capable to be upstanding and chuck a bucket down your gullet. To us!'

There was much scraping of chairs as they all stood up. 'To us,' they chorused.

Gus felt warmth flood through her. Probably the alcohol, she realized, but she felt part of a family – albeit a strange, drunken and disparate family. But right at that moment, she felt she loved them all!

Flora and Gus managed to pour themselves into a cab.

'I haven't had such a load of laughs in ages,' Gus confessed. 'It's so good to see everyone, and to catch up. I hope Kate and Sarah get their tenancies confirmed soon. Aren't we lucky, Flora, to both have ours settled in the same month? You got yours first. I can't help feeling envious that you're going to be where all the action is.'

Flora had been accepted into the radical set she had joined as a pupil. The set was famous for its tenacity in taking on supposedly no-win cases and emerging victorious. Most were legally aided so there was little money but plenty of satisfaction in the work.

'I know. I'm loving every single minute of it.' Flora hugged Gus's arm. 'It's been an interesting year, hasn't it?'

'Most interesting,' Gus giggled. 'Just remind me the next time I go falling for someone like James that I'm supposed to be an intelligent woman.'

'I have a feeling,' Flora confided in a slight slur, 'that whoever you fall for next will have to be pretty bloody special! And I can't wait to meet him!'

'Flora!' Gus screeched. 'Men and me are finished. I have my career mapped out. I shall be a QC by the age of forty, and I will be a forbidding, scarey old spinster registrar by forty-five. Then I shall go on to become an extremely eccentric and sexually frustrated judge who will take out all my regrets on the person in the dock. I shall be renowned for my catchphrase: "OFF WITH HIS BALLS".'

The cab driver looked over his shoulder and then slid the dividing window firmly closed. Flora and Gus glanced at each other and burst into fits of uncontrollable giggles.

Piers had finally managed to extricate himself from the voracious appetite of Giovanna. She kept him in her bed for almost twenty-four hours, insisting they make love again and again and again . . . Piers was too old for that sort of business. For Christ's sake, he was nearly forty-seven! By the time they were through the first twelve hours he couldn't tell whether he had an erection or was just plain swollen. He would certainly never forget her, but he didn't think he could survive another session. Next time Gulio asked him to deliver a painting he'd make damned sure he could think of a good excuse. Being seduced by Giovanna was almost as big a health risk as upsetting Gulio!

He had stopped off in London before returning to Guernsey, in order to meet another, and thankfully more legitimate, client. He was just ushering the gentleman out of the gallery when he caught sight of Frank Thompson through the front window. No matter what he was wearing, Thompson always managed to look shifty. He just had that sort of face. That he should be a policeman was so ludicrous as to be almost laughable. Piers shook his head to himself as Frank sidled through the door. God help the public with the likes of Thompson protecting them!

It was with a leaden feeling, though, that Piers turned to Thompson, wondering what little deal he'd fixed up this time. So much for Piers's resolve to have a quiet life now he'd finished with Capeletti.

* * *

187

Winston Davis was just putting the finishing touches to his painting. Taut with concentration, his tongue poked out very slightly between his lips as he held the tiny paintbrush over the last of the flowers which decorated the foreground of the little cottage garden. Two or three dashes of crimson lake and he'd be there. Sighing with satisfaction, he raised his head and proudly eyed the finished work at last. He straightened out the tired muscles in his neck and stood up, taking a couple of steps backwards in order to view his picture, letting its full impact settle upon him. Yes, it was good. He was justly pleased with it. He had started it several Saturdays before in order to complete it in time for his daughter's birthday. She would have it tomorrow. He picked up the small canvas and placed it on the tiled mantelpiece so that it would catch the heat from the electric fire which glowed on the hearth. Andrea would be pleased with his efforts, not least because she had been the one to get him started on his first painting-by-numbers kit. Initially he had laughed at the thought, but he had always yearned to be artistic, and had never been able to draw even a stickman, let alone actually paint a picture. And so Andrea had almost jokingly presented him with the tempting little box with its pretty pots of paint and carefully numbered pictures. It would have plenty of time to dry before tomorrow morning, and then he would wrap it up in time for her lunch-time visit. He had managed to change his driver's shift around so that he would be able to spend Sunday afternoon quietly with his daughter and her husband. She hadn't been married long – what, six months? Time, despite the fact that he missed her terribly, had passed remarkably quickly. Since Andrea's mother's death just three months before Andrea's wedding, Winston had struggled to keep as busy as possible, doubling up on the amount of overtime he had put in before Priscilla died. Then he had liked to spend time at home with his wife and only daughter. Now the house was empty. A huge, unfillable void had been created by the loss of the two women he cared about above anything in the entire world. But Winston was not a miserable man by nature. He had the natural West Indian optimism that the sun would shine a little brighter and, indeed, the world was ultimately a benevolent sort of place provided one gave a little loving here and there. And he'd sure given a lot of loving in his time!

As he busied himself in the kitchen, switching on the kettle for a nice cup of tea, and checking that the capon was settled happily in the fridge ready for tomorrow's lunch, he suddenly heard an ear-splittingly loud, terrifying exploding sound – which his mind told him at the same time he couldn't be hearing – remarkably but unmistakably, the sound of an automatic weapon firing a round of shots. In astonishment, he dropped the mug onto the floor where it smashed into several pieces. As he bent to pick them up, still unsure as to whether he had been listening to the next doors' television, the cracks rang out again like fragmented thunder. This time Winston had no doubt of what it was. Feeling sick with apprehension he stood for several more seconds as his ears rang with the noise, frozen into stillness, waiting for a third ... As he waited, he realized he was breathing fast. Fear filled his senses. Of course Winston had read about the increase in street crime, about these so-called Yardie louts and the crackhouses they controlled, but so far in this quiet little Wandsworth enclave, the most threatening crime was the theft of the Ford Cortinas and the occasional new Vauxhall or Escort – nothing that particularly bothered Winston or his family. But serious crime – no, that took place way over on the south side of Battersea, not here.

Ignoring the smashed pieces of china, Winston made his tentative way to the front door. He pushed the net curtain to one side and peered cautiously out. His breath caught in his throat as he realized he could just see the end of a pair of legs protruding past the front gate. He watched for a few seconds, feeling the blood rush through his ears in fear, his heart pounding in his chest. The feet didn't move. Winston again listened to the silence. Then, cautiously, slowly, he opened the door a couple of inches. Not a sound could be heard save for the distant rumble of the stream of cars rushing around the South Circular Road. Winston crept down the short pathway and poked his head around the gatepost. After that everything went black ...

Frank Thompson's thin-featured face had tightened into a snarling, threatening, almost feral mask. His brutality was legendary amongst his chosen men. He stood behind the desk, his hands squeezed into threatening balls which he looked as if he might throw in several directions at once. As he barked his words out, spittle flew from his lips. Martin Coles took a step backwards, fearing that the man had taken leave of all his senses and was, indeed, capable of murdering them all.

'What do you mean you haven't got a confession from the bastard yet? Harry Chapman has been murdered by a crack dealer ... a known Yardie ... using an Uzi semi-automatic machine gun and the murder was seen by two of my officers and you haven't got a confession out of him yet?'

'No, sir.' DC Cromwell shook his head.

'I don't suppose it's escaped your notice that we have news crews outside the station from every imaginable media source? That the Commissioner is taking a personal interest in the fact that one of our own has been murdered? That the public are baying for Davis's blood? And you haven't got a fucking confession yet. I guess you realize what the implications are ...'

All five of the men gathered in the room looked at him sharply.

Thompson watched as they nodded their understanding. 'Then get back down there and nail the bastard. No pussying about. I want that cunt nailed, no matter what it takes. Do I make myself clear?'

'Sir,' came the communal mutter.

'Good,' he eyed them viciously. 'Do not disappoint me this time or I shall be forced to take disciplinary action.'

Martin Coles's eyes settled nervously on Chris Thompson who slouched almost nonchalantly by the door. He was as big a bastard as his father and Martin knew he was probably even more dangerous. And like his father, he was a vicious bully with an overblown sense of his own power. No, Martin corrected himself, that's where he was wrong. The Thompsons did have all the power and he had known that from the beginning when he had first agreed to join them. Total and absolute power and control. And that poor black bastard in the cells downstairs was just another anonymous victim who would assist in keeping the Thompsons just where they wanted to be. Martin Coles had almost forgotten what it was like not to feel afraid. Afraid of being caught, afraid of Frank and Chris Thompson, afraid of his conscience and most of all, afraid for his family.

The taste of vomit sat on his tongue as he opened Winston Davis's cell. 'Get up, you black bastard!' he yelled. Then, knowing that Chris Thompson stood smiling in the doorway, he aimed his reinforced toe cap at the man's balls, trying not to imagine the pain, trying not to hear the cries, trying not to notice the sickening crunch of soft flesh against bone. Easy, easy, he told himself. Take it easy or he'll be dead. Lying dead like the poor bastard he had seen gunned down this afternoon.

'I think it's time we went back up to the interview room, don't you, Mr Davis? I expect you've probably got something to tell us by now.'

191

Winston Davis shook his head, but Coles and Thompson pulled him up from the floor. 'I want a solicitor,' he said feebly.

'He's on his way. I told you that this morning.'

Winston was pushed into the stark interview room for what he thought must be about the fifth time. His mind was cloudy, thoughts just wouldn't seem to crystallize properly. He vaguely remembered being at home, walking outside, waking up with a headache in a police car. Being taken somewhere, maybe another station, where he was beaten until they thought he would say what they wanted. But Winston wouldn't say. He knew, he remembered, what they could do to him. They sat him down at the small wooden table. A bare lightbulb shone overhead, the only illumination in the grim, windowless room. His clothes had been taken from him and he wore a grimy overall. He shivered with cold. He hadn't eaten for more hours than he could remember and every inch of his body ached. 'I won't say anything until I have a solicitor present,' he repeated.

'It's not necessary for you to say very much. You were seen by two police officers, Winston. We know your involvement with drugs. Your prints were all over the Uzi. You're a real celebrity now, Winston – you're making world news. Life looks pretty finished for you so you just might as well make what's left of it easy on yourself. Even if you say nothing, Winston, we've got enough evidence to nail you. But the more helpful you are, the more helpful we can be. Just tell us what happened. We know anyway, but once you tell us we can get you out of here, let your daughter know you're safe. We know you were probably set up to do this, Winston, but the fact is you were seen. You might just as well admit it. We've now got five independent witness statements that say you did it. Now don't you think it would be better for everybody if you were seen to be helping us? Think of the pressure your daughter's going to be under. The sooner you tell us, the sooner the public interest will be off her. I'm sure your daughter would want you to do that, Winston. You don't want to get into even more trouble than you're in already, do you . . .? Now shall we switch the tape on and you can tell us what happened?'

'I have a right to remain silent!' Winston knew he was weakening. He was hardly aware any more what he had and hadn't done. He had stepped from the real world into some nightmare where black was white, right was wrong and he had done something which he hadn't. Perhaps he had . . . had he, was he, having some sort of breakdown? Had he really not been capable of knowing what he was doing?

The door opened and a smart young man joined them in the interview room. The two police officers nodded to him.

'I'm the solicitor on duty.' He barely looked at Winston as he shrugged off his coat.

Winston's relief was palpable. 'My daughter . . .' he said immediately. 'I must speak to my daughter, and explain –'

'All in good time, Winston,' the policeman interrupted. 'After we've got your confession . . .'

The duty solicitor glanced at Winston distastefully. He put his briefcase down heavily onto the floor and took the seat opposite Winston. 'Right,' he began coldly, 'let's make this easy for everybody, shall we?'

Chapter Eighteen

When Gus stumbled into chambers the following morning she almost fell over a man wielding a small paintbrush. Removing her Raybans, she squinted at the list of names and then realized that her own name was being added to the list of barristers within the set. Feeling suddenly much less hungover, and rather pleased with herself, she almost skipped up the three flights of stairs.

Had she been a few minutes later, she might have noticed the rather lanky, shabbily dressed young man also showing an interest in the latest addition to the tenants of 96 Queen's Bench Walk.

Frank couldn't believe how bloody stupid his men had been. His group, his specially selected band, had acted like a bunch of playground bullies and instead of leaving the Harry Chapman matter to him to deal with personally, they had taken matters into their own hands and bumped the poor bastard off. In principle Frank agreed with them. Harry had been bloody stupid, trying to set up his own little patch of action. He deserved what he got. But Frank would have done it in another way. He would have been a bit more subtle about it. The entire episode had taken up the newspaper headlines for three days. Chapman was being hailed as a national hero and the force was repeating their demands for adequate protection in the form of arms. Having Brickwell at the centre of all this attention meant Thompson was faced with the possibility that certain of his activities might come under undesirable scrutiny. Already he'd seen one very shady-looking bloke in particular hanging around the place. Frank had decided to pretend he hadn't noticed the man. It wouldn't have been very cool, very professional, to go up to him and ask which of Frank's contacts the man was working for. Frank always had many irons in the fire and the timing of the Chapman fiasco was just fucking awful. All Frank could do was try to hurry along the conviction, get the evidence planted on this Winston Davis character and hope the whole thing would tick along quickly and then soon be forgotten.

Winston Davis's defence solicitor was climbing the wall with frustration.

'I'm sorry, Mr Parfitt,' the inspector in charge of the Davis case insisted when Clive telephoned him again, 'but you mustn't try and interfere with police procedures in these matters. These continual demands of yours really don't help matters at all. The normal practice is that you will be supplied with forensic samples once the committal papers are ready. Perhaps if you'd conducted a murder investigation before –'

'Detective Inspector Cromwell, I have conducted many murder cases before, and I am fully aware of what exactly I am entitled to and when. I am entitled to receive forensic samples for independent examination prior to receiving the committal papers because, as you well know, samples deteriorate with the passage of time and vital evidence may well be lost as a direct result of these interminable delays.'

'Aldermaston is a busy place, Mr Parfitt. Our forensic labs are working flat out. You can't expect us to go jumping the queue just because you're getting a little impatient, now can you?.'

'No indeed. But I find it hard to believe that in this case of all cases any of you would be dragging your heels. I shall continue to ask you for them until you supply the information required. Goodbye.'

Clive just managed to stop himself from slamming the phone down. He felt sick. This bloody case was giving him sleepless nights and uncomfortable days. Contacts he had previously relied on in the force had suddenly become unavailable to him. He had had hints that he was going to make himself extremely unpopular, that in effect he'd be blackballed from the 'club'. He hadn't ever thought of himself as a radical before now. Just and fair, yes, and with a balanced attitude towards every story he heard, but not some Establishment-fighting leftie who would be pushed out in the cold when it came to a little helping hand in the community every now and then. This case was leading him further and further into the Mr Unpopular Club. Unfortunately things were looking pretty bad for his client, too. Clive knew the defence were going to have a difficult time convincing a jury that Winston didn't commit the murder. Especially when there was a blasted confession to back up the evidence. It was such a pity that the duty solicitor who had first been called by the police on Winston Davis's behalf hadn't advised Winston to exercise his right to silence. A signed confession was going to be very hard to retract.

Then there was the mystery of the photos. Clive had tried to get photographs of the bruising on Winston's body but the film had mysteriously gone missing from the developers.

Clive decided to have another go at locating potential witnesses – witnesses who hadn't yet given their statements to the prosecution. Together with Lisa, his legal executive, and a good quality personal stereo-sized tape recorder he set off for Lavender Rise. They must have knocked on ten doors at least, and in each case the answer was the same. These people looked absolutely petrified. Doors opened by the merest six inches or so in cautious suspicion. Clive was usually good at getting people to open up their doors to him, and with Lisa's presence alongside him he shouldn't have had any problem. It wasn't that the people didn't know what he was talking about. As soon as he mentioned Harry Chapman's murder their eyes filled with fear and they tried to close the doors against the pair of them. He hardly managed to get the briefest farewell from them.

One man, who lived directly across the road from Winston, snapped at Clive viciously: 'I told the police already. They got my full statement, now you go away and leave us alone. Folks round here been put to enough trouble by this whole damn thing, man.'

Clive returned his grim expression. 'I know, sir. I can imagine. But I believe an innocent man is going to be tried for something he didn't do,' Clive knew he was sticking his neck out, but he was getting desperate, 'and I want to find out the truth of what happened on that day.'

'Well, I can tell you one thing for sure, man. The truth's the one thing you won't find down here. Now do us all a favour and leave us be.'

Lisa turned to Clive and shrugged dejectedly. 'They're terrified, Clive. They know what happened, but they're too frightened to tell. Nothing you can say is going to make them feel any different about that.'

'I expect you're right, but I'm not beaten yet, Lisa. This street's got a hundred houses in it, and I intend to visit every single one. Come on, we've got a lot more talking to do.'

Back in the office two days later Clive ploughed through the pile of already opened post. An official-looking letter with the CPS logo on the top spilled out from the huge pile. Clive pulled it out, the sinking feeling in his gut growing as he began to read.

'Jesus Christ!' he swore, his breath whistling between his teeth. 'What the hell are they going to try next?'

He cast the letter aside and put his head in his hands. Apparently the CPS were about to refer him to the Law Society as he was in breach of the code of practice established between the Law Society and the Prosecution by not having a member of the police with him when he attempted to carry out interviews with witnesses, and unauthorized interviews at that! Clive almost laughed. He hadn't got anywhere near getting an interview. Fear had gagged the whole bloody street!

Gus had almost viewed James's wooing of the latest pupil with amusement, so detached did she now feel from him. She had packaged him up into a little parcel that was somehow connected with her training, like a rite of passage, an initiation – a farewell to naïveté – a necessary diversion to educate her in what to avoid. Her charitable side had been tempted to warn the new pupil of James's reputation and probable intentions, but she had decided not to on the basis that she recalled being rather offhand herself when Flora had tried to tell her the exact same thing. Let the pair of them get on with it. After all, she had more important things to worry about than where James was pointing his penis.

Now she remained seated as James stroked his cuff nervously, gazing at him levelly, enjoying the look of guilt which was so clear in his eyes. He always seemed to squirm when they met up. Then he would quickly recover himself and attempt to assume his role of master. But Gus knew him too well now . . .

'This brief, it looks rather complicated, Gus, but I feel you might enjoy it. I thought I might pass it on to you. I shall lead, of course, but I want you to explain to Mr Parfitt that you are my junior and you will be overseeing things in my absence and naturally you will be coming to me if and when necessary.'

'When's the by-election?' Gus knew damned well he was setting her up with the case so that he could slide off to canvass for the newly vacated seat. Unsurprisingly – in view of Mirabelle's just-screened documentary – he had breezed through the selection process after Max Fowler's death and now seemed well placed to win the by-election.

'Four weeks' time, so I'm going to be a little tied up.'

'I see.' Gus kept her voice brusque. 'You have to get your priorities in order, I suppose.' James frowned, but didn't rise to her taunt. 'Between that and Mirabelle you must be awfully busy. Do you know much about the case?' Her voice rose sweetly. She remembered how quickly she'd discovered, when he'd 'borrowed' her from Henry for the rape case, how manipulative he could be.

'I've scanned the papers. I've put them on your desk so that you can have a look at them before Parfitt comes in.' James checked his watch. 'Oh dear, in about three minutes' time, as a matter of fact.'

'Three minutes!' Gus cried. 'That's no time –'

'I know. But don't worry, Gus, he's perfectly charming. I think you'll get on well with him.'

'Thank you,' she sighed. 'You will be attending the conference, won't you?' Suddenly she felt suspicious.

'No, er, I have to be down in the constituency by five, canvassing and all that,' he hopped awkwardly from one foot to the other, determined not to apologize for his absence, and yet feeling guilty nevertheless.

'Then you'd better run, hadn't you?' Gus's eyes glittered with annoyance.

'Keep me informed, Gus.'

She didn't bother to reply as he shot out of the room.

Clive Parfitt waited a little nervously in the plush reception area for his appointment with the great James Kentish. He had instructed Mr Kentish on three previous occasions, and had been most impressed by the legendary barrister's performance. He was always impossibly busy and it had been hard to pin the clerk down to an appointment time for the case conference. Just as he reached the end of the tastefully reproduced brochure depicting the various members of the chambers, a young woman appeared whom Clive assumed to be a clerk. She stuck her hand out towards him.

'Mr Parfitt, how do you do? I'm Augusta Lawrence. Would you like to follow me ...' She led the way back to her room. She waited until Mr Parfitt had settled himself into the seat on the opposite side of her desk and then sat down herself.

Clive Parfitt regarded her in some confusion. There were only two chairs in the room, and they were now both occupied. Where was Mr Kentish to sit? Had someone made a mistake?

'I have an appointment with Mr Kentish,' he said politely, not wishing to offend the young woman.

'Did Mr Kentish not tell you ...'

'Tell me?'

'About your seeing me.' Gus felt her cheeks flush. Bloody James. He had a terrible habit of doing things like this. He never seemed to take on any responsibility for his actions, but was content to let the flak fly in everyone else's direction. The client was looking pissed off, and understandably so. Thanks to James it was now up to her to appease him!

'I'm afraid James was called out.' She hoped the familiarity might help. 'I'm actually his junior. I gather you've instructed James as leader, Mr Parfitt, but James wanted me to take the brief and then report to him. I'm sure I can be of assistance to you. I might be able to keep the wheels of communication oiled and running between us. You see, James can be terribly elusive at times. And I was his pupil,' she added brightly.

Clive could barely believe his ears. 'Do you have any idea which case this is?'

Gus returned Clive Parfitt's stare equally coldly. 'No, but I trust you are about to tell me.'

'Winston Davis. The alleged police murderer!'

Gus swallowed hard. Inwardly she shrivelled. Fuck James! Of all the cases ... Her mind raced on as she struggled to appear calm and professional. No wonder James had wanted her to front the case. This was one hot potato he wouldn't want to touch! It might damage his chances with 'the people' by being seen to defend one of the public's biggest bogeymen. This was one hellishly high-profile case and James hadn't the balls to take it. He had really landed her in the shit this time. The poor solicitor was right to feel appalled by being palmed off with a junior. Winston Davis needed every advantage he could get. The guy was already tried and hanged so far as the public was concerned. Difficulty in getting him a fair trial might be the only thing the defence could use after the huge publicity surrounding it all.

'Mr Parfitt,' Gus took a deep breath and struggled for her career, 'James will lead and I will give you my assurance that I will do my utmost to successfully assist with this brief. I trust we can now proceed with this conference. If you should feel dissatisfied after that then you are free to take matters up with Mr Kentish. Shall we ...?'

Clive didn't know whether to be disappointed or plain angry. He had really wanted James Kentish to take on the Davis case. He should have thought through the very likely possibility that Mr Kentish's proposed second career might affect things. Clive had nearly fallen off his chair when he had first learned of it. There was Kentish with his apparent love of advocacy and his feel for justice. Funny, Clive would have thought that politics would have been far too much of a scrum for Mr Kentish. Still, having seen him on that recent justice series, all ponced up and his hair so obviously lacquered, Clive could perhaps understand that the man had a larger ego than had at first been apparent. It worried Clive that the girl seemed so young – barely out of her pupillage – but now he thought about it, the clerk had mentioned her name before and he vaguely remembered reading that she'd had two or three big successes with some tricky cases, pulling flankers at the last minute and not being intimidated by her senior colleagues. And, of course, she had been James Kentish's pupil. She was also very attractive – not that he tried to think of women he met professionally in sexist terms. But he wouldn't have been a normal male if he failed to notice. She was slightly above average height, say five foot eight, brown hair and soft grey eyes which were concealed behind austere tortoiseshell-rimmed spectacles. Although the severity of her plain black suit and white shirt did everything to deny the fact that she was a woman, her scent – a warm floral fragrance – hinted at her underlying femininity.

She had taken over the room next to Kentish's. The small fireplace was full of fresh flowers and there was an immediate feeling of cosiness and welcome, although the books which lined two of the four walls gave a clear indication that serious business was carried out in here. There was something about Augusta Lawrence, about the relaxed feel she had cast over the room, about her understated presence, that inspired confidence. She gave the impression of being serious-minded, but at the same time warm. She smiled encouragingly as he laid out the committal bundle on the desk between them. There was nothing to be gained by making a fuss at this stage. But if she didn't come up to scratch he'd have no hesitation in getting hold of James Kentish personally.

'I received the papers at the committal last Friday. I assume you know most details of the case?

'As does the whole country,' Gus murmured, 'but please, go on . . .'

'The accused, Mr Winston Davis, is charged with the murder of Mr Harry Chapman. The murder was witnessed by two police officers who were with Mr

Chapman, but were at the opposite end of the street when the alleged murder took place.'

'Reliable witnesses?'

'So it would seem. They apparently saw everything. Mr Chapman was murdered with an Uzi machine gun. As I'm sure you know, the inference is that this was a Yardie murder.'

'Is there evidence that Mr Davis was a crack dealer?'

'No.'

'Was he a user?'

'Not so far as we can ascertain.'

'I see. And the weapon? What's the forensic story?'

'If you must know it's been an absolute nightmare trying to get stuff from Aldermaston. I appointed an independent expert to check things over, but it was tough going getting the exhibits released from the police laboratories. Every time I chased the police, they said it was up to the CPS, and then the CPS said it was up to the police. It's been like a game of table tennis. But I think I'm satisfied with what we've got now in the way of the report.'

'Fine.' Gus was thinking fast. She pushed her spectacles back up onto the bridge of her nose, a movement Clive would become familiar with.

'And what about defence witnesses?' Gus had read all the details of the story in the newspapers, but she needed to hear things from the solicitor. Anything else was hearsay.

'Well, that's rather interesting because I attempted to check out potential witnesses the prosecution might have missed, and we obviously came across a number of witnesses who had already spoken to the police. However, at least one and possibly two of those statements have not been disclosed in the committal bundle.'

'So we'd better ask for those. Now, what about previous record, history of the accused and so on?'

'Absolutely impeccable,' Clive said. 'Up till now he's been absolutely squeaky clean. Good work record. Never off sick, continuously employed since he arrived from the West Indies thirty years ago. Due to retire shortly. Daughter's a teacher, wife was a nurse, recently died of cancer.'

Gus twirled a pen in her fingers and watched Clive Parfitt's expression. He had a pleasant sort of a face, sandy-coloured hair which was neatly parted to the side, quite thick and with a tendency to curl up at the ends. He had a tanned, almost ruddy complexion reminding her of someone who spent a good deal of time out in the fresh air. He wore a blue and white pinstriped shirt underneath his dark city suit. She sensed his unease about the case.

'Is something bothering you?' she asked frankly, getting straight to the point.

He looked at her with a sudden intensity. It was almost as if he were afraid to speak, to voice his opinions. Gus knew he was weighing her up, working out whether he could trust her, trying to judge what she was made of. Finally he spoke. 'I think it's a frame-up.'

Gus didn't reply, but returned his stare evenly.

'I think the police have set him up,' Clive added, watching to see if there was the slightest flicker in Gus's eyes.

'That's quite a thought, Mr Parfitt.'

'A dangerous thought, Miss Lawrence. Perhaps you might like to convey my thoughts to Mr Kentish? I have a feeling we could have a rather tricky time ahead of us.'

Much later, long after Clive Parfitt had gone, Gus ran through the papers for the fifth time. She had already made pages of notes and suggestions. The statement from Winston Davis was poignant in its simplicity. Several things bothered her about the committal papers; things which had come up in the forensic reports, and various inconsistencies in the witness statements which would have to be explained. They had a great deal of work to do. Despite James's reticence, she should brief him straight away. This case would need his direction, however much she might personally wish to avoid it.

Boy, had he gone down even more in her estimation! Frightened little toad – unable to say no to the Davis case, but foisting it off on to her on the pretext that he was too tied up. She'd bet a few thousand pounds that if they ran a successful defence he'd soon step in to take all the accolades! But in a case like this a successful defence could only result in public disgrace. The Davis case was a political case – good against evil, law and order against anarchy, and if there was the slightest foundation to Clive Parfitt's fears then they had the fight of their lives ahead of them. Winston Davis would need the best defence in the business. Until a few weeks ago she would have believed he'd got it in James. Now she knew that for all his posturing and skill, underneath it he had no moral fibre or principle. He was a weak, self-serving sham.

Chapter Nineteen

Tom Silverthorn had a hunch about this story. Jim Carter, the News Editor, had threatened to pull him off it more times than Tom cared to remember, but after eight years in the business, Tom knew when to trust his nose, and there was a bloody sour smell coming in from several directions. He had been investigating the case on and off for several weeks after he'd received a tip-off from some disgruntled criminal about the goings-on down at Brickwell police station. Scenting a potential serious exposé Tom had dug deep into the files to find out about arrests and prosecutions, and some rather alarming discrepancies had jumped out. Then, just as it was getting really interesting, the Davis murder had come along. And somehow Tom didn't believe that the Brickwell boys' involvement was mere coincidence. He smelled a bloody great rat. Trying to interview anyone in Lavender Rise had been like asking an investigative journalist to name his source. No chance! He'd had the door slammed in his face a dozen times, been told to fuck off twice, and just seen the twitch of a curtain in the rest of the street. Then he'd given up. The fact was, they were all shit bloody scared!

If his hunch was right, then there was a lot more to Frank Thompson's little network than taking a few bribes. Every time Tom thought he was getting near to the bottom of the story, some other twist came up, making him bide his time a little longer, just to see . . .

But this latest one was something to be believed. He'd been ferreting around, finding out whether the Davis

Trial had been set down. Old Don Trellick, one of the court reporters, had all the gen on it, including (through Don's intelligence sources) the name of the barrister who would be representing Mr Winston Davis: none other than James Kentish – whose sidekick was Augusta Lawrence. The same Augusta Lawrence who was the daughter of Piers Lawrence. And Tom just happened to know that Piers Lawrence was somehow involved with Frank Thompson, because he'd been tailing Thompson long enough to know how he liked his egg fried for breakfast, let alone who he associated with. Tom couldn't believe his luck. Jesus, this story was going to be fucking big! If only he could split himself into three. He wanted to watch both the Lawrences *and* Thompson.

But he had to keep his cool. He had to keep the stuff to himself or it could blow sky-high. Even Adam, his young photographer sidekick, couldn't be told every-thing. Just a little longer! Tom felt as if he were playing a fish, giving a bit of line, and then a bit more, and eventually he'd reel in the big bastard.

It had been a tricky decision whether to watch Augusta Lawrence, or stick with Frank Thompson for the next couple of days. But when Thompson ended up at Heathrow, checking on to the Guernsey flight, Tom felt a dangerous thrill go down his spine.

Tom and Adam Worth were the last to board. Tom made sure their seats were right at the very back where he could observe Thompson and not be observed by him. He suspected they were in for an interesting trip.

Frank was glad he'd done some research into Davis's representation. His taxi pulled up outside Pete's gallery at the smart end of St Peter Port. He hadn't announced his visit to Pete, but he'd checked with his secretary that he'd be in Guernsey for the next couple of days. If Frank missed him here, he'd catch up with him at home ... after lunch. There was a rather nice little fish restaurant down by the harbour which produced an excellent sea-food platter. Frank's mouth watered at the thought. Then maybe a swim in the hotel pool, a little rest, then business – if necessary.

Frank strolled around the towering, white-walled room. Vast canvases of vibrant colours were hung in an exhibition of contemporary works. Definitely not Frank's style. Bar some woman and the receptionist, he was the only person in the gallery. Frank knew that Pete spent most of his time upstairs, in the offices where he carried out his mega deals. Having satisfied his curiosity, Frank approached the receptionist. 'Tell Mr Lawrence that Mr Thompson would like to see him.'

Frank paced in irritation while Pete kept him waiting. Some fifteen minutes later he finally appeared, just as Frank was deciding to go off for lunch and make Pete catch up with him later. More for the sake of the receptionist than any degree of civility on Pete's part, he made a show of welcoming Frank before ushering him up the stairs to his office.

Once behind the closed door, Piers turned on Frank angrily. 'Just what the hell are you doing here? This is becoming too much of a habit, Frank, a rather bad one. Aren't your superiors going to wonder why you're spending so much time following me around? Don't you have work to do solving crimes instead of pestering me?'

'That's exactly what I'm here for – solving crimes. It concerns your lovely daughter . . .'

Piers' eyes narrowed suspiciously. 'What about her?'

'Augusta, isn't it? I remember meeting her at that delightful anniversary party you held – what, nine months ago now? Doesn't time fly? Must be our age . . .'

'Get to the point,' Piers snapped impatiently.

'The point is that your daughter is involving herself in a case which is a little sensitive. She'd do better to give it up, or at the very least not put too much effort into it. She could do us all a big favour if she toed a certain line . . .'

'You're suggesting that Augusta is bribed into some nasty little scheme of yours?'

'Well, I wouldn't exactly have said "bribed". More persuaded for the good of her family – especially you, now Pete . . . sorry, Piers. You wouldn't want her to know about things, would you?'

Piers put his head in his hands. It had always been just a matter of time until Thompson tried to get his hands on Gus. He had been naïve to think she could be spared the shadow of his past. But he couldn't influence Gus. There was no way he could suggest any kind of deal to her. He knew his daughter too well to believe that anything he, or anyone else, could say to her would influence her professional life. It had been Piers's life's ambition to keep her protected from his shady dealings. He never wanted her to know the truth about any of it and he would do anything to protect her from it.

'You're wasting your time. Whatever it is you're asking me to do, she won't listen to me. She's a grown woman, Thompson. She's always been headstrong and I just wouldn't have any influence over her.'

'You just might if she was in some kind of danger . . .' Frank stood up and stared out of the window, leaving the threat hanging in the silence.

'What the hell do you mean?' Piers hissed, standing up, closing the gap between Thompson and himself. Before he could stop himself, he grabbed the lapels of Thompson's blazer and pulled him close to his face. 'You dare even begin to think of harming a hair on that girl's head, then you're dead, Thompson. Dead, remember.'

Frank raised his arms and brought them down heavily on the crook of Piers's elbows, freeing himself. 'I wouldn't be too sure about that. Think about it, and then have a word, would you? We're friends, you and I, Pete. I know you'll remember all the things we've done together over the years and you'll think of something.'

'Get out,' Piers rasped angrily. 'Just get out of here!'

As Piers listened to Thompson's footsteps receding down the stairs, he shuddered. There had been a time once before when Thompson had threatened his daughter . . .

Chapter Twenty

1970

Piers gazed into the tiny cot and marvelled at the small pink bundle lying asleep, so peaceful and contented. He ached to reach out and stroke the beautifully rounded head with its coating of soft brown velvety hair, but he dared not in case he was too rough. Instead, he leaned forward and listened to the regular, shallow breathing of his infant daughter, so close that the could discern the delicious scent of baby.

The nursery nurse finally took pity on him. 'Would you like to hold her?' she asked needlessly.

Piers straightened up, and smiled his gratitude: more than anything in the entire world. Carefully, tentatively, he cradled the tiny bundle against his chest, treating her more reverently than if she had been made of the finest, rarest piece of Baccarat crystal. Now he knew what all the fuss was about. It was an odd feeling, this thing called parenthood. A mixture of pride and happiness, of joy and amazement, yet at the same time it brought with it a kind of pain, a kind of vulnerability which he hadn't known before. To care about something so much that the thought of the smallest hurt to it could bring such pain and torment. His heart and his soul had been captured by his tiny daughter.

'Augusta,' he whispered her name. Such a big name for such a tiny creature. 'I shall call you Gus,' he said to her conspiratorially. He wondered at her tiny button of a nose, the perfection of her skin, the neat little rosebud mouth and those smooth near-translucent eyelids so still and peaceful in sleep, so totally trusting. The warmth generated through the blankets to his chest. He could have stayed for hours, just gazing down at her, just admiring all the bits he could see, and wondering about all the bits that he couldn't. But he hadn't seen Cat yet, and he knew she would be waiting for him.

He reluctantly handed the tiny bundle back to the nurse, and headed down the corridor towards room number 5. There were so many flower arrangements around the bed that he wondered where he could find space to stand. Yet there, in the centre, looking radiant, was his wife. He picked his way to her side.

'Darling,' he cried, 'I'm so proud of you! I've sneaked a look at her already, she's absolutely beautiful.'

Cat's face was perfectly made up, with her signature eyeliner sweeping up from her eyelids out to her temples, for ever like her namesake. He bent to kiss her, but she turned her cheek at the last second. Piers frowned, hurt by her rebuttal. But at least he knew this was nothing new. He had just hoped that maybe the birth of their first child might have mellowed her somewhat.

'Ugly little thing, isn't she?' Cat sighed, eyeing him disdainfully. 'All she ever does is shit and yell. And my God, Piers, if I'd known what was going to happen to my tits! They've swelled like bloody bullets. I feel like a champion cow. It's the most ghastly thing that's ever happened to me in my whole life. Leaking all over the place, stinking of sour milk. Well, I'm not breastfeeding, and that's that. The whole idea just completely turns my stomach. I've arranged for a nanny who'll take over as soon as I come out of hospital. I've done as you asked, you've got your blessed child. And she'll be the only one you ever have with me! I am never, never going through that agony again, Piers. It was terrifying and hateful.'

Piers had already taken a step back from her. He couldn't quite believe his ears. All through the pregnancy Cat had protested that she would hate this child. Even after he had finally bullied her into going through with the pregnancy she had continued to say awful things about it, but he had hoped, indeed had known, that once the child was in her arms her maternal instincts would take over. All the doctors and specialists he had consulted had told him exactly that. The mothering instinct was there in everyone – it just needed time to come out. After a few days' rest at home, with the newly appointed nanny taking care of Augusta, she would feel differently towards her baby.

Piers tried to let himself be soothed by the advice, but he couldn't help feeling anxious for the tiny girl who was so dependent upon him for everything. She was the only really good thing in his life. Everything up until now was tainted by his past. Maybe now was the time to concentrate on a different future, a life that he could one day be proud of, not something that he always had to hide from those he loved. This tiny creature deserved more and he would do his damnedest to make sure she got it!

And so they had gone home – the four of them – the nanny, Cat, Augusta and Piers. Piers had been told to give it time, Cat would soon come round. First of all her attitude was put down to postnatal depression, then tiredness ... Piers had heard all of the excuses in the book as to how it was his wife could be so indifferent to her own baby. They moved to a large country house in Sussex to accommodate the growing paraphernalia of family life. Gus got bigger and stronger, she learned to crawl and then to walk. Eventually she started to talk.

213

Piers was the only one who took notice of her. Yet all the while the child was obsessed by her mother. She cried for her, searched her out, sat outside her door crying for her, called for her when she woke in the middle of the night, even though it was always Piers who went to her, who listened to her garbled attempts at conversation and interpreted her words to the rest of the world; Piers who read her stories at night, and cuddled her when she was cutting teeth, or had bad dreams. It was almost as if she had an in-built defence mechanism which thankfully was unable to interpret her mother's lack of care or concern as rejection. It made Piers' heart ache to see little Gus trot after her mother and to see Cat completely ignore her.

As the months passed, he ceased to have anything to do with his wife. Since the pregnancy they had not slept together. Cat, whenever she was at home in Sussex, seemed to have an entourage of hippies around her, all of whom appeared to Piers to be completely spaced out. Occasionally she would go off on what she termed her pilgrimages to some exotic-sounding place without so much as a hint of when she would be back. Piers had considered divorce, but part of him rejected the idea because he feared Augusta's reaction.

A stream of nannies arrived and left in quick succession. There was no problem with Gus, but Cat usually managed to make them feel so uncomfortable and unwanted as to scare them off. Piers had long since ceased to be surprised by a tentative knock on the door from the more serious-minded ones, suggesting that he should get some help for Augusta – or for Mrs Lawrence! But Piers hadn't bothered to get specific help for her. He'd got to the stage where she disgusted him so much that he wished she'd rot herself from the inside out. At the rate she was going with all the rubbish she was pumping inside herself, he wouldn't have to wait long. By the time Gus was three years old, he could barely bring himself to look at Cat, so strong was his hate and disgust.

George Kennedy-Hughes III usually enjoyed his trips to London, but today was not going at all well. His eleven o'clock meeting was already ten minutes behind schedule. Oil company or no oil company, he didn't like to be kept waiting. The receptionist at WestPet gave him his second cup of coffee and invited him to read some glossy magazine. Trying to calm his irritation he flicked through the pages, barely glancing at the contents. Then he caught an item on the Crowborough Collection. Anything to do with art was always worth a look . . .

Photographs of the paintings were spread across two double pages, and George squinted at the reproductions. His attention was drawn by the small impressionist study beneath the Rembrandt. It was remarkably similar to the Manet . . . He peered more closely as his pulse rate trebled. It couldn't be! Jesus Christ, it was the same fucking painting!

George threw the magazine aside, jumped up from his seat and without the slightest nod to the confused girl, he rushed out of the executive offices of WestPet.

Within an hour his taxi was setting him down outside Hollyworth House. A rushed call to Lady Crowborough explaining that he was on a flying visit from the USA and was anxious to see the collection had met with surprise, but a dignified invitation to spend thirty minutes with her secretary.

The only explanation for the fact that there were two identical Manets was that one was a fake. Question was, which one?

'I've just had a very interesting call, Frank. I think you'd better come over and see me. It concerns that little deal you put together for me a couple of years ago. Yeah, sooner rather than later, if you don't mind, Frank.'

Stephen Wallace put the phone down and snarled angrily. By the time he'd finished with Thompson he'd wish he'd never been born. Right out of the blue he'd taken a call from that fucking American. Unbelievable. Bloody unbelievable. If he himself hadn't gone and opened up his big mouth about how it had been his painting the bloke had bought – if he hadn't offered to take him out for a celebration drink and ended up swapping cards, then maybe Mr George Kennedy-Hughes might not have been so quick to pick up the phone to him. It had taken a while to remember who he was, and just what he was talking about. Stephen hadn't given the painting much thought since then, there'd been so many others. But to find out that it was bloody nicked! What kind of an idiot goes and launders money through hot paintings, even if a fake were supplied to replace it? Fuck it, if it wasn't so bloody sick it would be laughable. So, the American geezer had the original, but the copy was hanging on the wall amongst the Crowborough Collection, where Hughes's Manet should be. So Hughes, not surprisingly, wanted half his money back! Otherwise, he said, he would shout his mouth off about exactly where the painting had come from. Provided everything was handled quietly, and he got his 'compensation', Hughes said he would forget the whole episode. They were bloody lucky he hadn't demanded *all* his money back!

Frank Thompson walked briskly down the path towards the Sussex house which Lawrence had recently acquired. Frank had already given Lawrence notice that he'd be collecting the money today. Although the wind was biting through his thin raincoat, he didn't notice the cold. He was deep in thought, very angry thoughts about what he was going to do with Lawrence. The double-crossing bastard had really stitched him up with the Wallace deal, and now he would bloody well pay for

216

it. He still hadn't managed to piece together the jigsaw – whether Crowborough himself had been in on the deal, or whether Lawrence had simply swapped the paintings to cover up the theft, but the fact was Frank now had to pay half a million quid back to Wallace so that he in turn could pay off the American. Otherwise Frank knew there would be a contract out on him. Lawrence would have to come up with the money and fast!

Frank reached the house. He stopped by the gate and leaned on the curved railings. Smug bastard in his mansion! He would make sure Lawrence regretted his little scam for the rest of his life. Now Lawrence really owed him!

Frank's hot rage pumped through every vein in his body. Never, ever before had he felt so murderous, so outraged. All these years it had taken to build up his contacts with Wallace, all the money he had been raking off as commission – and Lawrence too – now all of it had come to nothing, thanks to this little prick. Oh he was smug all right in his smart Sussex house, neat little flowerbeds and dolls' house windows. A right little lord of the manor. And what of Frank? His name was mud with Wallace, and would probably soon be mud with every other contact he'd spent the last five years cultivating. Fucking little shit . . . he'd *have* him.

'Look, how was I to know the painting would appear in some blasted magazine – and that the bloody American would just happen to be in England the month it was published? So far as I was concerned, everyone was happy.'

Piers remained seated behind the desk in his large book-lined study while Frank paced up and down over the oak floorboards.

'The point is,' Frank stopped and wheeled around to point his nasty little weasel face into Piers's, 'that you flogged me a stolen painting in the first place. The

Manet belonged to the Crowborough estate trustees and wasn't Dickie Crowborough's personal property. And how many more of your paintings can I expect to crash around me in the future?'

'That was the only one. All the rest were legit.'

'Oh thank you, how fucking good of you!' Frank spat. 'You realize I've fucked up with Wallace, thanks to you? You realize that I shall be breathing down your neck even more closely from now on? Damages! That's what you owe me, mate, bleeding damages!'

Frank was almost stamping his feet, he was so beside himself with anger. His face was mottled with red and spittle bounced off his mouth as he shouted at Piers.

'First of all you give me half a million – in cash – otherwise we're both dead. Then I shall decide just how you make amends to me!'

Piers knew he was, for once, in a corner that he simply couldn't get out of. The money was a blow, but he could afford it. It meant it would reduce the amount he could spend on the Van Gogh which was about to be auctioned in New York – Piers looked at his watch – in just a few minutes' time! He needed to get Frank out of his study otherwise he'd miss the sale.

'Okay, okay. I'll agree. Only cut all the insults, Frank. I've done you more favours than you'll ever know with all the other stuff you've put through me. I don't take kindly to your insults.'

Frank looked apoplectic with rage. He was about to burst forth again but Piers was already by the safe. He turned his back on Frank while he worked the combination. He counted out the cash and then handed the large wad into the policeman's hand. 'Let's just put it down to youthful inexperience, shall we?'

'Any more like that and you're dead, Lawrence –'

The telephone trilled into life and Piers picked it up. 'I need to take this call. You've got your money, now leave, Frank. Don't hurry back.'

218

Frank slammed the door so hard behind him that the panelling shook. Then he saw the little girl coming towards him. She couldn't have been described as an attractive child – too solemn and pale-faced.

'Have you come to see my mummy or my daddy?' she asked in a husky little voice.

'I've just seen your daddy!' he snapped, causing the little girl to flinch backwards. But as she started to scamper off into the shadows of the corridor he called her back. Frank made it his business to know all about Pete's family. Very soon it would be payback time.

'What's your name?'

'Augusta.' She turned and shyly clutched at the drape which hung at the hall window.

'Where is your mummy, Augusta?' Frank concentrated on trying to keep his voice soft.

'Mummy's in the garden.'

Frank forced a smile, 'Good, would you like to show me where?'

Frank could tell by the way she dragged her little legs that she was reluctant, that she sensed there was something scary about him. Well, she was right to be frightened. He patted his pocket, checking that the heroin was still safely tucked inside. It had been tricky getting hold of such pure stuff. Pure caviar for Mrs Lawrence. The purest of the pure. One little hit of this could put her out for days.

They stepped out into a courtyard and Gus pointed in the direction of a walled enclosure. 'Mummy's in there,' she said and then disappeared back into the house. Frank could hear her small feet trotting as fast as they could back down the corridor.

The walled section turned out to be the original kitchen garden. It seemed rather incongruous to find Cat with a hoe in her hands, bending over a row of seedlings. She didn't see Frank until he was within a few yards of her. She grinned at him and straightened up.

'I'd never have thought gardening was your style,' he said.

'Marijuana, dear Frank. I should have a decent crop here in a few weeks' time. Maybe I can count you as a customer?'

'I shouldn't think it'll be up to my usual quality. Talking of which ...' He dipped into his pocket and pulled out a small brown envelope. 'A gift for you, Cat. Take care with it, you never know how strong this stuff can be.'

Cat rubbed the soil off her hands and took the package. 'Payment in kind then?'

Frank smiled. Exciting as he knew she could be, he didn't feel in the mood. 'Later maybe, I've got all day. Perhaps we should take a walk. Why don't you show me the famous Sussex Downs?'

'Okay. I'll get the dog.'

'I expect you'll want to, er, try out your present, too, won't you? I'll wait.'

'You're a very bad influence, Frank. That's why we've got such a lot in common, you and I. You understand me, don't you?' She stroked his chin suggestively. 'Hang around, and I'll be right back. If I'm not here in the next twenty minutes, start without me.'

Piers had the telephone pressed tightly to his ear, listening to the ascending bids courtesy of the girl on the other end who was on one of the bank of telephones in the sale room. Piers could guess that interest in the lot would be at fever pitch. This time he didn't think he'd be lucky, but even so it was worth a try. One could never forecast what the market might do – it was all a question of nerve!

Waiting for the moment when he would join the bidding, Piers spotted the little troupe through the window. Cat and Frank Thompson, with Gus trotting after her mother, were climbing over the gate at the top of the garden which led to the open countryside of the Downs and the sheer cliffs above the sea. For some reason Piers suddenly felt a chill of fear run through him. He watched the figures growing more distant, and then had to pull his attention back to the telephone. It was time to enter the auction.

Fast as it was, to Piers the whole thing seemed interminably slow. He stood up so that he might see the party more clearly. The bid was with him, then against ... just a few more moments and then he would go after them ...

Finally, after several unsuccessful minutes, Piers ran from the house, taking the short cut which led through a gap in the hedge, and across the field. His leather-soled shoes slipped over the grass, but he kept on running until he felt his lungs would burst. Way ahead in the distance he saw them – the tiny figure of his daughter, and Thompson several yards behind. Piers continued to run. He tried to call out, but his words were carried away on the breeze. Then he realized the dog had seen him. The little creature came careering across to him, followed by Gus. Piers waved in relief to his daughter, but there was no sign of his wife. Only the sinister figure of Frank Thompson standing with his back towards them, looking down over the cliffs to the rocks far below.

Holding tightly to Gus's hand, Piers approached Thompson. When they were almost upon him Thompson turned. His face looked ghostly white and his lips started to move.

'Something terrible has happened . . .!'

Gus pressed her face against the window. The glass was cold, freezing cold. Her forehead had gone numb, aching with the chill, but she didn't mind. She had been told to stay upstairs and play some games. Nobody thought she knew or understood what had happened, but she knew something had happened to Mummy. The glass in the window had strange little bubbles inside it, like those in a fizzy drink. The square bits, when they got cold, would bleed water, which she would sweep off with her forefinger and then draw shapes across the glass until it made nice squeaky sounds.

But she wasn't drawing pictures that day. She was watching the big black car reversing into the drive, and the box which had come out. She'd seen a box shaped like that in a book. She knew that they put people in them when they went to heaven. She didn't exactly know where heaven was, but people seemed to think it was a place everyone went to sometime. Nobody ever seemed to come back from there. As she stared out, her breath kept clouding the window, making it difficult for her to watch. She'd used the sleeve of her cardigan to wipe it, and now that too was growing soggy. She watched as the box was taken across the garden, out of the gate, wheeled on a funny little trolley, like a big pram without the top. She wanted to open the window and ask what was in the box, but she wasn't allowed to touch the catch. She knew that whatever it was, it was very sad. And that somehow it would have a very bad effect on her. She knew this because everyone started to whisper whenever she was around. And everyone looked so sad.

Chapter Twenty-One

1993

'I've looked over the papers, of course.' Gus pushed her specs up on the bridge of her nose, and patted the bundle of papers which Clive had given her earlier in the week. 'I must say, it's a most disturbing case. Naturally without having met Mr Davis it's difficult to crystallize my initial ideas as to his character, and what sort of a defendant he comes over as, but from the instructions you have given me he seems to be one of the mildest of men, with a previously unblemished record, an admirably long-service employee, a professional daughter and son-in-law and no connection to any form of drugs whatsoever, bar the odd paracetamol I should think! Hardly a number-one suspect for the Yardie crackhouse-linked murder of a policeman.'

Clive nodded, but remained silent. It was, after all, her opinions he was after and he knew better than to disturb someone's train of thought.

'I agree with your decision not to have had an independent autopsy carried out. PC Chapman was murdered by a semi-automatic machine gun – an Uzi – found at the SoC, and no further weapons are being sought. That seems straightforward. So, what else do we have to go on?' Gus placed her fingertips together and raised them to her lips thoughtfully. 'Any news on those missing witness statements?'

'None at all, but we do have a statement from one of

the witnesses confirming that he actually gave a statement.'

'Then we shall issue an application for it.'

'Against who?'

'Against the CPS, of course!'

Clive swallowed hard. It was all right for Miss Lawrence up in her eyrie where the élite existed in an entirely cloistered environment, removed from the real world. He was on the bloody ground and he wasn't very comfortable. The trouble was that deep down he completely agreed with the way they were fighting their every corner. They had no other choice at all if they were going to run a decent defence. It was the very least they owed their client. Poor sod. It was hard getting access to him at Risley. Every paper that Clive sent up there would be scrutinized by third parties. There could be no confidentiality between solicitor and client. Even when Clive made the trip up to see Winston, they had a guard present who might well be reporting their conversations back to some opposing interest. It was a sad business to be defending someone so obviously innocent when the odds were stacked so highly against him. Justice ... sometimes Clive felt very cynical about the whole system. What had the Legal Aid Board said? 'There does seem to be a lot of evidence against the defendant. Do you really think you should be seeking independent forensic reports, Mr Parfitt?'

In other words, don't defend the poor old sod too vigorously. He's going to end up guilty and we don't want to throw good money away on him. God, the system made Clive sick at times.

'Now I see we're set for trial in three months' time, in September. Naturally bail was refused, and poor Mr Davis is languishing in Risley. North Cheshire's hardly convenient for conferences with you, is it? And impossible to maintain any kind of confidentiality through

224

the remand postal system. Still, we'll just have to make the best of the situation.'

'And your initial opinion?'

'That Mr Davis is as innocent as you or I and that he's been the victim of a setup. But by whom at this stage, I have no idea. Let's get to those witnesses and maybe they can throw some light on just what happened outside 52 Lavender Rise that day.'

'And what about his signed confession?'

'Yes, well that does give cause for concern, doesn't it? It's a shame that you weren't called in earlier. I feel the duty solicitor was rather careless. He didn't make much of a job of advising Mr Davis of his right to remain silent. In fact I gather he convinced Mr Davis that a confession was the best course to follow. Such a pity! And as for Mr Davis's allegations of police brutality – you'd think that the duty solicitor would have seen fit to comment upon his wounds. Unfortunately as it stands, and without any material evidence, we have nothing to corroborate those allegations other than Mr Davis's daughter's word – and I don't think she'd be classed as an independent witness. So I think for the moment we should concentrate on these witnesses. See if you can trace any irregularities or inconsistencies. The results might prove very interesting!'

Tom Silverthorn sat on a bench enjoying the May sunshine looking for all the world like some vagrant, though admittedly a somewhat clean vagrant. There was something about Middle Temple's hallowed calm, its pretentious, self-important, arrogant posturing, that annoyed the pants off him. Even the façades of the barristers' chambers looked haughty. Privilege and elitism. Tom shoved the remaining half of a Mars Bar into his mouth and threw the paper onto the grass in a show of rebellion. Then, unable to reconcile his ecological principles with his disdain, he retrieved the black paper and pocketed it. He looked at his watch and wondered idly what time Miss Lawrence would appear. It wasn't an unpleasant way to while away a couple of hours, but he had promised to meet up with one of the researchers later on and therefore it would suit him if she came out sooner rather than later.

He tried not to feel cocky but it was tough not to. Piers Lawrence's daughter, like the icing on something from the Gloriette Patisserie. It was a funny old world. It never ceased to amaze Tom how a story could drift on for weeks, months even, following just a hunch, finding nothing and then, suddenly, everything just fit into place, like a jigsaw when it gets down to the last few pieces.

This lady had to be bent. And Tom intended to find out just how bent she was. He took a Marlboro out of the battered packet in his jacket pocket and fondled it between his fingers, running it beneath his nose, inhaling the sweet, spicy smell of tobacco. Sod it, he smiled. He deserved a treat today. Feeling like the smug twit in the Hamlet ad, he lit up his fag – Tom Silverthorn, the King of the News. Thompson ... Lawrence ... they didn't stand a cat in hell's chance!

Half an hour later the woman he was waiting for appeared in the doorway. She appeared older than twenty-three, but then she was hidden behind those serious-looking glasses. Her face was pale, no make-up, soft skin. Classy-looking. Good bone structure, neat brown hair scraped back into one of those large black bow things. She carried a beige raincoat – no doubt a Burberry – over her arm and in her other hand a battered briefcase like the one he used to have for school. He stood up and sauntered after her.

She walked along the narrow passageway which led out on to Fleet Street and then stopped briefly to consult her watch. She turned to the right and headed in the direction of Ludgate Circus. Tom paused to look in a few shop windows, increasing the distance between them, and then carefully following twenty or so yards behind. Eventually she disappeared inside El Vino.

Tom bought himself an *Evening Standard*, and then waited five minutes before ducking his head below the narrow lintel and stepping into the dark interior. He paused for a few moments, letting his eyes become accustomed to the gloom, and then he glanced quickly around, looking for the woman. Damn it! Where was she? He stood at the bar, using the mirror, as he waited to order a drink. Then he spotted her, seated in the corner by the window, talking to a very attractive black girl. It was obvious from the other girl's dress that she, too, was a barrister in the obligatory black suit and white shirt designed to remove all sexual identity. God, what a load of crap! Tom thought derisively. He ordered himself a glass of house red.

As Tom watched, and quietly sipped, they were joined by a couple of blokes – also barristers by the look of them. What a cosy little foursome they made, laughing and joking together. Augusta Lawrence looked relaxed and confident, obviously very easy with her mates. Funny how people had hidden sides that even their closest friends never suspected. Tom knew all about that. *He* wasn't easily fooled.

Unfortunately for Tom it was not going to be a good time to introduce himself. Ever the pragmatist, he knew there'd be other opportunities. He downed his wine and walked out of the bar.

Frank Thompson epitomized the essence of successful Surrey man. Comfortably relaxed in his pale blue Lacoste polo shirt and his soft pink cashmere V-neck pullover, he smiled easily at the gathering in what he and his wife called the 'games room'. The lighting was suitably dim, coming from the green canopied lamps which were suspended over the full-size snooker table.

They were expensive repro, none of your old rubbish. A thick-pile red carpet ate up the sound of the rather large feet stepping over it on this particular evening. Although there was a fully equipped bar, Frank was circulating amongst his nineteen men with a bottle in his hand. He knew better than to offer them free run of his stock. They'd be on the Scotch and the Bacardi like suckling babes if he let them. Besides, he felt it was something of an extended duty of his to try to give them some kind of extracurricular education. Tonight he was tickling their tastebuds with a rather nice little number that he had picked up from a Spanish trip a year ago. It hadn't been laid down because it was a relatively young little red. Just good enough for this bunch, but not for his other associates. Everyone was relaxing, beginning to chat and tell jokes. That was good. Just as he wanted it to be. He winked at his son, Chris. Impetuous young buck! Just like Frank himself had been at that age. Needed to get it out of his system somehow though. Frank should have had him boxing or something, instead of letting all his energy bubble up, contained like a bottle of fizzy, ready to burst when the pressure got too much.

'First a toast, lads,' he called when he had filled everyone's glass. 'To our dear friend and colleague Harry. A brave and loyal comrade. May he rest in peace.'

They raised their glasses. 'Harry!' the voices said in unison.

Frank held a cap above his head. 'For his widow. I'm starting a fund at the station, but we'll get it going here tonight. Dig deep in your pockets, lads. Remember what a good man he was.' Frank placed a fifty-quid note in first and then handed the cap to his son. Without a moment's hesitation, Chris matched his father's donation and passed the cap on.

Frank continued: 'And to a successful operation. I would like to thank you all for your co-operation in these difficult times, and to say that your tact and diplomacy

228

requires devotion beyond the call of duty – for which I am truly grateful. Well done!'

He beamed at the eager faces around him, Frank prided himself on his ability to motivate such a closely knit team. Each man could be relied upon to fulfil his chosen duty to the last. They were brave in the face of adversity and danger. He knew he could count on them to carry out any orders he gave them, however dangerous or unorthodox. He knew without any shadow of doubt that he would be obeyed unquestioningly. He knew this, because if there were any dissenters in the group, they too would be having a cap passed around on their families' behalf. Harry had been a good man, his only fault being that he had been too greedy. While Frank still regretted the way the boys had handled the affair themselves, he was, in a funny kind of way, proud – especially of his son, Chris.

'And so to business.' Frank drew the double-lined floor-length red and green patterned velvet curtains. He had already swept the room for electronic devices. The men were completely contained in these headquarters of his. Anyone who happened to know about this little gathering would only think that Detective Sergeant Thompson's team were having a friendly get-together. Good for morale. Besides, it was clear that this particular division worked very well together. They were a good bunch of lads, Frank thought proudly. During his years in the police he had seen many such men rise through the ranks, and now they occupied various posts around the entire force, some in very high positions indeed. It gave Frank a huge sense of security to realize just how widespread his select little network had become.

Frank turned off the lights and moved to the overhead projector. He had a number of transparencies ready. He used a long white cane to indicate areas of the diagrams.

'Here is the back entrance to the house,' he began, pointing. 'You will see that there is a low wall over which suspects may try and escape. I suggest that three of you remain in that vicinity, and that as we break the door down at the front, another four of you rush in through the back door at the same time. I shall obtain authorization for the use of firearms, as usual. All drugs found on the sight are to be confiscated and dealt with in the usual way. The higher the number of casualties, the better. As we all know, London will be a much safer place if we can reduce the number of these crack gangs . . .' and, he could have added, our competition!

Much later, as the boys prepared to leave Frank's little soirée, he called Chris back.

'I've got a little job for you, son. It's a bit sensitive, but I think you can handle it . . .'

Flora twiddled the tap with her toe and luxuriated as the tub heated up, letting the hot foam swirl around her. She was busy thinking about exactly what she would wear for her date. The music from the CD belted out Annie Lennox. She turned the tap off and closed her eyes. As the song blared out she opened her mouth and shrieked along with the chorus. The truth of it was, she had rather mixed feelings about the evening ahead. While she was looking forward to the actual going out, she hadn't managed quite to rationalize her feelings about the person she was about to go out with. He was good company – or so she thought from what little she knew of him – and he was a copper. The problem was that part of her couldn't decide whether she had misgivings about going out with him because he was a copper – and because her newly acquired middle-class ethics warned her that this was not the sort of bloke she should be going out with, the other part of her had decided that because of her suspicions about herself and her potential snobbery, she absolutely had to go out with him in order to prove to herself that she wasn't becoming a snob.

They had met through work – sort of. She had almost fallen into him coming out of the Old Bailey. She had had such a large pile of papers to stagger under that she could barely see over the top. He had very kindly offered to help get her into a cab – which, owing to the rain, had taken a good fifteen minutes to find – and he had been easy and ordinary, and refreshing compared to the usual hothouse flowers she had to endure all day long. He was nice-looking too. Black hair and brown eyes, like a tall version of Tom Cruise only without the big nose.

Yes, she was looking forward to it, she told herself. She'd wear jeans, and a white shirt and her big brown leather jacket. She laughed as she stepped out of the bath. Chris would probably have a fit when he saw her out of her usual penguin garb. Funny how she'd been thinking to herself that it was about time she got a bit of romance into her life again.

Gus arrived back just as Flora was heading out. She tried to hide her disappointment. Quite frankly the Davis case had really been getting her down and she'd been looking forward to an evening talking things over with Flora.

'Have a great time,' Gus called after her.

She opened up a bottle of white wine and sat down at the kitchen table, trying not to mind her solitary status. At least she avoided ghastly complications this way. Gus was beginning to despair of any form of romantic involvement ever working out in her life. All she had to remember was a stream of disasters ending in total unhappiness. Luckily James's new parliamentary career was taking up most of his time and he was rarely to be seen in chambers. She could now view him, and many of his contemporaries, as rather egotistical, highly opinionated, and possessing the same degree of human fallibility as ordinary mortals. The realization had done wonders for her confidence and her maturity. While she still had the utmost respect for his skill, the respect no longer went hand in hand with deferential, almost blind obedience. The spirit of confidence had helped her through difficult courtroom clashes, where she had been pitched against more experienced counsel and found herself able to spar and parry without being affected by novice's nerves.

She wondered how James was getting on with Mirabelle – *if* they were still getting on! Gus fully expected that Mirabelle would have lost interest as soon as she knew Gus had dropped out of the race. Mirabelle knew only jealousy and competition. She was a pathetic figure who should be pitied. Gus was perceptive enough to realize that Mirabelle had not found happiness through her actions. While she thought she was using the men to hurt Gus – as she had thought by 'stealing' James, even after Gus had found out about Esme the superwoman – she was at the same time hurting herself, using her own body as a tool of malice. There was no pleasure or fulfilment in that. But that was something only Mirabelle could find out for herself. Mirabelle was as much a victim as Gus had been, in an odd sort of way – a victim of her own insecurities.

It was the thought of the men themselves that fuelled the anger in Gus's heart, of the trust she had bestowed upon them each time. And the simple act of betrayal, so unnecessary, so selfish and ultimately transient. Mirabelle's style wasn't to form lasting relationships with any of them. She just wanted to hang around long enough to let Gus know that she had scored another few points over her. No, what angered Gus more than anything was the fact that Jonathan and James had been too weak and too selfish just to say a simple 'no'. Somewhere on this earth, somewhere, sometime in the future, there had to be an exception. Trouble was, the way she felt about men right now, even if she fell over him in the street, she probably wouldn't want to know!

Chapter Twenty-Two

Tom Silverthorn waited in the swanky reception area of Maverick Productions while the receptionist told Mirabelle Angeletti of his arrival. He hoped maybe he'd get a feel for the family through Mirabelle, if he played the chummy media bit on her. It had been one of the researchers back at the paper who'd come up with the connection. Coincidentally she had a friend who'd temped for Maverick Productions and they had gossiped about what Mirabelle Angeletti had been like to work for. Apparently she was an absolute bitch, but Tom didn't take too much notice of that. In the media world a lot of women were bitches. Some women didn't just file their nails to make them look pretty, they honed them into offensive weapons in order to beat off the competition as they climbed the ladder of ambition. Tom was not unused to the type. Indeed, some of his best friends were bitches!

A direct approach to Mirabelle had got him immediate results, with a meeting arranged over the phone.

He picked up a copy of the Maverick promotional brochure. There were mug shots of Maverick personnel, and rundowns of their previous work. Mirabelle didn't seem to have a very long history. She'd studied at film school and then become a researcher at the BBC, then on to senior researcher at Maverick. No doubt she'd either screw the boss next or move on to some other independent – if she was any good, that was. Her credits listed the *Justice on Trial* series which he vaguely remembered. That prat Kentish, who'd just gone and won the candidacy for Bulsworth, had fronted the thing. Tom studied the small picture of the attractive blonde cynically. She'd certainly given him a leg up – and possibly a leg over as well – for his career. That was something else Tom had to find out: what was the connection between Kentish, Augusta and this sister? Was it just that Augusta happened to be Kentish's pupil or had Mirabelle Angeletti's programmes bought Augusta a tenancy? Was Kentish somehow involved in some shady deals? Tom was beginning to feel just the tiniest bit confident about his story proposal. He hated Establishment hypocrisy and self-seeking so-called public servants and he had enough leads now to blow several things apart!

He put the brochure back on to the coffee table just in time to see Mirabelle Angeletti walk into reception. She paused at the desk without looking in his direction, and checked through what he assumed to be a pile of messages. His first impression was that she looked like a Sindy doll. All long blonde hair, so blonde as to be almost artificial, but for some reason he sensed that it probably wasn't. She had endlessly long legs, which were bare and tanned, ending in the sharp points of black stilettos. She wore a short red dress, belted at a waist so slim he felt he could have squeezed both hands around it and found his fingers and thumbs meeting in the middle. She flicked her hair back over her shoulder and turned towards him. He was too much of a shrewd cookie to miss the initial contempt which crossed her too-perfect features. As the veil lowered over her turquoise eyes and her scarlet lip gloss stretched into a smile, Tom wondered idly if she'd had a nose job. It seemed so small, so neat, so taut that he felt it couldn't possibly have just formed like that. Still, he wasn't particularly interested in whatever arrangements Mirabelle had or had not made with a plastic surgeon. He wanted to know all about her family.

'Let me buy you lunch,' he said quickly, before she had even managed to get out a 'hello'.

'No, no, I don't think I can,' she said quickly, taking in his battered donkey jacket and his very nearly threadbare green cords.

'Then how about we just trot round to the local wine bar?'

Mirabelle relaxed. That was a far safer option. The last thing she wanted was to lumber herself with this tramp for too long. At least in the wine bar she could hide him in the shadows, away from everyone's prying eyes.

'Sure, that's a good idea. I'll collect my bag and join you outside in two minutes.'

'Great,' Tom grinned back. His usual ploy had worked. Give them two ghastly suggestions and then they'll opt for the lesser of the two evils, which is usually the one you wanted them to do in the first place. If Tom had breezed in and invited her out to the wine bar, she'd no doubt have told him she could just about manage a quick coffee in the office. All set and ready to go . . .

So different had Tom Silverthorn been from all her expectations that Mirabelle had decided to invite him back to her place for a home-cooked meal that evening. He had turned out to be very interesting. What she needed more than anything was ideas and be they borrowed, shared or just plain stolen wasn't important so long as they were ideas. She needed to get John Stapleford stroking his bloody nose again and Tom Silverthorn might be just the person she was looking for to fire up her imagination. A bottle of champagne was chilling in the fridge, and a further two bottles of red wine were breathing next to the hob. Mirabelle loathed cooking, but that wasn't a problem as the caterers had delivered the supper ten minutes earlier and it was now sitting in the warming oven, ready for whenever they felt like it.

Mirabelle turned the music down a shade, and started

236

to light the many candles dotted around the apartment. Then she disappeared into the bathroom, gave herself a last spray of Poison and, after checking her cleavage, decided to undo yet another button on the dark blue silk shirt which was tucked into her tight, white satin jeans. The doorbell rang and she looked at her watch: he was a mere five minutes late. Keen!

When she opened the door she noticed that he had discarded his disgusting old corduroys in favour of blue denims, and a black shirt which was buttoned up to the neck. His hair, which curled to his shoulders, was a rather nice shade of honey, like pale butterscotch, making him look younger than twenty-nine. Mirabelle noted a long lean face; piercing delphinium-blue eyes above chiselled cheekbones; a slightly unshaven chin; long rangy legs, slim hips and waist, but broad shoulders. He had a good body. His fingers were long and delicate; artistic-looking. Watching them curl around the glass she wondered whether they were indicative of the length of his cock.

'Let's just drink and relax before we eat,' she said, inviting him to sit down. 'It's ready whenever we want it. The salmon's poaching in the oven. I do hope you like hollandaise sauce.'

Tom took a large drink from the glass. She was just the sort of woman his mother had warned him about: mad, bad and dangerous. But his northern upbringing had well equipped him to deal with Mirabelle's sort of high-class tart.

'I've been thinking about what we discussed earlier.' Mirabelle's voice was silky and seductive. 'About the justice series and possibly expanding it to cover reconstructions, the victims, maybe even getting the victims to confront the perpetrators, that sort of thing. Could be sensational . . .'

She rolled her tongue around the outside of an olive and then popped the green orb into her mouth and crunched it between her teeth. Tom laughed inwardly. If he didn't watch himself, he'd be part of tonight's menu along with the salmon.

'Maybe,' she continued, 'we could involve the police too. Perhaps do some sort of exposé on the way they work . . .'

'Oh I don't think I'd be interested in working on anything to do with the police,' Tom lied smoothly. 'That's really not my sort of field – no, what I'd be interested in getting into would be the dichotomy between what's known as white-collar crime, such as fraud, insider dealing, computer stuff, the difference between what sort of sentences are passed for white-collar crime and the sort of common or garden crime the rest of us mere mortals get involved in. What do you get? Three years in an open prison. Half-time remission for good behaviour, or if you've gone a bit bonkers you get out straight away. Well, that really pisses me off, Mirabelle. But I'm keen on getting to know how these guys work. Where do they come from? Where do they hide their money? How do they get away with it? How many payoffs do they have to make and is it still worth it, even if they get caught? I mean, your stepfather probably knows loads of these sort of guys. I bet he's swimming with them. Maybe he might have some contacts he could suggest to you, Mirabelle.'

He paused, waiting to see if she'd take the bait.

'My dear Tom,' Mirabelle splashed some more champagne into his glass. 'I wouldn't be at all surprised if my stepfather was one of those men you're talking about!' She giggled at him. '"Course I'm only joking, but he is such a mystery man. No family, no relatives at all. To this day my mother and I have simply no idea of where he came from. And he absolutely refuses to discuss it. No, I think you're absolutely right, Tom. Maybe Piers could be helpful . . .'

Tom leaned back into the sofa as Mirabelle warmed to

her subject, and briefly wondered what it would feel like to be coated in warm hollandaise sauce.

Gus was late. She broke into a sort of half-run, burdened by her case full of papers and the umbrella which kept catching the freak July wind and threatening to turn inside out. Her eyes were fixed on ground level, watchful of water-filled potholes. She'd been caught out before on Fleet Street's worn pavements. Holes three inches deep lurked invisibly under the puddles, ready to swamp one's shoes.

'OOPS!' she cried out involuntarily as her bag tumbled to the ground, sending her tripping over it and half falling into the wet. 'Aaah!' she cried as she hit concrete.

The idiot responsible bent over her, trying to pick her up. 'God, I'm sorry,' he cried. 'How clumsy of me. Let me help you. Here, take my arm.'

'Well, really,' Gus snapped. 'You could have been looking where you were going.'

'I know, I know, I'm terribly sorry. Look at you, all wet. And your knee – oh dear. You've grazed it.' A large strong hand went under her elbow and gently pulled her back to her feet. Then he stooped to collect her briefcase. Gus was trying to brush the dirt from her skirt.

'My umbrella,' she shouted as the thing blew clumsily towards an oncoming bus. Too late. It crunched miserably under a giant tyre. 'Great! That's just about all I need.' She straightened up and found herself looking into a pair of the bluest eyes she had ever seen. The rather rugged-looking face was regarding her sympathetically.

'I'm awfully sorry.' His voice was deep and gentle. 'Where are you going? You can share my umbrella – in fact why not have my umbrella? It's entirely my fault that yours got crushed. It's the least I can do.'

Gus pursed her lips, about to snap some clever retort, and then something about the face, a gentleness in it, stopped her. 'Don't worry, I'm not going far. Just down to El Vino. It's only a few yards away. I can manage, thanks.'

'Well, that's good, because that's exactly where I'm headed. Come on, we'll walk together.'

'Oh,' Gus said, somewhat taken aback. But she couldn't think of a good reason why she shouldn't just walk with him. 'Okay. That's fine.' She grinned up at him. He was at least six inches taller than she was, and although he brought the umbrella down to rest on top of his head, the rain still swept sideways underneath it, towards her face.

'Dear oh dear, this doesn't seem to be working, does it? I'm too big. Here, you take the umbrella and I'll walk behind.'

'Then you'll get soaked.'

'So? What's a little soaking every now and then? It's the only way.'

'Thanks.' Gus took the handle as they walked the last few yards to the bar.

'My name's Tom, by the way, Tom Silverthorn,' he said, holding the door open for her.

'And I'm Augusta, Augusta Lawrence. But everyone calls me Gus.'

'Hello, Gus. Would you let me buy you a drink as I seem to have got you soaked and bleeding in the first five minutes of our acquaintance? I'd like to made amends somehow.'

'Well, I'm supposed to be meeting someone . . .' Gus scanned the tables but there was no sign of Clive as yet. That was a good omen. Perhaps he was actually getting somewhere with this witness of his.

'A quick one with me?'

'Oh, okay, thanks. Dry white wine, please. Shall I grab a table?'

'Sure, I'll come and join you.'

The only free table Gus could find was way over in a dark corner, out of sight of the door. She wondered if Clive would be able to see her. Still, she hoped he knew her well enough by now to realize that if they'd arranged to meet, she'd be there. He'd have enough sense to search for her.

Several moments later Tom ambled over to her, clutching a bottle under one arm, and a glass in each hand. 'I thought as I'm having the same it would be easier to get a bottle. I hope you don't mind.'

Gus's eyes narrowed briefly. She hated any kind of pick-up and if this guy thought that he could push her over with a couple of glasses of wine . . . Hell, what was she thinking about? It was a filthy night outside, the place was packed, and so what if she had a couple of drinks with him? He folded himself down on to the stool opposite. His knees scraped the underside of the table as he struggled to tuck them underneath. Gus caught the table top as it lurched threateningly.

'Sorry,' he murmured. 'Nobody ever seems to make stools or tables for people my size.'

She smiled at him and watched as he filled her glass to the brim. He had long stringy hair which fell around his shoulders in an untidy mess, no doubt made worse by the rain. His hands were large, with delicately tapering fingers, like those of a musician. She wondered vaguely what he did. He looked rather artistic, sort of unconventional – and interesting, she caught herself thinking. But definitely not her type.

'How's your leg?' he asked, glancing underneath the table.

Gus wriggled her left leg out and was surprised to see a bloody trickle escaping down towards her shin. 'God, I am bleeding, what a nuisance.' She delved into her pocket and pulled out a handkerchief, then proceeded to dab at the graze. A large hole had appeared in her

241

tights. She suddenly realized what a wreck she too must look. Suddenly feeling self-conscious, she touched her hair, smoothing it back into its bun.

To Tom, she had a much softer face than he had at first realized. From a distance she had looked coldly efficient, stark and sexless. But then he hadn't been able to see her soft grey eyes, and the way they sparkled so intelligently at him. She certainly wasn't as plain as he had imagined. The voice was different too – not loud or overbearing like some of these super-educated women who had a habit of wanting everyone in their vicinity, immediate or otherwise, to appreciate just how educated they were. She was rather softly spoken, with a nondescript accent, obviously southern in origin, but vowels not too rounded. He noticed she wore no jewellery: no bracelets, rings or trinkets – unlike her stepsister who had been literally dripping with assets – just a simple pair of knotted gold earrings in her ears. Her nails were filed short and her hands were small, neat, capable. She had a steady, unflinching gaze which was directed fully on him.

'Are you meeting someone?' she asked, suddenly wondering why he had been coming here too.

'Yes, except I'm very early, and they're invariably late. So, just think, if I hadn't fallen over you, I'd be sitting over there and you'd be sitting over here, each of us with nobody to talk to, and having nothing better to do than stare into space trying to look comfortable about it.'

Gus laughed. 'Well, I would have been comfortable about it. I've got a load of papers to read. My time wouldn't have been wasted.'

'You're a barrister, aren't you?'

'How did you guess?' she said, looking down at her stark, soggy black suit.

'Oh, by the wig, I guess.'

'Very clever, seeing as I'm not wearing it. So what do you do?' Gus was surprised at how easy it was to talk to this rather bohemian-looking stranger.

'Guess. I did.'

'Well, it was hardly difficult, seeing as how you fell over me opposite the High Court, that I'm wearing a black suit and white shirt, and that I've got a ton of papers which must make me walk like Quasimodo. Definitely nothing to do with the law,' she said decisively. 'Let's see, how about advertising?'

'No way.'

'You're in a rock band, playing lead guitar or something?'

'No, although I must confess I have played some pretty mean guitars in my time.'

'Photographer? Am I getting warm – some sort of artist?'

'Maybe. A tiny bit warm.'

'I know. You're a sheep farmer down from Lincolnshire.'

'No, Gus, I'm not a sheep farmer, and I'm from Nottinghamshire.'

'A cow farmer?' The wine was going to her head. She suddenly remembered, too late, that she'd skipped lunch.

'Now you're not being serious.'

'Unfortunately I have to spend almost every waking minute being serious and it can get awfully tedious at times. Anyway, I've got it. You're a journalist, aren't you?'

'Very good. How did you guess?'

'Because you've got those ridiculous pink *Financial Times* socks on. And as you're clearly nothing to do with the City, you had to be something to do with the newspaper. You're on the *FT*, right?'

'Used to be. Now I'm on the *Sunday Journal*. On their investigations team,' he said, watching her reaction very carefully.

'You mean you're one of those journalists who spend their time crawling through other people's rubbish, training obscenely large lenses on poor unsuspecting innocents in the hope of getting some tawdry little scoop on the front page of your newspaper in return for ruining some poor wretch's life?'

Tom smiled at her, unruffled. He was well used to this turn of conversation. 'Absolutely right. We're the ones who expose the bent MPs, inform the public about the way their revered – and salaried – royals really behave, who weed out naughty public servants who've misappropriated funds, tell the voters about gerrymandering politicians ... that sort of rubbish. It's a great service to the public, and I'm proud of it.'

'I suppose one would need to justify your distasteful occupation in some way.'

'And what about you, Gus? How many guilty criminals do you try to get off? How many innocent men and women are you going to fail in the years to come? What documents will you neglect to reveal to the other side in order to suit your client? And how do you sleep at night? Or does the uniform and the silly hat absolve you from all that? Why do barristers need to hide, after all?'

'So what are you saying, Tom? That we both perform a necessary function which at times is distasteful and dishonest in order to serve the interests of the great British public? The difference is that I can only work on facts. The trouble with your lot is that a lot of your damage is based on rumour and supposition. I limit while you engineer.'

'But sometimes it must be difficult for you, to stay a disinterested party, to remain independent when dealing with certain sectors of the criminal fraternity?'

He was sticking his neck out to see what kind of a response he would get. He watched her closely for the smallest flicker of guilt, or fear, or whatever.

'I don't see what difference there should be to my independence when dealing with any sector. Unless of course you're banging on about the boring old chestnut

244

of how could I possibly defend a rapist, or wife batterer or such like. You know the answers to that.'

'Of course. Innocent until proven guilty, et cetera, et cetera. That wasn't quite what I meant, but never mind.'

She was either being deliberately obtuse, or she really didn't have a clue what he was driving at. So far he had found no evidence to link Augusta with any of her father's past activities. Her schooling, her time at university, her friends and associates and so on were all squeaky clean to the point of dullness. She had an impeccable educational background, winning prizes at every junction of her career so far. She led a fairly quiet existence, out of the limelight, away from the gossip columns, with little outward trappings to show she was heiress to an immense fortune. So far as Tom could gather she lived rather modestly, albeit it in a rather smart mews house, but she drove a sensible little Peugeot, dressed soberly, didn't smoke and had had so few romances in her life as to be almost virginal. Hardly the archetypal bent lawyer image he had expected to find. Unless of course she was just plain clever – which, of course, he knew she was!

Whatever, he didn't have further time to pursue the thought because Gus's date had turned up. Tom eyed him lazily, taking in his rather rotund figure, his neat haircut which had been ruffled by the rain and his beige trenchcoat. Whoever he was, he certainly didn't look too relaxed about something. As Gus introduced them, the guy he now knew to be called Clive sat down beside Gus, hardly acknowledging Tom's presence at all. Gus looked vaguely uncomfortable, obviously hoping that Tom would now make his excuses and leave them. Tom had no such intention.

Gus had expected to find Clive exuberant after the weeks and weeks of hitting his head against a brick wall. But he looked ghastly – ashen!

'Clive, whatever is it? What happened? How did the meeting go?'

Tom played nonchalant, staring at his shoes.

'The meeting didn't go at all, Gus. I didn't arrive in time . . .'

'What do you mean? You were late? Well, can't you see the guy later?'

'No. He's dead, Gus. I've just seen his widow. He was killed in a freak accident this morning. It seems he stepped in front of an articulated lorry by Wandsworth Common. He was killed instantly.'

Gus's face crumpled with disbelief.

Tom butted in quietly, 'I'm sorry. Obviously someone you knew . . .'

'Would have liked to have known, if I'd had the chance,' Clive said darkly.

Gus's mind was racing, all sorts of terrible thoughts flashing through her imagination. 'I think we'd better go.'

'Sure, of course,' Tom said, his voice full of concern. 'What happened? Who? God, how terrible for you.'

'Sorry, Tom, but Clive and I really must . . .'

The sort of conversation she intended having with Clive was not for the ears of anyone – and certainly not a self-confessed investigative journalist. She stood up and Tom stood also.

'Here's my card. If you ever need a journalist, this is where you'll find me.'

Gus just managed to smile weakly. 'Thanks, Tom, for the drink and the chat. It really was nice meeting you.'

Tom nodded and watched them go. Whatever was going on between those two, it had certainly shaken up that solicitor bloke – for Tom had guessed immediately that was what he must be – and Gus. And somebody had been stiffed. He would head straight back to the newsroom and find out whoever the victim was, and also try and find out why Gus and her sidekick Clive were interested in him. Never a dull moment, he thought to himself as he picked up his soggy umbrella.

His file on Thompson and his team was growing fatter by the day, Piers Lawrence's history was almost completed, now all he had to do was solve the riddle of the connection between Lawrence's daughter and the Harry Chapman murder. It wouldn't surprise Tom to learn that Thompson had set the poor Davis bloke up with a duff defence in order to make sure he was convicted for the murder. That was the obvious scenario. But somehow, having met Miss Lawrence, the image that came over didn't sit happily with the possibility that she could be extremely bent. Unfortunately, he had found himself actually liking the woman. He shook his head to himself. No doubt he'd have a few more meetings with her before the end of the case!

Chapter Twenty-Three

Winston had been told that he'd be placed on a Section 43 'for his own good'. He'd almost felt grateful, so naïve was he. He wished now he'd had the foresight to refuse this little courtesy the prison system had extended to him. Section 43 was where all the sex offenders ended up: the rapists, and the child molesters and other depraved individuals who were kept locked up separately for their own safety. The trouble was, when Winston was allowed to spend time with the other remand prisoners, he was invariably beaten to a pulp on the mistaken assumption that he must be some kind of sexual demon.

Winston just couldn't seem to find any peace in his heart or his body any more. The screws kicked him almost hourly, he suffered a constant stream of humiliation and oppression, other prisoners spat in his food or worse, and he was completely isolated from anything and everything he had taken for granted in his previous life. He had no pride, no sense of self any more. He was dirty and abused and felt no good. Most of the day he just sat on the bed, staring into space, wishing it would all end, that something would release him from this living hell. There didn't seem to be anything to live for any more. He was an embarrassment to his beloved daughter – making her life as much of a nightmare as his own. She had been so good, coming up to Cheshire for the short visits allowed on Saturday afternoons. Poor Andrea. What a birthday present he had given her. He shrivelled back on to the hard bed and tried to remember the good things, the happy times in his life. Only the life inside his head had the power to soothe and comfort him any more. Everything on the exterior was cruel and alien. He just wanted to retreat, to disappear into the world inside himself. If only he could just do that for ever, block off everything else, just like dreaming, drifting in the warmth of his subconscious, away from the world.

Mirabelle was in a particularly ratty mood and Alice, her secretary, was trying very hard to keep a low profile. Mirabelle's mood usually came in two assortments: bad and not quite so bad, but today was extremely bad.

'Are you sure there aren't any other messages?' Mirabelle had come out of her office for the third time in an hour and was looming over Alice's desk. She drummed her long red fingernails on the blond oak surface.

'I told you, Mirabelle, you've had them all. There aren't any others.'

'And none yesterday either,' Mirabelle snapped, half to herself. 'And no faxes?'

'Well, yes, there have been several faxes. But none from Tom Thornthingy.'

'Silverthorn! Huh!' She whirled away from the desk and stomped back into her own office. Dammit. She'd rung Tom's office at least half a dozen times in the past three days and still he hadn't returned any of her calls. Damn, damn, damn! She needed his help, she needed his ideas so that she could get something together for John Stapleford. Since the James Kentish series had finished, she was on a bit of a low simmer as far as her career was concerned. The series had been highly successful and the programmes had received well above average ratings for an early-evening doc spot, resulting in Mirabelle's promotion from senior researcher to assistant producer. Now she needed a decent follow-up, and Tom's idea of a crime series could be developed very nicely. But it would be difficult to research it by herself, and at this early stage she didn't want to sow the idea in anyone else's mind. She picked up the phone and tried his number again.

'Tom Silverthorn? Yeah, he's here somewhere ... who's calling?'

'Mirabelle. Tell him Mirabelle Angeletti ...' She waited, listening to the frantic sound of a newspaper news desk filtering through the earpiece. 'Tom ...' she sighed at last as someone retrieved the phone at the other end.

'No, sorry, love. He seems to have disappeared ...'

Mirabelle threw the phone back down in frustration. The shit was obviously avoiding her. She'd have to go and see him, catch up with him at his office. She had to get him to help her. Even though she hadn't managed to seduce him the other night, she knew he'd found it difficult to tear himself away. This time she'd make sure that she got to know him a whole lot better before letting him escape. No man avoided Mirabelle – at least not once they had discovered the depth of her charms.

She was wearing one of her shortest skirts – a Jasper Conran pink stretch jersey number which clung to her perfectly conditioned butt – sheer tights and high heels. Her hair was brushed straight and long, held back in a pastel pink Alice band. She stood in the doorway of the news room and searched for Tom. A smile spread over her face as she spotted him on the far side of the room. She crossed the room, weaving in between the islands of computers and serious-faced hacks swapping their attention between banks of telephones and VDU monitors. As always, she was conscious of the curious and admiring looks she was getting. She swung her hips lazily, knowing her bum was keeping most of the journalists mesmerized.

Tom looked up just as she reached the far side of the room. Mirabelle's eyes narrowed as she could have sworn she saw him curse silently. Then he smiled, but only briefly. Remarkably he turned his back on her and continued with his conversation. Dammit, he was hardly going to acknowledge her. What the hell did he think she was doing here?

'Tom,' she called out, 'darling ...' louder. She'd embarrass him unless he paid her some attention.

'Hi ... you okay?' he said stepping towards her. She tilted her cheek, expecting at the very least to receive a peck on it, but instead he grabbed her elbow and pulled her to one side, and out of his way. 'Excuse me, I've got to catch someone. You weren't looking for me, were you?'

Mirabelle felt her cheeks colour, aware that the entire staff of fifteen or so were watching the pair of them. 'Of course I was looking for you.' She kept her voice low. 'You didn't return any of my calls and I felt we should talk some more.'

'God, Mirabelle. I feel bad about that. But the thing is, I'm really busy. I've got a story to finish off for tomorrow –' he looked at his watch – 'and my deadline's in an hour's time. Tell you what, I'll call you when I can. Oh, by the way,' he called as he strode away, 'thanks for a great supper.'

Unable to stop herself, she called after him, 'What about tonight – later on?'

'Can't. Sorry.'

'Tomorrow?'

'Got to stay loose, Mirabelle. Can't say at the moment. I'll call you. See ya around.'

Mirabelle bit her lip angrily and stomped out of the room. Bastard, bastard. Absolute bastard. He'd used her. She'd gone to all that trouble giving him a champagne dinner and he'd bloody well used her. Well, people didn't get away with that so easily. If he wouldn't help her with the story, she'd bloody well do it on her own and show him ... Keeping her waiting for his bloody phone call, making a fool of her, making her feel like some cheap tart. She was Mirabelle Angeletti and people didn't treat her like that.

By the time she got back to her office she had decided on her first plan of action. She punched out a telephone number and waited for the recorded message to finish.

'I'd like to commission some independent research of a rather sensitive nature. Call me.' Doug Sanders was one of the best private dicks she had come across. Expensive, but thorough. And unless she wanted to do the dirty work herself, she had no choice but to make use of him. Above all, this idea Tom had inspired had to be kept secret from her colleagues.

Flora was feeling the teeniest bit apprehensive as she finished the salad off. She threw the croutons into the bowl and then dolloped the blue cheese and garlic dressing over the top. She felt starving. Hopefully Chris would turn up soon. This was the first time she had cooked for them. In the last week they had been out for a pizza, a Chinese, taken in a movie, and been clubbing on Saturday night/Sunday morning. And all while Flora had been trying to keep her work up to date. She was feeling pretty exhausted, but that was one of the perks which went with the job. She hadn't really been out with anyone like Chris before. He was not how she'd imagined a typical cop to be. For one thing he was a graduate – a humanities degree from Sheffield five years ago – which at twenty-six put him at just two years older than she. As yet, she hadn't learned too much about his background. They seemed to have spent most of their time talking about her, and her life with Gus. Every detail of it seemed to be fascinating to Chris. She had found it mildly flattering to discover the kind of awe with which he viewed the almost secret world of barristers and courts. They had shared, and giggled over, their courtroom experiences. It was refreshing to find someone who didn't feel they had to pretend that there was nothing remotely intimidating about the corridors of justice. She assumed from his accent that Chris was probably originally from London, but which part she didn't know. So far they hadn't discussed families in any detail.

Perhaps she'd ask him tonight. At last the doorbell buzzed and Flora skipped down the stairs to welcome her guest.

Chris Thompson let out a gasp as he stepped into the sitting room. 'This place is quite something ... your friend Gus must be pretty loaded. When am I going to meet her?'

'She'll probably be back soon. Her father's pretty wealthy. I'm just lucky enough to be able to share it with her. Come on into the kitchen and I'll find you a drink.'

Chris's eyes were everywhere, taking it all in – the furniture, the paintings, the trinkets around the place. He stopped to look at the small round table over which Gus had arranged a selection of photographs, and where the telephone sat. Then he followed Flora into the kitchen.

'What's Gus's father do?'

'Has anyone ever told you you're very nosy?' Flora teased.

'I'm a cop. I have this need to know everything.'

Flora giggled. 'He's an international art dealer. Piers Lawrence. In the art world he's pretty well known.'

'Never heard of him,' Chris grinned as Flora passed him a glass of white wine. 'Cheers.'

'Tell you what, Chris, why don't you go and relax in the sitting room while I finish off in here? Switch on the box, if you like. I'll join you in a few minutes.'

'Can't I do anything? It smells great. Let me help ...'

'No.' Flora shoved him towards the door. 'This is my treat tonight. You just go and put your feet up.'

Chris seated himself down next to the little table,

listened carefully to Flora bustling around the kitchen next door, and got to work.

Much later, when Chris and Flora were clearing away the last of the plates, Gus appeared. Flora greeted her cheerfully.

'Gus, come and meet Chris. Chris, this is Gus.'

Gus smiled at Flora's new man. 'Hi, Chris,' she said warmly. 'Welcome to our home. I can tell you guys must have had a great supper – I can smell it.'

'And guess what – there's some in the oven for you. I thought you'd be hungry. I'm afraid we polished off all the salad, but there's still plenty of spicy chicken. Help yourself.'

'Flora, you really are an angel. I think I'll take a tray upstairs. I'm absolutely bushed. Today's been hell –' She broke off as the phone rang. 'Oh God, I bet that's for me,' she sighed, grabbing the receiver. Flora continued to sort out the cafetiere while Chris got the cups off the dresser.

'Clive!' Gus's voice rose in surprise. 'Good news?' she paused. Flora and Chris kept politely quiet. 'You say you've found a witness who'll talk?' Gus glanced at Flora and Chris. 'Hang on a minute, Clive, I'll just move next door. Excuse me, you two,' she explained, 'but it's business. I'll take it in the other room.'

Chris hovered by the door, listening easily to Gus's voice carrying across the corridor. His lips tightened as the conversation came to an end.

'A quick coffee and then I'd better be off,' he murmured apologetically to Flora as they sat themselves down at the kitchen table once more. 'I've got an early start tomorrow.'

'Good idea,' Flora said brightly. 'Me too. I still haven't recovered from crawling in at 6 a.m. on Sunday morning.'

'You ladies work hard, don't you? There's poor Gus still taking calls at 10.30 at night.'

'She's got a big trial coming up. No doubt she'll be working through many nights from now on. This is nothing unusual. Anyway, let's forget about work. Tell me again about that friend of yours – the one who's sailing round the world. That sounds like a lot more fun than working!'

Reluctantly Chris turned the subject. He'd much rather have been talking about work – especially Gus's.

Chapter Twenty-Four

The receptionist announced the caller to Clive. Clive's nerves were feeling shattered and frayed. He had other clients who needed servicing, but most of his waking hours were taken up with the Davis case. He had a committal to attend this afternoon, and a sentencing tomorrow morning, though neither of the cases required him to do much in the way of paperwork. He was completely *au fait* with the cases in hand. He dreaded speaking to Andrea Coleman, Winston Davis's daughter, because he never had any good news to give her. She was a charming girl, well educated, polite, and so trusting in Clive's ability to secure her father's freedom and sort everything out.

It had been Andrea who had instructed Clive in the first place, after discovering that the duty solicitor provided by the police had been worse than hopeless in looking after Winston's rights. Andrea and her junior doctor husband had come to see him and told him of their father's version of the events which had led up to his arrest and subsequent murder charge. In a way, Clive would have found it easier if Andrea had occasionally lost her temper and screamed and railed at him, like many of his other clients had done in the past. She seemed to be so passive, and so trusting that it made Clive feel even more impotent. With a heavy heart he spoke into the mouthpiece.

'Mr Parfitt,' Andrea's voice sounded distant, muffled and hollow, 'it's about my father . . .'

'Yes, I was just thinking about him. The file's here in front of me.'

'He's dead, Mr Parfitt. He was found early this morning. It seems . . .' her voice cracked, '. . . he hanged himself.'

Clive held his breath, unable to think, to breathe. A lead weight pressed on his chest. His mind spun. 'Andrea . . . I . . . I'm so sorry!'

'I thought you should know, Mr Parfitt. I'm afraid I have to go now. It's all too difficult . . .'

'Yes, of course, I understand. Goodbye, Andrea.' He replaced the receiver, feeling as if he would throw up.

Some hours later, Gus reread the fax which had just arrived. It was professional, straight to the point. 'The case against Mr Winston Davis will not be proceeding as I regret to tell you that he appears to have taken his own life. Would you please therefore return all relevant documents to my office. Clive Parfitt.'

Woodenly she collected up the papers and tied them into a neat bundle. Then she organized for them to be DX-ed to Parfitt and Brownley, Solicitors. So, that was that. End of case. No more worrying about lack of disclosure, missing witnesses or police obstructiveness. She could concentrate on other things now. She wouldn't have to lie awake at night thinking of the surrounding implications of the whole Davis affair. She was, after all, a professional. Distance and objectivity intact! She had not allowed herself to become emotionally involved. She had, as with all her other cases, simply been going through the motions. Then why, she suddenly asked herself, did she have tears streaming down her cheeks?

Gus had just stepped out of the bath when the telephone rang. She had left chambers early, feeling grotty and depressed. She had treated herself to a long soak in Flora's new bubbles and was thinking of curling up with a good video to try to take her mind off her work and the nightmare of Winston Davis.

'Hi, Daddy,' she sighed, too tired even to register surprise at his call. She listened while he spoke, noticing that he sounded agitated, nervous almost – which was completely out of character. It seemed he wanted to see her about something which he couldn't discuss over the telephone. He would meet her at Claridge's.

'But I've just got out of the bath – my hair – I'm ready for bed . . .'

He listened to her protests but was insistent. Reluctantly she agreed. She would be there in an hour. As she quickly got herself ready, Gus wondered whether he had, at last, decided to talk about the past – but if so, why now?

Gus sipped slowly at her brandy, while Piers was clearly struggling with whatever it was he had to tell her. She waited patiently, not wishing to interrupt his thoughts. Whatever he had to say, it was obviously important, and she very much wanted to hear it.

'Gus, I'm sure it comes as no surprise to you to realize that over the years I have done business with many people from all walks of life . . .'

Gus raised an eyebrow. The image of Frank Thompson's face, hazy as it was, swam into her mind, together with Dickie's comments.

' . . . some grand, some not so grand, some, well, old money and some new.' He flicked her a quick glance. 'Thing is,' he continued hesitantly, 'unfortunate as it may seem, I do have some so-called shady connections, some –' he put up his hands in case she should interrupt – 'good customers, but I guess one could say that one might be dubious about the origin of some of their money. Naturally one never really knows just what sort of a client one is dealing with. After all,' he laughed awkwardly, 'one can hardly go asking, can one? So unwittingly, you might say, I have been involved with certain factions over the years.'

Gus took a deep breath and another slug of brandy. 'I'm not a fool, Daddy. I guess it's the same with any business, isn't it? Anyone with serious money – new money – has either come by it by fair or foul means. It's not always easy to know the difference. And I suppose sometimes there can be a very fine line between the two.'

Piers grinned at her and leaned back into the sofa, appearing to relax slightly. Gus was always full of surprises. He hadn't expected her to be half so understanding.

'And I do learn what the criminal fraternity gets up to, so you can hardly think of me as a naïve, can you?' she added.

'Absolutely not,' Piers confirmed. 'Thing is, Gus, this is all very difficult, but without putting too fine a point on it I've had a bit of a scare lately.'

'Oh no!' Immediately Gus was filled with concern. For all his faults, she loved him dearly and anything which upset him would also upset her! 'What? Can I help?'

'Well, actually you probably can. I've been approached by someone and the awkward thing is, darling, that the whole messy issue concerns you.'

'Oh?'

'Oh God, I don't know how to put this so I'll get to the point. I've received threats, and I'm frightened to tell you the truth, Gus, really frightened. These people mean business. I wouldn't be here if I thought they didn't. I had to come to warn you, to stop you . . .' It all came tumbling out in an almost incoherent stream. 'There's a case you're working on. I don't know what it is. I can't tell you anything else, but I've been told to warn you off. And these people are serious.'

Gus put her empty glass on to the table in front of her, fighting the urge to laugh. 'Don't be ridiculous. This is ludicrous. What sort of people are you dealing with, for God's sake? You're being hysterical. Warnings and threats. You'd better tell me exactly who's spoken to you and what you're talking about.'

'Gus,' Piers' face was ashen now, 'if I told you *that* your life would be at risk. Believe me, darling, I am absolutely serious. Do you really think I'd be having this conversation if I didn't have to? Do you think it pleases me to have to talk to you like this, to frighten you, darling? I'm doing it because I know these people are serious. They have asked me to warn you off. I don't have the resources to protect you from them, bar locking you up somewhere.'

'Don't you realize what my life's about?' Gus hissed, angry almost beyond words now, shock covering any fear she might otherwise be feeling. 'My oath is about justice, to uphold it, to let it be seen to be done. Any fights that I may have will be carried out honestly and fairly. Let your bullies threaten me and they'll wonder what's hit them!'

'I knew you'd react like this. You've always been a stubborn girl. But, Gus, I beg you, be careful. If you can get out of what you're doing, then for my sake and for yours, do. I know I've brought this on you, it's all my fault for doing what I do . . .' His voice tailed off. Gus had no idea just how ashamed he was feeling right now. And this was the very tip of the iceberg. If ever she got to find out about who he really was . . .

Gus's hand flew to her mouth. 'It's Winston Davis. It's the Winston Davis case, isn't it?'

Piers shrugged helplessly. 'I don't know, darling. I really wasn't given the details.'

'Well, you can tell your friends,' Gus hissed bitterly, 'that they wasted their time. The guy hanged himself yesterday. Satisfied?'

She collected her bag and stood up. 'And just for the record, even if he hadn't, I'd never give up a case because I was threatened. You should know me better than that.'

Piers stood and grimly watched her leave. Bloody Thompson. Over the years he had somehow managed to sour everything in Piers's life. After tonight, Piers was afraid his relationship with Gus might never be the same. Suddenly he felt very old and tired. Always looking over his shoulder, always aware of his past – and afraid it would betray him. And always afraid for his daughter. Perhaps the safest thing for Gus now was to have nothing to do with him. Should he try to remove himself completely from her life so that she might never have to learn the truth? But even then it wouldn't protect her from the likes of Thompson. Besides, he couldn't bear not to see her, even if she did despise him.

Clive sounded as miserable as she did. 'Look, I know this is probably out of order, Gus, but do you fancy meeting up for a drink? I really need to talk about this to someone. It's bugging me. Hard as I try to get it out of my mind, I just keep going over and over things that I found out. Of course I'll understand if you say no. I've been driving my wife round the bend because I haven't been able to talk to her about it, and she knows there's something very wrong with me. I thought maybe we could meet up at that wine bar in Victoria, the one we both mentioned the other day?'

It was just a couple of days since Gus had spoken to her father. The fact was that she too had been finding it impossible to stop thinking about Winston Davis, and whatever connection her father might have with the case. She had been wondering just what to do about her feelings. The case was officially over so she should just forget about it, get on with her next job. Be professional. 'The truth is I feel just the same way as you. I'm very unhappy about lots of aspects. I could be there in, say, an hour's time, seven o'clock?'

Clive sighed gratefully. 'Great. I'll see you later.'

They were into their second bottle of wine and both of them were feeling a lot better for it.

'Let me get this straight, Clive. You think that Winston Davis was actually driven to suicide by the police?' Augusta's voice was a low whisper of disbelief.

'I know it sounds outrageous, but I do. And there's an awful lot to it. My investigations have come up with some terrifying stuff, half of which I haven't dared tell you before now, until I'd got some sort of concrete evidence on what was going on. But the plain fact is that no fewer than eleven officers attached to Brickwell have had malpractice allegations made against them, ranging from physical violence to misuse of drugs – offering them to witnesses in order to influence their evidence, planting them and fabricating evidence. None of these men has been prosecuted, due to lack of evidence.'

'What are you saying, Clive?' Gus was hoping with all her heart that Clive was wrong, but the trouble was, all the time she had guessed these must be the missing links. Now the whole setup would fall into place. Lack of witnesses, obstructiveness from the police, poor Winston's story of how he had been in the kitchen innocently making himself a cup of tea, the discovery by two policemen, the weapon – the Uzi – would have been accessible to the police, especially if they'd taken it in a raid. All of it fitted, and it was horrifying in its implications. He lowered his voice to a murmur so low that Gus had to bring her ear almost to his mouth. She could feel his warm breath on her earlobe.

'I think you know what I'm saying, Gus. I believe the police killed Harry Chapman – one of their own colleagues. Why, I have no idea. But Winston Davis just happened to be too close to the scene for his own good. And that witness, the one who met with the "accident" ... he was murdered because he was going to tell me what had happened. They got at him before he could talk.'

'So what do we do now? We can hardly report the matter to the police. Just how far do you think this bent little network goes?'

Clive shrugged. 'I have absolutely no idea. It could be just a dozen men in that station, it could go further. I don't know how we find out. This really isn't our field, is it? More in the line of police work. However, I think we could put a file together for the CPS. I'm sure you feel the same way as I do: my conscience will not allow me to accept that the case is closed simply because the police are not looking for any further suspects. Think about it, Winston's suicide must have been extremely convenient for them.'

'Clive, you do believe it was suicide? You don't think he was –'

'No. I don't think so. At least not at the moment. According to Andrea, Winston's daughter, he was suffering from severe depression. Indeed, he had mentioned being free of it all many times. But I'll keep an open mind on it. So I shall be putting together a file and I may well ask for an opinion from you to go with it.'

For a moment Gus wondered whether to tell Clive about her father, so that he should know just how sinister the whole business was becoming, but to do that she would have to expose that her father was implicated in the terrible events, and she wanted to find out for herself what his role was before talking to anyone else.

'Sure, you can have an opinion with pleasure. Let me know how you get on. Anything at all I can do to help – just let me know.'

James was in exceptionally high spirits on the day that Gus suggested they have dinner together. His campaign had been a success and he was now, at last, an MP. He was spending a considerable amount of time mulling over just what topic he would choose for his maiden speech. Gus was dressed rather austerely in a dark grey woollen dress which James thought did nothing for her colouring. She looked terribly white. He hoped the poor girl wasn't overworking. She had, as he had always known she would, turned out to be a bright young advocate. He was well pleased that he had decided to steal her from Henry all that time ago. Shame about the affair but she seemed to have worked it all out. James had actually been wondering if they might resume their relationship on a sort of ad hoc basis. Bed with Gus had been very satisfying. He had given Mirabelle the elbow shortly before the by-election. James guessed that the girl could be a bit of a liability if left unchecked. She had been useful over the TV business, but he had had to clean up his act for the sake of the party! Esme had been quite right to point out his vulnerability. But with all that behind him maybe he could have the odd little liaison now and then. Sadly his latest pupil hadn't been half as accommodating. But Gus was being tiresome. She kept wanting to talk about work, while James wanted to talk about them, about what they would do later . . .

'James,' Gus's voice sounded bossy and school-marmish. 'This is serious. The man hanged himself.'

'I know all about it. Don't think just because I wasn't around I didn't learn things. I know every twist of that case. I made it my business to take an interest.'

Gus knew he was lying. 'He was innocent.'

'My dear Gus, I'm not disputing that! But the silly man didn't hang – oops, sorry, no pun intended – hang around long enough to let us get him a fair trial.'

'Which he wouldn't have got!'

'It's too late to do anything about it now, the poor man is dead.'

'Clive Parfitt thinks we could present the case to the CPS again. He thinks there's enough evidence to open the file up once more. I think Clive's right.' Gus's grey eyes blazed at James challengingly.

'Then Clive Parfitt is very stupid, Augusta. And I know that you are not. Be professional, for God's sake. The case is closed. Our brief is finished. I happen to know that you've got a pile of new briefs on your desk and that you would best serve yourself if you looked after them instead of going off on wild-goose chases on some silly whim.'

'But what about Winston Davis? What about his reputation? His family? The police ...? Don't you care, James?' Gus's voice rose accusingly. People in the small restaurant were beginning to look over at their table.

'Gus, keep your voice down. I'll be recognized.' James hissed.

'Don't be pathetic, James. What the bloody hell did you get yourself elected as a Labour MP for? Aren't you supposed to be a representative of the people? Aren't you supposed to be fighting against injustice, standing up for people's rights?'

'That's precisely what I do, and will do. There's no question of that.'

'Oh I can see straight through you, James. You only wanted to be an MP for self-advancement. You wouldn't know a moral principle if it came up and socked you on the nose. You are a sham, with no more substance than a wet cardboard box. You should be ashamed of yourself!' Gus stood up and threw her napkin on to the table. 'If you won't help me, I'll do it on my own. Just remember, James, you'd better keep on your toes because the papers will be watching you, to catch you out ... the old sleaze police! And one day someone might just tell them what you're really like. The great James Kentish – man of the people! Huh!'

Gus spun on her heel and left the restaurant, feeling a lot better than she had done in several days!

* * *

Chris Thompson shot the car round the bend at approximately seventy m.p.h. Martin Coles was catapulted towards the passenger door, then his seat belt caught him, bruising his chest, but thankfully holding him perpendicular.

'Chris!' he screamed. 'Slow the fuck down, can't you? You'll kill us both!' They were what Chris termed joy-riding in one of the unmarked Rover mean machines which could outrun most things. Chris was celebrating and unfortunately Martin had agreed, under heavy persuasion, to accompany him. All Martin really wanted was to get home. He'd been on duty for three shifts of twelve hours over the last four days, and then he'd had to work overtime on top of that. He felt knackered – completely fucked. And besides, he wanted to see his wife, and daughter, little Amy, just eight weeks old. Smiling and holding her head up already – any time now she'd be rolling right over and he didn't want to miss it. How she'd grown in such a short time. And he had to get all the progress second-hand from Sharon. She was pissed off with him too, quite understandably. Take last night: he'd promised that he'd be back in time to do the shopping for her – stocking up on the nappies and the washing stuff. He'd got home after eight, too late to go, and she'd had to ask her mum to go out this morning. He'd got an earful from her, as well. It was all right for Chris. He was still footloose and fancy-free. No steady women for him. Half the time he'd try his luck on the new WPCs doing job training. Martin felt like warning him if he didn't watch his step he'd be done for sexual harassment. But Chris didn't seem too worried about anything, really. He thought he'd get away with it, get away with murder if necessary.

Martin looked across at him. Like his father he was, with that same tight black curly hair, 'cept his father's was grey now. They were both big men, taller than Martin. Big in stature and character. Loud voices which they could put to good use when they wanted something. Scary, it was.

Martin hadn't known what he was getting into when he'd first been assigned to Brickwell. First of all it had started with DC Cromwell, his superior, buying him a drink while on duty. Don't worry, he'd said. We all do it, it's part of the job, we need to relax. Until we get provided with a therapist as part of the job, we can't be blamed for having a little snort now and then. Then there'd been the little gifts for Sharon. First of all a little camera, then a watch, then a pair of earrings, and before he'd stopped to think, cash. Just a bit to begin with – twenty quid for this or that, 'overtime perks' Chris had called it. Then it had got bigger. Fifty quid, and what with the baby and all, well it had been pretty useful. Sharon wanted everything to be just so. New cot, new pram, buggy, clothes – the list went on for ever. They seemed to be getting through money like water, and his meagre PC's wage wouldn't cover anything like what she wanted and pay the mortgage and all the bills. So these little perks had come in pretty handy. God, he'd been so thick, so stupid! He shouldn't have been surprised the first night they'd done the drugs bust – when Chris had explained what they were going to do with the stuff. 'Where do you think your perks have come from?' he said. 'What about Sharon's pressies, and all the stuff for the baby? 'Course you're going to have fun explaining all that away, ain'tcha, if you decide not to join us? You in or not?'

What choice had he had? Thus it had started, his life of fear and intimidation. Of always looking over his shoulder, wondering when he would meet the same fate as that poor bastard Harry Chapman.

It had been Chris's idea to teach Harry a lesson, but Martin hadn't realized just what sort of a lesson Chris had in mind. Just because the guy had tried to sneak more than his fair share of the profits over the Clapham job. And that was it. Bye-bye, Harry. God, it was disgusting. He and Chris had been the ones to go around and tell Harry's widow what had happened. Martin glanced at Chris again. Evil bastards! And he was no better. God, he hated his life. But there was fuck all he could do to change it. All he could do was try to keep himself and his little family safe until maybe, just maybe sometime in the future, he could see a way out for himself other than in a box with fake brass handles!

Clive's nocturnal telephone calls were becoming a regular occurrence. Flora had taken to ignoring the telephone at times when Chris was present. He, too, had established a regular pattern of visits to Flora and over the past two weeks he had started to stay overnight a shade more often than Gus would have liked. It wasn't that she had anything against him – he seemed a nice enough man – it was just that he always seemed to be around where she wanted to be. If she was in the sitting room, Chris would come and chat or even just flick through a book; and if she was in the kitchen he more often than not would come in and get himself a coffee and then stay around. She felt a bit mean feeling so claustrophobic about him, especially when he was obviously going out of his way to be friendly – not to make her feel excluded from his relationship with Flora, Gus supposed. But really she would have much preferred it if he left her alone so that she could regain her sense of space and privacy once more.

The trouble was he didn't seem to be terribly sensitive to gentle hints about wanting to take phone calls in private, or disappearing when Gus was entertaining her own visitors. Gus picked up the phone and felt grateful that at least for the moment he appeared to be occupied elsewhere.

'I heard back from the CPS this afternoon!'
'And?'

'Not much hope there, Gus. So far as they're concerned the case against Winston Davis was pretty watertight. They say it wouldn't be in the public interest to open it up again.'

'But what about the police involvement?'

'Not a chance. I got the letter, then I called the solicitor involved and talked it over with him. He says the last thing they want is a witch hunt within the police force.'

'You mean it's political!'

'Well, what do you think? Public confidence in the police is at an all-time low as it is.'

'But that stinks, Clive. So much for justice!'

'Well, unless you've got any bright ideas I really don't know what to do or where to go next.'

Gus was thinking fast. 'Send me the report tomorrow. I know someone at the CPS – George Lavenham – I went to Bar School with him. I'll send it off to him. Maybe he can drum up some interest in it. It's worth a try.'

As Gus replaced the receiver, she noticed a shadow move across the doorway.

Half an hour later Flora was surprised to find herself saying goodbye to Chris. 'But I thought you were staying . . .' She was nonplussed rather than upset. Flora had never had a particularly possessive nature.

'No, not tonight, darling. I've got work to do. Didn't I tell you yesterday? I've got some reports to draft out and then I need an early night. Heavy day tomorrow.' He bent and gave her a warm kiss on the lips and then collected his coat. ''Bye, Gus,' he called as Flora held the door open for him.

It had been a most interesting evening, and now his father would be keen to know the latest developments. Chris guessed he'd probably blow a gasket when he realized this bloody woman wouldn't give up on the case.

'How're you getting on with Chris?' Gus asked when she noticed Flora's bemused expression. 'Everything okay?'

'Yeah, sure. It's just that I thought he was staying. It's no problem, just odd that he turned up with stuff for tomorrow and then just upped and went. Perhaps it was something I said.'

'Well, what did you say?'

'To be honest, not very much. We were too busy watching *Brookside* – his favourite programme.'

'Oh God!' Gus roared with laughter. 'Do you find you have lots of other things in common as well as *Brookside*?'

'Don't be a cow, Gus,' Flora warned, but her voice was warm and Gus knew she was semi-amused. 'He's very sweet.'

'Ugh!' Gus shuddered. 'Sweet, almost as bad as nice. That's a real put-down in my book. He's so sweet.'

'Are you trying to tell me you don't like him?' Flora suddenly looked hurt. Gus noticed the warning sign of her arms folded firmly across her chest, one leg crossed tightly over the other.

'I think he's very ni – I mean swee – Oh God, charming and likeable. How's that? He seems very fond of you, judging by the amount of time he's spending here. It's not many weeks since you guys met. Talk about whirlwind romance. What are his friends like?'

'I haven't met any of them yet. We've been too busy getting to know each other.'

'What's he do? You haven't actually told me yet.'

'Umm, I thought I'd mentioned it,' Flora hedged. She purposely hadn't told Gus because she thought Gus would only make fun of him. Flora knew that Gus had a thorough disrespect for a lot of the police, particularly through this last case of hers, which she'd dropped a few hints about and Flora had managed to fill in the gaps for herself. She knew enough to understand that

270

now was not an opportune time to introduce a policeman into Gus's life!

'God! I've just remembered I left a pizza in the oven.
Shit! I bet it's really burned by now!' Flora leaped up out
of the chair and rushed into the kitchen. Hopefully Gus
would have completely forgotten what she was talking
about by the time Flora reappeared. She was so preoccupied with other things these days that Flora knew
most of the conversations they had were conducted
with Gus on automatic pilot, and that were Flora to ask
her in ten minutes' time what they had been discussing,
she would not have had the faintest idea.

Elena Lawrence snapped the heads off the faded roses
with a vicious sense of purpose. The secateurs sliced
satisfyingly through the wilting stems. The decapitated
blooms lay in the basket hooked over her arm. The
fragrance was quite delectable, sweet and heady, with
the vaguest hint of apples. She inhaled and enjoyed, but
her mouth remained tight-lipped. Ever since she had
received the telephone call she had held herself taut, in
check, upright, stiff and contained. She also had to keep
busy. After the roses she would check over the veget-
able garden. The gardener would no doubt be surprised
by her visit, but she might find some late strawberries
ripe for the picking, or some early globe artichokes
which she might include in a flower arrangement. After
that, she would swim and then she might visit a friend.
It was important not to stop, to keep going, not to think.

Ah, the sun. She held her face up towards its warming rays. How good the heat felt, melting her tension,
easing her strain. Piers should be home from the gallery
at six. She could kill time until then. Everything must
wait until his arrival. As it had done since she had
received the call from that woman early this morning.
The nerve, the absolute bloody gall of the woman,
calling her up like that.

271

Elena remembered exactly who she was – the tart that Leo Fiorenzi had brought to the party. Elena had disliked her on first sight – obviously with good reason. Elena had known she was making a play for Piers even then! But she still found it all so hard to believe. Piers was no gigolo! He didn't womanize! He was, in fact, quite a moral person. While it was true to say that he had had many women since Catherine's death, he had only ever had one woman at a time. Throughout their six-year marriage Elena had never had cause to doubt his fidelity. Piers had been steadfastly loving and generous towards her. Appreciative and caring. She only had to think back to the anniversary party ... and then there was the fabulous necklace he had presented her with. It was so out of character for him to play around. Perhaps because of that she felt deeply afraid of this other woman. For Piers to have paid her so much attention – if what she said was true – then she would not be some sort of short-term fling. She must be something serious. She must mean something very special to her husband.

Elena suddenly felt chilled, although the sun continued to burn down on her. What sort of woman could say those things? How could she have called up and given Elena such explicit details of their fling? Elena had been over the conversation a million times in her head. She knew exactly what she would do. She would pour them both a drink, and then she would ask him, quietly and unemotionally. She would ask him whether he was having an affair with Giovanna Lucciani. And if the answer was yes, then she would leave him. Immediately!

'Gus, darling, how nice. You look marvellous!'

'Thank you, George.' Gus acknowledged the compliment graciously. 'You're looking very well yourself. Crown prosecuting obviously suits you.'

'Now now, Gus, enough of your naughties, what'll you have to drink?'

'Dry white wine would be nice.'

'I'll join you.' He called the waiter over and gave him his order. 'Now what's all this about? Obviously I've read your report, but am I to understand that you and your solicitor colleague believe that a policeman actually committed the murder of Mr Chapman, and tried to frame Mr Davis?'

'Yes, in simple terms, that is what the circumstantial evidence would point towards.'

'And yet there is clear forensic evidence which confirms the presence of Mr Davis's fingerprints on the weapon – an Uzi, I believe – and that he was witnessed not only by these two police officers, but also by several members of the public.'

Gus could tell that George was as sceptical as his colleagues had been. 'I know how it appears, George. But Winston Davis had no previous convictions in his life – no violence, no possession, not even a parking fine. He was widowed not very long ago, his daughter is a teacher, his son-in-law a doctor – he's just squeaky clean. What possible motive could he have had for gunning down a police officer in broad daylight?'

'As much motive as one police officer wishing to shoot another police officer,' George sighed. 'And what about all these witnesses the prosecution were able to come up with? All to a man say they saw Davis gun Chapman down. Just what are you suggesting? Intimidation on a massive scale? Come, come now, Augusta, you've been reading too many of those American novels.'

Augusta wisely decided to ignore George's patronizing attitude. 'No fewer than eleven police officers at Brickwell police station – the station to which Chapman, Thompson and Coles are attached – have had charges made against them by the public. These charges range from: planting of drugs by the police; attempting to bribe witnesses with offers of drugs; brutality, and several others. To date, George, not one of those officers has been suspended or even transferred. Documents have gone missing – even whole files! And not only that, Clive had a meeting planned with a potential witness and the man met with a fatal accident before Clive got to talk to him. And,' she hesitated before continuing, 'I've had threats.'

George sat up. 'What sort of threats?'

'Oh, just the odd message on the answer machine, the odd call in the middle of the night. All thinly veiled, of course.'

'What you are suggesting is inconceivable.'

'You sound like Lord Denning. Please remove your blinkers, George, and look at the file again. Poor Winston Davis committed suicide because he was so ashamed of the false accusation. I'd hate to think that whoever is responsible is laughing out there somewhere, knowing they've got away with it. Please help me.'

George squeezed Gus's hand. 'All right, as you're obviously so convinced there's something here, I promise I'll have another look.'

Chapter Twenty-Five

Mirabelle was not frightfully thrilled to receive her mother's distraught telephone call saying that she was on her way and would be spending a night or two with Mirabelle, and so had responded by booking her into a suite at Claridge's. She had telephoned the airline explaining that Elena should meet her for drinks in the bar of the hotel. That way Mirabelle wouldn't have to risk having her style cramped by her mother's presence. Mirabelle was fond enough of her, it wasn't that she didn't like her or anything ghastly like that, it was just that Mirabelle liked her own space, liked to feel that she could do things on the spur of the moment if necessary, like asking the odd man back if she felt like it, cavort around with no clothes on, that sort of thing ... things which she wouldn't be able to do if Elena were around. It was far more satisfactory for the both of them if Elena was independent. Besides she always stayed at Claridge's when she came over with Piers so she could jolly well do that now. Why they couldn't buy a house like normal people did completely exasperated Mirabelle. Piers had some daft notion that he'd only be saddled with more staff worries and more security worries, because knowing the Lawrences they'd end up filling it full of priceless artworks. But whatever the reason, it was bloody inconvenient!

The ice in Mirabelle's cocktail was melting fast, diluting the drink. She stirred it with the wooden cocktail stick. Next time she'd have to tell them to strain the ice. There was nothing worse than a watery Alexander. She was wearing her new Versace suit and she knew she looked very cool. The skirt was unbelievably short, but then most of Mirabelle's skirts were unbelievably short. Her motto had always been if you've got it, use it, and she knew just how much leg to show, how often to cross and uncross those legs, with just the right degree of whisper as her thighs slid together.

It had been a shame about Tom, but fortunately for Mirabelle she'd managed to find young Adam, Tom's photographer, a lot more helpful than his colleague. She'd been seeing Adam just a couple of days and even though he was young – he was only just three years younger than Mirabelle – he was certainly keen to learn. She had made the happy chance discovery that Adam wanted to break into films at some stage, and learn about movie cameras as well as stills. It hadn't taken much to convince the ambitious young buck that Mirabelle might be able to give him a helping hand within a certain production company. So it wouldn't have fitted frightfully conveniently into Mirabelle's scheme of things, as it were, to have Elena around the place just as Mirabelle was about to get the lovely young Adam between the sheets.

Elena dabbed her eyes prettily with the delicate lace handkerchief. Mirabelle thrust the double gin into her hands.

'Take a drink, Mummy, you'll feel much better.' Mirabelle hated public shows of emotion. She was now wishing that she'd stuck to Elena's original plan and met her at the airport. 'Perhaps we should go upstairs?'

'Why should we go upstairs?'

'Um, because I've booked you into a suite here, Mummy. I thought you'd be far too uncomfortable in my poky old flat. Anyway, you love staying here. You and Piers always stay here.'

Mirabelle was horrified to see Elena's eyes fill up once more. 'Oh God, please stop crying, Mummy. Come on, a large swig, it'll do you the world of good.' She almost thrust the glass at Elena's mouth and then prodded it upwards. Elena fought valiantly not to choke and eventually succeeded in just producing a gentle splutter.

'It's Piers, he's got a mistress.'

'Don't be ridiculous. He can't have!' For some inexplicable reason, Mirabelle felt a stab of jealousy shoot through her chest. 'Who and when? And how did you find out?'

'Earlier today. She called me and told me. I mean she must be completely ghastly if she could just call up out of the blue like that and be so viciously cruel.'

'Well, who is she?' Mirabelle's voice was rising indignantly. How could he? Piers didn't have affairs, he was married to her mother. And Mirabelle was realizing, somewhat bizarrely, that she was angry because if Piers was going to have an affair with anyone, it should have damned well been with her! 'Who is this woman?' she repeated once more.

'Giovanna Lucciani – that tart who came to the anniversary party with Leo Fiorenzi. I thought she was ghastly then . . .! She told me she completely exhausted him.' Again Elena crumpled. 'They were in bed for two days!'

'Good God, I didn't know he was so fit!'

'Unfortunately he's not, darling. At least not with me! But as soon as I confronted him he just went to pieces, telling me how terrible he was, how I didn't deserve him. If it wasn't so awful it would have been pathetic. It really was most out of character – you know how tough he usually is. The least I would have expected would have been a string of lies. Mirabelle, you don't think he's about to have some sort of nervous breakdown, do you? Is this what they mean by a mid-life crisis?'

'But, Mother,' Mirabelle took hold of her mother's rather cold little hand, 'this is quite ghastly. Whatever are you going to do?'

'Leave him, I suppose. I really don't think I want to be married to someone I can't trust. And the trouble is I love him so desperately. He's the loveliest man I've ever met – apart from your father, of course,' she added quickly, wanting to spare her daughter's emotions. 'But what else can I do? I really don't think it would have been right just to say I'd forgive him and forget about it, do you?'

Mirabelle studied her mother's face for a few moments before she answered. Luckily the situation had never happened to her. It was always the other way around in that Mirabelle was the other woman and some other poor bitch was left feeling hurt and betrayed. 'I guess I'd want to get my own back!' she said simply.

'What do you mean?'

'Well, if someone hurt me like that, I guess I'd want to hurt them back, let them see what it feels like. That's what I'd do. I wouldn't just walk away from it and give him the satisfaction of being comfortably able to get on with his seedy little affair. Oh no, I'd make his life jolly difficult. Question is, what's the best way to go about it?'

'No, Mirabelle, I don't think revenge is really what I'm after. It's not a very pleasant way of going about things, is it, darling? I think a cooling off period would be best, and then if I still feel I can't trust him – depending on how he behaves during the coming days and weeks – then I shall have no alternative but to consult a lawyer, and think in terms of getting a divorce.'

'And do nothing apart from that?' Mirabelle squeaked incredulously. Why were these women so weak? Gus was just the same. She hadn't once tried to stop Mirabelle from doing what she was doing. Why hadn't she ever come after her and threatened to wring her neck? That's exactly what Mirabelle would have done – not

278

literally, of course, but metaphorically speaking; she'd have thought up some subtle little course of revenge, and that's precisely what her mother should now be doing.

'It wouldn't be becoming, darling, to do anything else.'

Mirabelle suddenly lost her temper. 'God, why do you come out with all this shit, Mother? What do you mean, it wouldn't be becoming? This is 1993, you know, and women don't live their lives according to what's becoming any more.'

'I'm sure women don't,' Elena snapped, recovering some of her inherent self-restraint, 'but I can assure you that ladies do.'

'Oh come off it, Mother. Step into the real world. I bet you Piers' new mistress doesn't exercise the same restraint as you. She called you up, didn't she? Seems to me she's prepared to play a very dirty game to get what she wants. You're just going to sit back and let her, are you? Okay, that's fine. But in the meantime he's my stepfather, and his playing around affects me too! I intend to pay him back even if you don't, and I've got an idea I know just the way to do it. To hell with this passive, ladylike shit!'

Elena looked at her daughter aghast. She had no idea she used such language. She was behaving like some common little street trollop. 'But, Mirabelle,' she said weakly, 'you must not do anything without my permission . . .'

'Save it, Mother. I'll call you tomorrow!'

The object of the conversation was just setting foot on British soil as Mirabelle was hailing a taxi to take her from the West End back to South Kensington. Giovanna pulled her silver fox round her shoulders, hating what she felt to be the cold damp night air of an English July. Two very large men closely accompanied her, but she spoke to neither of them. They made their way as quickly as possible through the arrivals hall, oblivious to the frenzy they had put the security team into. Giovanna was used to being searched. It was just another bore to be endured when crossing international borders. She waited, tapping her feet, as her luggage was X-rayed and picked over with a fine-tooth comb. Idiots, they should know better than to expect any of her family to be transporting anything they shouldn't. They had plenty of eager people willing to do that for them. They were squeaky clean. Even her bodyguards were unarmed. It was easy enough to get them kitted out once they reached London. There was simply nothing that couldn't be done if she demanded it.

Some three annoying hours later they were released with the surliest of apologies. Giovanna brushed the security people off with one of her withering looks. The limousine was waiting for her, long, sleek and black. Her bodyguards slid into the front seat, together with the chauffeur. Giovanna settled herself down in the comfort of the back, knowing that she was invisible from the outside, and she could do what the hell she liked on the inside. As the car slid away from Heathrow, Giovanna's glass gave the merest tremble. She drank half the champagne and then watched the cars to either side of her speeding towards London.

It had been almost two months since she and Piers had discovered their mutual admiration for one another, and he hadn't been in touch since! Giovanna never could get used to waiting around. She knew he was going to be in for a lovely surprise!

Tom Silverthorn was aching to stretch his legs out. Four hours' worth of surveillance and the only thing to show for it was two dead legs.

Then suddenly everything changed! Tom shot down in his seat. He saw a movement round by the doorway.

He blinked to refocus his eyes. That wasn't Gus coming home. Whoever it was was acting very peculiarly indeed. The door was open but for some reason Tom couldn't see the faces of the two people. There was no light reflected off them at all. Black, Tom thought. Maybe the other girl. Then as he watched the house he realized that no lights had been switched on. Both figures had entered, but they hadn't bothered to use the lights. Tom's sixth sense told him to get out of the car and see what was going on. He quietly opened the door and moved closer to the house.

It was set over three floors and he could swear that he could see what appeared to be a torch light play across the window in front of the open curtains on the first floor. Burglars? Burglars with keys! His mind tried to sort out the facts. What the hell were they doing? He stepped back into the shadows just fifteen yards from the entrance and waited, straining his ears to pick up the slightest unusual sound. The front door remained slightly ajar – for a quick getaway, Tom guessed. He could barely hear a thing, save for the slight banging of a door inside, and the scraping of wood against wood.

Then, to his horror, he recognized Gus's car coming into the square. Rooted to the spot, he watched as she expertly reversed the little Peugeot into a space. She unhooked her seat belt, collected up some bags and opened the car door. Tom didn't know what to do. He hovered, his foot poised to move, then he acted. He ran over to her, almost knocking her to the ground. He put his hand over her mouth to stop her screaming. As she struggled to face him, he saw the fear in her eyes. Not surprisingly she tried to bite the hand.

'Gus,' he whispered loudly, 'Gus, it's okay.' For a moment she stopped struggling, trying to see who it was, who knew her name. 'Listen,' he whispered urgently. 'Don't say a word, don't scream. Let's get back in your car. There's two men in your flat and I really don't think they look the sort to have got a cup of cocoa ready to welcome you back!'

For a moment Gus was too shocked to respond. She was still trying to make sense of what was going on. So suddenly had the man grabbed her that she couldn't remember where she'd seen him before. Now, to be sitting in her car – with an almost complete stranger – and to be told that two burglars were going through her house was too much to take. She opened the door and lurched out.

'Augusta, don't!' Tom's hand grabbed so hard that she cried out in pain. Tom was caught at an awkward angle, leaning over towards her, off balance. He pulled as hard as he could. 'Listen to me, for Christ's sake!'

'No! Why the hell should I be sitting here listening to you while my place gets the going-over? I've got to stop them.'

'You might get yourself killed. If I were you, I'd sit here quietly until they've gone and then we'll both go in.'

'Get myself killed?' Gus was angry – angry enough to storm right in and sort out whoever had dared to violate her space. Anger, she knew, provoked irrational behaviour. She took a few deep breaths while she thought.

'I must call the police . . .'

'No point. By the time they arrive these guys'll be long gone. Besides, I'd like to know who they're working for before we call the police. They just might be on the same side.'

Gus glowered at him, but realized he was making sense.

'Anyway, what are you doing here? You might well be something to do with them. I bet you're the bloody lookout, aren't you?' Again Gus lunged for the door.

'Gus, you've got to trust me, please. I'll explain everything later.'

282

Would he? Just exactly how would he explain that he'd staked out her house, and that he knew so much about what was going on inside? Tom had some quick thinking to do if he wanted to prevent himself from getting arrested.

Chapter Twenty-Six

Mirabelle cracked open another bottle and splashed more champagne into Adam's glass. The poor boy was almost incoherent with drink ... almost, but not quite!

'My God, Mirabelle, if Tom knew I was telling you all this, he'd have me strung up, oh, yes ... oh that's wonderful. No, don't stop it's ... mmmm.'

Mirabelle groaned softly to show Adam how excited and contented she was, and carried on with her licking, teasing and sucking alternately. Using her tongue to press tightly against his cock, sucking, letting it slide so slowly in and out of her mouth, she trailed her fingers over his soft but wonderfully firm belly. She released him for a moment. 'So, you were saying about this character called Piers turning up. About discovering that he was a famous art dealer ... do you really think he's something to do with Thompson's network?'

'I don't know, Mirabelle ... don't stop, please, just go on a bit ... oh yes,' he sighed as Mirabelle put her tongue to work once more.

'But you reckon you found out quite a bit about his past.'

'Bermondsey ... he started out on the street market ... oh God, oh God, oh God, yes ... oh Mirabelle, yes ... that's it ... that's just ...' Abruptly Mirabelle stopped moving. Adam's disappointed pelvis sank back to the mattress.

'And graduated to a spot of burglary?'

Adam's eyes remained closed as he nodded. When would this bloody woman stop talking and get on with the job? 'Something like that. I believe that's how he got into art. Now for God's sake, Mirabelle, shut up and let's fuck!'

'Sure,' Mirabelle sighed with satisfaction. Adam had corroborated what Doug Sanders, the private investigator had uncovered. Mirabelle knew she was on to something hot.

Giovanna allowed the manager to shake her hand. She gave him the barest of smiles. She was tired, hungry and cold, and all she wanted to do was get to her suite, have a long hot soak, and have dinner brought up. Then she would fall into bed – after arranging for Piers to come and see her, of course – and get a good night's sleep. She felt as though she had been travelling for a week. 'Choose something for me to eat, would you?' she snapped imperiously at the manager. 'Not too heavy, but delicious, and perhaps a little something to finish . . .'

'Of course, Signorina Lucciani. I shall show you to your suite.'

'Very good,' Giovanna's smile deepened a little. That was the thing about Claridge's – one was almost seduced by the excellent standard of service. She let her coat slip from her shoulders, confident that someone would not only catch it, but would carry it, too!

By the time she got through to Piers it was well after midnight. 'Darling,' she crooned into the telephone mouthpiece, 'I've missed you so much. Tell me you've missed me too!'

'Giovanna? Is that you?'

'Of course it's me – your little lovebird Giovanna. Why I not hear from you, Piers darling? I am very hurt. So I think to myself I come to you. And now I am here. Come to me, darling.'

Up until the scene with Elena late this afternoon, Piers had hardly thought about his exhausting encounter with Giovanna. It had been a diversion, a pleasant fling

– a one-night stand. He never, in a million years, expected the woman to call Elena and start squealing about the
whole business. For God's sake, it had been weeks since
they'd seen each other. He would have thought she'd got
the blasted message by now. He tried to hide his anger,
harbouring the fast-growing suspicion that the woman
may well be a few cylinders short of an engine.

'I have a wife, Giovanna, as you well know. I believe
you spoke to her earlier today. She's not terribly happy
about that, Giovanna.'

Giovanna giggled. 'But she had to know about us,
didn't she, Piers? We couldn't go on pretending. You
must know that I couldn't just be the other woman? You
didn't think that I . . . that we – oh no!' Her voice cracked
tearfully. 'You thought that I would be your piece on the
side? You thought so low of me, Piers, that was all I was
to you?'

'No, Giovanna, no.' Piers tried to calm her. The last
thing he needed was a hysterical woman after his blood.
What if she tried to engage the sympathetic ear of Gulio
Capeletti? 'But we have to talk.'

'I know, my darling,' Giovanna sounded immediately
brighter. 'We must. I have to see you urgently. How
quickly can you get here?'

'Er, where is here?' Piers could feel his panic gathering
momentum. A continent between them would have been
the best he could hope for, but he had a terrible feeling
she was a little closer . . .

'Claridge's, darling. I've only just arrived. Come and
see me tomorrow as early as you can. I shall be waiting for
you. I shall die without you. Tonight I will dream I am
with you again, that we are together . . . you know what I
mean, Piers. Think of me when you close your eyes,
think of my body next to yours, together, making such
sweet . . . such exciting . . . such passion . . . such sex
we shall have. I am melting right now, Piers. I must have
you or I shall die!'

'Yes, yes, Giovanna.' Piers cleared his throat, trying to get the vision of her lithe body out of his mind. His penis was already betraying him by throbbing into action. 'I'll see you for lunch. In the restaurant. At one o'clock . . . no, not in the room. We must talk first. Goodbye.'

Why did life have to be so bloody complicated? Now he had to sort out Elena and Giovanna.

At least Tom could be grateful that the suspense was keeping Gus from asking just what *he* had been doing there. The two of them sat slumped down in her car, straining their eyes on the upper floor of Gus's house, where the arc of a torch beam occasionally crossed the window. The lights remained off, but Gus now knew that Tom was telling the truth about the intruders.

'We should call the police now! We can't just sit here doing nothing.'

'No point. By the time they got here the burglars would have gone. Besides, I'd like to have some idea of what they're after before we call the boys in blue.'

'What on earth do you mean?'

'I'll explain later.' Gus shook her head in total incomprehension. They lapsed into silence for a few moments.

'We *should* go in there,' she hissed. 'This is just awful. They're stealing my things and I'm just sitting here doing nothing. I just can't bear it.' Gus stuffed her hand into her mouth to stop herself from screaming with frustration.

'Look,' Tom urged from the shadows, 'the light – it's come down a floor.'

'The sitting room,' Gus cried. 'They've done the bedroom and now they're in the sitting room. Bastards!'

'I think they're on their way out. Get down!'

'But I want to get a good look at them,' Gus protested, but Tom put a hand on her shoulder and pushed her further down towards the dashboard.

'I don't think we want to let them get a good look at us, do we?'

But even from her crouched, uncomfortable position Gus could see the two masked figures exiting from her house. They looked tall, and broad, and menacing as they walked stealthily away, disappearing into the shadows of the street.

'Did you notice something odd?' Gus turned to Tom after they had vanished from sight.

'Apart from the obvious, you mean?'

'They weren't carrying anything. Burglars have bags and sacks and suitcases. Whatever they took, it must have been very small.' Gus knew the mechanics of burglary very well. 'Maybe something disturbed them. Do you think they saw us?'

'No, I don't think they saw us. I just wonder what they were up to?' Tom's voice sounded ominous. 'Come on, let's go and see.'

Gingerly Gus put her key in the lock, feeling rather grateful that this tall semi-stranger was standing behind her. She may not know what the hell he had been doing there, but at least he was making all the right noises, for the time being.

'I'll go in first,' Tom volunteered. Gus stepped aside without argument. 'That's Flora, my flatmate's, room,' she said as they entered the ground-floor bedroom. Gus switched on the light. Everything looked in its place. Gus was half afraid, half eager to go on upstairs to see what had happened.

Again the sitting room looked untouched. Gus's eyes flicked over the paintings – bizarrely still in place. The fax machine, the video, the CD player, all were still there. Odd that such easy pickings should be left by opportunist thieves. 'Strange,' she breathed, 'but everything looks okay!'

'And upstairs?' Tom had already started climbing the next flight of stairs.

'My bedroom.' Gus followed close on his heels. The large rosewood marquetry box where she kept her

288

jewellery looked untouched. She opened the lid – there were her trinkets, all safely intact: the choker her father had bought her, the Cartier watch. She shook her head, not understanding. 'Odd,' she thought aloud. 'What the hell were they doing here?'

Tom was standing in the middle of the room, scratching his head.

'It's as though there was never anyone here.' Had she not seen the two men with her own eyes then she might have thought Tom had made the whole thing up. 'What were they doing here?' Gus repeated.

'Shit! Why didn't I think of that before?'

'What? What is it?' Gus felt out of her depth. She hadn't yet got to the bottom of what he was doing outside her flat.

'Drugs! I bet it's a bloody plant. And if I'm right, you're about to be busted!'

Gus looked on helplessly as he started pulling out drawers, throwing the contents on to the bed.

'Help me,' he commanded. 'There's got to be drugs somewhere and if we don't find them, you are going to get done!'

Gus dropped on to her knees, looking under the bed, feeling under the mattress, emptying her shoes from the bottom of the wardrobe. 'Bathroom!' she shouted as she raced to the door. She stopped to look around. Wicker Body Shop baskets full of goodies, sachets of bath salts – bath salts! She picked up a polythene bag which sat on top of a pile of soaps. 'Tom!' she called. 'I think I've found something.'

Tom was at her side just as they heard the knocking on the door. Neither of them spoke, but Tom slit the bag open with his fingernail and then sucked. 'Coke,' he confirmed, and then he swiftly emptied the white powder into the lavatory pan before flushing it away. Gus rinsed out the bag and buried it in the wastebin. The cistern was simmering quietly as the police broke through the door and charged up the stairs towards them.

They found Gus brushing her teeth and Tom doing up his flies. 'I hope you've got a damned good reason for being here,' Gus said haughtily.

'Would you mind if I made us both a drink?' said Tom. 'I guess you've got some Scotch somewhere in this joint of yours? I don't know about you, but I could certainly use something strong.'

The police had left, apologizing and muttering about an anonymous tip-off. Gus threatened them with charges.

'Er, yes, I suppose I probably could.' Gus took the glass and sank down on to the sofa, suddenly shivering with the cold. She huddled into her thin jacket. Tom disappeared for a moment and then returned with her duvet which he carefully draped around her.

'Shock, I expect. The drink should warm you up a bit.'

Gus was surprised to notice that the glass shook. Her hand was actually trembling! And yet inside she felt so calm, so in control.

'How did you guess about the drugs?'

'Oh, just the sort of methods these guys employ. I'm getting a feel for the way they operate.'

Gus felt she was in way over her head. Nothing in her life was normal any more. Threatening phone calls in the middle of the night, drugs plants – it was all becoming ridiculous. She wanted her life back again, to be just where she was before this blasted case.

'What's going on, and what were you doing here?'

Tom swallowed. 'Watching you.'

'Watching me?' Gus shrieked. 'What on earth were you doing watching me? I thought you were watching them – the burglars, or planters, or whatever you call them. What have I done to deserve your spying?'

'I'm working on a story. Er, somehow it crossed your path.'

Light was beginning to dawn on Gus. 'The other night, when you fell over me in the street, that was deliberate, right?'

Tom nodded, feeling ashamed. He didn't want her to feel set up. It was important for her not to feel that he had used her, that he had enjoyed falling over in the street. But what was he to say? He couldn't deny that he had barged into her on purpose and that he had wormed his way into buying her a drink. What was the girl supposed to think of him?

'You'd better tell me about this story of yours.' Gus had assumed her professional voice: cool, no-nonsense.

'You must know already.'

'That's a fairly huge assumption, Mr Silvertongue, seeing as how I know absolutely nothing about you bar the fact that you're a total sleazeball.'

'Oh come on, Gus, don't play the innocent. You know exactly what you've been getting into.'

'I beg your pardon?' Now she was getting seriously pissed off. The whisky had brought colour back to her cheeks, and she was beginning to feel strong enough to claw back some control of her life.

'Your father?'

'What about him?'

'Harry Chapman's murder?'

'What the hell do you know about it?'

'Probably not as much as you do. But my guess is you might be out of favour at the moment, otherwise why would they be interested in doing you over?'

'Who the hell's "they"?'

'Are you naturally this obtuse? Is this part of what they teach you at Bar School? Thompson's men, of course.'

'Oh for God's sake. I think you'd better leave. I have absolutely no idea what you're talking about.' Gus stood up. The telephone rang. 'Clive? Yes, I'm fine, but the flat isn't.' Gus's eyes narrowed at Tom, who made no moves towards the door. 'You've what?' she cried in disbelief. 'Your office too? Just an hour ago? Sure. I'll take care. Thanks.'

'It seems I'm not the only one to have uninvited guests this evening,' she said, sinking back on to the sofa.

'That doesn't surprise me. Perhaps it might be an idea if you and I could perhaps pool our resources, find out what we know? Try and figure out the pieces? Look, I don't know whose side you're on, Gus, but I do know that for some weird reason I quite like you, and for some even more bizarre reason which I am unable to fathom, I want to help you!'

Gus was too tired to argue. What the hell, she had nothing to lose. The Davis case was no secret anyway. So what if the papers got hold of the story? It might even help the cause to let the facts into the open. The public had a right to know what had gone on, and how an innocent man had been made desperate enough to take his own life.

'Okay, I'll tell you what I know,' she began.

By the time Gus got to the end of the unhappy tale Tom was feeling extremely bemused and confused as to exactly what Gus's motivation really was. Taking her purely on face value, she appeared to be very cut up about the entire incident, and incensed by the prospect that whoever set Winston up would remain untried. Tom couldn't work it out. If she was involved, as her father appeared to be, then how could she be looking after both sides? There had been nothing in her demeanour, her eyes or her words which gave the barest hint of duplicity. She seemed to be one hundred per cent on the level. But it couldn't just have been coincidence Thompson was visiting Lawrence in Guernsey. Even hoods had art collections – there were probably more art collections in the hands of hoods than in the world's museums. But Thompson didn't somehow seem the type. No, there was all the stuff from Piers' early life – his connection with Levy and his abrupt rise to fame and fortune. There was something bent about Gus's father. But Tom didn't feel at all convinced about the daughter.

'Now, Tom, it's your turn. Tell me what you know about all this, and exactly why you felt it necessary to stalk me.'

'Couldn't it wait? Maybe we should try and get some sleep. What about tomorrow morning?'

'I'm in court tomorrow morning. And besides, I think you should tell me now.'

Tom swallowed and helped himself to more of Gus's whisky. 'You might not like what you hear!'

'I'm a barrister. I've probably listened to worse things than you are able to imagine. I've got a strong stomach. Now I agreed to trust you . . . so do me a favour and talk.'

'Question is, where to start?'

'At the beginning?'

'I've been watching Frank Thompson for several months now –'

'Frank Thompson?' Gus gasped, and then bolted her mouth shut. She didn't want to give anything away before she knew what it meant. But that name again – that man. Her mind spun.

'He's a detective sergeant at Brickwell nick. His son, Chris, is a detective constable at the same place.'

'And Chris Thompson was one of the witnesses to Harry Chapman's murder!'

'That's right, along with Martin Coles, wasn't it? Well, I picked up the story way before that when snippets began to filter through from people about nasty goings on between the police and the public over at Brickwell. I decided to check it out, and my investigations – without wishing to sound like a policeman – have uncovered a whole bucketload of worms!'

Gus was still trying to slot everything together. Frank Thompson must have been the one to warn her father. That was what this was about. The Thompsons were involved with the Davis murder, and Frank Thompson had used her father to warn her off. Gus felt nauseated. Did that mean that somehow her father was involved too? Was that why Tom had been watching her? She needed space to think, to fit it all together. It was too much to take in at once, too frightening. But she couldn't let Tom know just how frightened she was. She had to act normal, until she knew the facts. She couldn't afford to trust anyone, and she wanted to test what information he had, what he thought.

'So you think Winston Davis was murdered by the police too?'

'Yes, Gus, I'm afraid I do.'

'But why? What motive could they have had for murdering a colleague?'

'I'm not entirely sure, but my guess is that it's something to do with drugs. You see, Frank has a team of about twenty heavies who are involved with the distribution of a large percentage of London's crack. They control a lot of these so-called Yardie gangs, in terms of keeping them supplied, protected and in business.'

'But this is horrific! So you're saying that practically an entire police station is not only bent, but is running a drugs empire! And why Harry Chapman? Why Winston Davis?'

'Harry Chapman must have been about to squeal . . . or maybe he had a policy disagreement, who knows? I think Thompson junior and Martin Coles gunned down Chapman, and Winston just happened to turn up.'

'Well, that's certainly what he maintained all along. He received a damned great hit on the head and woke up a murderer.'

'So, that just about brings us up to date. You know

what I know, and I know what you know. Question is, what do we do next?'

'You mentioned my father, Tom.' Gus steeled herself. She had to get as much information as she could.

Tom should have known better than to expect her to have forgotten that little slip of his tongue. He might have guessed that she was so used to assimilating facts on the hoof that she wouldn't miss a thing.

'It was just something about his early days . . .' he hedged. Maybe Gus might fill in the gaps for him.

'Early days? What do you mean?'

'Before he was so rich and well known. His background, where he came from.'

Gus frowned. Her brain was trained to think ahead, but for the life of her she couldn't guess what Tom was getting at. 'I'm not sure what you mean. Daddy's always been rich. His parents died when he was young – seventeen, I think. He got started up in business thanks to his inheritance. He doesn't talk about it much. I guess it must have been pretty painful.'

Tom took another slug of his whisky. This was not the kind of thing he was used to dealing with. 'He never mentioned his days in Bermondsey? On the market-stalls?'

'Don't be ridiculous, Tom. Daddy would no more work on a marketstall than conduct a London bus! You must have the wrong man!'

Tom had got his facts muddled. She felt immensely relieved. To suggest that he had been some market trader! What a silly idea.

'He inherited a stall from his grandfather. His father was a drunk and his mother left home when your father was very small. Then, when he was seventeen, he met up with Maurice Levy.'

'The gallery owner. I knew him. He was like a second father to Daddy. I remember when he died, Daddy took over his business.'

295

'Maurice Levy was a well-known fence. Your father helped him shift stolen stuff!'

'That's rubbish. I've never heard such a load of crap in my life. That's the trouble with you so-called investigative journalists – you just don't investigate the facts.' Gus felt as if a lead weight were pressing down on her chest. She was fighting for breath.

'Gus, I have photographs of him with Thompson.'

'Thompson used him to try to trace stolen stuff. My father told me that,' she blurted. Her head throbbed as she struggled to think through the fog of confusion.

Tom watched her face, realized her shock – her lack of comprehension. He gently put his hand on her arm. 'This must all be very hard for you.'

'Look, you may be right about Thompson, but I know you're wrong about my father. He's no crook, Tom. Thompson's just a nasty little villain trying to play out of his league, but I know my father. He's not the man you think he is!'

But as Gus said it, she doubted her own words. Did she really know what kind of a man her father was? Did she really know *who* he was?

She had to be alone. To think. 'Would you mind going now? It's been a tough evening . . .'

'Will you be okay if I leave you?'

She nodded. Then she remembered that despite what he'd told her, she owed him some gratitude. 'Thanks, Tom. I appreciate what you did tonight. I'd be in a cell right now if you hadn't been here. And then I'd be looking at the end of my career.'

'You've got my card,' he said. 'Call me when you feel like it – off the record, as they say!'

'Thanks. I'll do that.'

But when later Gus lay in bed, sleep wouldn't come. She huddled into a tight little ball, unable to escape from the nightmarish thoughts skidding around her brain.

Chapter Twenty-Seven

Giovanna was by far the most conspicuous of all the
diners. She had chosen a table, centre stage, near the
door, to enable her to see the comings and goings of
all. She was dressed in a skin-tight suit of kingfisher-
blue leather. Her slim but shapely legs crossed daintily
to the side of the chair, receiving many admiring
glances from the various males around the room.

She smiled broadly when she spotted Piers. He
waved and joined her. Leaning forward he brushed her
cheek with his, mouthing the smallest, most discreet of
kisses. Giovanna grabbed him by flinging her arms
around his neck and almost pulling him off balance as
she placed an enormously sensuous kiss smack on to
his mouth. He looked around the room self-consciously.
He knew the staff here well, and he guessed he'd
probably know many of the diners. He had been kicking
himself ever since Giovanna's call last night that he
hadn't suggested they meet somewhere a little more
discreet. The main reason he hadn't called her back to
insist upon such a change of plan was because he had
subsequently decided that if he were to meet her in
such an open venue, then the psychology would be that
they couldn't possibly be up to no good. What he
hadn't reckoned upon was Giovanna's total lack of
subtlety. Or maybe not so much her lack of subtlety, but
the simple terrifying fact that she was reckless enough
not to have the remotest care what anyone should see,
or think.

'Darling,' she crooned loudly, 'how I've missed you.

Why don't we skip lunch and go straight upstairs? I can't tell you how desperate I am for you.'

'Giovanna, please, keep your voice down. You will embarrass everyone!'

'Embarrass you, you mean, Piers. You English are so stuffy. Now, I have decided what we are going to do. I am so excited and so will you be when I tell you. Waiter!' she called loudly. 'Bring the champagne now.' She turned to Piers and smiled at him. She had a generous mouth, perfect, ivory-coloured skin and eyes as black as a moonless night below eyebrows shaped into neat, dark, curving crescents. Giovanna was unquestionably beautiful and her body was undoubtedly alluring, but Piers was no longer interested. He was far too old for this kind of thing, and since Elena's departure yesterday evening, his main desire was to catch up with his wife and attempt to explain himself. Damn this bloody woman for placing him in such a tricky position. Didn't he have enough problems in his life without having to cope with Giovanna, obviously an unhinged nymphomaniac? He realized that if he didn't let her down gently, she could make the scene to end all scenes, and then he'd end up with his face plastered all over the tabloids – something he could well do without.

He had not wanted to hurt Elena. While she wasn't exactly the most intellectually stimulating of wives, she had been loyal and loving to him during their six-year marriage. She deserved better than this shabby little incident which could hardly have been called an affair. It was a pity that he'd decided to come clean yesterday afternoon. But having heard about Giovanna's descriptive chat on the telephone to Elena, he really thought he'd had no alternative. The cat was well and truly out of her cage!

He needed to sort his life out, and persuade Elena that he was still the same attentive, loving and caring husband he had always been.

'I have the plane on standby,' Giovanna was gushing triumphantly after the waiter had filled their glasses. 'We are going to Nice, and then we are going on a cruise, just the two of us, for as long as we wish. We shall leave tomorrow morning, darling. That should give you time to get your things together. Mmm, aren't you excited? Just think, we can lie in the sun, swim, have the most amazing sex all day long. It will be so wonderful, Piers, it just makes me shudder to think about it. My God,' she lowered her voice, 'I'm so ready for you . . .'

Piers coughed. What the hell was he to do with this woman?

'Giovanna,' he began, 'there's nothing I would like more, but I'm afraid I simply can't join you. I have commitments I must attend to: offices, clients, meetings. My schedule is full. I can't just leave like this. I'm sorry, you must understand.'

'It is arranged,' Giovanna said decisively. 'The plane is scheduled to leave the airport at 10.50 tomorrow morning. You simply cannot let me down.' She smiled her most seductive smile.

Piers was beginning to lose patience. She was taking an awful lot for granted. 'Giovanna, I cannot, and there is simply nothing I can do about it. Now when I left you in Italy, we discussed no more about our relationship. You have taken the decision to make your own arrangements, and I'm sorry, but I simply cannot spare the time to flit away with you. I have things to sort out.'

He stared at her and Giovanna flinched from the anger in his eyes. He noticed the moisture welling up. 'Look,' he said more gently, and placing his hand over hers, 'I had the loveliest time when we were together. And believe me there's nothing I want more than to spend time with you. But I have another life which I must sort out. Calling up Elena was not something I would have wished you to do, Giovanna.' Now the

299

tears were beginning to spill down her cheek. Piers passed her his handkerchief. 'Please,' he said gently, 'don't.' Then against all his better judgement and for want of anything else to say: 'Perhaps we should go somewhere private and discuss these matters.'

Giovanna daintily blew her nose, and stood up, immediately brightening.

'But, Piers, that's what I wanted to do from the beginning.' She linked her arm through his and together they walked to the lift. Piers' mind was racing. Just how was he going to get out of this one?

'Mummy!' Mirabelle cried urgently. 'Mummy! Quick! Look . . . over towards the lift. It's Piers . . .' Her voice was an urgent hiss. 'Look, for God's sake, it's Piers and that woman. Can you see?'

Elena swivelled her head round. She and Mirabelle had been sitting having cocktails, deciding on where to go for lunch.

'Oh no,' Elena choked emotionally. 'I can't believe this. Mirabelle, where are you going, what are you doing?'

'This is too good to miss, Mummy. Just watch.' In half a dozen strides Mirabelle was behind the pair. Neither Piers nor the woman had noticed her approach. She tapped Piers on the shoulder. When he turned, she gave him the most beatific smile. The expression on his face was one which she would take a long time to forget. He looked as if he'd just been caught flogging a forgery of the *Mona Lisa*.

'Piers, I thought it was you,' Mirabelle grinned. 'It's Giovanna, isn't it?'

'Giovanna's just a client. Er . . . I'm valuing something for her. Now if you'll excuse us, Mirabelle . . .'

'Oh not so fast, Piers. You must say hello to Mummy.'

Giovanna, subtle as ever, glowered at Mirabelle, having looked her up and down twice over. 'I am no client,' she snapped. 'I am his lover!'

300

'Then perhaps you might recognize the lady over there – my mother. She is his wife!'

Gus waited and waited, then in frustration she replaced the receiver and redialled George's direct line. Eventually, after several rings, her call was answered.

'George?' she wasn't even sure it was him. He sounded so strange.

'Who's calling?'

'Augusta Lawrence.'

She waited again for several moments. 'Augusta?'

'George,' she said with relief, 'at last. I was beginning to wonder if you were avoiding me.'

There was a silence on the line. Then, 'Of course not, Augusta. Why would you have possibly thought that? Now, how can I help you?'

'You can't have forgotten already, George. The file, remember, on Winston Davis? You were going to have a look at it for me.'

'Oh yes. Nothing doing I'm afraid.'

'What do you mean, George?' Gus asked cautiously. There was something in George's tone, a hesitancy, that made her think he was on his guard. 'That can't be your considered opinion, George. I know the file backwards and I'm sure there's plenty of evidence.'

'Take my advice, Augusta, and forget it. The case is over. I'm sending the papers back to you. Now I really must go – there's another call waiting for me.'

A hollow click and the line was dead. There could only be one explanation: George had been got at. Without any doubt Gus was sure of it. She shivered involuntarily. Just how far did this network go?

That night, once again, the nightmare returned. Gus, her mother and her father walked along the same clifftop path. The wind was blowing Gus so fiercely, pushing her about, playing with her, as if she were a piece of

301

litter. It rushed around her ears, stealing the sound of her parents' voices, but every now and then she could just hear them shouting, whether in anger or to make themselves heard above the wind she couldn't tell. Her parents were always shouting at each other but she didn't know why. They seemed so far away, their figures growing smaller, drifting nearer and nearer to the edge ... the terrifying closeness of the edge. She screamed out at them but no words would come. She tried to move but her legs were rooted to the spot. She couldn't breathe, her fear stifling and strangling, suffocating her. Again she tried, but she was powerless, unable to do anything. She tried to see them, to see where they were. She knew she was lost, they were lost, she was going to lose them both for ever ... Then she saw her father. Her voice struggled to cry out. Mummy! Mummy! she shrieked in her mind. Her soul filled with anguish. Mummy . . .!

She woke up. The darkness swirled in around her. Had she called out? She felt her chest heave, her breathing coming thick and heavy, filled with fear and dread, leaving her so shaken, that she could barely focus her thoughts. She fought to return to consciousness and sanity!

Then she sat up with a start, feeling shock flood through her entire being. Suddenly she knew without a shadow of a doubt what had happened all those years ago. He had murdered her. He had pushed her over the cliff. Gus lay back on to the bed, pulling the duvet up tightly under her chin as the terrifying thoughts pushed into her mind. This time there was no stopping them. It was time to face up. Tom's revelations had released the lock to her subconscious, the riddle of all these years. The thought was too horrifying, too ghastly to assimilate, but she knew it was true. That was why he'd never talk about her mother. Every time she had tried to raise the subject he had avoided telling her anything. All she had to go on was the vague memories of a three-year-old and a sparse assortment of old photographs.

She pulled the pillow up to her face and pushed it against her mouth. She wanted to scream out loud, to shout her pain. Her father was a murderer! Her beloved father had murdered her mother! She slid out of bed, clutching her sides, feeling actual physical pain. What the hell was she to do? Who would she tell?

Mirabelle had a bird's-eye view of Gus from the public gallery. So far Gus was unaware of Mirabelle's presence. It had been quite a while since Mirabelle had last sneaked in to take a look at what her stepsister was up to, not least because it required a great deal of patience actually to find her. This particular case had appeared in today's papers, naming Gus as defence counsel for the accused. Mirabelle couldn't help smiling at the irony of it all. There was the perfect Miss Augusta Lawrence – daughter of art criminal Piers Lawrence – all decked out in her black gown and ridiculous wig, going through the age-old motions of conducting a trial in front of a jury, the picture of Establishment propriety, holding the jury's attention rapt as she cleverly undermined the main prosecution witness. The theatre of the courtroom couldn't fail to fascinate the lay observer. To Mirabelle's left, at one end of the courtroom, was the judge, sitting in her elevated position alone. On the wall behind her the huge coat of arms of the Order of the Garter with the legend 'Honi soit qui mal y pense'; the accused sitting in the sectioned-off dock at the rear of the courtroom to Mirabelle's right; directly in front of the judge sat the clerk and a stenographer, whose fingers were flying over the keys of her machine, taking down every word that was uttered. In front of them were two vast tables for counsel: the prosecution on the left, and the defence on the right. Just below the public gallery was the witness box, in which an articulate but nervous girl stood facing the courtroom and the jury who occupied the two rows of seats against the wall to the judge's left. Her back was turned towards the public gallery to avoid having to meet the eyes of the accused's threatening relatives. The furniture was covered in green leather, including the desks; a vivid green carpet covered the floor. Oak-coloured tongue-and-groove panelling ran laterally around the windowless room.

Gus's voice rang out clearly. The assortment of men and women who made up the jury watched her lips intently. The accused, a small wiry man hiding behind steel-framed glasses, hunched down in his chair, staring at his feet, as if the proceedings were nothing to do with him. Occasionally, he picked at his fingernail, or changed position slightly, crossing his leg, or glancing up at the public gallery to the three people who sat in the row in front of Mirabelle. It killed Mirabelle to admit it, but she did have a very slight admiration for the way in which her stepsister could turn around what had seemed like very satisfactory and solid evidence from an eyewitness. Mirabelle, too, listened intently as Gus continued with her cross-examination.

'And what colour eyes did you say the accused has, Miss Lloyd?'

'Brown. They are definitely brown.'

'I see. And what time of day was it when the accused allegedly entered the shop?'

'About 4.30. It was just beginning to get dark. I hadn't put the lights on at the front of the shop.'

'I see,' Gus pulled the line in a little, 'so would it be fair to say that the shop was a little shadowy?'

'It would be fair to say that, yes.'

'Thank you, Miss Lloyd,' Gus continued encouragingly, and turning to one of the clerks: 'Please could you bring me exhibit number eight? Now, Miss Lloyd, you also said in your statement that the accused was wearing glasses. Were these glasses clear or were they coloured.'

'They were dark.'

'I beg your pardon, Miss Lloyd, but by dark does that mean they were shaded, like sunglasses?'

'Yes.' The clerk handed Augusta a small plastic bag. She held it up for both the jury and for Miss Lloyd to see. 'Are these the glasses you allege you saw the accused wearing?'

'I think so, yes.'

'Sunglasses with very dark lenses. But you are sure you could tell, in spite of the fact that it was dark, that the shop was in shadows, and that the accused was wearing dark sunglasses, that the accused has brown eyes.'

A barely discernible ripple went through the jury. Ten points to Gus!

'Now turning to your statement that you gave to police following the robbery, you stated that the accused was in his early thirties, is that correct, Miss Lloyd?'

'I wasn't sure but I guessed that was about his age. He looked younger, it was difficult . . . as I said . . . it was dark.'

'Well, I would just like to point out, Miss Lloyd, that Mr Johnson here is forty-five years old, and I would suggest that there is a considerable discrepancy between early thirties and forty-five.'

'Look,' Miss Lloyd was beginning to get angry, rattled, just as Gus wanted, 'I told you, it was difficult to see, and I'm not very good at telling age. But I do know it was him, without any shadow of a doubt it was him!' she cried, looking over at the hapless Mr Johnson in the dock.

'Miss Lloyd, I am not in any way doubting your word,' Gus soothed gently. 'I am simply trying to establish the facts. Now if you are ready may we go on?'

The girl nodded and took a sip of water. Mirabelle watched, riveted, as the girl's hand shook, betraying her unease.

'In your statement you also state that the suspect had brown hair.' Like the audience on Wimbledon centre court, all heads swivelled in unison towards the dock. 'Mr Johnson has distinctly grey hair.'

'He was wearing a baseball cap,' Miss Lloyd blurted.

'So it must have been difficult to see what colour his hair was?'

'No! I could see it at the sides. It was a sort of brown. When I said brown I didn't mean a sort of solid brown, I meant salt and peppery brown, like grey.'

'So, although you said brown, you actually meant grey!' Gus was doing pretty well – another ten points to the defence.

She continued in the same vein for the best part of an hour, systematically questioning and dissecting the witness's statement, casting doubt on each and every aspect of what Miss Lloyd allegedly saw. Mirabelle would have hated to be on the jury. They could only find the poor bastard guilty if it was beyond all reasonable doubt, and Gus was giving them more doubts than a bent politician.

She pounced when Gus came out of the court, head to head with her instructing solicitors. They were smiling at each other, no doubt pleased with the way the morning had progressed.

'Gus,' Mirabelle called out softly. 'Gus, hi, I wonder if I could talk to you.'

Gus's face crumpled into a frown of disappointment. All she bloody needed was a dose of Mirabelle. She whispered something to the man she was with and marched over to her stepsister.

'What do you want?' she said gruffly. Gus had only seen her in the distance since the James affair. The sight of her hadn't improved with absence!

'I have to talk to you, Gus. It's about Piers. It's very important.' Her voice assumed a suitable note of urgency. She patted a bundle of papers under her arm pointedly. 'I really think it only fair to warn you of what's going on.'

Gus felt a hand of steel clutch her stomach. She had tried to push her father to the back of her mind, just so that she could get through the day ahead. The trial had occupied all her mental and emotional energy and that had been just fine. Now here was Mirabelle revelling in the fact that she'd got something no doubt ghastly to reveal to Gus.

'Whatever it is,' she said tiredly, 'I really am not interested.'

'But, Gus,' Mirabelle went on doggedly, 'it's about his early life. About how he was a common little criminal. A thief and a swindler. Don't you think you'd be interested to know more about that?'

Gus exercised a supreme effort of will and continued walking away from Mirabelle.

'Don't you believe me?' Mirabelle tried once more, running to catch up with her. 'Do you think I've made it up? Because I haven't . . .'

Gus stopped in her tracks and turned, squaring her shoulders at Mirabelle and at the world. 'No, as a matter of fact I don't believe you've made it up, Mirabelle. I expect you're probably telling the truth. But the simple fact is that I am not interested. Now if you don't leave me alone I shall have security throw you out. Goodbye!'

Gus just managed to make it to the robing room before the sobs took over her body. She had to continue, she had to get through the day, she could not allow herself to give in, to let go . . . She struggled to control her racked shoulders, to keep her breathing even. Think of the case, she told herself. Think of the witness and what you're going to do this afternoon. She bit her lip until she tasted blood. At least the pain felt real, something she could concentrate – focus on.

She pulled a tissue out of a box in front of her and mopped at her tired eyes. Enough, she told herself. It must wait until she was good and ready to deal with it.

Chapter Twenty-Eight

❧❧❧

Piers heard Giovanna's voice drifting through the half-open door. He heard his secretary valiantly trying to persuade her that Piers was out. Giovanna's deep Italian voice was rising indignantly. Just as Piers was contemplating diving under the desk, Giovanna pushed her way through the door. 'You rat!' she hissed. 'I knew you were here, hiding from me like a cowardly piece of vermin.'

Piers stood up. 'I told you the situation yesterday, how I felt. I cannot commit to the sort of relationship you need, Giovanna.' All the time he had tried to be utterly reasonable. He felt it was very important to try to take as much sting as possible out of his rejection. But even the gentlest form of rejection was too much for Giovanna to take. It was a word she simply did not have in her vocabulary!

'You wish to change your mind and come with me?'

'I'm sorry, I cannot.' Piers faced her steadily, his steely blue eyes hard opposite her glittering, challenging, black ones. 'I am afraid that I am not in a position to fulfil your needs, Giovanna. I find you very charming, and definitely irresistible. But I cannot give up my life to be your full-time lover.'

'And that is your final word . . . your decision? I come for you and this is what you do to me?' Her eyes blazed with anger.

'Giovanna, I . . .' he began, but she spun on her heel and marched out of the door, slamming it so hard that Piers could have sworn the entire building shook. As the peace settled around him once again, he breathed out. Thank God he'd managed to get out of that with his skin intact. Now he had to set about trying to mend what was left of his marriage with Elena.

Tom stood in the middle of the room, surveying the chaos around him. His eyes started to focus on the damage to individual areas. The sofa had knife slashes through the cotton ticking. The black ash dining table had been smashed down the centre. The carpet had bleach poured over it. The walls had been sprayed with red aerosol paint, which had run in ominous-looking blood-like droplets down the magnolia emulsion. Tom walked through to his bedroom. His computer lay in a shattered heap, wires burned and scattered. All his precious books had been cleared off the shelves and lay in a pile on the floor, which had then been urinated over. He felt like throwing up. His files had been emptied from the cabinet and the contents spread around the floor where that too had been sprayed with piss. Tom picked up the phone and called Adam; and then Clive Parfitt. Lastly he called Augusta.

Augusta and Flora were stealing a rare supper together. They had a favourite, out-of-the-way, Italian restaurant the other side of Chelsea Bridge which served excellent homemade pasta, had cheerful blue-and-white checked tablecloths, a decent house wine and a funny little Italian owner called Marco who always greeted them warmly even though they only managed to visit the place about once every six months. The restaurant was always buzzing with advertising types who made a lot of noise, making it easy for Gus and Flora to have confidential conversations without the slightest risk of being overheard.

Flora was pleased and a little surprised that Gus had issued the invitation. If she'd been Gus she'd probably have thrown her out of the flat and never spoken to her again. It had only been last night that Flora had learned of the break-in. Flora had felt a total heel, suddenly realizing how selfish she was being spending all her time with Chris. She would hate to be taken for one of those women who dropped everyone and everything the minute a man walked into their lives. And she had been in danger of doing just that, partly because Chris was so damned persistent and persuasive. Flora felt ashamed, too, that she hadn't noticed before just how much weight Gus had lost. Flora studied her face more closely, albeit with difficulty through the dancing shadows of the candlelight. Gus looked so pale and delicate, fragile and translucent, almost deathly in the whiteness of her skin. Her eyes were surrounded by purple bruises and her cheekbones appeared more prominent than usual. Her face had certainly grown leaner, making her look older, far more serious.

Flora realized, guiltily, that she hadn't actually checked to see that Gus had got over that business with James Kentish properly. But the thing about Gus was that she always seemed to be so damned capable. She wasn't the type to swap confidences over a croissant at the breakfast table. She didn't let on about her anxieties and her innermost feelings. Maybe Flora should have been more pushy but they both led such busy lives! It was hard enough struggling to get through the workload without taking on each other's problems too. Now Flora felt utterly selfish.

Gus was staring out of the window absently, her eyes unfocused, and Flora realized she was miles away. 'Gus,' she said, 'hello . . . come back to earth!'

'What? Oh sorry, Flora. You're right, I was miles away. What did you say?'

'Nothing. I've been thinking rather than saying. You look terrible!' she said bluntly.

311

Gus forced a laugh. 'Straight to the point as ever. Thanks, Flora, that makes a girl feel really great. Good job I'm not out on the pick-up, then.'

'Gus, I can't imagine you ever out on the pick-up. But you do look unwell. You haven't been sleeping, have you?'

'Sleeping, eating, thinking – I don't think I've been doing anything properly for weeks, Flora.' Her soft grey eyes stared out at a point way past Flora's left shoulder, then she sighed heavily and neatened up the knife and fork in front of her. She looked so desperately sad, suddenly. Flora instinctively reached out and placed her hand over Gus's. 'Want to talk about it? I guess the break-in, on top of everything else. On top of James . . .'

'James!' Gus sounded totally astonished that Flora could have suggested anything so moronic. 'James! Why on earth should I be –' Then, seeing Flora's shocked look, she immediately apologized. 'Oh Flora, I'm sorry. It's just that I haven't really thought about James for some time. Several other matters seem to have taken over the space he once occupied. In actual fact it's all rather difficult to talk about.'

'Oh please,' Flora said quickly, 'don't let me pry, Gus. I don't want you to feel I've put you in a tricky position.'

'No, no, I didn't actually mean difficult in terms of privacy, I meant in terms of it being so much of a problem – not knowing where to start. Not really being able to understand it all myself; not knowing whether by talking about things it'll actually make them worse. I don't suppose I'm making any sense at all.'

She helped them both to some more Valpolicella. Gus enjoyed the way the wine warmed her, relaxed her head, made her a little drowsy. She'd have to watch it or she'd be hitting the bottle too much, but for the moment it seemed to be helping her.

'It's the Winston Davis case,' she said, swallowing some more wine and then snapping a grissini stick in two.

'I thought it had to be. He committed suicide in the end, didn't he? I read about it in the press.'

'Yep, that's exactly what he did. He didn't kill that cop, of course. Some other cops did.' She popped the grissini into her mouth and crunched it.

'I knew that's what you were thinking, but it all sounds so bizarre. Are you really sure, Gus?'

'Oh, sure as I can be. I get the feeling I'm being watched all the time. And then there's stuff about my family – my father – but I really don't want to get into any of that at the moment. It's all too painful. So I guess you could say I feel generally pretty screwed up about a few things.'

'I'll do what I can to help, Gus. Perhaps you need a break – a few days away somewhere. Maybe a health farm or something, what do you think?'

'Nice idea, Flora, but I've got a pile of cases coming up. Besides, I've got a feeling I need to stick around London and see what develops. Don't worry about me, I'm pretty tough really.' She smiled crookedly at her friend. Flora had already decided she would talk to Chris. He might have some good ideas about how to test out Gus's suspicions. Maybe he might have heard rumours, something about what had been going on with Winston Davis, Gus's lay client. It had to be worth a try!

Frank Thompson had called a meeting of his three top men. This time they weren't having a tasteful little soirée at his home, though. They were in a little room over the top of Lennie Coone's boxing club down the Angel. Frank had arrived on his own, then Martin Coles; then finally Chris and Gary Bell. Gary checked the door and then the windows. The room was thick with ribbons of grey smoke hanging in horizontal layers. The acrid smell of stale nicotine permeated everything: the drapes, the mock-velvet upholstery on the chairs, the red and gold carpets and the green hessian-covered walls. Two bottles of whisky stood unopened on the leather-covered desk, with half a dozen glasses. But as usual, Frank didn't offer any alcohol to the gathering of his chosen men. He wanted them to keep their wits about them. He wasn't about to repeat, or write down, any of the instructions he would give them tonight.

Martin slouched up against the wall, next to the doorway. Frank sat behind the desk, leaning backwards in the swivel chair. Chris stood at the far side of the room, his face half in the shadows, while Gary perched on the windowsill in front of the Dralon curtains. They all waited for Frank to speak. Maybe it was a trick of the light, but he looked meaner tonight, his face thinner, more like the weasel they knew he was. But without him they would have been nothing, worthless members of an increasingly impotent force. Frank gave them power and money and it was an addictive mixture. Even the danger they encountered as a result of their activities was addictive. The rush of adrenalin as the fear subsided, the thrill of combat, and then of overcoming, of being utterly in control, could grow into a hunger that was almost sexual in its urgency. Animals – that's what they were. Finely trained, effective and terrifyingly powerful. Chris Thompson felt himself grow erect just by thinking . . .

'So,' Frank began, 'Piers Lawrence. I want a file put together by Friday – just three days' time. I want details of his bank accounts, and I want everything you've got on potential money laundering. I've got a whole load of contacts you can chase up.' His beady, rodent eyes scanned the faces. 'That clear to you all?'

'Yes, sir,' they answered in unison. Frank liked to keep things disciplined, a sense of order in the ranks, otherwise he knew all sorts of identity problems might arise.

314

'Right, Chris, you can go now. I want to see you tomorrow morning, usual place. And Gary and Martin, you two stay here. I've got another couple of jobs for you. To work, boys, and good luck.'

Gus first noticed the car on her tail just as she pulled out of Sloane Square and headed down King's Road. The headlights dazzled her. What the hell was it doing, trying to drive right up her backside? She accelerated slightly and flicked the rearview mirror upwards, so that the light reflected indirectly. She had been to the gym with one of her old university friends. It had been a long-standing appointment for a game of squash, and Gus had decided to keep it no matter how lousy and tired she felt, thinking the change would do her good. It *had* been good to see Tanya, but Gus hadn't given her a decent game. Tanya had absolutely thrashed her and Gus had guessed that Tanya had been frustrated by the ease with which she had taken every point from Gus. But she was far too polite to mention it. In the past they had had some fierce confrontations, with Gus giving every bit as good as she got. After showering, they had grabbed a quick bite to eat and a couple of glasses of wine. Gus felt tired, as usual, and had cried off early.

That damned car was almost touching her! Gus pulled up at the traffic lights and drummed her fingers impatiently on the wheel, keeping her eyes firmly in front of her. Then she saw something come out of the shadows towards her passenger door. She made out the shape of a man as the figure came closer. Then a gloved hand moved for the door handle. Even though Gus knew the door was locked, she shoved the car into gear and slammed her foot hard down on the accelerator. It was a quiet junction and she knew she was safer jumping red lights than sticking around to find out what was going to happen next. She flicked her rearview mirror back down and watched as the figure raced back into the car and started to follow her. Gus spun the car into the next left-hand turning, screeching down the residential street, dodging between the rows of parked cars, all the while keeping an eye on her rearview mirror. She had driven several hundred yards before she finally relaxed her speed, realizing that whoever her would-be attacker was, he had decided to give up.

Gus continued her journey home, thinking only of being safely locked behind her own front door – but even that wasn't safe any more – just three nights since the break-in! She could go and stay in a hotel, be anonymous, where nobody could find her ... No! She would not allow herself to become intimidated. She was going home and tomorrow she would feel stronger and better able to deal with all these strange incidents. The figure in black was probably completely unconnected with the Winston Davis case, probably just a thug prowling the streets – there were enough of them about, for God's sake – an opportunist mugger who had misjudged his timing. Pure coincidence.

Arriving home, Gus bolted the front door behind her. Then as she walked up the stairs the telephone started to ring. She picked it up. 'Hello?'

A male voice sounded breathy and harsh. It was the same voice she'd heard half a dozen times before: 'Next time I won't give up so easily. Now just lay off the case or else ...'

'Who is this?' Gus cried, but the line had already gone dead. She sat down on the sofa, kicked off her shoes, and then huddled into a tight little ball. Eventually she drifted off into a fitful sleep, tormented by new nightmares.

They were sitting in the tiny bar of some seedy Earl's Court hotel which Tom knew of, the reason being that no one would be able to overhear their conversation without their being aware of it. They had the little room to themselves and the door was firmly closed. The barman had access to the bar in the room in which they sat, and to the much larger bar in the main lounge. Having fulfilled Tom's order, he had largely ignored them, being kept busy on the bustling other side.

Tom had made a judgement, rightly or wrongly, that Gus was not involved with anything her father might be up to. She was just too squeaky clean, and the fact of her victimization hardly pointed to her being on the wrong side of things. A burglary could have been set up, but she was pretty shaken by last night's 'phantom' mugger, and the night caller. She looked ill compared to when he had first met her. Not so much composed counsel now. She was so much more vulnerable: she even seemed to have shrunk in stature. Had Clive not been there he might have been tempted to take her hand; to try and reassure her. He watched as she ran her neat little teeth over her bottom lip. She was just a bundle of nerves. Who could blame her? It was pretty ghastly for all of them not knowing what tricks were going to be pulled next.

'The ring leader is Frank Thompson – he's been in the force some thirty years: East End boy through and through. Joined when he was eighteen and worked his way into the CID. Now he's a detective sergeant – never particularly ambitious, in the force, that is. His son, Chris, is the one with the ambitions ... No, Frank seems to be happy staying a big fish in a small sea – in his own little empire. He's got five chosen men around him at Brickwell, and a further nine scattered around various London nicks. That number excludes the seniors involved. He's got bribes running through the CPS, and through the most senior channels of the Met at Scotland Yard. I have a list of most of those names,' Tom continued in a deadpan voice. 'And I guess that's what they were looking for when they visited my apartment. Needless to say they didn't find it. I have the list in my

317

head, and I also have it locked away in a deposit box which nobody knows about, and I don't propose to put either of you two at risk by telling you. However, in the event of my death I have made arrangements for the list to be made . . . let's say available!'

'But that's just incredible,' Gus choked. 'You're saying that this guy Thompson has connections even within the CPS?'

Tom nodded.

'And the mugger last night? You think he was out to kill me?'

'To be honest, Gus, and this may sound brutal, but if they were intent on killing you, I think they'd have done it by now. I rather think they're counting on the fact that either you'll get scared off, or you'll drop it because everyone you come up against won't want to know.'

'So why don't you publish the facts?' Clive, who had been thoughtfully silent, spoke up.

'Well, I rather think that's what I'm going to have to do. I just want to get the entire story together, to be sure of my facts, before I do. The legal implications of my getting anything wrong are pretty heavy. And,' he glanced sideways at Gus, 'I had a few other leads to check out, things to follow up.'

'Like me, you mean?' she said miserably. 'My connections to my father?'

'Well, yes, but I suppose I could have put it more gently. I didn't know what you did and didn't know about him.'

Gus glanced nervously at Clive. If at all possible, she really didn't want poor Clive to have to hear all the muck that lurked in her family background.

'So what are they actually doing – apart from murdering their own kind? And what motive did they have?' Gus was trying to piece together the facts, so far as she knew them.

'Drugs, racketeering, protectionism, Yardies – you

name it, they're into it. What really amazes me is how no one has thought to question how it is that a humble detective sergeant such as Frank Thompson can be living in a house worth over three hundred grand. And he's not the only one. You only have to look at the cars they're posing about in in their spare time. It's like nobody dares to take the lid off. Nobody dares to question them . . .'

'I'm not surprised, given the level of intimidation we've been through.' Clive rubbed at his jaw where he'd been socked by the intruder he'd had so thoughtlessly interrupted at his office.

'So what do we do now?' Gus faced them both, her grey eyes tired and earnest.

'I vote I finish off the story – then once it's published all hell will break loose and Thompson's lot should be arrested, an enquiry will follow and we can all relax.'

Gus almost laughed. 'If they haven't hopped it first!' Tom made it all sound so ridiculously easy. Of course it wasn't going to be as simple as that. 'And what do we do in the meantime?' It was a loaded question meaning: are we all going to get killed while you do this, Tom? How much more aggravation are we going to get?

'Carry on as normal.'

Gus nodded. What else had she expected him to say? Besides, she had cases to sort out, trials coming up. She could hardly take up Flora's suggestion and run off to a health farm. 'Clive,' she said eventually, 'got any better ideas?'

Clive looked at her for a few moments grimly. He would have liked to suggest that they go straight to the police . . . to the CPS . . . to the proper authorities to get this whole thing sorted out. But the trouble was they didn't know who they could trust. Gus's friend had hardly been helpful. Clive didn't have any better suggestions than to leave fate in the hands of this scruffy so-called investigative journalist. They knew hardly anything about him. He could have been leading them right up the garden path. He might be completely unscrupulous – even a stooge for Thompson's lot, if it were indeed true about Thompson's lot.

Clive shook his head to try and clear it of all these confusing and contradictory thoughts. He had nothing else to go on, no other ideas of his own, so he might just as well try and trust this Silverthorn bloke. In the meantime he intended to get his nose into anything and everything but the Winston Davis case. He felt like putting an announcement in the national press about how he would no longer be pursuing anything along those lines. Clive was not a campaigner, he had never thought of his views as particularly liberal, yet here he was acting like some committed radical when really he would have liked to crawl home to his wife and put the entire thing behind him. But thanks to both his and Gus's efforts, it was almost too late for that. They were in it. And for better or for worse, he had to be grateful that this Silverthorn bloke at least had a plan which might do some good. More good than the proper legal channels, Clive thought disdainfully. It said a lot for the British legal system when the only hope of bringing someone to justice was through the pages of a Sunday newspaper!

Clive finished his drink. 'I've got to go. Let me know how you get on, Tom, and I'll let you know if anything else happens, though I hope to God things quieten down a bit. I'm not cut out for this kind of cloak-and-dagger stuff. You'll be okay, will you, Gus?'

'Sure. Never been better.' She attempted to smile. In truth she couldn't remember when life had ever been this shitty. Even Mirabelle's antics paled into insignificance compared to what was now going on in her life.

Tom bought her another mineral water. 'Sure you don't want anything stronger?' he asked.

'No, this is fine. I daren't risk it. Besides, I was

320

beginning to find the numbing effects of alcohol really quite pleasant.'

'You want to talk about it?' he said, matter-of-factly.

'My father?' She sighed heavily. 'I don't know. I guess I've spent the last few days trying not to think about it. My delightful stepsister seems to be conversant with all his activities as well.'

'Mirabelle?'

Gus eyed him warily. 'You know her?' Here we go again, she thought. It was really quite amazing how Mirabelle could be so successful at insinuating herself into nearly every corner of Gus's life.

'I've met her. I had to find out what she was all about in the interests of the story.'

'Did you sleep with her?'

Tom nearly choked on his pint. He was about to say it was none of her business, but there was something in her face that stopped him. A kind of wariness, like that of a cornered animal. He could almost feel the tension in her body. 'No, as a matter of fact I didn't.'

'Not through want of Mirabelle trying, I'll bet,' Gus said flatly, staring into the depths of her mineral water.

'I suppose she would have liked to ... develop the relationship.'

'Well, I guess that explains how she knew about my father. You must have passed on all the information to her. Well done, Tom. That's really put the icing on my cake. You have no idea what a pain in the arse that woman can be. Of course she's delighted with this new bit of information. Thanks for being so discreet!'

'Now just wait a minute!' Tom snapped, angry at Gus's automatic assumption that he and Mirabelle had been ... well ... intimate. 'I didn't tell her anything. She told me little enough, too. I didn't know where she was coming from. She might have been in on whatever he's up to. I played it very carefully ...'

'Like you did with me in the wine bar that night. How

do I know when you're on the level? All of this support now – how do I know it's not just another ruse to strengthen your story, to get near to my father? Am I going to wake up one morning and find myself splashed all over the front pages in some sleazy piece about my family?' She stood up and grabbed her coat. Her head ached so much. She didn't know what to think any more, who to trust, what to do.

'Gus, wait ...' Tom followed her out of the hotel and into the street.

She quickly unlocked her car and jumped in, then in a replay of the previous evening she put her foot down and sped away from him.

Why was her life falling apart? What the hell had she done to deserve all this? Was this what her mother had found out all those years ago? Was that why her father had murdered her – because she knew too much – her poor dear mother whom she had missed every day of her life? God, he had a lot to answer for and, she suddenly decided as the anger fired her blood, she would make him pay dearly for what he had done!

Tom jumped into his ancient MG and followed as close on Gus's tail as he could. She'd really got to him tonight, making him feel somehow responsible for the state she was in. Well, he *was* responsible. She could have remained blissfully unaware of her father's circumstances if he hadn't started digging around. Maybe Gus was right, all he was fit for was sleaze and rolling about in the muck he'd so successfully raked up. He had to catch her. He wanted to know that she was safe. He couldn't remember when a woman had last got under his skin like this. Maybe just once, many years ago, he'd come pretty close to caring. The woman was older than he, more mature, very different to Gus. She'd been in the business, editor of the local paper he'd started out on. She'd had her fling with Tom, then gone off to New Zealand with the new man in her life. Tom hadn't let on how upset he'd felt. He just decided after that that he wouldn't fall quite so easily again, move on before things started to get serious.

He put his foot down, trying to stay with Gus, watching her rear lights. Eventually they made it to her street. Tom pulled in just after Gus had parked. She was getting out of the car when he screeched to a halt behind her. She squinted at him, and for a second he felt guilty for being the source of the fear he saw across her features. He pulled the window down and called out, 'It's okay, it's me, Tom. I wanted to make sure you got home all right. I didn't want a repeat of last night. I was worried . . .'

As Gus stood on the pavement, recovering from the thought of yet another onslaught, all the fight went out of her. Tom got out of his car and walked up to her. She seemed to slump, her shoulders sank down and her head drooped. He put his arm around her slim frame and held her close to him. She buried her head in his chest and he guessed she was crying. He leaned forward and brushed the top of her hair with his lips. It smelled of spring mornings.

'Ssssh,' he whispered tenderly. 'Come on, let's get you inside.'

Obediently, she let him lead her to the door, feeling grateful for the warmth and strength of his support. She handed him the key, he unlocked the door and together they climbed the stairs. Tom sat her down on the sofa, and then helped them both to a glass of whisky. Gus shook her head when he handed it to her. He put both the glasses down on the coffee table and seated himself down beside her on the soft feather cushions. Then, silently, he gathered her up in his arms once more and started to kiss away the path of wet tears down her cheeks.

Gus couldn't remember when she had last felt so warm and safe, cocooned in the tender circle of such strong arms. She relaxed against his firm body, lifting her face to his kisses. She could have pushed him away, but she seemed to have no will to summon; she was beyond fighting. It felt right to be like this with him. For all her bitter words, she did trust him. She could feel his warmth seeping into her own tired limbs. There had been no one at all since James, no thoughts or desires other than simply to get through. Tom's mouth explored her cheeks so gently, carefully, almost fearfully. She lifted her mouth and their lips met. She was astonished to feel the sudden fire shoot through her breasts, through her belly, right to her core; that wonderful melting, drowning, spinning sensation as her mouth yielded under his, opening up to his searching tongue, losing herself completely, forgetting where she was and barely who she was. She was vaguely aware of Tom's fingers sliding up underneath her sweater. She held her breath as he delicately reached round her back, deftly unhooking her bra, then she felt her breasts released, and the joy as Tom's hands cupped first one and then the other, his hands at once curious and tantalizing, teasing the tips of her nipples, squeezing and massaging until she was crying out for him, pulling his head harder to hers, bruising their lips harder together, squirming against him, her body taking over in its need for him.

Her fingers were clumsy with desire as she struggled to undo his button fly. Then she found him, proud and hard and aching. Gus ran her fingers over the silken shaft, and then round his testicles, loving the way Tom's tongue responded with such ferocious wanting. He slipped his hand inside her pants and pulled them down over her legs. She helped kick her feet free of them and then lay back, her legs gloriously open, urging him towards her. The joy of feeling him push into her was almost painful, creating and at the same time assuaging the ache deep inside her. She urged him deeper with her hips, rising and arching against him. He needed no encouragement as he rode into her harder and more ecstatically. Gus thought she would die. She was gone to some faraway land where all that existed was this wonderful feeling that she and Tom had created. She wanted to hold the moment, to freeze it, for it never to stop, to go on for ever and ever. She tried not to come, she tried to hold her body back, to prolong the ecstasy, but her body betrayed her, shuddering into vast paroxysms of bliss. She felt Tom stiffen against her, then she felt him deep inside her, coming and coming and coming, filling her until he too cried out.

'Gus, Gus, Gus,' he whispered as he sank down on top of her, his body spent. 'Thank you . . .' he sighed, closing his eyes and snuggling his face against her shoulder. His arms held her as if he were afraid she might disappear if he ever let go. She closed her eyes and let her hand stray over Tom's naked back, delighting in the way the skin rippled underneath her touch, as if it had a life of its own. She couldn't remember ever feeling this good, ever being loved so totally. She had been transported somewhere totally new by this strange, wonderful man. As she lay drifting, almost sleeping, feeling Tom shrink inside her, she realized that for a short while she had forgotten all the many things which troubled her. For a few idyllic moments she had been lost and removed from all the shit in her life.

Suddenly feeling cold, and maybe a little awkward, she started to shift her weight, making Tom move with a start. She guessed he had been just on the point of sleep. They had made the most fabulous love together, but they still needed to talk. Now Tom had to tell her every detail he knew about her father's past, no matter how bad.

Chapter Twenty-Nine

Giovanna waited on the terrace for Salvatore's arrival. The best way of getting over a lover was to take another one. Salvatore had been wooing her ever since she had first met him at Gulio's. Funny how Gulio had provided such opportunities for her! Her call to Salvatore's home in Switzerland just hours before had prompted him to suggest flying over immediately. What a nice change to feel wanted by a man! Unlike that bastard Piers. She had tried very hard not to think about Piers Lawrence and the way he had betrayed her like that. Leading her along, making her think that he really cared about her, when it was clear that she actually meant nothing to him. She thought with bitterness of that scene with his wife, when Giovanna had watched him almost grovel to the woman outside the lift, leaving her, Giovanna Lucciani, standing like some cast-off rubbish for all the world to see her shame! And what was it the girl had said? That she was a tramp, a little piece of pussy on the side! Huh! She was so angry ... so humiliated. Nobody, nobody ever treated Giovanna like that. She would have to teach him a lesson. She would enjoy thinking of something suitable.

'My darling,' Giovanna welcomed Salvatore with open arms. He planted a huge kiss on her lips and swept his left palm across her right buttock, squeezing his fingers into her bottom.

'Salvatore, you are a naughty boy,' she chastised him gently.

'Surely my little Giovanna hasn't changed towards me!'

'Of course not! Why would I have asked you here?'
She teased. 'But I have ideas for us, Salvatore. Like
bathing first. You are tired and hot and need refreshing.
Join me in my bathroom in fifteen minutes. I'll be
waiting for you!'

Salvatore was already naked when he entered the
bedroom. He saw that Giovanna had cast her clothes off
in a trail leading into the bathroom. He picked up the
gossamer-fine stocking and ran it under his nose,
savouring the smell of hot bitch. He let the stocking
graze his stomach as it floated back to the floor. He
wanted her very badly. His bare soles slid soundlessly
across the black marble floor. He could see the back of
Giovanna's head just poking above the edge of the giant
Jacuzzi. The sound of churning water drowned out any
sound he might make. He stepped up onto the edge of
pool and gazed down at Giovanna's body. Her eyes
were closed dreamily, her mouth half open in erotic
enjoyment. Her voluptuous breasts floated in the current, the tips of her brown nipples breaking through the
foaming surface tantalizingly. He could see the shadow
of the triangle at the top of her legs. She had one hand
draped over her belly, her fingers teasing into the crease
of her cunt.

Salvatore stepped into the hot water and settled in
beside her. He brought his mouth down almost savagely around her nipple, sucking on it as hard as he
could. Giovanna's eyes flew open in surprise.

'Salvatore!' she shrieked. 'You are a very naughty
boy.' Then; 'Mmm, Salvatore, do that some more, oh
you're so gooood . . .' as Salvatore's hand brushed hers
aside and slipped easily inside her. She opened her legs
to accommodate him further. Then he lifted up her
buttocks so that her belly floated to the surface.
Giovanna balanced herself by spreading her arms along
the edge of the tub, letting her body go limp and
relaxed, moving as Salvatore dictated. Her hips floated

on the surface, bucking gently with the thrusts of the water. Salvatore grasped a buttock in each of his hands and squeezed as if she were a ripe peach. Then he lifted her pelvis higher and brought his head down to meet her cunt, closing his mouth directly over her clitoris, sucking hard, swirling his tongue over and around, teasing and licking and driving her crazy. She pushed herself further into his face, grinding herself towards him. Then she began to climax. 'Salvatore ... oh, yes ... please ... do it to me ... fuck me ... oh yes ...' she cried, willing him to go on for ever. Then as soon as the waves had subsided, he pushed his body between her legs and nudged his way inside her. She wrapped her legs around his back and let the water take them. She was feeling better already ...

Afterwards, as they sipped ice-cold champagne, Giovanna took Salvatore by the hand. 'Come,' she whispered, 'I have something to show you.' She led him to the salon. 'Sit here,' she instructed, placing him on a sofa. 'Wait ...' She pushed the buttons on the console and the wall over the firebreast started to swivel. The Daubigny disappeared into the void behind and the Vermeer magically appeared.

'But ...!' Salvatore sounded amazed. 'What happened? I never thought Gulio would get rid of it. He was so desperate for the thing, pestered me to death for it. How did you come by it, Giovanna my sweetest?'

Giovanna's laughter gurgled in her throat. 'Gentle persuasion of course, my darling. I gather I can be quite good at it!'

'I can't believe any man would deny that, but the Vermeer ...'

Salvatore stood up and drew closer to the painting. He stood gazing into it, marvelling at the symmetry, at the technical perfection. He remembered back to how close it almost came to total disaster, just after he had hung it himself. The plaster hadn't held and the canvas had tumbled forward, falling against a wooden chair. A dent had formed. But the restorer had done an excellent job. Nobody but Salvatore would ever know the difference. He ran his hand over the right-hand corner of the painting. Amazing what a marvellous job had been done. His fingers searched more carefully the exact spot where the lump remained. Giovanna was watching him, at first just thinking he was lost in admiration, but there was something about his frown, the way it deepened, the way he was so earnestly stroking the canvas.

'Giovanna ...' Salvatore stepped back and looked again at the entire canvas. There was no doubt it was a masterpiece – but it wasn't a Vermeer. 'Your painting, it is a fake!'

Giovanna's mouth opened and closed but no sound came. She sank down on to the sofa. At last when her breath returned she managed to croak: 'Salvatore, you are joking. This is some kind of fun you are having with me. But it is not funny, it is cruel! Do you know how much I paid for this thing?'

'I can guess. But I promise you it is not the Vermeer that I sold to Gulio.' She listened to him, deeply shocked, as he recounted the tale of the restoration. 'So you see, my love, I have no doubt.'

'Piers Lawrence! He should have told me! He must have known. He brought me the painting – he's the expert. He must have been in league with Gulio. Why, the bastard! Salvatore, I have been betrayed.' She paced the floor angrily, throwing her fists around her taut body. 'This has cost me dear, but I vow, Salvatore, that Piers Lawrence will pay a higher price!

Piers's secretary put the call from Thompson through. As soon as Piers spoke into the mouthpiece Thompson rasped viciously: 'Listen to me, Lawrence. I told you to sort out that daughter of yours and she's still interfering in my business. You'd better call her off or she's dog meat! Get the idea? She's upsetting some pretty serious people, and believe me, they mean business. Oh, and by the way, as well as burying your daughter, you'll be burying your career. I've got quite an interesting file together already for the boys at the CPS. Got it?'

Piers snarled back, 'I go down and you join me, Thompson.'

'I wouldn't be too sure about that, Lawrence.'

Piers slammed the phone down feeling as if someone had kicked him in the stomach. Gus meant the world to him. Before she was safe, away, removed totally from his seedy world. None of this should touch her. He'd tried so hard all through her life to keep her shielded.

'Gus, I have to talk to you.' Piers's voice was almost pleading with his daughter. He couldn't understand why she was being so damned cold to him. 'Darling,' please, try to listen. I have something very, very important to say to you.'

'I don't want to see you,' Gus snapped coldly. 'There's only one important thing you've got to tell me, and I can't believe that that's what's on your mind.'

'What?' he said cautiously, wondering if she had pre-empted his warning.

'About my mother. I'd very much like to know what happened . . .'

'Oh really, Gus. Now is not the time,' he said impatiently. 'Darling, I must insist that you see me. It is a matter of life and death!'

'Most things are, it would seem,' she said, betraying little emotion. She was barely able to keep her voice level. His call had come right out of the blue: 'I'm in London. I must see you!' She hadn't expected to have to confront her feelings so abruptly, to work out just how she would deal with her suspicions. It was all so unplanned. She hadn't sorted things out yet. But it was hard not to hear the note of fear in her father's voice. Funny – he was always so cool and composed, so very much in charge of things, and here he was pleading with her on the opposite end of the telephone.

'Very well. You can come here. In one hour's time.' She put the phone down, not waiting for his answer.

At the other end, Piers shook his head sadly. They had shared such a special bond, the two of them. It had to be special – after all the time they had spent together, just the pair of them, a real little team. Although Gus may not have realized it, he had followed just about every inch of her progress through school and through college with the most immense sense of pride and, yes, adoration. She was everything he could never be. Honest, open, full of integrity, so clever and ambitious. She had the opportunity to make it in the legitimate world, not for ever hiding behind some thin veneer of respectability, waiting for something to come out of the shadows of his past, to catch up with him and find out the real man inside. Was this the approach of his Armageddon? Suddenly, from everything in his life being pretty nearly perfect, it was all going wrong. Gus's life could very possibly be in danger if he didn't sort her out quickly, Elena was filing for divorce, the Lucciani woman had departed vowing vengeance, Gus didn't want to speak to him, and it looked as if his earlier life of crime was about to be exposed. All in all, things didn't look too bright.

He jumped into his car, but was soon sitting stationary in a queue. Even the bloody traffic was conspiring against him!

Gus had decided just what she would do. She had everything she needed and she had an hour to prepare herself. She set to work, using the meagre bits of information she possessed, driven on by the thought that her father was about to have the biggest shock of his life. She just hoped that the shock would be great enough to get the truth out of him.

Chapter Thirty

The door of the house stood ajar. Strange, Piers thought. He called out Gus's name before entering, then hearing no response, he started to climb the stairs. 'Gus!' he called once more. He felt very uneasy. The hairs on the back of his neck stiffened, but he refused to let dark thoughts enter his mind. She must be here somewhere. He called again.

'Up here,' came back the faint reply.

He poked his head around the sitting-room door just to check. He thought her voice sounded as though it were coming from up the stairs, but he looked in just in case. The room was empty – save for the usual piles of books spilling all over the place, and open notepads and general academic chaos. Both girls seemed to use the place as one big study. He started to climb the next flight of stairs which led up to the bedrooms.

'Gus,' this time loudly, but not a shout, 'you up here?' He didn't really think it seemly to go charging into his daughter's bedroom unannounced. 'Darling . . .?'

He stood at the doorway and the scent was the first thing that struck him. The room was filled with the all-pervasive smell of lilies, sickly sweet and cloying. So strong was the smell that he could almost taste it in the back of his throat. It was a perfume he hadn't been exposed to for, what, twenty-odd years?

He stopped in his tracks, staring at the figure on the other side of the room. Her back was turned towards him, silky brown hair brushed into curls which fell down her back. 'Gus?' he whispered, wondering why she didn't turn to look at him. Then, slowly, agonizingly slowly, she started to turn her head.

Piers felt the wind knocked out of him. 'My God,' he whispered, feeling his knees crumple underneath him. The face looking back at him, that expression of total disdain, belonged to a time so long ago. The eyes with the thick liner – cat eyes – staring contemptuously at him. 'Cat . . .' He was looking at a ghost. She stood up, and he recognized the dress she was wearing: Pierre Cardin – black and white – a minidress. They had chosen it together in Paris. The lipstick, everything, he was staring at his dead wife. He stumbled towards the bed, and then folded down onto it.

'Why?' he asked, as the tears sprang to his eyes. 'Why?' His voice cracked into gravel. 'Why, Gus?'

'Because I wanted to see your face!' she cried triumphantly. 'I wanted to see the guilt on it. I wanted to know you for what you truly are! You killed my mother!'

Piers head slumped down to his chest. Suddenly he felt very old, much older than his forty-seven years. He had been transported back to another time, another world, when his life had been turned upside down by the woman. Oh yes, he felt guilty. Had done ever since she died. He knew that he could have done more, that if he'd tried harder then maybe . . . but it was no good thinking in 'if onlys'. He couldn't do anything to make things different now. He had tried to push her from his mind, almost to erase all trace of her existence. He had wanted to protect his daughter so much. For Gus not ever to find out, not to feel the hurt that the truth would surely bring. He had wanted to keep the secret about Cat for ever.

'I have carried the guilt with me all my life, Gus. I just wish things had been different. That I had acted differently.'

Gus stood looking at him contemptuously. 'Aren't you going to deny it?' She couldn't believe that he wasn't screaming his denial at her. Surely he would tell her that she had got it all wrong? Then she could know her nightmare had been just that, a vicious childhood nightmare that didn't mean anything. But he wouldn't look at her. He just hung his head, refusing to meet her eyes. Gus felt as if she might throw up any second. Yes, she believed he had murdered her mother. But she had wanted so much to hear from his lips that it was all lies, that he hadn't done it, that there was some other, plausible explanation that she could believe, so that everything would be back to normal. Well, as normal as normal could be right now. She stood facing him, her voice filled even now with disbelief.

'You admit you killed her?'

Silent tears were streaming down Piers's face. Please deny it, Gus willed him with all her heart. Every atom of her being wanted to hear his denial. She felt ridiculous, all done up like this. Cruel and perverse. But she had done it because she had to find out. 'Daddy! Please tell me you didn't do it!' She too started to cry.

Piers shook his head, unable to speak. He could have saved her. If he hadn't been so busy, if he'd paid more attention to his young wife and less attention to his empire-building and criminal activities, then maybe she wouldn't have turned out the way she did. He just hadn't been able to give her the support she needed, and then the inevitable had happened. Yes, he had killed her. He was responsible.

Slowly he nodded, feeling the knife blade twist deep into his heart as he struggled to speak. 'Yes,' he whispered so quietly that Gus could barely hear. 'Yes, Gus, I killed her.'

Gus stood immobile, staring down at him. He had always seemed so strong, so powerful. She had respected him so much ... now here he was a pathetic figure, sobbing self-pityingly. A common murderer. He had been responsible – of course he had – and her subconscious had always tried to tell her, to make her

335

understand. How did she feel about him? Empty, cold hard emptiness. She shivered, slightly at first, and then her teeth started to chatter. Then her shoulders began to tremble. She knew the signs. She'd seen them happen to poor clients. She was suffering from shock. She stuffed her fist into her mouth to stop herself from crying out. Then she rushed from the room and down the two flights of stairs. She had to get away from him, to put some space between them. If she stayed in the same place as him a moment longer she'd be tempted to knife him. She was filled with a cold hard hatred. A calculating rage. She would bring him down. He would be brought to justice. Her mother would be able to lie at peace once he had been dealt with.

She fired up her car and then accelerated out of the square. Where she was headed, she didn't know, but she had to get away, be by herself for a while.

How long Piers remained on the bed he didn't know. Time didn't seem important any more. He had no idea until now just how strong his daughter's hate was. Her eyes, once he had dared to look into them, showed nothing but contempt. He should have told her years ago, but he never quite had the courage. He'd always tried to pretend to himself that she was too young to understand – and now he had failed Gus completely. He hadn't even managed to tell her why he had needed to see her so urgently. She would never speak to him again, now. But somehow he had to get to her, to make her listen. He stood up and brushed down his trousers, then taking a clean linen handkerchief from his breast pocket, he blew his noise loudly. He couldn't remember the last time he had cried. Certainly not at Cat's funeral. He had been too angry then. Maybe all those years ago when his granddad had passed on. He walked slowly down the stairs, his legs feeling leaden and awkward, as if he had just walked ten miles. He saw the shadow cross the doorway at the bottom. Then, freezing against the wall, he waited as the tall frame came into view.

'Who the hell are you?' he cried, as the long-haired freak came up the stairs towards him.

'You're Piers Lawrence, aren't you? Gus's dad!'

'Have we met?' Piers regarded the younger man uncertainly. He couldn't remember ever having seen him before, and he felt sure he would have remembered him.

'I'm Tom, Gus's friend.'

'As in boyfriend?' Piers asked suspiciously, amazed to feel the stab of jealousy in his gut, despite the previous scene with his daughter.

'I guess you could say that. Where is she? Upstairs? Gus ...!' Tom called out. 'Hi, it's me! Hey, do you know where she is?'

Piers continued down the stairs. 'No. I ... er ... we had a bit of a set-to. She rushed out. She didn't say where she was going.'

'You look pretty awful, mate,' Tom called after Piers. 'Why don't I make us both a cup of tea? It's about time we met and perhaps we might be able to work out where she is.'

He used his best coaxing voice. Tom wanted to know just what had sent Gus out of the house, and what it was that had happened between them. His nerves were so fucking jumpy at the moment, he didn't need any extra puzzles to solve on top of the ones he'd already landed himself. He'd just finished giving Adam, that bloody cub of a photographer, a right bollocking for blabbing his mouth off to Mirabelle. Jesus, all that time and effort put into the story, keeping it secret, planning it all, and the jerk risks it all for the sake of a bonk with Mirabelle. Mirabelle – the biggest tart in TV. Well, he deserved to have picked something up apart from Mirabelle. And that's exactly what Tom had told him. Mind you, the look of terror at a thought which clearly hadn't occurred to him before did make Tom feel a tiny bit guilty. The jerk still needed to be taught a lesson though.

Piers came back up the stairs. 'Okay, Tom. I imagine you know your way around this place better than I do. I am in your hands.'

'Must be a funny feeling for you, then, seeing a strange man in here. I guess you probably bought this place for Gus, didn't you?'

'It was a gift. I don't think of it as being mine, if that's what you mean. A gift is a gift in my book.'

'So, you and Gus: you had a fight?'

'You're very direct,' Piers sighed as Tom passed him a mug of tea.

'It's my job to be.' Tom spooned three sugars into his own mug. 'Sugar?'

'No, thanks.' Piers sipped on the hot liquid. 'And what job is that?'

'I'm an investigative journalist.' Tom watched Piers's face over the brim of his mug, waiting for the faintest flicker of something ... anything. But there was nothing beyond a sort of polite interest.

'I guess you must have met through Gus's work.'

'Yeah. Sort of, I suppose. One of her cases crossed over with mine.'

'Funny. I'd never imagined Gus fraternizing with the press. She's always been fairly wary of the media.'

Tom smiled and Piers couldn't fail to notice the affection on his face. 'You're right. She wasn't sure of me at first. But here I am. She seems to have warmed to me.' Tom stood up and crossed to the kitchen window which looked out onto a small brick and stone courtyard at the rear of the house.

'This story,' he decided to play one of his aces, 'it's quite an interesting one. It involves some of London's underworld. Bent coppers, really gritty stuff. I've been doing quite a bit of research into London in the sixties,

338

the gangs, the scams, really quite revealing . . .' He turned around and looked directly into Piers's eyes.

Piers's jaw twitched as he stared back at Tom. 'Oh?'

'Yeah. You might even be able to help me, come to think of it,' Tom continued guilelessly. 'You were part of the swinging sixties and all that.'

'This case you say you have joint interests in, which one was it?' Piers had the feeling they were playing a game of bluff, each trying to pump the other. He knew this young man held the key to whatever it was that was bothering Thompson so much.

'A black guy who was set up for a murder he didn't commit. Gus, the solicitor and me think it was the police who did it. Trouble is, nobody wants to know.'

'Thompson!' Piers hissed.

'Of course, you'd know all about it, I was forgetting.' It was time to stop the game. 'Stupid of me. You see, I know about you, Piers. You've been involved.' Tom started to edge towards the knife drawer. If Lawrence pulled a gun on him he'd be dead. Not much of an investigative journalist if he were in a body bag.

'Thompson came to see me.' Piers stood up but he turned from Tom. He started pacing up and down the small room. 'He told me to warn Gus off. He told me that if I didn't stop her he'd kill her. I guess he'll probably kill you as well.'

'Yeah. I guess. We've already been burgled and harassed. Look, Piers, if you're in on the deal, why should Thompson come to you? I don't believe that. I think you're here to protect your own neck. That's why you and Gus have fallen out, I'll bet. The reason you came to warn her off was to stop her finding out about you!'

'Look, you moron! I don't know what you're talking about, but the fact is I came here to warn Gus and before I had the chance to do so she ran off. Now I'm frightened for her. I think she's got herself into some pretty murky water and she's got to get out of it. I came to help her.'

'You can help her. You can help get these bastards stopped. Isn't it time you did something decent in your life, eh, Pete? Oh yes, I know all about you and your humble beginnings – Bermondsey and the rest – and you could save Gus by confessing, shopping all your friends. I know you're involved.'

'Don't be so bloody stupid,' Piers was almost shouting. 'I told you, Thompson came to tell me to call Gus off.'

'You're playing me for an idiot. I know Thompson keeps in regular contact with you. What's your role?'

Piers slumped lower into the seat, feeling completely defeated. Everything was closing in around him. 'Look, mate, I've tried to build a legitimate business over the years, to get away from the old days. But they've always been there, just a few paces behind me, always jumping out at me, haunting me. I can't ever get away, but I don't want Gus to know, to suffer, to find out just what my life was ... is.' He stopped and put his head in his hands, trying to control himself. After a few moments he continued, 'I want to help Gus in any way I can. Maybe we might get along a lot better if we pooled our resources. Maybe we could work something out together.'

'Find out exactly what I know and then bump me off, I suppose.' Tom moved in front of the drawer, ready to pull it open. The bloke sounded so convincing but he wasn't taking any chances.

Piers watched Tom's face, as if he could guess what was going through his mind.

'Do you love Gus?' he asked after several moments of silence.

'I don't know. I guess I haven't thought about it.' He stared at his battered trainers for a second or two. 'I suppose I do, yeah.'

'I love her more than my life. She's the only thing that

340

really matters to me any more. Can you understand that, Tom? Ever since she was born, I felt I had to protect her, to be there for her. Always to let her know how loved and cared for and safe she was. And look now ... she has everything going for her, a spectacular career, full of opportunities after all her hard work – everything, her youth, her whole life ahead of her. Can you imagine how it makes me feel to have the seediness, the utter disgusting dirt of my past dredged up and used as a weapon against Gus? I've been threatened too, Tom. If I don't warn Gus, or if I don't manage to stop her, then my whole past will be revealed. You know what bothers me more than anything? The shame that Gus will suffer because of that. I'm tired of always looking over my shoulder, waiting for someone to jump out and say, hey I remember when you masterminded that robbery, or when you fenced this painting. I want some peace for me, and for my daughter. If you think I'm here to trick you, or entice her into danger, then you must be a complete fool – and poor Gus's judgement has failed her again.'

Tom stared at Piers for a long time, trying to read the real motives, to judge what was true and what was false. He was fighting with instinct. Everything had pointed towards Piers being with Thompson. The connection went way back. But he sounded pretty convincing about how he felt for Gus. She was his only child. Wouldn't Tom himself feel the same in such circumstances? He sighed and walked right up to Piers. 'If you're lying and you get Gus hurt, I'll kill you.'

'If Gus gets hurt I couldn't see much of a reason to carry on anyway. So, shall we talk?'

'Okay. Let's start with what you know about Thompson.' Tom pulled out a chair and sat down at the kitchen table. He invited Piers to do the same. This could take some time.

* * *

Gus pulled into the lane and studied the map once more. Strange that she'd never been back. She'd always known the address, but something had stopped her. Maybe her nightmare had subconsciously made her feel that something dreadful would happen – or be revealed – if ever she tried to retrace the steps in the dream. She followed the B road with her finger. Then she saw the little hamlet of Westcote and the old church. There was a lane behind the church leading across the Downs. Winford Lodge was marked about a mile further along. Her heart thumped hard in her chest. She felt sick with nerves. Now she would go back and retrace those steps and remember.

She slid the car into gear and set off. She passed pretty cottages with chocolate-box gardens, an old pub, The Hop Pole, made of herringbone bricks mellowed by a couple of hundred years or more, looking warm and inviting. She was starting to climb higher. She could see hills rolling out to either side of her. She saw the church first, its square tower rising above the roof, grey stone solid and somehow depressing. She turned right into the single lane, staying close to the left side where the overgrown hedgerow brushed the sides of the car. She passed two or three houses close together behind the church, one the Rectory, and a couple of fifties-style council houses. She felt the entire atmosphere making her feel oppressed, constricted, pushing down on her. She changed down a gear as the lane climbed steeper. She felt the prickle of sweat, cold and clammy around her neck. Too late to turn back now.

She slammed on the brakes. She had passed it. She reversed back a few yards and read the sign. Forged from iron, and painted in bargeware colours, it looked garish and out of place: 'Winford Lodge'. She swallowed hard, noticing how dry her mouth had become. Vague pictures from a memory long grown distant, faded, hazy and dreamlike, were flooding back in Technicolor clarity. She knew that just around the bend was the field with the old wooden gate that she used to climb when she wasn't forced into one of her twee little dresses. If she crossed the field, she'd reach a little copse at the far side where the farmer had erected huge wire cages to rear baby pheasants. She remembered the cool shadiness, the quiet inside the copse, except for the rustling of the wind through the bracken, and the sound of the birds calling overhead. Both she and her father had listened to the birds together, trying to work out how many sang. It was really difficult. Sometimes a tiny little sparrow could sound like ten birds as it flitted from tree to tree. The copse was like a strange, enchanted sort of place, where her imagination ran away with visions of foxes, badgers and even wolves. She always thought that she'd never venture there alone, even when she was bigger.

Then she saw the rooftop. The trees had grown so tall, so much higher, so that the front was almost completely hidden now, but through the leaves of the magnolia, she could see one of the square mullioned windows on the first floor, and then up to the four gabled windows set into the slate-tiled roof.

Gus walked around the house and stood looking at the view, feeling the breeze on her face, breathing in the smells, the scent of salt-laden air. Seagulls shrieked in the distance as she thought back as far as her memory would let her. She had been so young, barely old enough to remember anything. Whoever lived here now had let the place get overgrown. The walled garden was a mass of nettles and docks. Gus remembered helping her mother to thin out tiny seedlings, getting gritty soil down her fingernails which then had to be scraped over the soap and scrubbed until they were pink and shiny again.

Gus's feet carried her towards the worn path which led up to the cliffs. Her heart beat rapidly as disjointed pictures came back to her. The dream – this was it; all her life she had been plagued with the scene. She could close her eyes and see the little dog, her father running towards her. Her mother disappearing. Gus strode woodenly onwards, steeling herself, pushing herself closer and closer to the terrifying cliffs. Gus had never been able to stand high places. She walked on and up. When she could at last see the sea way below her, she stopped and listened to the sound of the gulls crying as they sailed on the wind overhead. She closed her eyes, tuning herself to the elements.

She saw herself running, legs flying, unable to cover enough ground, desperate to get to her mother's side. 'Mummy, stop, stop!' she was shouting. Her mother was dancing, reeling around and around, screaming to the wind. 'I can fly,' she was saying. 'Look at me, I can fly.' She wheeled closer to the edge. Gus was screaming. Her father was beside her. Gus's eyes flew open and she sank to the ground as her knees gave way.

It wasn't her father. It was Frank Thompson! That was the connection. The man with her mother that day had shouted to her, 'Go on, you can do it, Cat! You can do it!' And she had. Right over the edge.

Gus lay down on the ground, pressing her cheek against the cold grass, feeling the unyielding solidness of the earth. The cold filtered through her clothes, but she was beyond noticing. Her hair whipped around her face, hastening her tears, stinging her eyes, but she didn't care. She held on to her stomach and sobbed.

Her mother had thought she could fly. Gus now knew what that meant. She cried for her shattered memories, her delusions, her total misunderstanding, and for the loss of something she never had. Her mother had been on drugs, and no one had told Gus because they had wanted to protect her. So simple, but not simple enough for a child.

She didn't know how long she lay there, but she knew

she had to get the facts before she confronted her father. It was time now for the absolute truth. Slowly she made her way back to the car, feeling as though she had aged by ten years. All innocence had gone for ever. She knew! With stiffened fingers she dialled Dickie Crowborough's number on her carphone, and spoke to his private secretary. She would meet Dickie tomorrow. Tonight she'd stay at The Hop Pole, the comfortable-looking pub she'd passed.

When Dickie saw Gus he could barely hide his shock. She looked so tired, white as the roses upon the table. They were at his flat, where she had requested they meet. He'd had to cancel two morning meetings but the message had said something about her seeing him being of vital importance, and he knew Gus wasn't a hysterical girl, that it must be important if she said it was. Now, looking at her, he felt deeply concerned. The life seemed to have gone out of her. Where was her fight, her vitality and spirit that he knew so well?

'I have to speak to you,' Gus said, in a monotone. 'I know what happened, Dickie, when she fell off the cliff.'

'You were there, with her.'

'Yes, but I hadn't remembered. All I had was my recurring nightmare. I'd always thought my father was with us. Do you know, Dickie, I blamed him. All these years I thought it was his fault. I accused him of it yesterday morning. We had a frightful scene, and then I went down to Sussex, to the old house. I walked along the cliff and it came back to me. She was dancing ... and then she decided to fly!' Gus swallowed, trying to remove the painful lump in her throat. Then she cleared her throat and continued, 'My father told me yesterday that he had killed my mother. I thought he had murdered her.'

Dickie gasped. 'No, Gus! Never. That's absolutely ridiculous.'

Gus put her hand up to stop him. 'I know now. It was Thompson. Frank Thompson told her to jump and she did. What was he doing there? What was he to my mother? I have to know before I can face my father again, and you're the only one who can tell me!'

Dickie stood up and stepped quietly over to the drinks tray. Despite the earliness of the hour, he poured Scotch into two glasses and handed one to Gus. 'This may be unpleasant for you.'

'Please just tell me. Please . . .'

'Well, I hardly know where to start.' Dickie took a deep breath and began.

'Catherine got herself in with a very dubious crowd. She was a rather wayward woman, Gus. She was difficult – wild, even. Nobody could handle her. She used to do exactly as she pleased, when she pleased. Your father adored her from the beginning. He was completely head over heels in love with her, but he couldn't tame her unfortunately. Even pregnancy and motherhood didn't seem to have much of a calming effect upon her.'

'So what happened?' Gus was growing impatient.

'She started to take drugs, probably long before your father met her in actual fact. It got worse. Harder drugs – you know the sort of thing – cannabis, then LSD, then heroin. Latterly she was injecting it. She had overdosed on heroin before she died.'

'The flying,' Gus said, almost to herself.

'The whole drugs thing made your father so unhappy. He was desperate to know what to do with her. Every time he tried to help her she just pushed him away, got worse. Ridiculously, in my opinion, he always felt guilty about her, felt he didn't do enough for her. I expect that's why he told you he'd killed her. That wasn't quite what he meant, I don't suppose.'

'Was Frank Thompson her dealer?' Gus could guess the answer.

Dickie shrugged. 'Possibly. He was there on the day she died. You were the only witness. And your father never wanted anyone to ask you what you saw. He didn't want you upset, disturbed by having to think about it. He was pleased that your memory seemed to be protecting you from that day. Nature's way of helping you cope. Marvellous in some ways, but if it's been bothering you all these years perhaps we were all wrong, perhaps we should have asked you.'

'Frank Thompson told her to fly. He could have saved her. He as good as murdered her, Dickie.'

'A difficult one to prove, though, unfortunately.'

'I have my own plans for dealing with Frank Thompson. He's got away with far too much for too long. Listen, Dickie, I appreciate what you've told me. It all fits into place now. And please, I don't blame you for not telling me before. I understand you were trying to protect me.'

'As was Piers, darling Gus. Go easy on him, he was only doing what he thought best.'

'There's something else, Dickie, something that's bothering me about my father. Is he a crook?'

The question almost floored Dickie. He could just imagine Gus in her robes, slowly torturing the poor sod in the witness box.

'Of course not. Well, no more so than any of us.'

'So you're a crook too?'

Dickie looked at his goddaughter uncomfortably. Now what the hell was she getting at?

'How about Bermondsey, the marketstalls? I imagine you know about that?'

'No. I have to say I haven't a clue what you're talking about there.' He let out a silent sigh, hiding his relief.

'Apparently that's where my father started off his business.'

Subdued laughter rumbled through Dickie's chest. 'Did he now? Well, of course we all wondered where he'd come from. He was always a bit of a fixer, a bit of a lad

347

when I first knew him. A sort of East-End-boy-made-good. In those days it was trendy to have a cockney accent and hang out in East End clubs.'

'Then it's probably true?'

'That you'll have to ask him. I must say I've never bothered to pry into his history. He's simply one of my oldest friends, darling Gus. Where he came from is of no importance. But I wouldn't be at all surprised to learn such a thing.'

'The sort of man my mother would mix with? Was he into drugs too?'

Dickie knocked back some more whisky. 'No, Piers was not into drugs.'

Eventually Gus left, leaving Dickie Crowborough feeling like his guts had been through a spin-dryer. Not an easy session. But at least now Gus and Piers could sort out their differences once and for all. It was certainly about time!

Dickie called his office and learned that Piers Lawrence was on his way to see him. What a day it was turning out to be! Still it made a change from the politics of the Royal Opera House. No doubt Piers was coming to warn him about Gus. Well, he was too late and Dickie knew in his heart that he would have been wrong to avoid her questions. He'd deal with Piers, make him understand.

But what Piers had to say put all thoughts of Gus right out of Dickie's mind.

Chapter Thirty-One

John Stapleford put the draft script down and stared hard at Mirabelle. 'It's all about your stepfather!'

'Soon to be ex-stepfather. My mother's in the process of divorcing him. So it's no skin off my nose. It's good stuff, isn't it?' she said confidently.

'Sure. If it comes from someone else. It smacks too much of revenge – lacking in objectivity – from you, Mirabelle. No one would take it seriously.'

'But . . . that's ridiculous!' Mirabelle spluttered. 'Of course they'd take it seriously. It's the inside story. From someone close, someone who really knows. The real exposé.'

'I don't agree,' he said flatly. 'It's too much "in the family". I can't run it – at least not with your involvement.'

'You're saying you'd use it if I weren't assistant producer?'

'Sure, producing it, writing it, researching it, editing it. I wouldn't want you to have anything to do with it, otherwise it just might not be taken seriously.'

'But that's not fair!' Her petulant voice was rising. 'I'd have to take it elsewhere . . .'

'You're under contract to us, Mirabelle. That's an exclusive contract. You go touting your ideas elsewhere then I'll have to fire you.'

Mirabelle's aquamarine eyes narrowed into spiteful slits. 'You'd let me go, just like that?'

'Mirabelle,' John sighed, obviously trying to restrain his impatience, 'this is a tough business. You should have learned that by now. There's loads of people falling over themselves for your job. It's up to you,' he shrugged ambivalently.

'I shall have to think about it,' she said carefully, biting her tongue to stop herself from telling him to go fuck himself. She wanted time to think what to do about the story. She shouldn't make any rash decisions – end up with no job to go to. 'I hear what you say, and I shall consider it. That would seem only fair.'

'Your prerogative, Mirabelle. Only do let me know. I want to get this idea commissioned. It's good!'

She hung her head, letting her blonde tresses cover her anger. 'Sure,' she muttered and closed the door quietly behind her. She wanted to scream in irritation, but instead she picked up her jacket and left the studio.

It was time to catch up with her stepfather – let him know just what a shit she thought he was. She would relish the putting down she was about to give him. She wanted to see him squirm as she revealed all she knew. Mr high and mighty Piers. What a joke. The guy wasn't fit to breathe the same air as she was – or her mother.

Mirabelle hadn't broken the news to Elena yet. She would tonight, after she had witnessed Piers' reaction. Then she could report it all back to her mother and cheer her up. It would be good for Elena to know just how well off she was being out of marriage to that crooked bastard. Elena had mentioned that he was in London, though why her mother still kept track of his movements, Mirabelle couldn't understand. He would either be at Blakes or Claridge's. Probably the former, considering he was probably still feeling a little red-faced about the incident by the lift. Mirabelle quickly called reception at Blakes. Yes, they confirmed, Mr Lawrence was in residence, and yes, he was in his room. Perfect, Mirabelle smiled. If she jumped into a cab she might be able to collar him. The element of surprise was always a good thing to have on one's side.

* * *

Piers held the phone close to his ear and listened carefully as Dickie Crowborough explained developments.

'I've really had to stick my neck out, Piers, to get him to see you. You're damned lucky he's in town today. We've got an important debate tonight, so he'll be preparing for it, no doubt. Anyway I spoke to his PPS and had to do some real oiling to get you in. You'll have five minutes – that's all I could get you. You know where to go, don't you? Don't be late, old chum or you'll miss him entirely. I only hope that this vitally important secret of yours is of national importance. My name won't be worth a glass of mineral water if it's anything trivial.'

'Don't worry, Dickie. It's exceedingly important, and I'm afraid to say it's not at all trivial. He'll be extremely grateful to you for being so pushy. And so shall I. See you soon and thanks.'

As Dickie replaced the receiver, he realized that he hadn't once mentioned his visit from Gus. He'd been completely sidetracked by Piers' rather dramatic request. Oh well, perhaps it was best to keep Gus's visit in confidence for the time being.

Piers reverently scanned Tom's list once more. He had been astonished to see just how far the network had climbed. Several of the names were familiar to him, indeed he had dined with at least a couple of them. He was going to have quite a job convincing the Home Secretary that the list was for real. But Tom had briefed him thoroughly on the Davis case, on the drugs, and on several other matters which Tom had confirmed had enough evidence on them to make any half-intelligent person take notice. Piers had the tough task of making sure he was taken seriously. There was only one way that a ring like this could be broken up quickly, and that was by going straight to the top. Using ordinary channels – reporting it to senior police officials – would have risked members of the ring finding out, weeks of delays while authorization was sought to investigate, and then the appointment of outside forces to carry out an investigation. The whole thing could drag on for months – and Piers knew that Gus didn't have months. He had to act quickly.

Mirabelle called out to him as soon as he stepped onto the street.

'Mirabelle!' he cried in astonishment. 'What are you doing here? Not looking for me, surely?'

He had never admitted it openly, but he really didn't think too much of Elena's only child. He knew she could be very spiteful at times, and she had been positively venomous during the scene with Giovanna at Claridge's. Whilst Piers was the first to admit that a dressing down was fully in order, Mirabelle had been extremely vocal and extremely public about the whole thing, drawing the entire ground-floor area's attention to the four of them. Piers knew she had been enjoying herself immensely.

'I'm afraid I'm a little tied up.' He set off down the street, striding briskly. Mirabelle called after him. 'I can hardly hear you, Mirabelle – the traffic. I'm afraid I have to get to an appointment.'

'But it's desperately important, Piers –'

'I'm sorry, Mirabelle, but so's this appointment. I can see you later – at about three this afternoon?'

'No, now!' she said bossily. 'I'll come with you, we can talk in the car.' Piers had already unlocked the doors and Mirabelle jumped in. 'I've so much to talk to you about, Piers, it's a question of knowing where to start.'

Piers frowned at her as he slammed the car door shut and slid his seat belt into place. 'Look, Mirabelle, as I said, I have an appointment to get to and I really don't want to think about anything else before then. I can see you this afternoon – at the Ritz – we'll have tea.'

Mirabelle smiled angelically. Just perfect. What a wonderful setting in which to reveal her knowledge!

'All right,' she agreed. 'At three, Piers. I can hardly wait.'

She opened the car door and slid her legs out seconds before Piers turned the key in the ignition.

Gus had gone straight into chambers after speaking to Dickie. She was glad that she'd decided to spend last night in Sussex, to give herself time to collect herself. She needed some space before facing either Tom or her father. But now she must try to put things right. She would call Piers and try to arrange to see him later on today. It was time for everything to come out into the open, no more hidden memories or half-truths. She wanted him to tell her all about his family, his East End history – her history. His past. Whatever it was, she would somehow deal with it. She loved him too much to lose him. Too many years had been wasted by secrets and misunderstandings. She could hardly wait to see him, so that they could at last talk properly, openly.

Tom was waiting by the phone; waiting to hear how Piers had got on when the phones started going crazy. Jim Carter, the News Editor, shouted to Angus McDonald, one of Tom's colleagues, 'Get down to Fulham, there's been a bomb!'

Tom glanced at his screen as the Press Association message flashed across it: 'Two casualties, both white: one male, one female. Unconfirmed, but car that of Piers Lawrence, art dealer. Male killed outright. Female taken to Queen Mary's Hospital, Roehampton, suffering severe burns and other injuries . . .'

Tom could feel the blood draining from his head, the cold entering his body. 'Not Gus, please God, let it not be Gus,' he prayed, for the first time in his life. He had to get to her, had to see her. Roehampton was bloody miles away and it would take hours to get through the traffic.

'Jim, I need your bike. It's a matter of life and death. Please give me the keys.' The desperation on Tom's face was clear for all to see.

'My bike! My pride and joy? That's almost as important to me as my dick, mate.'

'Look, I've got to get to hospital. I know that girl – we're – well, we're an item. Come on, Jim, if I drive my car there it'll take me hours. Come on, help me, please!'

'Give us your car keys, then. And Tom, if you so much as scratch it I'll castrate you . . .'

Tom threw his keys at his News Editor and picked up the bike keys. It had been at least four years since Tom had owned his own bike, but he felt at home on the big black beast immediately. Within forty minutes he was turning down Roehampton Lane, heading for the hospital and the burns unit.

'Gus Lawrence. I'm a relative . . .'

The nurse looked at him disbelievingly. A huge crowd of cameras and journalists were hanging around the gate, but none of them had ventured inside the hospital. They were, for once, behaving themselves and waiting for an official statement on the welfare and confirmed identity of the patient.

'You look like a reporter to me,' the nurse said suspiciously, waving to the two security men.

'Look . . .' Tom was almost in tears now, so desperate was he to get to her. 'Just tell me then, is she alive or dead? How bad is she? I'm her boyfriend, for Christ's sake!' His voice cracked and he turned to the wall, thumping it hard with his fist.

The nurse softened. This was some act if he was pretending. 'Look, I'll go and get the doctors. Then they can tell you.' The next few minutes were the longest Tom had ever gone through in his life. All sorts of terrible pictures were conjured up in his imagination.

He had seen burn victims before. The pain was the most incredible pain imaginable. People peeled like boiled vegetables. He tried to stop the pictures, otherwise he thought he would go mad. He felt so afraid of what to expect, what to find, if she'd still be alive. Then the doctor arrived. A woman, young, around thirty. She looked anxious. Not good news, Tom guessed immediately. Hell, how could it be good news? The girl had just been blown up by fucking Thompson. 'You are ...?'

'Tom Silverthorn. I'm her boyfriend. Is she ...? Is she going to be okay?'

'We hope so, but it's early days. She's on the critical list. She's suffered severe burns ...' The doctor's voice tailed off and her eyes fell away from Tom's. She was avoiding telling him, Tom knew immediately.

'I want to see her,' he said.

'Of course. But she's unconscious at the moment. That, for the moment, is a blessing. You'll have to put sterile stuff on. I'll organize it for you. Come with me.'

A few minutes later, when Tom finally stood outside the ward, he hesitated in the doorway. He was so frightened of what he would find – just a poor creature in total agony. Forcing himself to be brave for her sake, he stepped into the room. His first glance was tentative. He took a small step towards the figure on the bed, then his eyes flew back to the pillow, and confirmed what he thought he had seen. It couldn't be ... not possible ... His heart leaped and he wanted to kiss the doctor. He wanted to jump and scream for joy and then even as the emotions hit him, he felt sorry for her. Poor Mirabelle, who valued her looks so much. The blonde hair spilled over the pillow. Slowly he backed out of the room.

'It's Mirabelle Angeletti Lawrence,' he explained to the confused-looking doctor. 'I thought it was going to be her sister, Augusta.'

'Wait a minute, Mr ... er ... Silverton, please,' the doctor called after him. 'Let me ask you for some more details.'

But Tom knew he had work to do. He had to find Gus, before Thompson did.

Gus was dictating notes on an advice into her Dicta-phone when a policeman and a WPC arrived. Immediately she stood up.

'What do you want?' She hoped this wasn't another of Thompson's frame-ups.

'I'm afraid we have some very bad news about your father.' The young woman spoke gently. 'He was in-volved in a serious incident earlier today and he died, Miss Lawrence.'

'What?' she gasped, unable to comprehend what they were telling her. Her ears were ringing, an extraordin-ary buzzing that wouldn't go away, making it difficult to hear. 'What did you say?' she asked again, sinking down into her chair.

'Your father. I'm afraid he's been killed.' The WPC came forward and put her arm gently on Gus's. 'Is there someone we can contact who can be with you?' she asked, hoping there was.

'What happened?' Gus ignored the question. She still couldn't quite grasp what they were telling her.

'There was a bomb ...'

'My father – he was near?'

'We think it was planted in your father's car. That he was the target. We need to find out if he had any enemies, Miss Lawrence. Anyone who would want to kill him? Or whether there's been some sort of mistake.'

Gus's eyes misted. She tried to blink, to refocus on the police, but their dark uniforms kept swimming in and out of focus. Any enemies, that was a joke! He was a crook. No doubt he had loads of enemies.

'No, I can't think of anyone right now. You must

356

excuse me,' she said weakly. 'But I think I have things to do. I'm afraid you really must excuse me . . .'

'I'll come with you,' the WPC was already following her.

Gus summoned up all her strength. 'There's no need. I shall be perfectly all right. I must get home. Don't worry about me, please. If I think of anything I'll call you. Now I'm sorry but . . .'

She raced down the stairs, out into the street, and hailed a cab. She fell into the back seat.

When the taxi pulled to a halt, she realized she had been completely lost in a dream world, thinking about her childhood, her dead mother, her father, now gone – the scene they had yesterday, her pilgrimage to Sussex. Everything had been fusing together at last, her questions answered, her confusion ending, and now this. Before she could resolve their difficulties he had gone and got himself blown up. Now she would never be able to apologize, to explain how wrong she had been . . . all those years of subconscious suspicion. He died thinking she hated him.

Her lips were tight-set, white, all colour gone. She felt completely numb. Woodenly she paid the cab, walked up the street. Fiddled in her bag for the keys.

Tom's voice. Gentle, reassuring Tom. 'Darling,' he said softly, 'I'm so sorry. Come on . . .' He gathered her small frame into his arms, felt her stiff against him.

She pushed him away. 'I'm okay, really I am.' She was shaking her head. 'I'm all right. If I could just . . . if I could just find . . .' The tears came, then great racking sobs that shook her whole body. Her moans were a strange keening sound, almost eerie in their depth of despair.

Tom cradled her to him, holding her head in his hands, whispering into her hair, taking the force of the trembling. 'Gus, let's go inside,' he coaxed her gently. 'You're freezing.'

'Why?' she said between sobs. 'Why, Tom?'

'Inside. We'll talk then.'

He led her into the house, poured her a large whisky and sat her down on the sofa. 'Thompson threatened your father. Told him that if you didn't stop investigating the Davis story, he'd kill you. That's what Piers came to tell you yesterday.'

Gus looked at him aghast. 'But he never said . . .'

'Maybe you didn't give him the chance. He didn't tell me the details, but I guessed you two had a fight. Then we couldn't find you, didn't have any idea where to look. God, the past twelve hours have been a nightmare – your going off like that, then going to the hospital, expecting to find you. Oh God, Gus! Thank God you're alive!' Tom grabbed her, pulled her tight against him. 'I love you. I don't think I mentioned it before, but I'm crazy about you, Gus. I know now's not the ideal time to mention it, but I just want you to know before anything else happens to us.'

'You went to the hospital? Why?' She was trying to make some sense of it all. Half of what Tom was saying was so muddled. She didn't understand . . .

'Mirabelle was with your father, in the car. It looks very bad for her, Gus. She might not make it. Even if she does, she's never going to be the same. She's pretty badly burned.'

Gus clapped her hands over her ears. 'Enough, Tom. I can't take any more. It's like some terrible nightmare – and I thought I'd got rid of my nightmares. Now it's all starting up again. What are we going to do?'

'First I want you to pack a bag – essentials – I don't know how long for. But we're going to get you out of here into hiding, away from Thompson and his gang.'

'But where?'

'A hotel's probably safest for now. Come on, hurry up. Get your things.'

'But my work – I've got cases to do; my car; Elena. I can't just abandon everything!'

'Gus, get real! You pack your bag, otherwise you're going to be joining your father. I don't want to sound brutal, but you'd better face facts. Now be a big brave girl and do as I say. Come on, I'll give you a hand.'

Five minutes later Gus was locking the door.

'Gus!' Flora came running up behind them. 'Darling, I heard on the news. I'm so sorry. What can I do? Are you okay?' She gave Gus a hug and Gus felt the tears welling once more.

'I have to go away for a while. Don't worry about me, Flora. Take care of the house, I'll be in touch when I can. I'll call you.'

'Sure, Gus. Only take care, huh? I want to help if I can.'

Gus nodded her appreciation. 'Thanks.'

'Come on, Gus.' Tom led her down the street, and then remembered the bike. 'Ever ridden shotgun?' he asked ruefully.

Gus followed his glance to the huge motorbike. 'Yours?' she said incredulously.

'Borrowed. I was in a hurry.'

She hitched up her black skirt and climbed on behind him. Tom resisted the temptation to tell her just how sexy she looked. Now was not the time. Then he kicked the beast into action and sped down the street. Neither he nor Gus noticed they were being tailed.

Tom flicked the curtains back and squinted down into the dark street some seven storeys below them. 'I've never stayed in the Savoy before. It's not bad, is it? Another whisky?'

Gus shook her head. 'I've had too much already. I feel completely senseless. Brain dead.' She was lying back on the large bed, shoes kicked off, skirt creased around her thighs and her hair hanging out of its pins. She

359

looked a complete wreck and Tom loved her all the more for it. 'Call Elena, Tom, and speak to her. Tell her you're a friend of mine. See if she's okay. I know I can't stand her, but I feel so sorry for her.'

Typical Gus, Tom thought. Her own world crumbling around her and she was worried about bloody Elena.

'Please, Tom,' Gus asked again, knowing he was trying to ignore her. 'Her mobile number's in my bag somewhere – in my diary. Just see how she is. Tell her I'll go and see her as soon as I can. And ask her how Mirabelle is.'

Tom shook his head, unable to hide his irritation, but even so he did as instructed. Soon he heard Elena's voice on the line – at least he assumed it was her. He'd never actually met the woman, for Christ's sake! He explained who he was – a friend of Gus's . . .

Within seconds the woman was blabbing down the line. It was hard to understand what she was saying. As he struggled to make himself heard, Gus grabbed the phone from him. She made several placatory cooing noises and then kept silent, obviously listening to the newly widowed Mrs Lawrence talk on.

'I see,' Gus said quietly. 'Are you sure? . . . Okay, Elena. Just sit tight. I'll send Tom round to see you. Everything's going to be fine. Mirabelle's going to be okay. Just try and keep calm. Sure, no, that's fine. 'Bye.'

'What do you mean you'll send Tom round? I'm supposed to be here looking after you, not that ghastly female.'

'You've never even met her!'

'No, but I've met the daughter!'

'She told me something important. She got a call this afternoon.'

'From Thompson? Gloating, no doubt!'

'No. Not from Thompson.' Gus stared into her glass. 'From someone called Giovanna Lucciani. Apparently she was my father's mistress. She told Elena she had a bomb planted under my father's car.' Gus's voice sounded remarkably calm, almost robotic. She gazed levelly at Tom. 'Not our friend Thompson.'

'Jesus Christ, some coincidence!'

'If it's true,' Gus added. 'I thought you might be keen to check it all out with Elena!'

Tom was already putting his shoes on. 'Too damned right. What did you say her address was?'

'She's staying at Mirabelle's. I think you know where that is.' Tom shot Gus a look of concern. 'Sure you'll be okay? Maybe you should come with me. I'm not happy about leaving you alone.'

'I'll be fine. I'll have a bath. Some time to think would do me good, Tom. I need to think things through, you know . . . a little space around me.'

He kissed her lightly on the mouth, then again on the tip of her nose. 'Don't let anyone in. I'll be back as soon as I can. Then we'd better plan what we're going to do next. Perhaps you might be able to keep that appointment with the Home Secretary instead. No doubt the Home Office will be falling over themselves to find out why Piers was blown up on his way to an appointment with them. They'll probably be thinking he was meant to drive the car closer to Whitehall and make a nice mess there.' Gus flinched. 'Sorry, darling. That was thoughtless of me. I'll see you later, huh?'

Gus waved. He closed the bedroom door behind him and the silence crowded around her. She dare not have any more whisky. And if she turned on the television she was afraid that she might have to witness news of the bombing. She felt very alone and vulnerable. She picked up the telephone and punched out Flora's number.

'Is that Chris?' she said, as the male voice answered.

'Gus. Hey, how are you? What are you doing? I'm really sorry about your old man . . .'

Gus hadn't warmed to Flora's boyfriend and wasn't in

the mood for his sympathy. 'Is Flora there? I need to speak to her, Chris.'

'She's in the loo. Can I give her a message?'

'Er no, no, it's all right, Chris. I'll hang on.'

'Sure. I'll go and get her.'

A few moments later Flora's voice came on the line. As ever, it sounded lovely and warm, filled with genuine affection and concern. 'Gus, how are you? Where are you? How're you feeling?'

'I'm okay. Tom and I are going to stay out of sight for a while.'

'This all sounds very cloak-and-dagger. Maybe you should tell me about it.'

'I can't, Flora. Not yet, anyway. Listen, I just wanted to let you know that I was okay. To say that you're not to worry.'

'Where are you, in case I need you?'

Gus hesitated. Tom had been adamant that they shouldn't tell a soul where they were. But Flora was different. Gus knew she could trust Flora. 'You've got to swear not to mention this to anyone, but we're at the Savoy, room 331. If it's life and death you can find me here, but Flora, you mustn't tell a soul!'

'You have my word.'

Flora brushed Chris's hand from her breast. He had been covering her neck with kisses all the time she had been talking to Gus. When she put the phone down she turned on him crossly. 'Did you have to do that? I was trying to speak to my friend, she's really upset, and all she can hear in the background is you slurping all over me. It's really embarrassing, Chris!'

'Oh for fuck's sake, woman, you're always bloody complaining.' Chris turned on her. 'Moan, bloody moan. That's what you do! Well, quite frankly I've had just about enough . . .'

'But . . .!' Flora couldn't believe this was happening. She never moaned at him, never complained. Mostly she just bit her tongue and ignored whatever he'd done to annoy her. This change in mood was just completely uncalled for. 'What are you talking about?' she asked incredulously.

'I've had enough, that's what. I'm off. You've got more time for your bloody friends than you've got for me. I've had it with you, Flora. Okay? Just had it!'

Flora didn't have chance to reply. He was already headed out of the door.

Gus was just dropping off to sleep. She cuddled the pillow tightly to her belly, her knees pulled up in the foetal position. Exhaustion was mercifully about to wipe her conscious mind, stop all the ghastly thoughts whirling around it, hold the memories, give her peace. She heard a movement at the door. At first she ignored it, forgetting where she was. Then as she heard a faint scrabble she opened her eyes fully.

'Tom?' she called softly. 'Is that you?' She looked at her watch. It was 8.30 p.m. He'd only been gone about an hour. Surely he couldn't be back so quickly? She watched as the door knob turned and then she shot up.

'Chris!' she said in confusion. 'What are you doing here? How on . . .?' It took her a fraction of a second to focus but then she saw! Chris had company – another man with him, and both had weapons pointing at her.

'Miss Lawrence, I presume!'

'Chris!' Gus couldn't believe it. 'What are you doing? I don't understand. What the hell's going on?'

Chris continued to point the weapon at her. 'I've been looking forward to this, Gus. It's been no fun stalking you. It's all been so fucking easy. Not even a guessing game as to where you and Silverthorn had gone. Where is he?'

Gus's glance shot to the bathroom, and then back.

'In there, is he?' Chris took a step towards the doorway. The other man, darker than Chris, chubbier in the face, kept his gun trained on her as Chris threw open the bathroom door. 'There's no one in here. He must be out. Well, we'll just have to deal with you and let Silverthorn have it when he comes back.'

'Why you? What are you to do with all this?'

'God, for someone who's supposed to be so clever, you're pretty thick, aren't you? I'm a policeman. Didn't I mention it to you? I know Flora didn't. She was embarrassed to. Thought you might think it a bit beneath her!'

'What?'

'Yeah. 'Cos you're such a snotty cow.'

Gus hadn't noticed before just what a mean-looking face the guy had. 'You're tied up with Thompson?'

He sniggered. 'You could say that. I'm Chris Thompson. I relied on the fact that it's a common name, didn't need to change it. Thought it wouldn't occur to you to work out a connection. In any event probably Flora never told you my surname. You made it all so easy for me.'

Gus's mind clawed through the confusion. 'You were seeing Flora so that you could get to me – spy on me, and what I was doing!' Her voice was barely audible. She shook her head over and over, unable to comprehend how stupid, how blind she had been. Tonight, calling up Flora. 'You were listening, weren't you, when I told Flora? That's how you found me!'

'Well, we had a pretty rough idea. Truth is we followed you and Silverthorn earlier, but we lost you in the traffic. That fucking bike was a lot quicker than a car. So you had a fighting chance until that call of yours. Very silly move. You see, your line's been bugged too.'

'You'll get caught. You'll never get away with this. You'll be put away for a very long time. Besides, Thompson pulled the trigger on Chapman, didn't he ...?' Gus started to use her brain. She had to play for time, play tactics. 'It wasn't you, Chris. You're not a

364

murderer – yet! You could do a deal. Think what kind of a deal you'd be able to put together with the CPS, Chris. Name names, help bring your father to justice. God, you'd almost be a national hero. I can just see the mitigation. Intimidation, bullying, coercion – a decent barrister could put together a really strong case to defend you. What else have you got going for you? A life of terror with Thompson. Soon to be cut short anyway . . .' She decided to gamble. 'You see, my father delivered a list to the Home Secretary yesterday. A complete list including Thompson and the men associated with him. There's about thirty all together, I believe, spread right up through the ranks. Thompson can't protect you any more. Kill me and it's another fifteen years on your sentence. It's over. It was over the day that Winston Davis was shot. We've got witnesses that Thompson didn't know about, didn't manage to get to.'

'You're lying,' Chris laughed. 'There is no list. And the CPS aren't interested in the Davis file. We know all that. We know everything you and Parfitt and that idiot Silverthorn have been up to. And there's something else you should know: I pulled the trigger on Harry Chapman.' He aimed the gun at Gus.

Martin Coles felt as though his chest might explode, he was hyperventilating so much. Keep calm, he told himself, just keep calm. What the girl had said was swimming round his brain. She'd put into words everything that scared him. Thompson had to be brought down. This was madness, murdering someone in cold blood in this place. They'd probably never even make it down the stairs. No one would believe the first-on-the-scene line again. It would be just too much of a coincidence. The girl responsible for the Davis case. All her approaches – there'd be papers, Parfitt – Jesus, it was all so fucking complicated. Madness. And he'd get done as an accessory, an accomplice. His hand holding the Uzi shook. He felt the cold sweat breaking out across his brow. He sensed Chris's arm muscle tightening. Now or never, he thought.

He turned the heavy barrel until it nudged Chris's spine. 'Drop it, Chris!' he groaned. 'Drop it or I'll fire this thing. I'm fucking serious.' He felt Chris's body tense, but the gun was still trained on the girl. 'I said drop the fucking gun, now!' He shoved the muzzle hard against soft flesh.

'What the fuck . . .? What are you doing, you stupid little cunt?'

Martin was almost sobbing with tension. 'It's over, Chris. She's right. It's all finished. We kill her and we're going to be in the worst shit imaginable. You drop the fucking gun or I'll shoot you.'

'Defending me in the line of duty,' Gus whispered. She was mesmerized by the barrel of the weapon. She watched as Chris's hand shook almost imperceptibly. He was unsure, wavering. 'Listen to him, Chris, he's right,' she murmured. 'Remember what I said about a deal.'

'Fuck you!' he shouted. 'You fucking little bitch.'

Martin squeezed and his whole body bucked with the kickback. A round thudded straight into his partner's flesh. Gus screamed, and dived under the bed. Chris's body twitched and jerked to the floor. Martin was sobbing, looking at the blood, the body, the mess. 'Jesus Christ, look what I've done!' His voice came in great gulping chokes.

Gus picked up the phone. 'Is there a squad I can call? Someone who's clean? Or will I just be handing you over to Thompson?' She looked at him challengingly. She had to keep in control somehow, keep on the upper hand, not let him lose his nerve or he just might turn his gun back on her.

'Yeah, call Mike Curtis at Scotland Yard. I was seconded to him once. He's okay. He's clean and he's good.'

Gus fumbled with the numbers, as footsteps came

charging down the hall. 'Show them your badge, for Christ's sake,' Gus hissed. The guy was in shock. 'Tell them you're calling for backup. Here, come and talk to him. Tell him to get here quickly with a team. Tell him to keep it quiet. You've got to make him understand!'

'Yeah, sure. I'll try.'

People were screaming behind them, throwing up. The scene was something out of a horror movie, blood splattered everywhere.

Gus watched the man's every move. 'Come on,' she whispered encouragingly. 'I saw everything, and I know the story. It'll be okay. Just do as I say.'

He spoke, said all Gus had told him to. Then someone was pushing through the doorway. 'What the fuck ...? Gus!' A male voice screamed. 'Gus! Where are you?' The voice was choking. Gus threw herself from the bed, racing across the room, through the blood, hurling herself into Tom's arms. 'I'm here ... I'm okay. Oh my God, Tom. Thank God ...' She crumpled against him and then she started to sob.

He held her to him as tightly as he could, surveying the bloodbath around him, the ashen-faced bloke with the handful of Uzi, the people standing in the corridor. 'Looks like I shouldn't have left you, huh?'

Gus couldn't speak. She just buried her head deeper into his chest, clinging on to him as if she were clinging to a rock face. 'We've got to get to the Home Secretary – tell him we're keeping Daddy's appointment. Come on, Tom, we've got to go now. We should have done it earlier. Hurry! We'll try and find Dickie, and if we can't we'll use my own contacts.'

James Kentish strode into the Central Lobby. 'Gus!' he said, almost unable to believe his eyes. 'What on earth are you doing here? It's a little late, isn't it? They're just about to ring the Division Bell. I'm afraid I haven't got much time to spare ...'

'Never mind all that, James,' Gus said urgently. 'This is one of the most important things you'll ever have to do in your life. I have to ask you to swear on your life that you'll mention this to no one but the people I ask you to speak to. It's vitally important, do you understand, James?'

'What's all this about, Gus?' He sounded more pompous than usual.

She felt profoundly irritated. 'Remember the Davis case we were working on?'

'Yes, of course I do ...'

'There is a police ring – a network. There are several important people implicated, James. There's a list. You have to get it to the very top. You know what I'm saying, James.'

'But my dear Gus, we went over all this before. Aren't you being a little hysterical? Besides, we don't have access just like that, you know. There are channels. This is most irregular.'

'For Christ's sake, James, listen to me. I was nearly murdered tonight. There's a policeman lying dead in the Savoy because his partner blew him up with an Uzi instead of the guy killing me! Now my father was coming here earlier today and he got blown up. How much more regular would you like this to be? Please, I beg you, James,' her voice cracked with emotion, 'you have respect for me, I know that. I have never asked anything of you since ... well ... you know.' James glanced at Gus's male companion who, although silent, was glowering menacingly at him.

'No, Gus and I do respect you, enormously. I trained you after all!'

'Take this list, and this letter and make sure that no one, absolutely no one but the Home Secretary gets it. It is of vital, national importance. Do you understand?' She spoke slowly, as if to a small child. James looked at the envelope suspiciously. 'It's not a bomb, James, for goodness' sake. It's not going to blow up in your face. I haven't turned into a terrorist.'

'One can't be too careful, and your friend . . .'

'Please, mate, just deliver the message. Explain that this is what Piers Lawrence was on his way to see him for when he got blown up. Maybe that will open the door for you.'

'I have to vote first.'

Tom felt he could strangle James any minute. 'Forget the fucking vote, just find him, James.'

Gus patted James's hand consolingly, thinking the two men were about to come to fisticuffs. 'We'll wait here, James. We won't move until you come and tell us what's going on.'

'Oh very well,' he muttered disgruntledly. 'This really is most irregular . . .'

For almost an hour Gus and Tom paced up and down and around the circular hallway. Then James finally appeared. He spoke rather grandly.

'The Home Secretary would like to see you now!'

Chapter Thirty-Two

❧❧❧

Tom's small flat was a wonderful, welcoming haven where Gus was attempting to gather her strength in order to deal with all the emotional turmoil she had been through in the past forty-eight hours. Her father had been murdered and she herself had been within a whisker of losing her life. She had revisited the coastal walk which invaded her nightmares, and she had finally managed to get those responsible for Winston Davis's premature death, Harry Chapman's murder, and that of the defence witness arrested. Thank God they had been believed.

What a terrible night it had been. Debriefing, they had called it, but Gus knew it was the closest she'd ever come to being interrogated. Men in dark suits had swarmed around her and Tom, asking endless questions, checking facts, acting as if they didn't believe anything. Then the phone calls had been made, checking more facts, death certificates, post mortem reports. Gus was astonished at how quickly things could be achieved when the orders came from the top. The smooth wheels of government – she'd have good cause to remember just how easy it was when she next had to prepare a complicated defence, when it took weeks of bureaucratic wrangling to get the smallest piece of information. It was impressive, heady stuff. She had somehow survived the ordeal through a strange sense of detachment. She was almost like an outsider looking in, programmed to act without feeling, speaking without emotion; that part of her soul temporarily barred. It was quite incredible the way the mind could deal with such terrible things. She found herself quite coldly and mechanically discussing her father's murder, the scene with Chris Thompson and Martin Coles. She'd even kept her promise to Coles and in her statements made sure that it was clear he had acted to save her life. Her eyes had somehow remained open, her body active. She would not let herself give in to her grief just yet.

Still when Tom had brought her back here, yesterday morning, she had acted normally, made tea, chatted about the flat and the weather. Tom, obviously deeply concerned for her, had asked her dozens of times if she were all right and each time she had replied that yes, she was perfectly fine.

But inside she felt she could crack into a thousand pieces. Okay, solid and functioning for the moment, but any more knocks, any more shocks and she could crumble completely. Tom had tucked her up safely in bed. He'd even given her a hot-water bottle and then he had left her to fall into a deep sleep with the help of the pills the doctor had insisted she have – the unconscious sleep of the completely physically and emotionally exhausted. Occasionally she had almost woken, able to hear the vague tapping of keys as Tom rattled away on his word processor. She knew he was putting the finishing touches on to his story. They hadn't discussed it. She didn't want to know ... it was all far too painful. She just hoped that they had a close enough bond between them for him to respect the parts which might hurt too much and stay away from them, or at least go easy on them.

Now she had to pull herself together. She must see Elena, help her with the funeral arrangements, speak to Flora who had been trying to get in touch.

Gus felt deeply sorry for Flora, for knowing that she had been duped, for the shock of having her lover murdered, for being the one to betray Gus. None of it

371

was Flora's fault, but even so it was hard to talk about it just yet. It was all too new, too sharp and painful. Maybe tomorrow. Today she had family business to sort out.

She finished doing her hair. As usual, and more out of habit than anything else, she had scraped it into its neat little knot at the back. Her face which stared back from Tom's small dressing-table mirror looked as white as the walls surrounding it. Her eyes looked larger, luminous in the deepened shadows surrounding them. She brushed her finger over the small lines which were beginning to show, albeit faintly, at the sides of her mouth. Not surprising as she spent most of the time with an expression of worry on her face! She had helped herself to one of Tom's huge fisherman's sweaters, which made her feel comforted, wrapped up, like when Daddy ... No, she mustn't, she couldn't think about it. She had to keep going, get on with things. No time to crack up. Mustn't let the mind wander. She bit hard on to her lip and stood up. Tom heard her movements and rushed from his desk.

'You're awake?'

'Yes,' she smiled weakly. 'I had a good long sleep. How's the story going?'

'Nearly done.'

'You don't mind too much, about not being able to publish everything yet?' Gus knew he had been secretly mortified knowing that once the Home Secretary had been told, and the arrests under way, he would no longer be able to publish the entire story in the newspaper until after the trial. Much of it would be sub judice.

'Sure I mind, but it's going to be a great book. I'm looking on the bright side. Just think, I can put all the trial stuff in, who knows what's going to happen next?'

He didn't let on just how upset he really was. A year's work down the drain. Still it was a risk he had to take, all journalists took. At the end of the day, justice was what was important! Or so he tried to tell himself.

'Ready?' he asked gently.

'Yeah. I've never made funeral arrangements before. Not that there's much left of him.'

'Let's just get on with it, shall we?' Tom started to bustle her out of the room. 'And remember, just stop thinking for once! When this is all over, we're going to go off on a nice long holiday, just the two of us. Do you realize we've hardly had the chance to get to know each other properly? All we seem to have shared are terrifying experiences. It's about time we found a bit of peace and quiet.'

Gus managed a rueful smile. 'I really don't think either of us is cut out for it, Tom. We wouldn't know what to do with peaceful.'

'I guess you're right. Anyway, come here. I want to tell you how much I love you!'

'Again?'

'Yeah. In fact again and again and again. I won't ever get tired of saying it. Ever, ever, ever . . .'

'That's a long time, Tom. I don't know that I believe in ever now. Things can be so damned transient.' Gus couldn't trust permanence. Not with her love record. She was like the kiss of the spider woman – everyone she ever loved had left her.

'Pedantic as ever. How about we just stick with I love you today, and I'll probably love you tomorrow, and I might even love you next week?'

Gus laughed softly. 'I can handle that. Feels more real somehow.'

'Come on, my brave girl. Let's go and start the rest of our lives.' He put his arm around her shoulders as they walked out onto the street. The August sun was blazing down on them.

'Look at that, Gus – think of new beginnings. There's a lot of baggage to leave behind you. A lot of it you'll miss, never forget, maybe wish you hadn't left. But remember, as long as you keep on walking forward

373

there's stuff out there that's going to help you deal with the missing, maybe even replace it, make you feel better certainly. That's the wonderful thing about life, it keeps going on no matter how shitty yesterday was. You are going to be a great lady, wise and successful, just and fair!'

'Some speech, Silverthorn. D'you read it somewhere?' Already the sun was getting through to her chilled heart, maybe warming her a little.

'No, it's just what I think. So, stick with me, kiddo, and we'll be okay.'

She beamed up into his blue eyes, snuggled against his shoulder. It felt very good to be with him. Who knew if it would last for ever. But he was certainly right about it feeling okay today.

Epilogue

❧❦❧

Gus stared down at the coffin, at the small pink rosebud which she had just thrown, unable to focus on the brass plate, unable still to believe that he had gone. Her arms hung stiffly by her sides. The bitter wind whipped through her. She shivered underneath her black wool jacket. It was fitting that the weather should turn today of all days. She stood for a long time, lost in her thoughts, unaware of the people standing behind her, concerned for her, unsure of whether or not to intrude on her thoughts. She was remembering their last conversation. She had been so cruel to him and now wouldn't ever be able to tell him how sorry she was, and how much she loved him. She had so many happy memories of the times they had shared, and she had blown it all with her suspicion.

It was too late for them now. Poor Daddy. Poor Gus. She felt the lump in her throat grow bigger, the tears prick. She had to keep a grip on herself. She had to get through the wake. Elena was in no state to handle anything – she had sobbed continuously and had been led back to the limousine by Tom as soon as the coffin had been lowered. She too felt guilty. Her last words to Piers had been in anger – in hate, even. And Mirabelle – she had been angry too. Poor Mirabelle, whose skin would split like old leather, was being cared for by the very best. She'd survive. With skin grafts she'd make it. But she'd be different.

Gus hadn't been to see her yet, but she intended to.

'Come on, my dear.' She felt a firm hand at her elbow.

375

She stepped back, away from the grave, being led obediently. She hadn't looked. She thought it was Tom and was surprised to see it was Dickie Crowborough. She smiled her thanks.

'My dear, I'm sorry. Your mother first, now Piers ... I am so sorry for you.'

'Thank you, Dickie.'

They started to walk down the grassy slope picking their way between the gravestones. Dickie's hand remained at Gus's elbow. They arrived back at the row of cars. He glanced down at his shoes, obviously feeling awkward, unsure of himself.

'Would you like to come in my car?'

'Thank you, I'll tell Tom. It's best if he goes with Elena. She's in a dreadful state.'

'Not surprising. This whole thing is a ghastly business. Too awful.'

Dickie was waiting for her next to the car when she returned. Neither wanted to get inside, yet. The chauffeur stood slightly aside, discreetly waiting for Sir Richard to signal when he was ready to move on.

'Your father adored you. You were his whole world. He was so proud of you ...'

Gus started to shake. She sobbed out loud, a great eerie, keening sound, as if she had been physically wounded, as if the knife were being twisted inside her. She thought her heart would break. How could she have got it so wrong? She moaned in agony.

'No!' she cried. 'It's not true. He can't have gone.'

'Gus.' Dickie sounded petrified. 'Gus, calm down, you're hysterical. Everything's all right.'

'No!' she cried. 'Everything's not all right, nothing's ever going to be the same again. I judged him – my own father – without ever hearing him, what he was saying to me.'

'Gus, darling!' Dickie cried. He pulled her small body against him, feeling the stiffness in her limbs. She was

376

shaking from head to foot. He stroked her hair as she sobbed into his shoulder.

Between gasps, she said, 'He's gone and I can't ever sort it out.'

'Sssh, he's forgiven you. I knew him so well, Gus, and he loved you more than his life. His death has had a purpose. He hasn't died in vain, you know, Gus. Someday you'll be able to see that.'

Now was not the time to tell Gus the kind of mess she'd have been in if Piers hadn't been blown up. As it was he had died almost a national hero.

Beyond the lane, the police were holding back crowds of mourners who were attending out of sympathy for the victim of a bombing. Piers' name would be uttered reverently in the future.

Had Piers lived, then the entire business about his former life would have come out, thanks to the forthcoming trials. Piers Lawrence had finally done the best thing for his daughter.

Dickie helped Gus into the car. Life would be hard, but he would see to it that she had all the support he personally could give her, and as for that young man of hers, it was abundantly clear how in love with her he was.

'Come on, Gus,' he said gently. 'It's time to go and meet your future!'